A Time of Confusion

Book 2 in the Bovey Tracey Saga

A novel set in Devon during
the English Civil War 1648 and 1649

Jim Marshall

Copyright © 2023 Jim Marshall

All rights reserved, including the right to reproduce this book, or portions thereof in any form. No part of this text may be reproduced, transmitted, downloaded, decompiled, reverse engineered, or stored, in any form or introduced into any information storage and retrieval system, in any form or by any means, whether electronic or mechanical without the express written permission of the author.

This is a work of fiction. The persons and events in this book may have representations in history, but this work is entirely the author's creation and should not be construed as historical fact.

The views expressed in this work are solely those of the author and do not necessarily reflect the views of the publisher, and the publisher hereby disclaims any responsibility for them.

Front cover image:
King Charles I of England
By Hendrik van Steenwijk the Younger, 1879

ISBN: 978-1-916981-30-0

This one is for my two daughters,
Sarah and Hannah

Contents

Characters
Those that really existed are in **BOLD CAPITALS**

The town of Bovey Tracey

Rev. JAMES FORBES William Garlick (Churchwarden), Ralph Goodes (Verger), Sam Fewings (Sexton)

John and Evelyn **Ramsey** (Bakers), Mary (daughter). James and Avril **Ramsey** (Apothecary), Nell (adopted). Gil and Ella **Ramsey** (smallholders) and Rosie (daughter)

Abel and Faith **Smith** (blacksmiths), Simon (son).

Dick and Sal **Allen** (tavern), Glory and Zachary (children)

Josiah and Alice **Grubb** (shoemakers), Imelda (daughter)

Will and Patience **Fletcher** (hedger and ditcher), May and Maud (daughters)

Adam and Olivia **Gates** (Miller), Kat (daughter)

Hubert and Mercy **Green** (Booksellers)

Peter and Lou **Crowley** (Carpenter), Matt (son).

The Parke Estate

Luke and Grace **Barton** (steward)

Peter and Laura **Cove** (bailiff), Harry (son), Hob (messenger)

Sam **Garvey,** Robert **Hook** (estate servants)

Bray **Cooper,** (Shepherd)

The Brimley Estate

Lady Violette **Charlton**

Thomas **Carpenter,** (Steward)

Luke and Meg **Farmer** (Assistant steward), Hal (son)

Kit **Warden,** Nick **Andrews** (gardeners)

Trusham

Michael **Brown,** Hugh **Ratcliffe.** (Hurdle makers)

Exeter

Captain Lionel **Brooke**

Sergeant Paul **Larkin**

Arthur Tamplin, Frank **Dellow,** Horace **Young,** Seth **Bell,** Malcolm **Fallow,** Edgar **Glass** (soldiers)

Westminster and elsewhere

JOHN NORTHCOTE County Administrator
THOMAS REYNELL JP for Devon
JOHN BRADSHAW Commission chairman
THOMAS FAIRFAX Parliamentary Commander in Chief
OLIVER CROMWELL Commander of New Model Army
HENRY IRETON Cromwell's son-in-law
Matthew **Kent** – roving Parliamentary Agent.

INTRODUCTION

England since 1641 had been riven by the war between parliament and the king.

King Charles I believed in his absolute divine right to rule, if necessary unopposed by parliament or by anyone else. Parliament held the view that it was entitled to both question and, if necessary, amend the edicts of the king. Today, we would never question that right. We return members to parliament in the fond hope that they will represent us fairly and equally. In the mid seventeenth century, this idea was slowly taking shape. Discrete areas of the country – much akin to our parliamentary constituencies – returned members to parliament. That is not to say that they represented all members of society. In the main, they represented the landowners, both large and small.

To that divergence of view was added the dread matter of religion. Charles was sworn in as 'defender of the faith' – the Church of England. Complication – he was married to a staunch Catholic – Henrietta Maria. It was widely felt, and also widely feared, that the queen exercised undue influence on the king. The fear was that he was being persuaded to relax strictures against Roman Catholics – even to promote its observance.

Therefore, Charles had a war on two fronts – one against his insistence of divine right, another on the fear of a resurgence of 'Romanism'.

Much of the country heard about all these 'goings-on' long after they had taken place. I have centred my stories around a small area of South Devon. News reached the small towns and villages of England only when it was relayed from elsewhere. It might be two or three days before news of a battle would reach a village from someone who travelled there from Exeter – and even Exeter could be days out of date!

I started with what was known as the Battle of Bovey Heath. The king's army under Baron Wentworth was routed and disgraced by an army under Cromwell. This happened early in

1646. It was followed by another resounding defeat at Torrington in North Devon, and by the final defeat at Launceston.

The South-West was predominantly for the king – and suffered badly in consequence. One has only to look at the ruins at Corfe and Berry Pomeroy to see the evidence. Bovey Tracey, now a thriving small town in South Devon, was no different to any other small, inhabited place in the South-West. I chose it as the centrepiece of my stories simply because it was the site of a 'battle' almost ignored by history – therefore, I became fascinated by it. Only a small marker stone reminds us of its happening. It can still be seen in what remains of The Heath – now at the northern end of what is another thriving community called Heathfield.

Like everywhere else, it received news well after the event. By the end of 1648, when this story commences, parliament had made many decrees. Some of these were widely ignored as policing every small town and village was wholly impractical. Where policing actually took place, it was varied in its execution. Some were strict, some were more relaxed. Any learned student of the interregnum is asked to forgive my interpretation as applied to Bovey Tracey. It is my fond hope that it makes for a better story!

I start again at the end of 1648 – my characters (both real and imagined) are nearly three years older.

CHAPTER 1

The service in the church of Saints Peter, Paul and Thomas in Bovey Tracey on the last Sunday in November 1648 had ended an hour earlier – and it had been a service conducted in a mood of trepidation. Some in the nave had been fatalistic – whatever Almighty God had in mind for them would happen anyway! Others of a more practical turn of mind had wondered what, if anything, they could do about it all. Near the end of the service, Reverend James Forbes had proposed the sign of peace (a few, a very few, still obstinately referred to this as the *Pax Vobiscum*). Neighbour turned to neighbour, family member turned to family member. The word *peace* reverberated around the old church – almost as a plea rather than a greeting.

That service might not have taken place at all. For months past, it was rumoured that parliament had decreed that all churches be shut. But then, rumour countered rumour until nobody really knew what was real or imagined. The king was a prisoner, the Prince of Wales fled abroad, the remnants of the royalist forces scattered around the country and useless. Parliament reigned supreme. They saw churches as places of *possible* idolatry, far too close to the Catholicism of Rome. Work should take place on Sundays, the people praising God by their private prayers and by their labours.

In London, Westminster, the other cities and the larger towns, the rules – whatever they were - were quite easy to enforce. Not so in the more remote parts of the country – small towns and villages up to two or three hundred miles from the seat of power. There, as in this particular small Devon town, they kept to their own old ways – as much as they thought they could get away with.

After the final dismissal, the congregation dispersed quietly. Most went back to their homes; some repaired with hastening steps to the tavern where Dick Allen and wife Sal presided over excellently brewed ale, roasted lamb, and assorted vegetables.

Whether in the large taproom or in the various houses, talk was confined almost exclusively to the subject of the Rector's address.

Three of the congregation went their own way. Gil, Ella and little Rosie walked down the village street to the bridge, then turned off to where the river tumbled over small rocks on its way to join the larger River Teign towards Newton Abbot. Gil and Ella had known one another since birth – they had been neighbours. Gil, son of John and Evelyn Ramsey, the village bakers; Ella, daughter of Abel and Faith Smith – village blacksmith. Gil, now eighteen years old, had married Ella (now seventeen) when he had reached his sixteenth birthday. Little Rosie – christened Rosamund – had been born a year after and was now nineteen months old – and a source of joy to the families - and to the wider village.

Gil and Ella sat on a fallen tree trunk close to the bank of the river. Although still only a few yards wide, it was nearly in spate from the draining of the moor. It had been a fair summer and autumn – no worries for the harvest that year. But November had come in with western gales and rainstorms that had battered the West Country all the way from the tip of Cornwall, across the moors, all the way to Dorchester and beyond. Then had come a few days of relative calm.

Gil suddenly jumped up and made a grab for his little daughter, who responded with a furious squeal at being restrained. She had been throwing little pebbles into the flowing river - but had been steadily getting closer and closer to the water which was only an inch or so below the lip of the grassy bank.

Ella gave her husband her usual grin, dimples at either side of her mouth.

"Well done," she laughed.

"'Tis no laughing matter," Gil remonstrated. "If she fell in, she would be swept away for sure. I doubt I could get to her in time."

"Aye – that is not to be thought of," Ella agreed with a shake of her head. "Rosie, you must not get too near the river. 'Tis very dangerous!"

Rosie favoured both mother and father with a furious scowl.

"Throw in the water – plop!" she shouted.

Gil handed a wriggling little girl to Ella, grabbed a stick and used it to drag a line along the grass parallel to the bank and at some two yards from it.

"There," he announced, kneeling in front of his daughter. "You must not cross that line!"

"Yes, dada," Rosie beamed her satisfaction, wriggled free and went right up to the line, turned and gave her young parents a triumphant grin, and threw her pebble into the river.

"Plop!" she announced. Then, honour satisfied, went back to Ella for a cuddle.

"Just like her mother," Gil laughed.

"And what exactly do you mean by that?" Ella demanded.

"I well remember a rather beautiful little girl climbing trees that her own dada said were too high and dangerous. T'would seem she has birthed another in her own mould!"

"Nonsense and piffle," Ella retorted. "Rosie – your dada is a dimwit!"

"Dimwit!" Rosie responded with a serious face.

Gil grabbed his little daughter, hoisted her high above his head and laughed at the delighted squeals from above. He settled Rosie on his shoulders and held out a hand to Ella.

"Come, wife – dinner awaits!" he said.

Ella sat where she was for a while, looking at the river and the large boulder that stuck up above the cascading water.

"Do you remember the day you and I sat here whilst you lobbed stones at that piece of pie that was on the boulder?" she asked.

"Aye – how could I forget it. Just a short while before we wed. I well remember you told me off then for wasting time!"

Hand in hand, as they had done for many a year, the two walked back to the bridge and up the village street to the blacksmith's forge, behind which was the Smiths' home. Along the way, their nostrils were assailed with the aromas of roasting dinners. By the time they arrived at the Smiths' parlour, all three were hungry for their meal.

Abel Smith was standing before a roaring fire. He was an enormous man, and not an ounce of fat on him. He was also the possessor of a laugh that could be heard the length and breadth of the little town. By his side was Ella's brother Simon – now sixteen years old and slowly assuming the size and strength of his father. Both held large mugs of ale, warmed by a heated poker.

"At last – I may now serve dinner!" came a voice from the doorway into the kitchen. Faith Smith was half the size of her husband, never able for very long to maintain a serious face. She was as invariably happy as her husband was loud.

Ella took Rosie out to the water trough and made her little daughter wash the mud from her hands.

"Cold!" Rosie screamed her objection, as she shook the icy drops from her fingers.

Seated atop a pile of cushions, she dug her spoon into her little bowl of mutton stew and managed to get most of it into her mouth.

"We would be very pleased to return this hospitality next Sunday," Ella announced as she finished her bowl. "I have been conferring with Gil's Aunt Avril about the way to serve our potatoes. She has shown me how they may be prepared and how some good flavour be added. Without, they seem very plain and bland!"

Gil and Ella lived in a small cottage some way down the village street. They had a large patch of ground in which they grew and sold a wide variety of vegetables – potatoes being the crop they had experimented with to start with. They had been delighted with the yield in that first year. They had managed to convert many families to this new and strange tuber – especially the tavern where Sal Allen had gleefully added them to her menu.

"Then we accept with great pleasure," Abel boomed. "Do we not, Faith?"

"Aye – that we do," Ella's mother gave her daughter's hand a squeeze. "Have you enough crop to see you through until Spring?"

"Aye, mother – we have plenty. Cabbages and kale, carrots, turnips, leeks, onions, even garlic. Potatoes we have by the sack full. We shall not starve, and neither shall our customers!"

"That is good news indeed," Abel gave a hearty belch that had Rosie giggling. He raised his mug of ale. "Here's to our king – wherever he may be – and may Master Pym fester in his grave - and his damned parliament!"

CHAPTER II

Bovey Tracey church was unique in one respect – it was dedicated to three saints. Originally dedicated to Saints Peter and Paul, another – Thomas – had been added following the martyrdom of Thomas Becket. It was widely believed that one of the de Tracey family had played a leading role in the assassination. Its rector, Reverend James Forbes, had also been chaplain to Charles, Prince of Wales.

Close to the church was the rectory, a comfortable house that had lacked a woman's touch since the death of Forbes' wife some years previously. It was a very masculine dwelling, with dark panelling and a lack of colour throughout.

That Sunday evening, the parlour was the scene for a small gathering, a not unusual occurrence. The rector sat slumped in a large chair with his feet on one of the iron firedogs. The fire in the large grate was aglow with a pile of embers, with a pile of logs at the side ready to add their contribution. On the other side of the fireplace sat old William Garlick, the churchwarden. He was an old soldier who had been with the previous king James. Like the rector, he was an avid royalist.

Sitting before the fire were four others. The first, Sam Fewings, was the long-serving sexton. Next to him was Peter Cove, bailiff of the nearby Parke Estate and right-hand man to Sir John Vickery. Next to them were two brothers – John and James Ramsey. John, the village baker, was Gil's father whilst James was Gil's uncle - and the local apothecary.

Between them all was a low table that held a very large pitcher of excellent Bordeaux. Each had a glass, and each sipped appreciatively. None of them had yet to adopt the habit of smoking a pipe of tobacco – a fact for which Forbes was very grateful as he was as vehemently opposed to the habit as had been old King James.

The only illumination came from the fire. Not one of the many lanterns in the room had been lit. This added to the solemnity of the occasion as the flames flickered and created fanciful shapes in the large grate.

All six were fully aware of what had happened in that and the previous year. King Charles had fled north to the supposed sanctuary of his Scottish Stuart followers. However, the Scots for whatever reason had handed him back to parliament. He had been held close at Hampton Court. Parliament and the army had tried to find some sort of settlement. Charles had used the time to endeavour to engineer a Scottish invasion. Parliament had somehow got wind of this which caused Charles to manage an escape from his confinement. In August of that year, Cromwell had led his army against the royalists under the Duke of Hamilton and had won a decisive victory. Charles had been recaptured and put into close confinement at Carisbrook Castle on the Isle of Wight.

"And still no sign of any settlement being reached, I suppose?" Peter Cove started the conversation from where it had left off some minutes earlier.

"Nay – and I fear none will ever be reached," Forbes shook his greying head. "The king will never bend a knee to parliament or its demands. He will go to his grave insisting on his divine right to rule alone and unfettered."

"But are parliament's demands so outrageous?" James wondered. "Could he not even listen to them?"

"Did his father before him?" William Garlick grunted. "Admitted, old James was just as insistent, but he at least had the grace to do so with a wave and a merry jest!"

"And James was not hampered by a Catholic queen!" John nodded. "His Anne from Denmark was content with her observance. Not like Charles' queen – Henrietta Maria is as Catholic as the pope – and would have us all attend her mass under threat of death!"

"The great fear, and that is what parliament wages so eloquent about, is that the king is just as ardent as she is. I know that to be untrue, but he does nothing to allay the fear!" Forbes stated with another shake of his head.

"Aye – and most of the country listens to that and is just as fearful of a return to popery!" Garlick muttered.

"Returning to the Scots," James broke in. "They are, after their humiliation at Preston, a broken reed. There will be no further sound from them."

The village – now really a small town – of Bovey Tracey had witnessed a rout of the royalists, followed in swift measure by the terrible slaughter at Torrington and then at Launceston. It was following on from that, the Prince of Wales had fled to the Isles of Scilly, taking with him nearly all his army commanders.

"There are two points at issue," Peter Cove raised fingers. "One – the demand that the king rules with the cooperation of parliament and, two – the matter of the religious divide. The first is a matter of negotiation which it would appear the king is adamant he will not do. The second is based on fear – rational or irrational – as are all matters of religion. That can only be settled by the king himself making a proclamation that he and the country will *never* return to the pope. And that again, he seems unwilling or unable to do."

"Then we are in for yet more years of stalemate," James sighed.

"I fear, not necessarily," Forbes sighed in his turn. "Parliament holds all the aces in this horrid game. They have the military might; they have the majority of the people demanding an end to the threat of popery; they have just cause to accuse the king of inciting rebellion by the Scots. Parliament might also hold the king to account for the misery and deaths caused by the wars that have raged these past seven years."

"But surely he was only upholding his right to govern!" John objected.

James, who was well known as a man of careful thought, gave them all a reason to go very quiet, then to disperse for the night.

"Is it possible," he wondered aloud, "is it at all possible that parliament might frame charges to be brought against the king? Kings have been arraigned before – or have had charges levelled against them. The second Edward was charged by his wife Isabella with the help of that scoundrel Mortimer. Admittedly, there was substance to those charges. I can see that charges *might* be laid against Charles – by a parliament set upon his emasculation!"

"There still remains what we all call the *Rump* of the Long Parliament," Garlick reminded them. "Rump they may be, but there are still many of them!"

And on that sobering thought, the meeting broke up – nothing decided or clarified – as most meetings were destined to end.

CHAPTER III

"May the Good Lord Above grant me strength and patience!" the old lady offered a prayer to the ceiling of the great hall – a ceiling that had already been cleaned and repaired. She expected no response to her supplication – had never expected one.

Lady Violette Charlton stood hands on hips and glared at the picture that sullenly refused to hang straight despite repeated shifting on its chain. The manor house in Brimley had stood vacant for some months before Lady Violette, a widow and heartily sickened by life in London – a place she detested for its noise and stink – had purchased it over two years before. She was a distant relative of the Courtenay family – one of the great Devon families. Bringing with her only her steward, her cook, her personal maid and a couple of serving girls, she had set about restoring the huge house into some semblance of order. She was a Lady who led from the front – as she knew the very best generals did. Often up to her elbows in dust and grime, the sixty-two-year-old had never been afraid of hard work – and she expected no less from those in her household.

She had herself ridden to nearby Bovey Tracey only two weeks after arriving – seeking materials needed for the beginnings of the restoration. Stopping at the blacksmith's, she had uttered one word.

"Nails!"

"And what kind of nails would you require?" Abel Smith had asked politely, holding the reins of the horse so that she could dismount. "There are short nails, long nails, thin nails, stout nails. It all depends upon what purpose they are to serve!"

"Ah! Then a very large bag of every conceivable type. I have a large house to put to rights. So, if I have a sufficiency of every type, then I shall be well equipped, shall I not?!"

Realisation had dawned on Abel's face.

"I shall set my son Simon on the task immediately, my lady. These would be for Brimley?"

"Indeed, they would. When may I expect delivery?"

"It will take three days at the most, my lady. Simon will deliver them as soon as it be possible."

And that was the way she had set about restoring the vast house and grounds – know what you want, go to the correct place, pay cash on the dot. She gave one more furious scowl at the picture and went to the door.

"Thomas!" she yelled.

A few minutes later, a grey head poked its way around the door.

"You bellowed, my lady?"

"Aye, Thomas – I bellowed. Find Farmer and send him in here."

Thomas Carpenter, one year younger than his mistress and her long-time steward, nodded and went in search of Luke Farmer. He found him at the bottom of the kitchen garden, turning the midden where all food scraps, leaves, cuttings and other compostable items were piled. The heap was the pride and joy of the head gardener, Rob Garside – a diminutive, little fellow who rejoiced in the nickname of Goliath.

"Luke – you'd better wash off the muck. My Lady needs you in the great hall."

"Aye, master Thomas," Luke Farmer replied. He and his close friend Kit Warden had teamed up with another ex-royalist soldier by the name of Nick Andrews and had sought work at various places, eventually landing up at Brimley – a house that was very seriously understaffed.

Luke stuck his three-tined fork into the midden and went to the nearest trough to wash the muck from his hands. Then he went through the kitchens to the great hall.

"You called for me, my lady?" he announced his presence.

"Yes – I have a job for you, young man. Go and fetch the set of steps and haul that bloody picture down. There is something amiss with its chain as it refuses to hang straight."

Farmer loped off and went to the shed by the kitchen door where he knew the set of steps was kept. Back in the hall, he climbed up and carefully brought down the large-framed painting – a portrait of her deceased husband. He propped it against the wall with its back to him and examined the chain.

"Ah – 'tis the fault of the chain, my lady," he announced.

"Yes – I already said that was the case. Now, what is the fault?"

"I would hazard a guess that the links be too wide, my lady. One like either way and it will not hang straight."

"Then go and find a chain with smaller links!"

"Certainly, my lady." Farmer stood up and prepared to go about his new errand.

"And how is that flame-headed wife of yours and the babe who has the lungs of an elephant?"

"Meg is very well, my lady – as is little Hal – I thank you for asking."

Luke and his mate Warden, both royalist soldiers, had witnessed first-hand the appalling rout of Wentworth's army at Bovey Heath in the January of 1646. They had tried to join again with their comrades but had failed in the awful winter weather – and had thus mercifully missed the slaughter at Torrington. They had ended up at the village of Lustleigh, working at restoring cottages. There, Luke had met and fallen head over heels for Meg, the red-headed daughter of the village woodcutter. He had given his word that he would seek permanent employment and would court Meg, if the woodcutter gave his approval. Meg had twisted her father's arm – and had married Luke some three months later. Lady Charlton, already his new employer, had allocated them a small chamber high up in the old house. Little Hal was the result – now a sturdy six-month-old. Meg had proved invaluable as a seamstress and had done most of the work on the curtains and fabrics in the house.

Kit Warden worked as a groundman, doing everything from scything grass to planting vegetables. Luke worked mainly inside the house as assistant to old Thomas Carpenter. Their other ex-royalist soldier friend, Nick Andrews, had proved himself to be a dab hand at carpentry and had spent many months repairing furniture, beams, and panelling.

The house and grounds were almost in a state that met with Lady Violette's approval – but not quite. She wanted the old stables torn down and rebuilt – a job that needed to wait for better and warmer weather.

The trials and tribulations of England passed by this slightly isolated little village. Lady Violette had had her fill of London, Whitehall, Parliament and its machinations. She required nothing more than a peaceful and quiet place in which to pass her declining years. Word reached Brimley from occasional visits to Bovey Tracey and Ashburton – but she steadfastly ignored them. Daily, she prayed for her king and cursed parliament – but that was the sum total of her involvement.

As for the three ex-soldiers, they were daily thankful for a quiet and peaceful billet.

CHAPTER IV

Luke Barton had been just four years old when Elizabeth, queen of England, had died. Grace, his wife had been born one year into the reign of the next monarch, James I. For the past ten years, Luke had been steward to Sir John Vickery, the owner of Parke Estate – a 'manor' that included Bovey Tracey and a host of smaller villages and hamlets. Much to their sorrow, Luke and Grace had never been blessed with children. They lived in a large cottage next to the bailiff – Peter Cove and his wife Laura. The bailiff's son Harry, eighteen years old, was now learning the ropes from his father.

Lord John was again absent on one of his mysterious trips, leaving steward Barton in virtual command of Parke. Not that he found this unusual, it was a regular occurrence since the civil wars had broken out seven years before in 1641.

Barton sat at his desk in the small parlour of Parke House, his head buried in a pile of paper. Bills from this and that supplier, messages from this and that servant – the head cook, the head gardener, the housekeeper. He hated paperwork.

He was a tall, spare man in his forty-ninth year. He was also a confidante of his lord and knew all there was to know about the current situation. And that was why he was buried in paperwork – to avoid thinking of the dire straits surrounding his king. He knew, as very few others knew, that the king was soon to be transferred from Carisbrook to Westminster where it was rumoured charges against him were being formulated. It had even been rumoured that a formal Bill of Indictment was being drafted. He wondered whether Reverend Forbes was also privy to that information.

One other piece of information had come his way, one that he knew that he *should* impart to the bailiff so that the bailiff in his turn could inform the people. A parliamentary force had been sent to 'garrison' the West Country. A contingent was at Exeter, another at Launceston, yet another up in Barnstaple. How long, he wondered, before smaller units were sent to places like Bovey Tracey, Tavistock, Teignmouth?

He sighed and pushed the papers to one side, sorely tempted to scatter them to the winter wind blowing outside. He donned a thick cloak against the chill and went in search of two servants who had yet to earn his trust.

Sam Harvey and Rob Hook were busy working in the woodstore. One job they had to do every week was to split enough logs to supply the fires and the kitchen range. It was no mean task. The wood came in the form of large logs about a foot and a half long. Mainly ash, but sometimes a variety of other woods. They longed for ash as it had such a straight, easily split grain. They were about half-way through the task that would take them most of that day. Once split, they had to be properly stored in the special log bins.

They stopped and straightened up as the steward came into the woodstore. Both knew they were still on probation, even though they had been there for over two years. They had been soldiers in Cromwell's New Model Army – until they had been separated from their unit following a long trek over the moor. Both were very experienced woodland trackers and had been a part of a special tracking unit spying out the royalist positions in and around Bovey Heath.

They considered themselves very lucky to have landed permanent jobs at Parke – given their background, parliamentarians were distrusted by most people.

"Tomorrow, I want the pair of you to scour the north wood – do what you are best at. There are wild boar there, or so I'm reliably told. They could be anywhere between Furzeleigh and Shaptor. I've had complaints that they are making a nuisance of themselves, rooting up fences and trampling new plantings. Find them, mark the locations well, and be ready to lead a hunting party the day after."

"Aye, master. If they be there, we shall find them," Garvey answered as he usually did for both of them.

Barton gave them a swift glance and went back to his desk, trying to think of other things he might do to keep himself away from that mound of paper. He gave a satisfied nod and went in search of the housekeeper – she had been on again about mice in the cellars. What he needed was a trip out to Hawksmoor where he would find an old chap who kept a pair of the most ferocious ferrets.

"So, out into the cold for us on the morrow," Hook grinned at Garvey. "Can't say I'll be sorry to get out into the woods again!"

Rob Hook delighted in the nickname of Haddock – his facial features were of a definite piscine cast.

"Will be a change, at least," Garvey agreed. "I wonder who will form the hunting party? Lord John is away again – and bailiff be too busy. No real hunting dogs neither – only that pack of lymers. They be good to sniff out prey, but that's what we are for!"

"Aye – and that long snout of yours be just the right length!" Haddock grinned.

"Pig's arse!"

"Some of them from Bovey might fancy a trip. That apothecary be good with a musket."

"And old Garlick would not want to miss out!" Garvey nodded.

They returned to splitting logs, trundling them in barrows to the respective log bins, and going back to work their way through the still impressive mound of wood.

* * *

Later that afternoon, about an hour before the light faded, Gil was busy hoeing the beds where cabbages and kale still grew. Every now and again, he looked up with a smile of happiness as shrieks of laughter came from his small cottage. Not for the first time, he wondered how he had ever been so lucky as to have known Ella all his life – and to marry her. Not only was she a beautiful young woman, she was his one and only love – and his best friend. And to have little Rosie was simply an added, wonderful gift.

As another shriek of merriment came from the cottage, he gave up and went back to put his hoe away, rinse his hands and enter the warm kitchen. One young woman in an apron and a mass of chestnut waves looked up at him and gave him a cheery wave. Kneeling on stools were two little girls, also wearing small aprons – and covered in flour. His little Rosie smacked her tiny hand down on a small pile of it so that a white cloud arose – and that was what was causing such hilarity.

"Look dada – wheeeee!" she yelled, causing another cloud.

Ella looked at him and gave a shrug of helplessness. Nell, kneeling next to Rosie also looked at him and wondered if it was all right for her to laugh as well. Gill gave a huge grin at the appalling mess, then smacked his much larger hand down causing a minor snowstorm of flour.

"You, husband, are going to help me to clear this mess!" Ella stated.

"And who is going to tell Aunt Avril why Nell is in such a state?" he asked.

Nell was now six years old. Two years previously, she had been simply abandoned by her surly grandfather, an itinerant tinker. The old man's son-in-law, and Nell's father, had sustained a head injury and had died in James' and Avril's house two days later. They had immediately adopted little Nell as their own – and it had proved the making of that little girl. She was a happy, loved and safe child – and a firm favourite with the village.

A delicious smell came from the oven where a tray of cakes was baking. More biscuit than cake, as they had been made thin and covered in raisins. Ella removed the tray from the oven and set it to cool on the stone shelf.

"And now, we all have to clear up the mess," she announced. "Nell – the little brush and tray. Sweep the table, please. Rosie – go out with your dada and shake all that flour off your dress and apron. Then come back so that I may wash you from head to foot."

"Cold!" Rosie stamped her foot.

Gil swooped, grabbed his daughter and hauled her kicking and yelling out of the kitchen. He peeled off the apron and gave it a vigorous shake, Rosie, captivated by the white cloud, started smacking at her dress to add to the cloud. By the time he had managed to get Rosie back into the kitchen, some semblance of order had been restored. The table was clean, as was the floor and the pots and pans that had been used. Even Nell looked passable.

"And now, young madam, it's a wash for you," Ella grabbed Rosie's hand and marched her into the parlour where a fire was burning.

"No, mama – cold! Brrrrrrr!"

"Yes, mama – hard luck!" Ella replied, hauling off one little dress and using a cloth soaked in warm water to remove flour from face, hands, arms and legs. Her hair had been brushed clear of flour.

A short while later, Rosie in a clean dress and apron was sat happily in front of the fire munching her way through a raisin biscuit. Nell sat by her side eating her dainty way through another biscuit. Every now and again, she would dust crumbs off Rosie's new apron. Ella always knew that Nell would look after Rosie – would be like another very young mother.

By then, the light had gone – and the lamps had been lit. Gil took Nell back home, Nell clutching a small bag of biscuits. He went into his uncle's and aunt's house and delivered his charge.

"We made little flat cakes," Nell announced, handing them around.

"And very nice little flat cakes they are," Avril said, giving Nell a hug.

"And Rosie smacked flour all over the kitchen!"

"Aye – and I suppose you thought that very good fun," James laughed.

"It made us sneeze," Nell grinned.

Gil went back home to see what Ella had prepared for their supper. He smelt it as soon as he went into the cottage.

"Vegetable pottage – or my nose has got it wrong!" he sniffed appreciatively.

"Your nose has got it absolutely right," Ella gave him a kiss – and caused the usual rumpus.

"Rosie wants kiss!"

"Rosie will have to wait!"

"Shan't!" Rosie toddled over to her mother and demanded her kiss.

"And who shall tell you a story at bedtime?" Ella asked, setting Rosie back on her feet.

"Dada! Dada, tell me about the little frog!"

"Oh – I've told you that one ten times already!"

"Want it again!"

CHAPTER V

Rougemont Castle had played a significant role in the history of Exeter and the West Country since the time of the Normans. Built in the north-east corner of the city, against the city walls, it earned its name from its 'red' appearance. It had been taken by the royalists in 1642 but had fallen to the parliamentarians four years later in 1646. Parts of it were in ruins.

On the first Sunday in December of 1648, Captain Lionel Brook surveyed his new command. It was raining – one of those typical Devon winter days where the fine rain lured you into a false sense of security. Believing it was just a sort of mist, within five minutes you were soaked through, cold and decidedly miserable.

Within the main keep, his office was warm. He had an abundance of food and supplies for the hundred or so soldiers he had brought with him only two days previously. And now, he had the job of sending small units to a few towns and villages that were considered by his superiors to be of significance. What that significance was, he had not been told – but he could guess. They were probably places where royalist sympathies still remained strong – and where trouble might just arise.

He had been ordered to send three small units; one to Teignmouth; another to Ashburton; the third was to go to Bovey Tracey. He decided to deal with them in reverse order. Consequently, he called for his 'runner' and told him to locate Sergeant Paul Larkin and tell him to report to his office.

Thankfully getting in out of the wet, he went to his office where his clerk was already setting out a glass of wine and a small platter of sweetmeats. Shrugging out of his topcoat, he sat down behind his desk and waited for his sergeant to appear.

Sergeant Paul Larkin was one of those men who could only ever have been an army sergeant. Just over six feet tall, shoulders like an ox and a voice that could probably be heard three streets away. He knocked, entered and stood rigidly to attention.

"Ah – Sergeant Larkin. Come in, sit down and get yourself comfortable. I have a mission for you that may take a while to explain."

"Now what?" Larkin said inwardly. He always drummed into his soldiers the old army maxim, 'never volunteer'. He had not volunteered for any mission and wondered what it would turn out to be. He removed his pot helmet, slipped off the baldric that supported his broadsword and removed the famous 'buff coat' – made of boiled leather and as tough as the hide of a rhinoceros. He sat down opposite his captain.

"First, tell me what you know of the current situation," Brook ordered.

"Well, sir – I know that there is no threat from any large force anywhere hereabouts. General Cromwell put paid to all that malarkey. I understand that Charles Stuart is being brought to Whitehall to face possible charges."

"Correct on both points. Now, whilst it's true that there is no chance of any mass attack on us, there still remains the distinct possibility of isolated, small attacks being made by those still fiercely loyal to him."

"Ah," Larkin thought. "Then I'm to be sent to look for and counter any localised resistance," he said aloud.

"Correct again, sergeant. I want you to pick six or seven of the old hands and get yourselves to the town of Bovey Tracey. Why Bovey, I hear you ask? Bovey is remarkable on three separate counts. One – it was the scene of a rout of royalist forces, hence bitter resentment. Two – it is the home of Sir John Vickery, whose present whereabouts are a mystery. Three – it is the home of Reverend Forbes, chaplain to the Prince of Wales. Two years ago, one of the inhabitants attempted to assassinate a couple of our soldiers. That failed due to the vigilance of the sergeant who was in charge at the time. Bovey probably *is* a hotbed of anti-parliament feeling."

"And what are we to do, sir? Patrol and watch? Impose military law?"

"Certainly not the latter! Doing so would only antagonise and probably generate the sort of response that we do not need. No – watch and remain calm at all times. By that I mean that the inhabitants are to be allowed absolute freedom to come and go as they please. They are not to be harassed – not even if you are mildly provoked. If, of course, you are seriously threatened, you are free to take whatever measures you feel appropriate. Treat them with courtesy, especially the women. I do *not* want to get reports of any attacks on, or raping of, females! I trust that is understood?”

“Completely understood, sir. What about enforcing any law on churches?”

“Use your discretion on that one. I’m sure it is being flouted throughout Devon! Now, another secret, I am sending two other small units. One to Ashburton and another to Teignmouth. They will have exactly the same orders as you. Now – go and select your unit and be ready to depart in the morning.”

Larkin gathered up his belongings, stood and walked smartly out of the office. He had no objection whatsoever to going out on his own small command. It would make a nice change from being part of a huge crowd.

An hour later he surveyed the six he had chosen. He sat them down in a small, stone-walled room in the castle’s lower floor. He had chosen them for their age and experience. He knew that, for a mission of that kind, new recruits and inexperienced soldiers would be more of a hindrance than an asset. All six had been in battle more than once. Therefore, he reasoned, they all knew the importance of reliance upon one another.

“I were at Bovey Heath, sergeant,” Trooper Fallow remarked, once their mission had been explained in detail.

“Aye – so were I,” Trooper Tamplin nodded. “We grabbed over four hundred horses. King’s men simply fled for their lives.”

Larkin overlooked the reference to ‘the king’. It had slowly become the norm in parliamentary circles to refer to that person as Charles Stuart. The leaders of parliament believed it somehow relegated him to the status or mere mortal – something they were eager to accomplish.

Along with Fallow and Tamplin, Larkin had picked Glass, Bell, Dellow and Young. The six knew one another and, as far as Larkin was aware, there was no animosity he would have to deal with.

So far, so good, Larkin thought as he sent them on their way to prepare for their departure the next morning. How they would be housed, how their mounts would be stabled, how they would be supplied – all could wait until they got there. The sixteen mile journey would take three hours at a leisurely trot. He would draw provisions for three days before they left.

* * *

Ella had been concerned that they would not have enough food for the promised Sunday dinner. Gil simply scoffed at the notion and earned himself a scowl from his young wife. So, as they were walking back down to their cottage after another Sunday service, Gil decided to make himself scarce – and to take Rosie with him. Ella was all in favour of that idea. Preparing Sunday dinner for twelve people would be difficult enough without the comments from her husband and the constant interference of one little daughter.

Gil put Rosie on his shoulders as they came abreast of their cottage and continued on down towards the bridge. Ella hurried indoors to start her preparations. She had studied the recipe which Gil's aunt Avril had devised for these new-fangled potatoes – and was eager to put it into practice. The first thing she did was to wash and dry the potatoes. Then, having stoked up the parlour fire, put a heap of them into the bottom embers and left them until she could poke a sharp knife into them and test that the insides were nice and soft. Then, leaving them in a row before the fire to keep warm, she went to get on with the other parts of the meal.

Gil reached the bridge and turned left. That immediately drew wails from above.

"Water, dada. Rosie throw stones!"

"Aye – and so you shall – just as soon as we have looked at the new ground."

That seemed to satisfy one demanding little girl. She stayed quiet as Gil took the path down beside the old mill and wandered down onto Bovey Heath. About a hundred years further up to his left was the plot he and Ella had rented so as to grow their crops. Beyond that was simply open heathland. The new plan was for them to rent more of the land, fence it off securely, and start to raise chickens. They would be able to sell eggs directly, and to offer some pullets to the local butcher to kill, pluck and prepare. First, he had to inspect the ground. Too wet and it would be useless; too hard and the fowl would not be able to unearth worms and grubs.

He set Rosie down on her feet and led the way to the prospective plot. Ideally, it would be a continuation of their own plot. He walked up and down, testing the earth with the toe of his boot. Rosie immediately copied him, but with the sole purpose of unearthing pebbles to throw into the river.

"'Tis ideal," Gil muttered. "I must get to see Master Bailiff and make an offer to rent this!"

Then, seeing the look on his daughter's face, he also gathered a pocketful of pebbles and led her to the river.

* * *

The little parlour seemed to be bursting at the seams. The table was just about large enough to seat four on each side and two at either end. Everyone was crammed together – and that had resulted in near mayhem as Ella, helped by Mary and Nell, had brought in platter after platter of food. Gil's mother and father, with Mary his sister; Ella's father and mother with Simon her brother; James and Avril with Nell; Gil and Ella with Rosie. Abel Smith was encouraged to sit at one end, his son Simon at the other end. If those two had chosen to sit somewhere in the middle, chaos would have ensued.

Ella had cut open the potatoes in their crusty skins, then had poured over them a mutton and vegetable stew. Everyone without exception said that the result was delicious. Mary, now a very pretty sixteen, had decided to act as surrogate mother to Rosie and had sat her on her lap. Rosie still insisted on feeding herself. The result was spectacular and caused gales of laughter. That was quite the wrong thing to do as it encouraged the little terror to plaster even more gravy over her face.

Evelyn and Faith had brought a dessert with them to ease the load on Ella. It was a large, sweet pastry flan filled with sliced apples and honey. Mary volunteered to take Rosie out so that the gravy and sticky mess could be removed.

After all the debris had been cleared away, and Ella roundly congratulated on a superb meal, the 'older' people were left in peace. Mary, Simon, Nell and Rosie all went for a walk, the weather being cold but dry. Gil produced a large jar of honey mead and small mugs. Talk naturally started with a summary of the four children.

"Simon seems to be totally smitten with Imelda Grubb. I wonder whether he is contemplating following in your footsteps, Gil," Faith said.

"He is certainly going to have stiff competition," Abel, her husband observed. "That Imelda is a very pretty maid!"

"He and Mary have been lifelong friends – just as Gil and Ella have been," James pointed out the obvious. "Both be sixteen now!"

"Aye – true enough," John nodded. "But that is all it has ever been – lifelong friends. Our Mary seems content to bide her time and wait."

"She comes to us every afternoon and is learning all about herbs and potions," Avril commented. "Soon, she will be competent enough to be an apothecary in her own right. Maybe she sees that as her future?"

"But have you noticed how she is with our Rosie?" Ella laughed. "I see in Mary the makings of a wonderful mother!"

Talk then veered towards others in the village, and then to what was happening in the country as a whole. Everyone looked to James – the acknowledged fount of wisdom.

"I have followed what Reverend Forbes has been saying, and what is slowly coming down to us here in Devon. The king has lost all authority, whilst parliament is ruling the roost. Bradshaw and the other members will not be satisfied until they have wrested all power from the king. How they intend going about it, I know not. But one thing is very clear – they will not relent now they have a stranglehold!"

"And how, uncle, may that affect us here?" Gil wondered.

"We will without doubt feel the impact. There will be some restrictions. There will also now be a slight relaxing of taxes – as the fighting has faded and the need for weapons and soldiers' wages decreased. We must simply bend with the wind – for otherwise it may break us."

CHAPTER VI

Sergeant Larkin and his small troop left the guardroom at Rougemont just after nine the next morning. He had instructed Tamplin to draw him a map of Bovey from his memory of his time there. Tamplin had drawn a wiggly, roughly horizontal line representing the main street through the small town. On the left, he had drawn another one vertical to the main street.

"Down the bottom of this one is Newton Abbot. To the left at the crossroads is the way up to Hay Tor, straight on north and you get to Moretonhamstead."

"I understand all that," Larkin answered, getting a trifle impatient at the longwindedness of the explanation.

"Ah, but that crossroads is important! Turn left and a little way on the right is the Parke Estate."

"Oh – yes – that is important," Larkin agreed. "Go on."

"Starting at the crossroads and going right into the town, the first thing you come to is the bridge over the river. Then, immediately on the right is the mill where we were stationed after the battle. Then there are houses and cottages all the way up to the church at the top on the left. There is an apothecary, a booksellers, a butcher, a chandler, a shoemaker, a smithy, a baker and a large tavern."

"There must be more than that!"

"Aye, sergeant. There are many more. Some are cottages for workers at the estate, some for farm labourers, I seem to remember that there are some that looked unoccupied."

"Hm – one of those would do us very nicely!" muttered Larkin. "Here's what we shall do. We shall take a slightly longer way around and come up from Newton Abbot. I shall visit the Parke Estate and see if we can take one of the empty cottages. There must be a bailiff or a steward who has authority."

Consequently, it was one o'clock in the afternoon when the troop arrived at the Parke gates. Larkin dismounted and walked to the first house he came across up the drive. He knocked and waited.

A tousle-headed lad opened the door, took one look at the parliamentarian soldier and let out a yell.

"Master bailiff – bloody soldier at the door!"

Peter Cove emerged from his parlour and took in the sergeant standing on the threshold.

"Pay no mind to Hob," he said. "Manners of a pig – and that's on a good day. What may I do for you?"

"I assume from what he said that I'm addressing the bailiff?"

"Aye – Peter Cove, bailiff to Sir John Vickery."

"Then, Master Bailiff, I have a request. Is there in the town any cottage that is unoccupied at present?"

Cove gave him a furtive look.

"You say it is a request. Is it more likely to be an order?"

"Request I said and request I did mean!"

"Then I can tell you that there indeed be a cottage that is unoccupied. I assume you want to use it for you and the soldiers I can see down at the gate."

"And we will pay whatever you deem the current rent."

"Well – that is more than your colleagues did some two years past. A Sergeant Franks was here with a small troop. They camped out by the mill. They also shot our night soil man."

"There would have been a reason for that!" Larkin sounded very sure.

"Aye, there was reason enough. Stupid bugger tried to take off the heads of two of the soldiers when they were sleeping – except that they were not sleeping."

"You have nothing to fear from us, bailiff. We are here simply to see that there is no plotting and planning."

"Then you will have a very boring time. I am sure that, whilst you will be resented for your presence, you will encounter no real hostility – as long as your men behave in a civil manner."

"That I can assure you. I have already told them that they are to behave properly – especially towards your womenfolk."

"Let me get my cloak – 'tis blowing cold today. I shall show you the cottage you may occupy."

Cove emerged from the house in a warm cloak. He walked down to the gates and led Larkin to the crossroads and straight across, making for the bridge about two hundred yards distant. The mill was working, the massive water wheel trundling away. He went slowly up the street as it bore around to the left. Just before the small square, he halted at a cottage that was larger than most. He handed Larkin a hefty key.

"This be the cottage. I shall inform you the rent when I have spoken to Sir John – and that may take some time."

He gave a polite nod to the sergeant and walked back. Adam Gates, the miller, was waiting for him as he passed to cross the bridge.

"Under occupation again, are we, bailiff?"

"So it would seem – although this chap seems civil enough. They're even going to pay rent for the cottage up by the square."

"Should have left them in the open freezing their bollocks off!"

"And what would you prefer, Master Gates? Soldiers cold, miserable and angry – or soldiers warm with nothing to complain about?"

"Ah! That probably be why you be bailiff and I remain a humble miller!"

"You humble, Master Gates? Have never seen evidence of that!"

"Aye – and you probably never will," Gates chuckled, and went back to hoist another bag of grain up to the chute loft.

By nightfall, the whole town was aware that they were again 'under occupation', as many saw it. The tavern was alive with speculation and not a little resentment. They all knew that they had no choice in the matter; parliament was in total control and could impose whatever it chose on whomsoever it wanted. But they did not have to like it. All except one member of the village.

Three of the soldiers came into the taproom that night – an hour before Dick Allen closed up. Two were short and dark – one was tall and had a shock of fair hair over a freckled face. He had a friendly grin as he ordered – and paid for – three mugs of ale. Glory, the daughter of the tavern keeper, brought the mugs to the side table and responded immediately to the thanks of the soldier. Glory was eighteen, a mass of red hair, full figure, and a keen sense of her own allure. She was quite taken with this soldier.

"My name is Glory," she whispered as she put his mug down on the table beside him.

"And never a maid more worthy of the name!" came the whispered reply.

Glory went back to the kitchen to see if there were any more orders to fill. Her mother, Sal, gave her a sharp look.

"I hope you not be flirting with that soldier!" she growled.

"Me, mother? Would I do such a thing!"

"Aye – you would. Be careful – they be here not for our good!"

"He cannot help being a handsome man!"

"And you cannot help being a flirt by nature! I warn you, my lass – be careful!"

Trooper Bell, known inevitably as Clanger, sat and gazed after the retreating Glory, noting the gentle sway of her hips – probably deliberately, he surmised.

"Remember what sergeant warned," Trooper Dellow warned him.

"Aye – he said treat with respect. Well, 'tis what I'm doing – respecting the way she walks and looks!"

"Lass like that must be spoken for," Dellow muttered.

"Aye – probably!" Bell replied sadly.

* * *

The next morning, both Gil and Ella went to see the bailiff with their plans for enlarging their business.

Gil was still helping his parents with bread deliveries. These were over by nine every morning, leaving him time to get home, gobble down a bowl of sweetened oatmeal, then scurry out to help Ella with the vegetables. During the winter months, there was not as much to do but they spent some time every day digging over and preparing beds for the early Spring planting.

They ran the bailiff to earth at the large Parke House, trying to get young Hob to remember a rather long message. He had almost given up and was on the point of writing it on paper when the two arrived.

"Have you two come to rescue me from this thankless task?" he groaned.

"'Tis not my fault, Master Bailiff," Hob complained. "There be words I have never heard before!"

"Aye – go and find cook and see if she needs help "

Hob needed no second bidding and scampered off, dreaming of fresh crusty bread he might just be able to snaffle when cook's back was turned.

"And now – what may I do for you?" Peter Cove asked.

"Ella and I have had a notion to add to our plot, Master Bailiff. We would need to extend our plot to do so."

"And what new enterprise may be in the wind?"

"Fowl, Master Bailiff," Ella explained. "Gil and I want to take more ground and erect small sheds for roosting, laying and resting the fowls. We need enough ground also for them to peck at grass, worms and grubs."

Cove was impressed.

"How would you plan to start this – given you get the ground and erect the sheds?"

"We would go to Lustleigh where there be a large flock already. We would purchase hens and a cock. Some eggs we would sell, others we would hatch out to increase our own flock. Then we would sell male fowl to butcher and keep all little hens – plus a cock or two. Would not be too long before we had a sizeable flock to supply eggs in plenty."

"And who is to tend these fowl when you are stretched in Spring, Summer and Autumn to tend your vegetables?"

"We would get little Nell to learn and take on the task. She would have the time between her lessons. James and Avril have said it would be good for her – and Nell is keen to do it."

"Nell – six years old? Yes – she's a very sensible little lass. It could work. I suppose you want me to come and see the additional plot you require?"

"Aye, Master Bailiff – if you could spare the time. I'm sure we could return the favour by delivering your message – the one Hob cannot understand."

"'Tis for Master Allen at the tavern. He is to make sure that the soldiers are treated with proper courtesy. He is also to keep his and his family's ears open for any unguarded comments those soldiers may have. It will not harm us to have foreknowledge of any plans they may have – or suspicions they may harbour."

"We can certainly deliver that for you," Gil promised as they made their way out of the estate and down the lane past the mill to where the two had planned the new enclosure.

An hour later, they had agreed on the additional plot – an additional twenty yards at the bottom of their existing plot. They had also agreed the additional rent.

"Next job – fence it off and put a small gate between the vegetables and the new fowl run."

"And do not forget that we need the roosting and laying shed!" Ella laughed, just in case Gil thought he had got away with it.

Peter Cove went back to his office and Gil went up to the tavern to deliver the bailiff's message. Dick Allen and his wife Sal were not in the least surprised at the contents of that message.

"We've been expecting something of the kind," Sal said. "We shall assure the bailiff that the soldiers will be treated as we would any other customer. And we shall keep our ears open for any problems from the locals!"

Two days later, the new area was fenced off – securely to keep out dogs and foxes that might be interested in young fowl wandering about. Gil had asked Peter Crowley, the carpenter, to help him erect the sheds – not that they were very large or hard to make. Gil just wanted them secure and weatherproof.

On the Sunday afternoon, Gil, Ella and Nell went to Lustleigh to see the owner of the chickens. They took with them a cage in which they hoped to bring back six hens and a cockerel. The four mile walk was nearly all gently uphill and took them well over an hour. The chicken farmer was a quiet man – almost morose - but agreed to sell them what they wanted. Nell had a merry time chasing the hens but all were eventually caged with a young cock. Gil paid the agreed price and was somewhat amazed when the farmer offered to drive them back on his cart – pulled by an ancient pony.

By nightfall, the seven new occupants were settled into their new home – a supply of water and grain put into bowls. Ella closed the shed with a sigh and took Nell back to Avril for her supper.

"Well," she yawned, sitting on the settle before the fire. "I suppose we are now farmers!"

"Wonder when we shall get our first eggs," Gil mused. "We need to let them be – we need many more hens before we can start gathering eggs for sale."

"And do not forget that the new chicks will not be ready to lay for nearly five months after they have hatched. We will need to keep a couple of extra roosters."

"Aye – 'tis going to be a long-term project to start with. I hope Nell will be able to cope."

"Oh – for the next month or so, there will not that many for her to look after. She will cope brilliantly!"

Gil pulled a long face. "We have no idea what we are doing, have we?" he grinned.

"Probably not," Ella grinned back. "But we have coped well enough so far. We have produced vegetables, and not to forget that little sweetheart upstairs!"

"Aye – Rosie is loud but is thriving. So, we must be doing something right!"

"Maybe she would like a brother or sister?"

"Yes – maybe she would!"

CHAPTER VII

The River Bovey wound its way south from Bovey Tracey down to meet the River Teign just to the east of the little hamlet of Ventiford. Just over a mile further south, the River Teign curved its somewhat tortuous route past the hamlet of Preston, before flowing further south to Newton Abbot. Small clay pits existed to the east of Preston, almost abandoned since the defeat of the royalist armies had deprived it of half of its menfolk. Three men lived in a run-down cottage on the edge of Preston. One of them looked out of the window of one of the two upstairs bed chambers. It was the third Tuesday of Advent, and the weather was cold, with a biting wind.

Lionel Hawkes was twenty-six years old, short and lean, with dark hair that had been left to grow well down past his shoulders. He and his two colleagues had found the abandoned cottage nearly three years before. They had fled south from Exeter when that city had fallen to the parliamentarians. It had not occurred to any of the three to attempt to rejoin the royalist army – and had learned some days after the event of the fiasco at Bovey Heath. That had made them doubly grateful that they had decided to abscond. Each still had his sword and pistol but had shed their uniforms as soon as they could locate and steal some ordinary clothes. They wandered far and wide, stealing what they needed. They had ranged across miles in their search for victims – from as far away as Ivybridge in the west to Starcross in the east. They had lived charmed lives, narrowly being captured in Ashburton – twice.

Hawkes went down the rickety stairs to the parlour where his colleagues were sat around the fire roasting chestnuts.

"Where to next?" Ned Thomas asked. He and Art Simmonds nearly always deferred to Hawkes. Thomas was tall and stout, Simmonds tall and thin. All three hailed from distant Gloucester and had joined the king's army together in search of adventure – certainly not for any reasons of loyalty to their king.

"Might take a stroll up towards Bovey," Hawkes replied. "Haven't been in that direction for some months now "

"Thought you said we should keep to small places," Simmonds grumbled.

"Aye – I did – but we've run out of them for a while. Might also have a look at Trusham and Chudleigh Knighton whilst we're up that way."

"They sound smaller than Bovey," Thomas nodded. "I reckon tis time we took a small pig. I quite fancy some pork and lovely crackling skin!"

"We'd have to kill it on the spot – it would squeal if we didn't!" Simmonds said sagely.

"I still say we hit Bovey first," Hawkes decided.

* * *

Two days later, towards evening on the Thursday afternoon, there was a small meeting in the church hall. They had spent the last hour discussing the decorations to be made to the church for the forthcoming Christmas services, totally disregarding any possible legislation. Sam Fewings, the sexton and on whose shoulders most of the work would fall, had been quite relieved that last year's extravagant decorations would not be repeated!

Ralph Goodes, the verger, was immensely fat. By rights, most of the work should have fallen on *his* shoulders, but everyone knew that he was both too rotund ever to climb a step ladder and too short of breath to do much of the lifting. Luckily, Hob was easily able to assist the sexton. Still only twelve years old, Hob was like a squirrel up and down ladders. Avril had brought Mary with her. Avril was always ready to volunteer at the church; her common-sense approach to things was much in demand. Mary, Gil's sister, was also one of those ready and willing to help. Henry Hogg, the saddler's son, was eighteen and two years older than Mary. Both Forbes and Avril thought that it was Mary's presence that had prompted Harry to volunteer, rather than any pious consideration.

The seventh and last member of the group was the churchwarden – William Garlick. He was sitting to one side in a large chair. And it was a remark of his that had prompted Mary to raise her hand.

"Can't have any serpents or devils polluting the church this year!" he had grunted in his usual manner. "Lowers the tone of celebration!"

Forbes saw Mary's hand waving, albeit a bit uncertainly. "Yes, Mary – you have a question?"

"Yes, reverend," Mary was uncertain whether her remarks would be treated seriously. "Why is evil always represented by a serpent? If God created everything in the universe, why would He create something that we are supposed to revile? Surely, we should be encouraged to revere *all* of God's creation!"

"Damned good point, if you ask me!" Garlick growled.

"Yes, Mary – it is a very good point. And have you thought of the answer? Has anyone?"

Hob's thoughts were centred solely on the beetle that he had in his pocket – and what prank he could play with it. The others looked to Mary to see how she might respond.

"Is it because *we* have made the serpent into an evil thing? After all, worms are like serpents – they wriggle along – and we don't hate them. They're far too useful!"

"In a sense, Mary, you have answered your own question. Almighty God gave us all the means to think and to reason. That means we also have the means to get things wrong as well as right. Perhaps the serpent *is* a harmless thing, but in our minds, it has become the embodiment of evil."

"But some people *are* evil!" Mary persisted. "I remember when there was that battle down on the Heath. I was peeping out of the windows at home, and I saw two soldiers fighting, and both were shouting that God was on *his* side and they were trying to kill one another! Surely, that's evil! And when little Nell's grandfather left her all alone here with her dada who was dying – that *must* be evil!"

"Two hundred years ago, you would be a novice with the nuns," Avril said with a smile. "You are a good person, Mary. You *want* to see the good in people. Unfortunately, some are very far from good! Some even revel in their wickedness!"

"Aye – that they do!" Garlick grunted. "I've seen my fair share of killing – done a bit of it myself. But I never *liked* doing it. I did it because I believed in what I was fighting for!"

"But so do the soldiers who fight for parliament!" Mary knew she was stepping onto dangerous ground.

"Again, you are right. They do believe in their cause. I believe they are wrong and will always say so. But that does not mean I want to kill them all!"

"I have to admit that I can see right on both sides," Avril admitted, knowing full well that Forbes and Garlick were staunchly against parliament. "The king believes he has the divine right to rule without reference to anyone else, He was anointed by the church."

"And that is an end to it, as far as I am concerned!" Forbes insisted. "There can be no argument against it."

"But what about the people he rules? Have we no say in anything at all? That does not seem to be right!"

"It goes against the natural order of things. We have a lord to whom we owe allegiance and obedience. The lord has a duty of allegiance to the king."

"But what if the lord – to whom we owe allegiance – orders us to do something we know to be wrong? If indeed the king orders us to do the same wrong thing?"

"Our anointed king would never ask us to do such a thing!"

"An anointed queen once ordered us to give up people like Archbishop Latimer – and then burned him. That was wrong!"

"But that anointed queen was a Catholic!

"She was still God's anointed!"

Mary was quietly thrilled to hear her Aunt Avril put forward points she had not yet the maturity or daring. She decided to support her – and hang the consequences.

"Parliament has asked that they be consulted – that we be consulted. Surely that cannot be wrong! If we are not ever to be consulted it would mean that the king is always right – and that cannot be so. He is not God – he is a human being like the rest of us – and we are not always right!"

"Well said, Mary," Avril gave her niece a pat on her hand. "If the king claims to be right all of the time, then he is putting himself level with God – and that is surely blasphemy!"

"But we, being loyal subjects, have to assume that whatever the king decides, is in our own interests – he does it for the good of his people!" Forbes argued.

"Against that, the king tolerates – even supports – his queen in her following the teachings of Rome. He swore to uphold the Church of England – he swore that at his coronation. The two things are not compatible!"

"I can see that we are not going to agree," Forbes sighed. "I know you to be a loyal and devoted servant to the church, Mistress Avril. Let us agree that we disagree – and part friends."

"That, Reverend, is tolerance and goodness – as Our Lord taught us."

Young Henry Hogg had listened attentively to the exchanges. His admiration for Mary had increased as he had followed her and her aunt's arguments. He had never before seen Mary in that light – a thinking, erudite young woman. He was quite bowled over.

"Er – Mary," he faltered. "May I see you safely home?"

Avril tried to hide a smile. Mary lived at the bakery that was no more than fifty yards from the church. She decided to advance the young man's cause.

"Aye – Mary. Let Henry escort you safely. I have to see to a few things here first or I would see you home myself."

"Oh, - then thank you, Henry. That would be most kind," Mary replied. It said much for her serious nature that she saw no ulterior motive behind the offer.

Mary donned her warm cloak and followed Henry to the main door of the church, which he opened and held for her. The two walked in silence for the two minutes it took to reach the bakery. Henry had taken those two minutes to rehearse his next speech.

"Mary – would you agree to accompany me to the Eve of Christmas celebration at the tavern?"

Mary was quite startled at this request. She had never thought that she might have sparked the interest of the saddler's son.

"I thought you had eyes for Glory," she said.

"Glory has eyes only for that young parliamentary soldier – or had you not noticed!"

"Nay – that I had not! I cannot see that Master Allen would be pleased were he to know that Glory had eyes for a soldier – especially one from parliament!"

"Glory will go her own way – even if Saint Peter himself told her nay!"

"Aye – I suppose she would," Mary giggled. "Then I shall be happy to go to the celebration with you, Henry – if you do not find me too boring and serious!"

Henry almost skipped the rest of the way down the main street and into his parents' house. He was a happy young man.

* * *

In the darkness of the wood that bordered Bovey Heath, three pairs of eyes surveyed the small town. They concentrated on a small flock of sheep.

"One of those would last us a week or more," Hawkes muttered.

"Ewes be ready to drop lambs in a month or more," Simmonds muttered back. "I will not kill a ewe who is with lambs!"

"Nor I!" Ned Thomas grunted. "'Tis not right!"

"'Tis not right that our bellies be empty!" Hawkes retorted. "There be no tup with them, so that means we have to go back and take one of the goats we saw back aways."

"Goats be not so easy to take quietly!" Thomas warned. "Goats fight back!"

"Goats make a lot of noise!" Simmonds added.

"Oh, for the love of Satan!" Hawkes groaned. "We cannot take geese – they raise heaven with their noise. We cannot take ducks as we have seen none. We cannot take ewes because they are with lamb. What can we take? I see no elephants nor lions!"

"Why do we not take bread, or meat from the butcher?"

"If you have eyes to see, there be no bread ready at midnight – nor be there meat displayed in the butcher's window!"

"Nay – but if we stay here hidden, there will be both aplenty come the dawn!"

"And how may we do that unseen?" Hawkes demanded.

"Why? The same way we take from houses! We are quiet; we have experience; we have daring," Simmonds reminded him.

"Then, be ye content to lie here in the bitter cold until dawn?"

"Aye – we are!"

"I am cursed with addlepates for friends!"

Nevertheless, that is what they did, burrowing into piles of leaves in the vain search for some warmth. Their night dragged past very slowly.

CHAPTER VIII

That Saturday morning started off like the three preceding days – cold, sharp and bright sunshine. By the time the bread delivery was over, and they had eaten their breakfast, Gil and Ella were as usual tending the vegetable plots. Nell had arrived to tend the chickens. She spent a little time each morning and evening with them – topping up their water and filling the bowl with grain in the morning before shooing them outside to peck whilst she cleaned out the coop. In the evenings, she again topped up water and grain and secured them inside for safety against any fox or other marauding predator.

Ella put down her hoe and walked quietly over to Gil.

"Hark," she whispered, putting a finger to her lips. Gil looked up and listened, then he grinned at his young wife. They both crept down to the gate that separated the potato beds from the chicken run.

Nell was inside the coop and was ushering the last of the six out to join the other hens and the rooster.

"Petal – do not be a nuisance. I need you outside with your sisters so that I may make your little house nice and clean. Out you go!"

The hen in question emerged with a flutter of wings, followed by a little girl who was brushing wisps of straw from her apron. She saw Gil and Ella and gave them a happy wave.

"That one is always the last to leave the coop," she said. "Now I can get on with cleaning up properly. Oh – and there are still no eggs!"

"No – we were warned that they might take some days to settle in their new home," Ella nodded. "We should get the first eggs soon."

"Shall I leave the hen who laid it with her egg?"

"Aye – we need chicks more than we need eggs to sell."

"Nell, you called that one Petal. Have you names for all of them?"

"Oh yes – I have named them all. The rooster is Trumpet – because he makes a very loud noise. That hen with the wobbly topknot is Prudence; the one with the brown tips to her wings is Poppy; the one with the black feathers in her tail is Polly; the one over there scratching at the twigs is Penny; the one pecking at the fence is Pippa -- and the one I chased out is Petal."

That recitation was brought to an end with a very loud call from the rooster.

"Aye – I can see why you have named him Trumpet!" Ella laughed. "He certainly makes a very loud noise. Luckily, we are all up and about before he starts in the morning."

"Mistress Green is not," Nell said with a grimace at a cottage two down. "She said I was not fit to look after hens if I could not control them properly."

"Take no heed of that miserable woman," Gil grinned. "Both she and her husband are like a black cloud on a sunny day – they bring misery wherever they go!"

Hubert and Mercy Green were what would best be described as ultra-puritan. They spent a goodly part of every day on their knees. They saw laughter, happiness – especially happiness in children – as signs of wickedness and un-godlike behaviour.

"Master Green said he would take a stick to me if I did not stop singing when I walked here."

"Did he, indeed!" Gil said, turning quite pale with anger.

"He also said that little Rosie made too much noise and that she needed teaching how to be silent."

Gil looked at Ella, then went into the cottage where Rosie was being looked after by young Maud Fletcher. Maud was nine years old and earned a few pennies a day taking care of the little one. She was the daughter of Wilf Fletcher, the ditcher.

Maud looked up as Gil entered the small parlour.

"Rosie wants to put logs on the fire," she said. "I told her that she must not and must stay away from the flames."

"Quite right," Gil nodded. "Rosie – you must do what Maud tells you or you will get hurt."

"Shan't!" Rosie yelled. "Put log on fire!"

"I must ask Ella's father to make us a stout iron guard so that she cannot get near it. I should have done that months ago."

Rosie stood up and toddled over to the log pile, obviously intent on doing what she wanted. Gil made a grab for her and sat her on the table, his face an inch from his little daughter.

"Rosie – listen and listen well! The fire is dangerous and will hurt you. Maud is correct and you must obey her. Look – I will show you what would happen."

He put Rosie down and found a small piece of cloth from Ella's work basket.

"This is like your dress, Rosie. Look what happens to it when I put it on the fire."

The cloth caught immediately and was burned to a cinder in seconds.

"That is what will happen to you if you go near that fire. Do you understand?"

Rosie, as was her custom, switched immediately from disobedient to winsome.

"Yes, dada – love you, dada!" she gave Gil a huge smile. "Rosie shall be good."

"Yes – and pigs may well fly past the window," Gil muttered as he left them to their play. He went down to the Greens' house and went into the bookshop – the front of the Greens' cottage. Hubert was sitting on a stool reading a passage from the book of Amos.

"Master Green," Gil confronted the sour face. "I hear tell that you made threat to take a stick to Nell because she was happy and singing."

"Aye – that I most certainly did. There is no place for such behaviour. Children should be quiet and have their eyes downcast. They should be taught the way to behave in a godlike manner."

"I shall tell you this just one time, Master Green. Should you lay one finger on Nell – or on our Rosie – I shall rip off that finger! Also bear in mind that Nell never had a mother, lost her father and was abandoned by her grandfather. If ever a child needed love and kindness, it is she!"

Gil slammed his hand down on the counter, raising a small cloud of dust, and simply walked back home. He left Hubert Green speechless. Mercy had heard the exchange and came to comfort her husband.

"We have work to do, husband – the day will come when sober and godlike behaviour shall be enforced on them all. We must redouble our efforts to spread the holy word."

* * *

Nell, her chickens and rooster were being watched by three pairs of eyes.

"Go away, little girl, and leave them unguarded," Hawkes muttered from behind a clump of hazel.

Ned Thomas and Art Simmonds were nowhere near as keen to have a go at the chickens – certainly not whilst they were being tended by a small girl. They would have to subdue that child, and neither was keen to do anything of the kind. Stealing was all very well – it filled their belies. Harming children was not at all to their liking.

"Cast your eyes to the right, further up the street," Thomas urged. "The butcher has plenty of meat ready for his customers. Then, further up past the smithy, is the bakers – and they have loaves, pies and cakes aplenty. All we have to do is to wait for the noon dinnertime and that will be our chance."

"Aye – I suppose you be right," Hawkes reluctantly dragged his eyes away from the plump hens. "But – what are those fellows down by the mill? They are soldiers in the uniforms of parliament. We have not seen any of them for many a long day!"

"Mayhap they are stationed in the town?" Simmonds ventured. "They are certainly not just passing through."

"That adds another complication to our quest," Thomas nodded. "They may well not keep to dinnertime as the rest of the town will!"

"Satan's bollocks!" Hawkes swore. "What if they set up patrols to watch the people in case of trouble?"

"Then our bellies will have to wait a bit longer," Simmonds grunted.

"Nay – we sneak to the back of the butcher's when they go for their meal. Take what comes easiest to hand and then straight into the woods and away."

A slight change in the direction of the wind brought Nell's voice clearly to them as they hid out of sight in the hazel clump.

"Which of you is going to lay an egg first? I know – I'll set wagers. One penny for a guess. My guess will be Poppy as she looks the biggest. *Ella!*" she shouted.

"What is it, Nell?"

"I wager a penny that Poppy lays the first egg."

"Then I wager a penny it shall be Penny. That seems likely – Penny for Penny!"

"What will Gil wager?"

"You had better go and ask him. He is within the parlour – probably stopping Rosie doing something!"

"Maud will stop her. Maud is very watchful."

Just then, Gil came out with Rosie on his shoulders. Maud was in the kitchen stirring the vegetable stew for dinner.

"I have told Master Hubert Green that he lays a finger of Nell or Rosie, and I shall rip it off."

"Nell wagers a penny that Poppy will be the first to lay an egg."

"Oh, does she! Then I wager a penny it shall be that Petal – she seems the most reluctant to leave the coop!"

He carried Rosie to the small gate and set her down on the other side. Rosie immediately toddled over to Trumpet and made a grab at his tail feathers. The rooster pecked angrily at one chubby little hand. Rosie squawked and burst into tears. Gil chuckled.

"That, my precious daughter, will teach you not to try to steal his feathers. You have to learn that you cannot have whatever you see."

Nell went over to Rosie and cuddled her. "See," she said, "no harm done. Trumpet missed your fingers." She wiped Rosie's tears with the hem of her apron. "Now – which one do you think will lay the very first egg?"

"That one!" Rosie stated firmly, pointing at Trumpet.

"That is hardly likely," Ella laughed. "Try again!"

"Then that one!"

"Rosie wagers one penny it shall be Pippa," Nell declared. "I shall remember all our wagers. I wonder when it shall be?"

"Ella," Came Maud's voice from the kitchen door. "Vegetable stew be ready."

"Then it be time for dinner. Everybody, wash hands first, please."

* * *

Troopers Fallow and Young had paused in their patrol. They were at the side of the gate that led to the church, munching their way through mutton and onion pies that they had bought from Evelyn in the bakery shop. They knew that what they were doing was not strictly in accordance with the rules — they were supposed to patrol for a whole two hours. Nevertheless, the delicious smells emanating from the bakery had proved too enticing. Therefore, they were half hidden behind the hedge that grew both sides of the large gateway.

Young, who was blessed with the sharpest eyesight, happened to glance across the main street, downwards towards the smithy and the butchers. He did a double-take and nudged his colleague.

"What do you think those two be up to?" he muttered, directing Fallow's eyes to the space between the smithy and the butchers. "Just saw them sneak past the side of the smithy."

"Let's stay silent and watch," Fallow muttered back.

Hawkes and Thomas, the two in question, peered anxiously around the corner of the smithy. They could feel the heat from the forge but could hear no sounds of movement either from the smith's workshop or from the butcher's shop. Simmonds, at the back of the smithy was keeping watch on the rear.

"Seems like as good a chance as we may get," Hawkes murmured. "Are you sure there is no bell on the shop door?"

"Aye — I watched and listened earlier in the morning. I heard no bell."

"Then we do as planned. You open the door silently and stay there with it open. I shall go in and grab whatever comes nearest to hand. Then we go back out and close the door lest whoever is in the back notices the cold creeping in."

"And we go back the way we came?"

"Aye — back past the smithy, across that field and straight into the trees and away."

Simmonds, earlier that morning, had proposed a different plan.

"Why do we not simply walk in and buy the meat? We have plenty of coin from that house we robbed!"

"And we need to keep that coin!" Hawkes replied. "We must only ever use it if there be no other means of obtaining what we need."

Simmonds was not happy – but Simmonds never was. Hawkes privately regarded him as a misery-guts – but most reliable in a fight.

Thomas edged towards the butcher's door and peered around it. He could see nobody in the shop – and the door to the back parlour was closed. He silently pushed open the door and beckoned to Hawkes who crept silently into the shop and reached immediately for a leg of lamb that was on the nearest hook. He took it down, hook and all, then crept back out again. Thomas silently closed the door. The two crept back to the smithy, all ready to make their escape.

"Time to interfere, I do believe," Fallow grunted, taking his pistol from his side holster. Young copied this action and the two burst from the gate and raced across the street.

"Stop where you are!" Fallow roared, seeing Thomas about to disappear down the little, dark passage.

Thomas, who was a few yards behind Hawkes, fled down the passage between the two buildings. He was a sitting duck. Fallow's pistol roared and Thomas felt a massive blow between his shoulders. He gave a shriek of pain and tumbled forward. Hawkes, simply dropped the meat and raced into the open, gathered a stunned Simmonds and the two fled to the cover of the trees – where they simply disappeared.

Within a few minutes, the street was thronged with people. Everyone in the little town had heard the pistol shot. Simon Dingle, the butcher, and his wife Stella were the first to emerge. Abel Smith the blacksmith, John and Evelyn Ramsey from the bakery, and a host of others congregated at the mouth of the lane. They watched as Young and Fallow examined the mortally wounded man. Young came back towards the throng with the leg of lamb.

"Yours, I believe, Master Butcher," he grinned. "I doubt you received payment for it!"

Fallow walked back more slowly. "I have no idea who he was – or who his friends were – but I believe this town will not see them again. That one," he gestured over his shoulder, "will never steal again. He is dead."

He could not fail to notice that a very few of the people thronged in the street crossed themselves in the old way. He decided not to make any comment – he had seen many people in shock at the killings that had taken place throughout the country as royalists and parliamentarians had slaughtered one another.

Reverend Forbes pushed his way to the front and, without asking leave, went straight to the dead Thomas. He fell to his knees and administered the last rites, then ordered the sexton, Sam Fewings, to fetch the small cart so that the body could be transported to the shed at the side of the church to be prepared for burial.

Sergeant Paul Larkin, who had arrived some minutes after the shot had been fired, made his presence known.

"Hold fast, Reverend," he said. "By all means get the body out here. But I need everyone here to view the man. I need to be told whether he be known to anyone!"

Forbes recognised that this was a perfectly legitimate order. He and his sexton lugged Thomas' body out and laid it at the side of the street. Larkin ordered everyone to walk past it - and watched the faces intently as they shuffled along. He was looking for any change in facial expression – and did not see the slightest flicker. All he saw was sorrow and shock.

He allowed the body to be carted away to the church hut, then asked everyone else to go back to their homes and businesses. He turned to his two troopers.

Young and Fallow gave him a detailed report of what they had seen, being careful to say that they had been in the church ground and not behind the hedge scoffing pies!

"Seems we have a small gang of thieves in the neighbourhood," he grunted. "I doubt if this town will see them again. You did your duty as you should. Well done."

Simon Dingle came across to the three soldiers holding the leg of lamb.

"I would have lost this had you not stopped those thieves," he said, holding it out. "One good turn deserves another – so please accept this with my thanks."

Larkin was a trifle taken aback by this gesture.

"But we are not of your loyalties," he pointed out.

"If you be here to uphold law and order, then I for one care not who you serve," Dingle replied.

That evening, the soldiers ate roasted lamb. Thomas was laid out, washed and shrouded. The town of Bovey Tracey went to bed with very mixed emotions.

CHAPTER IX

The following Tuesday morning was again cold, but the sun had disappeared to be replaced by lowering clouds that threatened snow – certainly over the moor.

Gil and Ella were busy as normal, wrapped up against the cold as they dug up potatoes and very late carrots. They were disturbed by a squeal from the chicken coop. Nell, wrapped up in layers of clothes, appeared at the small gate.

"Prudence is sitting on an egg!" she chortled. "Nobody won the wager!"

"At last – I wondered if it was ever going to happen," Ella was as delighted as Nell. "I wonder which will be next. Perhaps we should hold the wagers over to see."

"What do I do now?" Nell asked. "Do I leave her alone?"

"Aye – leave her all by herself and shoo the others out for the day. She will be quite content keeping her egg warm. In three weeks, you are going to have your first little chick."

"But it's going to be very cold," Nell said. "Do little chicks need to be kept very warm?"

"Aye, they do. I'll have a word with Aunt Avril. She will know how to go about it."

"When will the little chicks start laying their own eggs? They will be very tiny for a long time!"

"I need to check that also – but I think it's about six months after they hatch."

"I believe it's actually five months," Gil broke in. He gave a big grin. "I heard Aunt Avril talking about it some days ago – or I would not have known!"

"I wonder if Master Green has any books on the keeping and raising of chickens?" Ella mused.

"Well, if he has, I shall be the very last person to ask him!" Gil frowned.

"I shall ask my father to go and see," Ella smiled. "Can you imagine Master Green being rude to my father?"

"Nay – it would take twenty of Master Green to chance that!"

"We really should have done more research into the whole business," Ella said thoughtfully. "We seem to be all at sea – and we should not be. I well remember your Uncle James asking if we had planned it properly."

Gil did not answer that one. He knew that he was a bit impetuous. He was a great believer in the saying that things usually turned out for the best. He just hoped that this enterprise followed suit.

*   *   *

Sergeant Larkin had just finished his dinner in the cottage when he was alerted by the sound of rapid hoofbeats that clattered to a stop outside. Cursing, he put down his spoon and went to see what the fuss was all about. A mounted courier sat in the saddle, his horse lathered in sweat.

"That be no way to treat a good mount," Larkin remonstrated. "What can be so urgent that you made such haste?"

"A message and a notice from Captain Brooke, sergeant," the courier said, slipping down and patting the horse's neck.

"The first thing we do is to get that poor nag wiped down, fed and watered," Larkin insisted. He looked back into the cottage and yelled for Bell.

"Take this mount to the stables and see that it is properly tended. Now – what is this message?"

Bell led the horse away to the stables and Larkin led the way into the small parlour. The courier handed Larkin a paper that was folded and sealed. It was a large piece of paper!

"Message is that this paper is to be displayed prominently in this town, sergeant, and that all appropriate citizens be instructed to read it.!

"And that is the message?"

"Aye, sergeant – word for word."

Larkin examined the seal and saw that it was simply a blob of red wax, no imprint of a signet impressed into it. The inserted the tip of his dagger and broke the seal and unfolded the large paper. He read it through and gave a whistle of surprise.

"This cannot be the official notice – it is not worded in the usual manner of a clerk."

"I saw Captain Brooke write it himself – he seemed to be reading a large scroll at the same time."

Larkin called for a bowl of stew for the courier plus a mug of ale.

"Refresh yourself and leave that poor horse of yours for at least an hour before you return to Rougemont. And this time, pay more attention to your mount! A courier who loses his horse from exhaustion half-way along his route is of no use to anyone!"

Suitably chastened, the young courier did as he was told. Larkin went outside into the bitter cold to read the notice through twice more.

"That is not going to earn us any friends!" he muttered. "I wonder how the official notice reads. I'll wager it is written in terms more acceptable to a lawyer. This is blunt and provocative."

He shrugged and went back inside to wrap himself up warm for the short walk to Parke. That had to be his first port of call. He knocked at the bailiff's door and again was greeted by young Hob.

"Sergeant be here, Master Bailiff," he called out.

Peter Cove invited Larkin into the warm office and offered him a mug of ale.

"You may wish to withdraw that offer once you are aware of the purpose of my visit," Larkin grinned wryly.

"What can be so bad as all that?" Cove asked. "Surely you have not found armed insurrection in the town!"

"Nay – but when you and the town have read this notice that I must post, there could well be! Is Sir John here?"

"His lordship has yet to return. In truth, I have no idea when that may be. So, what is in this message that threatens upheaval?"

Larkin passed over the notice. Cove read it and did what Larkin had done – he whistled in dismay.

"I certainly take your point, sergeant. This is not going to be read with equanimity!"

He held the paper before him and read aloud.

"Be it known that Charles Stuart, present holder of the office of King of England, Scotland and Ireland, shall be brought from his place of confinement to face charges which shall be published in due course in the form of an indictment and that the said Charles Stuart shall be prosecuted at Westminster Hall according to the customs and laws that pertain at the present time."

"That hardly reads as an official announcement!" Cove observed.

"I agree – the courier who brought it from Rougemont said that my Captain wrote it himself whilst reading the official document."

"And you are presumably instructed to post this notice?"

"Aye, that I am. But first I must satisfy myself that it is indeed a fair summary of the official announcement. I shall leave immediately for Rougemont and shall return on the morrow – either to forget all about it, or to post it as instructed."

"And in the meantime, I keep this to myself?"

"I would deem it a favour, Master Bailiff. To post that in its present form would be dangerous to the maintenance of peace and good order. But should it be a fair summary, then I shall have to take measures to ensure that peace and good order may be held in place. And only the Good Lord knows how I may achieve that!"

Larkin downed the ale, gave his thanks to the bailiff and hurried back to the stables. He saddled his horse himself and, leaving Tamplin in charge, rode off at a steady pace, the notice securely folded into his satchel.

*   *   *

A notice did appear on the church gate that evening – a notice that had nothing whatsoever to do with kings, parliament, or impending charges.

"Beware the wrath of God. This church, so near to the idolatry of Rome, is no place for you! Turn aside from false gods. You are breaking the covenant and doing evil in the sight of the Lord. This is said clearly in the Book of Judges. Turn aside and follow the true path to redemption. It shall not be found within these gates!"

An hour later, before it was found by Will Garlick, someone had appended one word to it.

"Bollocks!"

Garlick grinned, took the notice and posted it under the front door of the bookshop, whence he was sure it had originated.

"Bloody Hubert and Mercy up to their games again," he muttered, wandering back up the street to the tavern where he sat and quaffed a large mug of mulled ale.

He was old enough and wise enough to realise that the Greens were far from alone in their ultra-puritan beliefs. He was fully aware that many who sat in parliament were of the same opinions as Hubert and Mercy Green. He also had grave misgivings about the real intentions of this parliament. Their war against the king and his insistence on sole rule was one thing. Their religious beliefs were another – and he was not at all sure where this was all leading.

CHAPTER X

Nell was giggling as she came to report to Ella the next morning.

"Poppy has laid an egg and is sitting on it – so I win the wager!" she crowed.

"Then that's two little chicks that you will have to look after when they hatch."

Ella sat Nell down.

"Nell, I have had a word with Aunt Avril. She says that what we must do is to make a small place in the kitchen where it is warm so that, when the chicks break out of their eggs, they and their mothers may be brought in here out of the cold. Gil is finding some timber to nail together a small corner coop for them. The hens will need water and feed, and so will the chicks. When you go home today, you must ask Avril what sort of grain and seeds are right for the little ones."

"We are lucky – Avril and James know so much! James tells me all about the stars and the planets and gives me books to read. Avril tells us all about chickens and also teaches me about herbs and medicines."

"Also, Nell – here is my penny and that of Gil and Rosie. You won the wager."

Nell took the three pennies and sat back on her heels.

"May we ask Master Crowley to make a wooden doll for Rosie with my pennies? It shall be my present to her. My dada made my doll for me, and it would be nice for Rosie to have one."

"That is a lovely thought. Aye – after dinner, you and I shall go to Master Crowley and ask him to make one for Rosie.

Nell blew Ella a kiss and hurried back to her chickens. Ella gazed after the little girl, wondering not for the first time, how kind and thoughtful she was. Given her dreadful luck with mother, father and grandfather, she would have been forgiven had she been self-centred. Instead of which, her thoughts were always for others.

* * *

Sergeant Larkin arrived back later that morning, saw to his horse, then walked back to the bailiff's house.

"From your expression, sergeant, you seem to be the bearer of poor news," Peter Cove ushered Larkin into his warm office. He again mulled a mug of ale for the sergeant who accepted it gratefully.

"Aye – you have the right of it. 'Tis not good news. I managed to look at the official notice – without my Captain being aware of it. What he has written is indeed a bald synopsis of it. I have no choice but to publish it as ordered."

"Although we be on opposing sides, we are both charged with the keeping of order in the town. Therefore, I shall make it known that all must gather before sunset at the square where I shall read it out – and make an appeal to all to keep the peace."

"That would be very welcome, Master Bailiff. It is my task, but it comes better from you. But I must add words when you have finished."

"Then let us both pray that we are able to put a firm lid on what will be a seething kettle!"

* * *

The news spread, like news always did in the small town – very quickly. There was wild speculation amongst some as to the purpose of the meeting; There were those who said that it was news of the king's reinstatement; others were equally as vehement that parliament were about to impose stringent new taxes; a few – a blessed few – who were convinced that the French and the Scots had united yet again and were on the point of invasion, perhaps had already done so.

It therefore came as a shock to have the notice read out to them by their own bailiff. Peter Cove folded the paper and handed it to Larkin.

"I am charged by Sir John Vickery to keep good order in this his manor. I fully intend to do so. Therefore, I urge all here present to abide by the law and refrain from any action that may bring dire consequences. Let us wait until we are told of the nature of the charges brought against our king. Until then, we do not know how serious they may be."

"Your Master Bailiff has urged patience and good order," Larkin added. "I also urge you to do so. I bear none of you any ill will – nor do my soldiers. But mark this and mark it well. Any sign of insurrection – be it armed or not – will be supressed. Go about your lives and your businesses as normal and I shall not have to take action. But action I will take should there be any violence!"

The meeting, attended by nearly all the inhabitants of the town, broke up into small groups – some angry, some resigned, some openly weeping. James and Avril immediately invited the Ramseys and the Smiths to their house where they sat and mulled over what they had heard.

Faith was the first to put down her small mug of mead and express her horror at what they had just been told.

"They cannot charge an anointed king with offences, can they?"

"They – and I mean parliament – can now do anything they choose," James said, holding up his hands in what amounted to a sign of surrender. "They have won battle after battle: they have the king in custody – or what amounts to custody. Prince Charles is fled, along with his advisers and commanders. Believe me, parliament is in sole charge. And as Gil and Ella will find out when they have more cock birds, he who crows loudest rules the roost."

"But is it even lawful that a king may be charged? Is there such a law?" Evelyn asked.

"I have no idea whether there be or not," James admitted. "But parliament has only to draft such a law and it is then enforceable – because they say so!"

"So, we are all powerless and must do as parliament decrees?" Avril was aghast at the notion.

"Let me play devil's advocate," James said, steepling his fingers – a sure sign that he was about to deliver a lecture. "Up until now, the king has ruled almost without any interference from parliament. What the king wanted the king took – because he claimed divine right. What parliament wanted never weighed a single feather with the king. Parliament claims to represent the people of this country – although in practise they represent only the landowners. Parliament argues that they have as much right as the king to make and amend laws. What is good for one, should be good for all – or so they claim. Are they wrong?"

"They must be!" John argued. "It has never been so. The king is anointed by God to rule."

"But what if parliament states that his rule is corrupt? We all know the history of this land. There have been corrupt kings afore now! The second Edward is just one example."

"Does anyone here believe that our king Charles is corrupt? Mistaken in many things he may be – the tolerance of his wife's open Catholicism is clearly mistaken. But that does not make his whole rule corrupt!" Avril argued.

"Believe me – if parliament decides the rule be corrupt, then corrupt it will be!"

There seemed little anyone could add to that conversation, so they decided to change tack and talk about the coming Christmas festivities instead.

* * *

Hawkes had followed Simmonds blindly as they ran through the woods. His main thought was for the loss of that leg of lamb rather than the probable loss of a colleague. They had been running in a zig-zag pattern for some minutes when Simmonds stopped and listened, signalling for Hawkes to stand still.

"Nothing – think they didn't follow us," he muttered, gasping to get his breath back. "What happened to Ned?"

"Dunno," Hawkes gasped back. "There was a shot – but you probably heard that. I think whoever that was, got him – and we've lost the meat!"

"I'm going back to the edge of the wood – see what's going on. Might be able to help Ned."

"Oh no, you bloody well will not!" Hawkes growled. "Whatever happened, he's either dead or a prisoner. Nothing we can do. Let's go due south instead of straight back to the cottage- just in case some clever bastard is tracking us."

"Suppose you're right," Simmonds realised that Ned was probably a lost cause.

They came to the far edge of that wood and immediately struck off along the edge of a large open space, heading due south instead of south-east. They kept going along a thick hedge and then crossed a stone wall to see a farmhouse, sheds and a barn ahead of them. They also saw a man and a woman plus two children repairing a gap in the stone wall about a hundred yards to the right of the house.

"Too good a chance to miss!" Hawkes grinned. "House or sheds?"

"Sheds, definitely!" Simmonds stated firmly. "Could too easily get trapped in the house."

The farm formed the centre of a tiny hamlet named Coldeast – not that either of the two men knew or cared. They kept to a tall hedge until they were just about level with the buildings. The four people intent on their work were hidden from view by the large barn. Hawkes led the way silently to the nearest shed, pulled open the door and stopped a whistle of surprise just in time. Hanging from hooks, out of reach of any wandering animals, were a flitch of bacon and a joint of pork – kept out in the raw cold to ensure they stayed fresh.

Two hours later, having lost their way a couple of times, they were back in the ruined cottage. Simmonds had hung the two large joints up, having cut off a sizeable piece of the pork. Hawkes had lit the fire and had used an old iron rod to fashion a spit which he arranged across two forked branches. After a while, the tantalising aroma of roasting pork filed the space, making their mouths water in anticipation.

As night fell, the two huddled into their makeshift beds, bellies filled – and hardly a thought for their missing colleague.

* * *

Christmas Eve that year fell on Sunday. A decree of parliament had ordered that Christmas Day was like any other – shops must open, and work must be carried out as normal. It was also widely suspected that all church services be stopped. The ultra-puritan parliament wanted each day of the week to be one of dedicated service to God – and no one needed to go to a church to acknowledge it. These new laws were rigorously enforced where there were enough troops to do the job. However, in far-flung parts of the country, it had proved impossible to enforce – there were nowhere near enough enforcers to do the work. Small towns and villages – like Bovey Tracey, far from Westminster – did have informers. But the bulk of the people in those traditional little places still were determined to go their own way.

The snow arrived just after ten in the morning. Everyone in the small town knew that just a few miles to the west up on the moor, it would be far worse than down in the Bovey River valley. By noon dinner time, there were two inches covering Bovey Tracey, blown on a strong and bitter wind. Nell arrived in the small kitchen and immediately made for the fire – and stood in a puddle of melted snow.

"How are the hens?" Ella asked, putting a pile of chopped herbs into the dinner stew which was bubbling in the large iron pot.

"Every one of them except Petal has eggs to sit on – and they are content. I have filled their water bowl and scattered seed and meal for them until the morning."

"I'll come out with you then," Ella promised. "Twill be Christmas Day and we must all get to church soon after we have tended to them, although we are not supposed to celebrate."

"And I must collect the doll from Master Crowley. He promised to have it finished today."

"Are Avril and James taking you to the service this evening?" Gill called out from the parlour – he was trying to get Rosie to sit on her high stool for the coming meal. Rosie, as usual, had far more pressing matters to attend to – throwing twigs onto the parlour fire – and decided to offer what resistance she could.

"Aye – we are all going," Nell called back. "Will you all be there?"

"We shall bring Rosie whether she likes it or not. She will probably sleep through it all as usual."

"I am not sorry that my mother and father are hosting the Christmas dinner," Ella said, giving the stew one last stir. "Next year, twill be our turn. Just maybe, Rosie will have learned to behave better by then."

"Do *not* place a wager on it!" Gil laughed, finally plonking his recalcitrant daughter on her stool. "There is much room for improvement still!"

"Rosie is a good girl!" the little one shouted in defiance.

"Aye, my precious – you can be a good girl. But not always!"

Rosie looked up at her young father and gave him her biggest grin – one that never failed to melt Gil's heart.

"Love you, dada," she said, and blew him a kiss.

Nell heard that distinctly and turned away to hide the tears that came immediately to her eyes. She well remembered saying that to her own dada as she lay beside him on the day before he died. He had never woken from the coma, having fallen from the back of the cart and cracked the back of his head. Avril and James had taken the young man and Nell into their home to nurse the injured fellow – and Nell had been with them ever since.

CHAPTER XI

The church of Saints Peter, Paul and Thomas was packed on Christmas morning – so full that people stood in the central isle as well as in the side aisles. The Reverend James Forbes beamed happily as he started the service; he hadn't seen so many in the church at any one time since the previous Christmas – not even at Easter, when it should have been overflowing. Forbes knew that he was flying in the face of what everyone suspected was the law. And so, he addressed the congregation at the very start.

"Good friends, we all suspect that this is *not* supposed to be happening – as all of you be well aware. However, tis the birth of Christ our Redeemer and we shall celebrate that come what may!"

That resulted in a rousing cheer from all within the church. When it came time for the gospel reading, he did something that had been on his mind for some time. He broke with convention – some said he broke the laws of the church – and brought up some children to read it, a paragraph at a time. Maud Fletcher, nine years old, went first, followed by Kat Gates, the miller's daughter. Forbes read the middle section himself, then called on Zachary Allen from the tavern. Last to read was Nell. Forbes had to pick very carefully from the few young children who could actually read and write – and there were not many from which to choose.

As Nell went forward to take her turn, Rosie piped up in her normal manner – totally oblivious to her surroundings.

"Where be Nell going?" she demanded. It says much for the example set by the rector that it was followed by loud chuckles – and not one voice raised to tell her to shush.

Nearly the whole of the small town streamed out of the church, each receiving a greeting from Forbes, Garlick, Verger and Sexton. Standing in the street at the gates were Hubert and Mercy Green.

"Shame on you all," Hubert bellowed. "Tis no time for hilarity. Tis a time for prayer and silent thanksgiving! Thou all knowest that the law of God forbids such naked displays of ribald worship. Mistress Green and I shall make it our bounden duty to inform the proper authorities – and ye shall all receive punishment. Get thee all to your homes, carry on your proper tasks and beg forgiveness!"

"You really are a miserable sod," Simon Dingle, the butcher, gave him a massive pat on the back. "Have you never heard the word happy?"

"Nay!" his wife growled. "That face might crack asunder if he smiled!"

She started what then became a ritual. One by one, the people walked past and slapped Hubert on the back and roared, 'be happy – tis Christmas!'.

The Ramseys and the Smiths all made their way to the smithy for the celebratory dinner. Faith had turned the large parlour behind the smithy into more of an open space. Chairs and benches lined one long and one short wall, the other long wall holding two large trestle tables. The room was decorated with holly boughs and ribbons of varied colours.

"I know tis not customary to celebrate like this until the morrow - Saint Stephen's day," she said. "But both Abel and I thought that we all needed some extra cheer!"

"Talking of extra cheer," Abel boomed. "Simon – come and help me bring in the wine and the mead. You can then mull the wine. Nell – would you find mugs and glasses for everyone?"

"Avril, Evelyn, Mary, and Ella can come in and help me to finish off the cooking of the meal," Faith rounded up her cohort of cooks.

John, James and Gil were thus at a loose end – until Rosie demanded that they all tried to find her when she had hidden. Gil prudently closed and barred the door to the smithy. Even though the furnace was cold, he did not want his little daughter to think she could pop in and out of that dangerous place whenever the fancy took her. There were tongs, hammers, cold chisels and other things in there that could do considerable damage in the hands of a twenty-month-old.

The three men sat and faced the wall with their eyes closed. Rosie, thinking they were completely unaware of her movements, toddled over to the long trestle and crawled beneath, pulling the covering cloth back in place. The three men, knowing exactly where she was, spent as long as they could vainly searching for her.

"She is not on that top shelf!" James announced, knowing full well that no little tot could possibly have climbed up there.

"And she's not in the log basket either," Gil announced.

"I wonder if she might be behind the linen cupboard, for she is not within it!" John said.

They studiously ignored the stifled giggles coming from beneath the trestle table.

Gil, realising that his Rosie would soon be getting fed up with the delay, suddenly pulled the cloth aside.

"Boo!" he grinned. "Found you!"

They were spared any more games with the arrival of a large pewter bowl of wine which Simon set down beside the fire. He took the poker – which he had fashioned himself a year ago – and thrust it into the heart of the fire. Rosie immediately made a grab for the protruding handle - but was snatched away by her sixteen-year-old, and huge uncle.

"That will burn you," Simon said. "Look – give me your hand!"

He took one very small hand in his own large one and held it out towards the fire.

"Hot!" yelled Rosie.

"Yes – hot!" Simon replied. "That poker is getting much hotter. It is dangerous and you must not touch it."

"Want to!"

"Yes – we all know you want to. Just wait and I'll show you why you must not!"

A few minutes later, Simon took the pad of cloth which he always had poked through his belt. He wrapped his hand in it and withdrew the poker and touched the end to a log in the basket. Immediately, it scorched a mark in the bark.

"See?" he said to Rosie, who was still clasped by one muscular arm.

"Hot! Made a big mark."

"Aye – think what a nasty mark it would make on your hand."

"Must not touch!"

"Clever girl. Must never touch!" Simon pushed the poker back into the fire and then thrust it into the bowl of wine. It bubbled and an immediate aroma arose to fill the parlour with the scent of pine and cinnamon.

To be on the safe side, Simon put the poker back into the fire now that he knew the lesson had been learned. Abel came in with a large jug of honey mead, followed by Nell with her arms full of mugs.

"Simon is going to make a brilliant father," John told him.

"Aye – just like his own father is!" Abel grinned, ruffling his son's hair. Simon went red with embarrassment and muttered under his breath.

It had been wondered for some time whether or not Simon would follow his sister Ella's example and marry Gil's sister Mary. The two had known about this for years and had always gone along with the pretence. They had been lifelong friends – and that was how both of them wanted it to continue. Gil was well aware of that situation.

"And how is the lovely Imelda?" he asked. That caused Simon to go an even deeper shade of red. Imelda Grubb, daughter of the shoemaker, was indeed a very pretty girl – and a year younger than Simon. Both were the same age as Gil and Ella had been when they had married.

"Imelda Grubb," Abel looked at his son. "Hmm – a very pretty lass. Have you asked Master Grubb's permission to keep company?"

"Aye, father, sometime past. He and Mistress Grub both gave consent."

"And why am I and your mother only just discovering all this?"

"Pray what am I just discovering?" Faith came in dusting flour off her apron.

"That our son, the secretive young hound, is paying court to Imelda."

Faith immediately gave her massive son a hug. "And why have you not told us – tis good news indeed."

"I have to admit that I knew," Mary came I, also dusting flour from herself. "I know everyone expected Simon and me to follow Ella's and Gil's footsteps – but we are friends for life and never destined to be wed."

"And who then *are* you destined to wed?" John asked.

"I believe you may be asked a similar question by Matt Crowley," Mary replied.

"And that I had suspected," Gil grinned. "Matt has spoken to me a few times, praising Mary to the heavens!"

"So – you are set to gain a daughter for the smithy, and we are destined to lose a daughter to a carpenter," Evelyn summed it all up.

"I can think of worse families for our Mary to marry into," John remarked. "Peter and Lou Crowley are good folks – and he is a superb craftsman."

Avril gave Nell a secret grin. Peter the carpenter had made the little doll that Nell wanted to give to Rosie the next day. Lou had painted the face and the hands. Nell was delighted with it and had kept it hidden in her bed.

"Merciful heavens," Faith exclaimed. "What with two families of Ramsey, another of Smith, yet a third of Grubb – and now a fourth of Crowley – we shall have to hire the entire tavern for next Christmas if all comes about!"

The dinner passed with much banter across the parlour – everyone sitting with platters of food on their laps. Even Rosie sat on a cushion on the floor, far too immersed into duck and vegetables to contemplate any mischief.

By the time the sun set that late afternoon, lighting up the relatively small amount of snow, the parlour looked like an armed horde had passed through. Empty mugs and glasses were strewn across the trestle tables; empty platters were scattered over the floor.

"Tis time Nell and I went to settle the hens," Ella announced, fetching their cloaks from the pegs by the door.

"How many are sitting on eggs?" James asked.

"Five now, and only two more weeks until the first one hatches," Nell said. "Or that is what we hope."

Ella opened the door to the smithy, letting in a draught of bitter cold air. Nell followed her out and, just as Ella was about to close the door behind her, everyone heard a scream from fairly close by, followed by another scream for help!

* * *

Earlier that afternoon, Sergeant Larkin and four of his soldiers had wandered up to the tavern for a Christmas Day drink. None of them had attended the service at the church that morning. They knew that, should they be reported, they would be in a bit of trouble.

"I do believe that you all are just here for a normal day of drink," Larkin gave the tavern keeper a stern look. "It cannot be that you be flouting the laws and are celebrating Christmas!"

"Nay, sergeant," Dick Allen. "Perish the thought that this town would disobey the laws!"

Larkin knew full well that, up and down the small town, Christmas feasts were being eaten. He was also a realist and knew that his task of keeping the peace would be made infinitely more difficult if he started banning this and that. As long as the peace was maintained, he was happy.

Bell and Young had drawn a short straw and had found themselves on patrol duty whilst the others had gone to the tavern. Tamplin and Dellow had been drawn into a game with three of the young children and had supplied 'horses' for the kiddies to ride around the large taproom. Larkin had been chatting to Dick Allen for a while – the tavern keeper surprised to feel no animosity for the tall soldier who was regarded by many as an occupying force.

As two more people entered the tavern to cries of 'Merry Christmas', everyone within heard the scream and the cry for help. Most of the men present scrambled out of the doorway to see what it was all about. A bit further down the street, the smithy emptied out – everyone peering this way and that. And then, out of the short passage that led between the butcher's and the carpenter's shop fronts, came a slight figure clutching a ragged robe around it. The figure within was sobbing and crying out for help.

Abel and James were the first to reach the bedraggled figure.

"Tis May Fletcher," James called out as everyone clustered around. "May – what has happened?"

The girl – just twelve years old – looked around, searching for any family member amongst the crowd.

"I'll go and fetch them," Simon volunteered, and raced off down the street to where Wilf Fletcher, his wife Patience and smaller daughter Maud lived. Even with the hubbub, all heard the loud knocking at the Fletcher's door. Within minutes, the ditcher, wife and little daughter were hurrying up to the crowd. Patience fell to her knees and clasped May to her.

"What's needed is calm," Dick Allen pronounced. "Let us all withdraw and see what Patience and Wilf may learn."

Everyone thought this sound advice and withdrew a way in silence. All they heard was May, gulping back tears and muttering to her mother and father. Little Maud stood to one side, wondering what had happened to her sister. After a few minutes, Wilf Fletcher left May in her mother's embrace and came across to the group.

"May was attacked as she walked down from the church. She says she was dragged down that alley, was beaten and her clothes torn. It was an attempt at rape! May the Good Lord be praised that she escaped that at least!"

"Amen to that!" Dick answered for all of them. He cast around until his eye lighted upon his own son Zachary.

"Zachary – run as fast as you may to the bailiff. We need him here as soon as possible. I suggest that the rest of us split up into groups of four or more and search for the culprit."

"Aye – that makes good sense," Abel growled. "But what does the bastard look like? Find him and bring him to the smithy and I'll hammer off his bits with my bluntest chisel!"

"Nay, Master Smith!" Larkin needed to exert his authority. "Find him by all means – and render him to me. Believe me, he shall not escape lawful punishment!"

"Was probably one of these bloody soldiers," someone at the back shouted.

"Twas certainly not one of these," Dick Allen stated loudly. "The sergeant and those other four were in the tavern the last hour or more!"

"Then must be one of the other two!" the same voice shouted.

All shouting stopped as running feet came up the street. Bailiff Cove, with Troopers Bell and Young.

Peter Cove was brought up to date by Larkin, his normally calm face broke into a grim scowl.

"Can young May give us any description?" he asked.

"What about questioning those two bloody soldiers first!" the same voice shouted.

"What – these two?" Cove scratched his head. "Nay – they have been with me patrolling the estate – some of the early lambs have gone missing. It would seem that it be either one who lives here amongst us – or that it was some vagrant creeping through the town!"

Larkin heaved a huge sigh of relief that all six of his men were exonerated from any blame. Patience then led a tearful May up to the bailiff.

"Cannot be one of they soldiers anyway," she announced. "May says the man wore a woollen cloak – not one of those boiled leather coats! He was cloaked and wore a hood and mask!"

"Might it be one and the same as tried to steal my leg of lamb?" Simon Dingle wondered. "Mayhap they've gone from a joint to a whole lamb!"

"Aye, tis possible," Luke Barton, the Parke steward had joined the throng of people. "But how would that match with an attack on the maid?"

"We are just wasting time discussing what might be. Let us set up a proper search," Cove instructed.

Groups of four or more immediately started off, going along the sides of houses and shops and searching outbuildings and the open ground of the Heath, all the way down to the river.

Patience led her two daughters home. Wilf Fletcher went with the group that was led by the bailiff. He was silent as they scoured every alleyway and garden between the bakery and the mill. They found nothing and nobody – and not a sign in the alleyways that the light dusting of snow had been disturbed.

Sergeant Larkin took two of his soldiers, along with Gil and Zachary. He did the obvious thing – went down the alley where the attack had taken place. He stopped where there was a mass of smudged footprints.

"Here is where the young maid was dragged," he stated the obvious. "Can anyone see signs of footsteps beyond – towards the open field?"

Zachary, being the youngest and lightest, was hoisted aloft on the shoulders of the two soldiers.

"Nay – not a sign!" he reported.

"Then the bugger ran back out the way he came in! Where would he most likely go from there?"

"If he had an ounce of sense, he would have got off the street as soon as he could," Gil answered. "The nearest way would be up the street to the smithy – there will be much mess in the snow there and would hide his footsteps."

He led the way back up the street and stopped at the smithy. There was indeed a trampled mess – and there had been many footmarks along the street. Gil, more familiar than any of the others with the smithy, went to the right side of the building and peered into the alley between that and his parents' bakery.

"There be something strange here," he called out. Larkin and the others joined him. "Look – the snow is hardly deep enough in here to take a footprint – the overhang of the smithy has sheltered the alley from the snowfall. But see at the side of the smithy – there be sliding marks – as if someone has shuffled down so as not to leave a footprint."

"Aye – you have the right of it," Larkin nodded. "Let's see what happens when the marks cease."

Gil led the way to the end of the short alley. The sliding marks continued to the left and continued up past the back of the bakery, and then left again to join the street just opposite the church. The marks ceased there and joined the many footprints in the light snow. None of them pointed up and out of the town.

"Crafty bastard simply joined everyone else coming down the street!" Larkin declared. "Is it possible he was one of the crowd that assembled with all of us?"

"Best place to hide is in a crowd," Trooper Tamplin stated. "All he had to do was to remove hood and mask and no one the wiser!"

Larkin turned to young Zachary.

"You were with us when we all came from the tavern. It was probably our group he joined. You are best placed to note who was in that group as you know most folks hereabouts. I need you to go back to the tavern in the warm, sit down in a quiet place and draw up a list of all you can remember."

"Aye – I can but try," Zachary nodded, and made his way back into the near empty tavern. He sat down with a mug of ale by the roaring fire to think.

Meanwhile, Larkin had dispatched his two troopers to summon back all the other search parties. It was doubtful indeed that they would find anything untoward.

A while later, the tavern was bursting at the seams. Dick, Sal and Glory were rushed off their feet fetching large jugs of ale to be mulled at the fire. Cove, Barton and Larkin huddled in a small back room with young Zachary. Luke Barton had found paper, pen and ink, and sat at a small table.

"Who can you remember?" he asked Zachary. "Start with all who came with you from the tavern – cannot be one of them!"

"Well – my mother and father, Glory and me. The sergeant here and his four soldiers. Then Master Goode, the verger, Mistress Goode and little Paul – your soldiers were playing with him – and also with Kat and little Felicity. Their parents were there as well – Master Gates and Mistress Gates, Master Dingle and Mistress Dingle – their parents. Then there were the two that arrived as we heard May scream – Master Fuller and his missus – cannot be them. Those were the ones in the tavern. In the group outside with us were Master Hook and his missus – they must have come directly from their cottage just away down the street – oh – and Master Burton. He lives down aways, so he must have been out walking."

"Gary Burton," Luke Barton mused. "Cannot see him doing aught to a young maid – he be sixty or thereabouts!"

"Aye – and his wife died some years back," Peter Cove nodded. "He is a lone type – keeps to himself most of the time."

"What did he do to earn a living?" Larkin asked.

"Oh – he were one like Hubert and Mercy Green – always praying and never joining in. Still, cannot see him having the nerve to assault a young maid, still less having the wits to evade like whoever did!"

"We cannot just dismiss him," Peter Cove decided. "I'm bailiff, and I must go and see what he has to say."

"Aye – that you must!" Barton agreed. Cove nodded to everyone and made his way out of the tavern.

"Still cannot see Burton be the culprit!" Barton shook his head. "He's none too steady on his feet – and uses a stick everywhere he goes."

* * *

Down at the ditcher's house, Wilf was still seething angry, but had the good sense to leave May in the care of his wife and sister Maud. May was calm and had settled down before the fire. Patience sat by one side of her, and Maud on the other.

"Now, May – tell me everything you can remember about the man who assaulted you."

May had a darkening bruise developing under her right eye where her assailant had delivered a punch.

"Start with when you were walking down the street," Patience added.

"I were just walking home," May was still shivering with the delayed reaction from her ordeal. "I got to the butcher shop when someone grabbed me from behind – and put a hand over my mouth. He dragged me into the ginnel between the shops."

"Let us stop there," Patience said. "Now – the hand that went over your mouth – was it covered or bare?"

"Twas in a woollen glove – and it was wet."

"So, we now know he wore a long woollen coat, wore a woollen glove, and had hood and mask. Go on."

"He kept his hand over my mouth and started to tear at my cloak and dress. I remember his hand slid from my mouth and I screamed as loud as I could. It was then he punched me in the face."

"Aye – near half the town heard that! It be what saved you from further hurt. Do you remember anything else?"

"After he had hit me, he seemed to just disappear. But I recall something else. When he was holding me close, I smelt that tobacco stuff on him. The smoke is different in smell from wood in our fire. He must have had a pipe of it sometime before he grabbed me."

"Well done – that all needs to be told to the bailiff."

"Aye – well done, lass," Wilf Fletcher growled. "I shall find bailiff and tell him word for word what you just said. It will help find him – and then I can rip his head off!"

Wilf grabbed his warmest cloak and went out into the cold. Little Maud gave her sister a big hug, whilst Patience went to get them all something to eat.

* * *

A mile past the gates into Parke estate, on the track that led up to Hay Tor and then to Widecombe, a man walked slowly through the slightly deeper snow, his hands under his armpits to keep any residual warmth. The track was a slight incline that would get considerably steeper the nearer one got to the tors of the moor. The snow would get thicker. In the deep pocket of his woollen coat was the hood and mask he had worn until removing them before joining the throng that had assembled outside the smithy. As he trudged slowly upwards, he muttered curses under his breath – curses that the wretched girl had been allowed to scream, curses that he had been unable to do more damage to the wretched child. However, he silently applauded himself that he had evaded any notice – or aroused any suspicion by his astute actions.

Reaching a bend in the wide track, he paused and looked very carefully around – especially back the way he had come. Satisfied that he was completely unobserved, he took a barely identifiable path to the right that led to the rear of one of the large fields behind the Parke Estate. Snow was falling again, snow that would soon obliterate his footsteps on the main track.

When he was satisfied that he was far enough away from the track, he fished out the hood and mask. They would keep his head, ears and lower face warmer than if they were left bare. A few more hundreds of yards, he climbed over a stone wall and startled the ewes that were huddled against it, keeping themselves and the very few early lambs out of the wind. The sheep, recognising who it was, soon settled down again as the man made his slow way across the large field to a hut on the far side. Unusually, there was no sheep dog to cause a fuss at his arrival. He slumped down onto his straw pallet and found his pipe. Plugging a wad of tobacco in it, he used his steel and flint to spark a few strands of dry straw into life, applied it to the bowl of his pipe and drew in several lungsful of smoke. He laid down, covered himself with some old blankets and stared up at the reeds that covered the roof. He dreamed of what just might have been.

* * *

Peter Cove had arrived at the door to Gary Burton's cottage, only to find the place in darkness. He used his fist to hammer on the door. Receiving no answer, he tried the latch. Shut and locked. Exasperated, he went back to the centre of the street and peered again at the cottage. Total darkness.

"Master Bailiff, hold there for I have more information." Wilf Fletcher ran towards him and slowly relayed all the new information that May had told them.

"Then tis even more urgent that I rouse him – even though it looks like the place is deserted," Cove stated. He went back to the door and used the large knob of his stick to pound on the door. Wilf stood and watched as a light flickered in the upstairs window.

"Master Bailiff – a light has just shown above," he called out.

Cove heard shuffling and then a voice came from within.

"Cannot an old man ne'er have peace," it said. "Who be it hammering on my door at this time of the night?"

"Tis Peter Cove, Bailiff. Open up and let me in for I have urgent need to speak with you."

The lock was turned, and the latch depressed. Cove was faced with the sight of the old man in his nightshirt holding one guttering candle.

"Come within and let me shut the door," Burton muttered. "There be little enough warmth in here without letting any escape."

Cove followed the old man into the main room. Burton lit an additional lamp from his candle and that allowed the bailiff to observe the untidy state of the place. Books were scattered over the floor, dirty platters and mugs littered the table.

"What words do you have for me, Master Bailiff?"

"You were with the group outside the tavern when we all heard of young May's assault."

"Aye – and why should I not have been?"

"Where had you been that you arrived at the tavern so quickly?"

"Where I always am before retiring to my bed! My old bones do not settle into sleep unless I walk for a while before retiring. Each evening, I walk up to the bend in the lane beyond the tavern, then walk slowly back here – it eases the aches that plague me."

"You were wearing a woollen coat, were you not?"

"Aye – it is the only one I have to keep the winter chill off me."

"And you also had a hood and a woollen face mask," Cove ventured.

"Nay – I have no woollen face mask. I did not have my hood with me."

"I do not smell tobacco smoke in this cottage," Cove ventured further.

"Nay – you do not! Tobacco - I regard it the same as strong drink – it is an abomination in God's sight!"

Cove had also noted the old boots by the front door. They were of an old pattern, with heels distinct from the soles. They could not have made the marks that had been spotted. He sighed in frustration.

"Master Burton, I am sorry to have intruded on your rest. I wish you good night."

He was half-way through the front door when he heard a gasp behind him.

"You believed it were me – the one who attacked the young maid!"

"Nay, Master Burton. "Just checking all who might have seen something."

He heard the latch and lock as he returned to the waiting Fletcher. He shook his head.

"For certain, twas not that man," he grunted.

"Then who?" Fletcher demanded. "Who?" he yelled angrily.

CHAPTER XII

The last but one day of December saw the beginnings of a thaw. The sun, a weak affair, shone low in the sky. By noon, the remnants of the snow had gone from the main street, although small piles still remained in the alleys and ginnels. Down on the Heath, sheep were able to graze without scrabbling to find it. Gil and Ella were able to dig into soil that was not frozen. Nell stayed in the hen coop all morning, chasing Trumpet away from the seed bowl – he had a tendency to grab everything, leaving little for the hens who were now all busy sitting on their eggs. Up in the smithy, Abel and Simon worked with the doors open wide – even shedding clothes down to shirts and breeches. The heat from the furnace was intense. John and Evelyn sat contented in the bakery, the remnants of their oven fire still radiating through the room, the smell of dough and fresh bread permeating the whole house. Soon, they would have to make a start on the meat pies. Even down the street at the apothecary's shop, there was an open window. Mary, now very well versed in the trade, ground garlic into a paste. James and Avril chopped herbs, infused seeds, filled jars. Soon enough, there would be a call for cough and cold remedies – plus the inevitable cuts and bruises occasioned by cold hands and sharp tools.

Just a few doors up from the apothecary's shop, Hubert and Mercy Green were poring over a new book that they had managed to acquire from a place in Dartmouth. It was all about the life of Job – a biblical person with whom they had a lot in common. They were also bemoaning their lot, if not all day long, certainly half of every day. All they could ever see was sin and wickedness in the small town. It was not helped that morning by the shrieks of laughter coming from the street outside.

Putting aside the book – a book that they had been commissioned to get for a customer in Exeter, and one from which they expected to make a handsome profit – Hubert opened the door and strode out, bristling with what he believed to be righteous indignation. A few paces up the street were Maud Fletcher with little Rosie. They were fashioning little snowballs from the remnants of a pile of snow.

Maud, a happy nine-year-old, spent much of her days being a sort of nursemaid to little Rosie. Gil and Ella had faith in Maud's sense and control over their daughter. Maud seemed to be able to control Rosie far better than anyone else.

The first the two girls knew of the intrusion to their game was when Hubert shouted at them, not six feet from where they stood.

"Be silent!" he shouted. "Be silent as children should be! Go back indoors and remain there or I shall administer a severe beating!"

Maud had one other attribute – she had a fierce streak of independence. She silently took Rosie's hand and made a dash past the irate bookseller. When they were some yards past, she stopped, turned, and poked out her tongue.

"Miserable old sod!" she yelled at him. "Beat Rosie or me and my dada will flay the skin from your back!"

"You be no better than that sister of yours. She probably got no more than she deserved!"

"Is that so?" came a voice from the open door of the butcher's shop. Simon Dingle came across to the two girls, a bloody cleaver in his hands. "You are exactly what young Maud called you – a miserable sod. And to say that a little girl of twelve years got what she deserved is a disgrace. I shall inform her father of your comments. He will not take them kindly I can assure you!"

Hubert blanched at the thought of having to face Wilf Fletcher, gave a growl and went back into his shop and bolted the door behind him.

"You pay him no heed, young Maud. You and little Rosie go on with your game. This town needs to hear children's laughter!"

Back in his own shop, he recounted it all to his wife Stella, who was stripping liver, kidneys and heart from a pig's carcase.

"You have the right of that, husband," she nodded. "The state of affairs in this country needs all the laughter and cheer that it may get. Fancy saying that young May deserved what was meted out to her! One of these days, Hubert Green will go too far with his misery and threats of eternal damnation. Will you tell Wilf?"

"Aye – that I will. In fact, I shall do so now."

Wilf Fletcher was clearing out a ditch by the side of the street opposite the church. It had been clogged for days and was causing water from the melting snow to flood over the street, down into the opposite gutter, and then flow down the hill to overflow again across into the front yard of the carpenter's workshop.

He relished the hard work of digging – anything to take his mid from the hurt to his elder daughter. May's bruise was fading to a dull yellow and would, he knew, have disappeared in a few more days. It was not that he was fuming about – it was the assault itself. Had May not been able to scream, doubtless she would have been raped, perhaps even killed to silence the girl. He imagined what it would be like to have his hands around the throat of the bastard.

That was where Simon Dingle found him – shovelling another mound of mud and filth from the ditch. After he had relayed to Wilf exactly what Green had said, Wilf went very quiet for a while.

"Thank you, Simon, for telling me. I shall visit Master Green when I have had my dinner."

He put his shovel and rake by the side of the ditch and walked home to wash and eat a silent meal. Then, taking his hand axe, he left the house and walked purposefully down to the bookseller's. He found the door locked. Raising his axe, he used the blunt side to hammer on the door.

"Hubert Green – get yourself out here!" he bellowed.

Getting no response, he hammered harder and bellowed louder. That caused many people to peer from their doorways to see what was happening. Simon Dingle went to Wilf and laid a restraining hand on his arm.

"Wilf – do not do anything hasty. Aye, twas a disgraceful thing to say, but does not deserve a split skull. You will be the one to suffer for that – and Patience, Maud and especially May need you home with them."

Wilf dragged his arm free and resumed his hammering and bellowing. By then, a large crowd had gathered, including

Sergeant Larkin and two of his soldiers. Larkin pushed his way through the throng.

"What is the cause of this disturbance?" he demanded.

Simon Dingle told him what had been said in his presence, and that he had relayed it to Wilf. Larkin grabbed Wilf's arm and made him turn to face him.

"Master Fletcher – this is not the way. You will be the one to suffer – and that will help your family not one iota."

He raised his voice. "Master Green. This is Sergeant Larkin. Open your door and come out to speak with me. That is an order. If you do not, my soldiers will break down your door and drag you out!"

After a few minutes, the lock was turned, and Hubert Green stood peering out. There was no sign of Mercy, his wife.

"I hear that you blamed young May Fletcher for being assaulted – said 'twas no more than she deserved," Larkin stated. "Is that so?"

Hubert huffed himself up in indignation.

"Aye – 'twas what I said and 'twas what I meant! Young women parading themselves shamelessly!"

"It was hurtful, untrue, and unnecessary!" Larkin barked. "You will now apologise for the remark!"

"What – apologise to a mere ditcher? I most certainly shall not!"

"Nay – you shall not apologise to Master Fletcher. You shall apologise before all here to the person you insulted. You shall apologise to young May! Someone – please fetch the maid here."

Hubert could only stand and gape. "You, sergeant, are here to support the laws of the parliament. Those laws are being openly flouted every day, with lewdness, drinking, fornication. I know that the church held celebrations in defiance of those laws. I shall make it my duty to inform the authorities of this defiance and your own laxness. Can it be that you are in sympathy with this open disobedience?"

"You, Master Green, are free to do whatever you choose. But you have no right to abuse a young maid in such a disgusting manner – and for that you *shall* apologise!"

"Nay – I shall not!"

Larkin loomed over Green, grabbed his shirt in both hands and hauled him off his feet.

"Here be young May. Now – apologise!"

Struggling proved absolutely useless, he could not shake the grip at all. Going slowly red in the face, he at last gasped, "I apologise."

"That, we did not hear properly!" Larkin remarked, hauling Green further off the ground. "Say it again, and this time address it to the young maid."

Going a shade of puce, Green managed to blurt out, "I apologise, May."

"There – that did not hurt, did it," Larkin lowered Green to his feet. "Now, go back within and keep your vile remarks to yourself in future."

Green scuttled inside his shop and locked the door. Larkin was very surprised to hear the crowd behind him clapping. Fletcher held May by her hand and touched the sergeant on the shoulder.

"That, I shall not forget. Thank you."

That evening, when his footsteps took him to the tavern, Larkin was handed a brimming mug of ale.

"There be no charge, sergeant," Dick Allen said.

* * *

Kat Gates, daughter of Adam and Olivia, was playing with her new kitten in the back room of the mill. The wheel had stopped hours before, and all that could be heard was the running of the river, the mill leat having been closed when the wheel had been stopped turning.

The kitten, chasing a little ball of wool, made a leap and landed on the windowsill, making a grab with one white paw for the ball. Kat knelt on the seat beneath the window and picked up the kitten as she had been shown – by the scruff of its neck. Cradling the little thing in her arms, she stared out at the dark Heath.

"Papa – there be a funny man creeping down the field," she announced. Adam Gates walked over and peered out. He was just in time to see a figure in a long coat and hood making rapid strides towards the trees on the far left side of the Heath.

"God's blood!" he muttered. "Can it be the same?"

Grabbing a large stave of oak that he used to lever open the wheel brake, he rushed out into the cold night.

"Stand ho!" he shouted, running up the street. "Stand ho!"

Many faces peered out of their doors, wondering what the fuss was all about.

"Strange figure in a long coat and hood making for the trees by the Heath!" he yelled.

He was soon joined by at least twenty other residents, all armed with a variety of weapons. Troopers Glass and Bell, halfway through their patrol, joined in the stampede, swords drawn in one hand and pistols cocked in the other.

By the time the mob had clambered over fences onto the Heath, it was a forlorn hope that they would catch whoever it had been. The search was called off after an hour.

* * *

Just before midnight, Bray Cooper arrived by a very circuitous route back at his hut. He was panting and livid with rage. He removed his hood, threw off his long, woollen coat, and hurled himself onto his straw bed. Plunging a dirty mug into an equally dirty pitcher of ale, he proceeded to drink himself into oblivion. Then, stretched out with filthy boots still on his feet, he fell asleep.

Glory, never knowing how close she had come to being viciously assaulted, walked back to the tavern. She had gone for a walk before bed, taking little heed of the warnings from her parents that it was not safe to do so.

* * *

The same messenger arrived in Bovey Tracey the next morning. This time, he had ridden with more consideration for his mount. He went straight to the cottage and presented Sergeant Larkin with another folded paper.

"Captain's orders, Sergeant. And you are to post this notice immediately and have it proclaimed."

Larkin broke the seal and read the notice. He grimaced, then sent the messenger to the tavern to rest both himself and his horse. The sergeant donned his coat and went straight down to find the bailiff.

Cove read it and gave a gasp. "This cannot be so!" he muttered.

"I'm afraid that it be so, bailiff. I have to proclaim it myself and post it prominently."

Once again, the people of the town were summoned to hear the notice for themselves. Larkin, not liking it one little bit, held the paper in front of him and started reading.

"Be it known that by act of parliament, Charles Stuart shall stand trial before parliament. The indictment reads as follows – that the said Charles Stuart following upon the recent wars, be guilty of treason, murder, rapines, burnings, spoils, desolations, damage in the said wars and mischiefs to this nation acted or committed in the said wars or occasioned thereby. The trial of the said Charles Stuart shall commence on the twentieth day of January."

He turned and nailed the notice to the post that stood in the square. His actions were accompanied by absolute silence – no one there able to comprehend the magnitude of that announcement – except for one person.

"Tis nothing he does not deserve!" Hubert Green muttered. Taking Mercy's arm in his, he hurried back to his shop and locked the door behind him.

Peter Cove stood and surveyed the small town for which he was responsible to his master, Sir John Vickery. He had to say something.

"Let us all go quietly back to our homes and businesses. Twill take time for us all to digest this news. Pray do nothing until we have all had time to reflect. Sergeant Larkin is charged with keeping order. I have no doubt he and his soldiers will do so. Go home now – quietly and in peace."

He went straight to the rector's house to sound out Reverend Forbes and Will Garlick. The rest of the crowd simply did as bid, and went back to their homes and businesses, too stunned to say anything.

"They mean to have his head," Forbes stated. "What else could it mean when they charge him first and foremost with treason?"

"Tis a nonsense!" Garlick shouted. "How can it be that an anointed king be held for treason against his own country? Makes no sense whatsoever!"

"Mayhap they are holding the trial as a way of bolstering their own importance – and hope thereby to subdue all opposition," Cove ventured.

"Nay – they are in earnest!" Forbes almost whispered. "Why else hold him prisoner, haul him to Westminster, and then frame the indictment thus? The only thing they mean to uncover is who will dare to come forward to defend the king."

"Is there anyone who might even dare to take on that role?" Garlick wondered.

"The only person with enough clout to do so would be General Monck – and he has played as great a part in the wars against the king as anyone," Forbes replied. "It is just possible that he will regard this as a step too far – but I am not at all sanguine that he has sufficient standing."

"The penalty for treason is beheading – and they cannot surely contemplate that!" Cove grunted. "Nay – if found guilty, the probable outcome is forced abdication and possibly banishment."

"That leaves us with another Charles – and I am, for one, not at all sure he has the stomach for it," Garlick had never been an admirer of the Prince of Wales.

Forbes, who had been Prince Charles' own chaplain, said nothing. Whether that signalled agreement with his churchwarden, or was silent disagreement, nobody was sure.

CHAPTER XIII

It was considered by most of the residents that it would be prudent to hold a service in the tavern – just in case!. The first day of January 1649, falling on a Sunday, was thought to be a reasonable excuse for some sort of a celebration. Enough of the people of Bovey Tracey were of like mind – that it was becoming too dangerous to flout the new laws – that the tavern's main taproom was filled to bursting.

Reverend Forbes conducted a simple prayer service that lasted only fifteen minutes. He ended it with a short speech in place of his usual homily.

"Good people – this is the first day of a new year. Only the Good Lord above knows what it may hold for us. I can only ask each one of you to offer what prayers you deem appropriate for the safety of this country. Mine shall be for the health and safety of our king. But we also face dangers much nearer to home. There be amongst us someone who needs apprehending. He has already frightened and hurt one of our children. Let us all put our thoughts towards identifying who it may be. But let no one take any action before it is known for certain sure who it may be. May the Lord Above bless us all and keep us safe."

There followed a rousing chorus of 'Amen'. And then the service came to an end, many people going back to their homes. The Allen family, who lived above the tavern, started serving dinner to those who remained. Bailiff Cove, his wife, son and young Hob, Steward Barton and his wife, the whole Ramsey family, churchwarden, verger and sexton – all sat down on benches before the tables and started tucking into the roast beef. Ella was particularly pleased to see some of their potato crop had been added to the vegetables.

"Young May seems to have returned to normal," James remarked. "Apart from the bruise which be fading, she is now as happy as before."

"Has anyone spoken again to Adam Gates – to discover what else he might tell us of the figure he saw?" John asked.

"Aye – I did the very next day," Bailiff Cove answered. "He could only say what he said on the night – 'twas a figure, tall, in a long, dark coat and wearing a hood. That could apply to any tall man in the entire town. Equally it could be any tall man from a nearby village – or indeed some vagrant. We seem no further forward."

"We can certainly eliminate any who were chasing him. Who was best placed to identify them?" Avril suggested.

"Probably not Adam himself," Steward Barton stated. "He were far too occupied in leading the chase. Peter Crowley were amongst them – and he is as level-headed as any of them."

"Aye – that is a good thought," Cove nodded. "Hob – when you are finished eating that pile of beef, hurry down to the carpenter and ask him to come back here."

Hob could only nod. His mouth was so crammed with beef and gravy that he dared not even open it. Instead, he chewed furiously, crammed another load into his mouth and shot off on his errand.

"I wonder if he will ever learn to walk," Evelyn laughed. "For sure, I have never seen him do so!"

The rest of them continued to eat the dinner in a more leisurely fashion, waiting for the arrival of the carpenter. Hob arrived back at his usual frantic pace.

"Master Crowley be on his way," he reported, resuming his place to start on a dish of pastry filled with cream and raisins.

Peter Crowley had brought his wife Lou and son Matt with him. with him. They sat down at the end of the longest table.

"Hob said you needed to have words, Master Bailiff," he grunted.

"Aye – that we did. You were with the search party that went out when Adam Gates raised the hue and cry. Are you able to tell all who were in that party?"

"I can but try – and Matt was also there, and his eyes are as sharp as anyone's. Adam Gates were there, obviously and us two as well. Then there were Simon Dingle, Wilf Fletcher, Jake and Henry Hoggs, Josiah Grubbs, the Hobson brothers from the dairy. That new chap and his son who took the Platt's old place."

Peter Cove had been busy with paper and pen, listing all the names. He looked up.

"That be only twelve. I heard tell that it were nearer twenty who went searching."

"Oh – there were the two soldiers who joined from their patrol."

"Two more soldiers came up from their cottage – they joined in as well," Matt added. "And surely the three from the tannery – Billy, Stephen and Cal. I remember them as they all carried large staves."

"That makes nineteen – I suppose tis near enough." Cove shrugged his shoulders. "So, we know for sure it may be none of these. It cannot be any of the children, nor any of the womenfolk. May said she thought him taller than her father – and thin. So, let us think of anyone who is not on our list, who is taller than Wilf Fletcher, and is thin. Let us start at the top of the town and work our way down.

"Well – Reverend and Churchwarden do not fit that bill," Lou Crowley chuckled. "Come to that, sexton and verger neither. Then, across the street, John Ramsey is hardly thin!"

"Abel and his son Simon cannot be thought of. They be far too big!"

And so it went on, each person considering the men of the village as they wandered mentally down the street. When they came to the mill, there was a silence. Not one man fitted the description.

"Then let us turn to the estate," Peter Cove was a bit reluctant, but knew it had to be done. "It were certainly not me – I'm shorter than Wilf by at least two inches – as is Master Steward. The male household servants are all too old. That only leaves the two ex-soldiers who work outside with the gardener. Old Colin can be discounted, as can the two soldiers. Both be shorter than me and neither be thin. So, we are looking for someone from further afield."

Bray Cooper the shepherd completely failed to register with the Bailiff. He was answerable to the steward and was very seldom seen anywhere near the grounds of the main estate. He was, to nearly all folks, almost invisible.

The meeting broke up at that point, all of them frustrated that they had not found anyone to fit the description, but secretly glad that they could not point the finger at anyone of their little town.

* * *

The next day, Nell was as usual looking after the hens and their eggs. She had with her little Rosie who had demanded that she see the inside of the coop, Rosie, who was never without her little wooden doll, was full of questions.

"Big Trumpet not making any noise. Why?"

"I don't know," Nell answered, pouring more grain into the large feed bowl. "He makes a loud noise every morning – but we're all usually awake afore he starts.

"Why is Penny looking sad?"

Nell peered at the hen in question and could not see any sign of sadness – nor any other emotion.

"She does not look sad. She does not look happy, either. She just looks like a hen."

The task finished, Nell led Rosie out of the coop and latched the door carefully. Rosie was peering through the fence at the bottom of the enclosure.

"Look, Nell – two men over by the woods."

Nell looked, following one little finger that was pointed at the tree line. One was short and the other tall and thin. She grabbed Rosie's hand and hurried through the gate to where Gil was again hoeing.

"Gil – two men are over yonder by the woods – and one is very tall and thin."

Everyone in the town had been instructed to keep a sharp eye out for any such character.

"I saw them first!" Rosie claimed.

"Then you be one very clever little girl," her father said. "Go indoors now and I'll see what may be done."

He went through the house, Ella yelling at him to remove his muddy boots – an instruction he ignored. Out in the street, he went from door to door, summoning as many men as he could.

Within minutes, a small group armed with anything they could find, was running up the street to get into the woods to start the hunt.

* * *

"Bloody cold," Simmonds grumbled as he and Hawkes emerged from the trees to gaze towards the backs of the houses that edged the north of the Heath.

"Why are we out in the open?" Hawkes grumbled. "We should be back in the trees and out of sight."

"Aye – I suppose we should at that," Simmonds was so hungry he just didn't care.

"Still no way we can get at those hens – not with those damned children and that noisy rooster. Can we dare have another try with the butcher?"

"The last time we tried that, it cost Ned his life. Nay – that we cannot try again. Why do we not wait until it be dark and see what we can get around the back of the bakery?"

It still had not occurred to either of them to spend one penny of their coins on buying anything. Stealing had become a way of life for the two men. Hawkes suddenly stiffened.

"We have been seen," he snarled. "Quick – back into the trees and let's lose them."

Simmonds needed no second bidding. He turned and followed Hawkes back into the wood just as the small band of pursuers burst into view. Hawkes, far fleeter of foot than Simmonds, was soon haring along a track, then plunging through thick bushes, across a small stream, and was well clear of any pursuit before he had gone a mile.

Simmonds, slower and more used to loping along, followed along the same track but was startled into leaving it well before he should have done so. He suddenly found himself stymied by a very steep bank. Although not more than twenty feet high, it made him stop to see which way offered the best ascent. That pause was his undoing. With a fierce yell of triumph, Gil aimed a vicious sweep with his stave at the man's legs. Simmonds collapsed with a howl of pain. By the time he was able to squirm upright again, he was surrounded by five irate men all brandishing staves, or in one case, a wicked looking sickle. He had no option but to surrender meekly.

Henry Hoggs, the saddler's son, produced a short length of rope and bound the man's hands behind his back. Simmonds was marched back along the track and into the field.

By that time, quite a crowd had assembled, and gave a ragged cheer as the captive was led back to the street.

"Well – that was excellent work!" Sergeant Larkin applauded the pursuers. "So, who do we have here then?"

"Only the one, I am afraid," Gil felt it necessary to apologise. "The short one got away – he was heading south when last we saw."

Larkin approached Simmonds, grabbed him by the belt and forced him to his knees.

"Name!" he demanded.

"Bugger off!" Simmonds spat at Larkin's boots.

With a bunched fist, Larkin gave him a massive, backhanded swipe across the face. Simmonds rolled sideways and lay in the street. Larkin put his boot on Simmonds' neck.

"Name!" he said again, quietly.

"Henry Tudor, you parliamentary piss head!" Simmonds growled.

"Ah, we seem to have a joker with us," Larkin grinned. "Someone, please bring young May Fletcher here. Let us find out if she recognises this piece of offal."

It was not long before the throng around the scene was nearly a hundred strong. Wilf Fletcher pushed his way through the mass of bodies, bringing Patience, May and little Maud with him.

"May Fletcher," Larkin called her forward. "Might this be the man who grabbed you? Take as much time as you need, for we have to be sure."

May turned to her father and whispered something.

"May needs him stood up," he said.

Larkin simply grabbed a handful of Simmonds' coat and dragged him upright.

"You can come as near him as you need," Larkin encouraged May. "Believe me, he will not harm you – not with my knife at his neck!"

May, fumbling for her father's hand, came forward and peered up into the sneering face, then let her gaze travel down to Simmonds' feet.

"Tis a different coat and a different smell," she said quietly. Then, with a small start, she looked directly at the face and said, "Boo!"

"Fuck off!" snarled Simmonds. May gave a nod.

"Tis even a different voice," she said. "The man who grabbed me said I was to stop struggling. His was a local voice. This one is not a local voice at all!"

"Well, May – thank you," Larkin gave her a smile. He turned to Simmonds again.

"You, friend, may not be the man we seek for assaulting this maid. But you are certainly not out of the woods. Why were you spying on the town, and why did you run away when challenged?"

"I give you the same answer I gave her – fuck off! Why cannot a man walk across open heathland? Why cannot a man run away when he sees danger from an armed mob? You have no cause to hold me!"

"Believe me, friend, I have every cause. Unless you give me a name and a reason for you being here, I will have you taken to Exeter for questioning – and the person doing that questioning will not be as gentle as I have been!"

Simmonds just stood there glaring at Larkin. He said nothing. Larkin turned to Trooper Dellow.

"Get three mounts. You and Glass take this long piece of garbage to the Captain and say he was spying on the town – and that he refuses to give us name or reason. Let us see if his tongue becomes loosened."

"Aye Sergeant," Dellow grinned. "And if he attempts to escape on the way?"

"Shoot him!"

Before long, Simmonds was hoisted into a saddle, his feet bound beneath the horse's belly. The two troopers led off at a steady trot. The large crowd slowly dispersed, talking quietly amongst themselves.

"I'm sorry that he was not the man," Larkin said to May.

"If that had been the man, what would you have done to him?" May asked.

"Why – sent him to Exeter where he would have stood trial. He would have been found guilty and hanged."

"It were not him, though!" May grabbed her father's hand and walked slowly back home.

"Damnation!" Larkin muttered to himself. "I wish it had been him. That little maid needs to be avenged!"

* * *

Three miles north of Parke, a flock of sheep grazed in a meadow that was surrounded by stone walls. The shepherd crouched in the shelter of the western wall and hummed to himself as he opened his pack and pulled out a small loaf of bread and a hunk of yellow cheese. Having chewed his way through a rough meal, he took out the stopper of his ale flask and gulped down a mouthful.

The sheep grazed contentedly, despite the cold wind. The shepherd sat and thought about the copper-headed tavern maid that he had missed.

"Soon," he muttered to himself. "I shall have you soon!"

He sat for another hour before calling his dog. Between them, they rounded up the flock and headed back to their usual field. The shepherd went to his hut, made himself a bowl of thick porridge, sweetened it with honey, the curled up into his bed and dreamed of the young woman with the mass of copper hair.

* * *

It worried Hawkes not one little bit that he found himself all alone. One lone man, he knew, could go where two or more could not. One could blend into his surroundings whereas two or three stood out. Apart from all that, he now could spend all the coin in his purse on himself. Sprucing himself up as best he could, he followed the river as it wended its way to the outskirts of Newton Abbot.

The one thing he could do nothing about was his accent – it was nothing like the Devon burr. Before he wandered down the main street, he wound a scarf around his throat and quietly practised a hoarse whisper. It was deep winter, and many had rheums and sore throats.

He stopped at the bakery and peered at the loaves and pies on offer. Meat would last longer than fish – or so he fondly believed. He opened the door and went to the small counter.

"Two of the meat pies and three small loaves," he croaked.

The young lad behind the counter, probably the baker's son, was a friendly sort and tried to make conversation with every customer.

"That throat sounds mighty sore," he said.

"Aye – tis mighty sore. Where may I find an apothecary?" That sounded very genuine to Hawkes.

"Just a further six doors down," he was told. He paid for the pies and loaves, put them in his pack and wandered down the street further. However, he didn't bother to stop at the apothecary, but continued down until he came to a tavern. The temptation was too great, and he went in. The pies and bread would keep. What he wanted more than anything was some hot food.

The taproom was a large rectangle. Unusually, it had a fireplace on both long sides, surrounded by benches and small trestles. It was packed. Hawkes cursed himself for a fool – he should have waited until the normal dinner hour was over before venturing inside. The drawback to that was that there might have been little left for him to eat. He managed to find himself a seat at the end of one of the benches. At his elbow was one of the small trestles. Three serving girls were threading their ways between benches, hands full of mugs of ale. One of them spotted Hawkes and pushed her way through the throng, slapping hands away from her as she passed.

"Ale?" she asked. Hawkes nodded and pointed to his throat. "Stew?" he croaked.

"Aye – there be some left." The girl pushed her way to the kitchen.

"Bad, be it?" his neighbour asked, having noticed Hawkes having difficulty speaking.

"Aye – bad enough," Hawkes managed a grin with the croaked reply.

"Not seen you hereabouts. Come far?"

Hawkes had rehearsed this.

"Aye – some distance. Finished the last job back in Dorchester and heard that work were going in Totnes."

"Aye – they're always wanting work done there. What work do you do?"

Hawkes had rehearsed that as well. He had chosen an occupation that he really did know something about. His ale and stew arrived. He took a mouthful of ale before answering.

"Been a stonecutter these ten years," he almost whispered, pretending that his throat was getting worse with all that talking. His neighbour nodded and took the hint, leaving Hawkes to eat a rather delicious mutton stew. He finished his ale and set his mug down.

"Another ale?" the same serving wench was back again.

Hawkes shook his head and took out the coins to pay. He was on the point of standing up to leave when the door opened to admit three soldiers in buff coats and pot helmets.

"Buggers cannot leave us alone for a single moment!" his neighbour grunted.

The three stood just inside the door, scrutinising faces. The leading one looked hard at Hawkes and pushed his way through to him.

"Not seen your ugly face here before," he grunted. "Passing through, are you?"

"Aye – on my way to Totnes," Hawkes croaked, holding his throat piteously.

"You will not get there before nightfall – tis too far."

"Tis only ten miles, sergeant," his neighbour piped up. "Strong young chap like this will do that in two hours – three at most!"

"Then you had better be on your way," the sergeant said. "There be a tavern in Ipplepen and another in Littlehempston should you not make it all the way."

Hawkes nodded and threaded his way out of the taproom to stand in the street. He simply had to start off to the south as he had no idea what eyes were following him. He counted twenty more parliament soldiers before he left the town. Newton Abbot obviously merited a larger contingent than Bovey Tracey.

It was after dark when he managed to get his way back to the cottage near Teingrace. He flopped down on his straw bed, ate a pie, then went to sleep. Even after that strange day, he spared not one thought for Ned Thomas – long dead – and Art Simmonds – now probably either dead or a prisoner.

* * *

The next day saw yet another light dusting of snow. Luke Farmer and his wife Meg had not slept well in their attic room at Brimley. Hal, seven months old, had kept them awake most of the night with a hacking cough.

"Do you think Lady Muck will allow me to take him to the apothecary in Bovey?" Meg asked as the first streaks of daylight penetrated their small room.

"Aye – I suppose she might. Do you think Hal needs physic?"

"Aye – I do." Luke Farmer knew better than to argue – Meg could be as stubborn as a mule when she had decided upon a course of action. "I'll first talk to Master Steward."

Luke also knew that his flame-headed wife could twist the old steward around her little finger. He grinned, gave Meg a kiss, then one on the top of little Hal's head, dressed hurriedly and shot down to get a slice of toasted bread and cheese before setting out for his work on the estate.

An hour later saw Meg, wrapped up against the cold, with little Hal clasped to her, walking the short distance to Bovey Tracey. She went into the apothecary's shop and talked first to Mary who was mixing something in a jar.

"Little Hal has been coughing all night long," Meg said. "Be there anything he might take?"

"First, I need to know what sort of cough it may be," Mary replied. "Is it a wet cough with phlegm coming up after? Or is it dry?"

"Dry – no phlegm."

"Then I need to see if he has a fever as well. May I put my hand on his chest to see?"

Mary poked her hand down the blanket and the layers of small clothes. She frowned and called over her shoulder.

90

"Aunt Avril – here be little Hal from Brimley. Dry cough and slight fever. His chest feels too warm."

Meg, by then, was starting to feel very anxious. Avril bustled into the shop and repeated the examination.

"Aye – you have the right of it, Mary. Hal be hot, but not burning. Tis a slight fever he has. What would you recommend?"

Mary knew that this was yet another one of the endless tests that Avril and James put her through. It was essential if she was going to be a practising apothecary in her own right.

"The soothing cough linctus – the one with honey for the sore throat. That will ease the cough. I would also give a small drop of poppy in a spoon of milk every few hours. That will ease him to sleep. The fever will take care of itself in a few days."

"Aye – perfect!" Avril went back and left Mary to finish up. Mary gave Meg a small flask of the linctus and a tiny one of poppy – she repeated the instructions.

"Never more than one drop of poppy – and never more often than every three hours," she cautioned.

Meg, much relieved, thanked Mary, paid coins for the medicines, gathered up Hal, and walked back to Brimley. All the way, she sang softly to the little mite. Hal looked up at his mother and gave a happy gurgle that turned into a cough.

As she walked purposefully along the track that led to Brimley, she was totally unaware of a pair of eyes following her progress. Those eyes took in the flaming red hair and the full figure.

"That be two of them now!" the shepherd muttered to himself.

CHAPTER XIV

Michael Brown and Hugh Ratcliffe stared out at the snow that was blowing in the wind outside the cottage in Trusham village. Very little seemed to be laying but was blowing into small drifts against any obstacle in its path. The door was closed, and they went back to sit before the fire.

Theirs was a very chequered history. Brown was an ex-royalist sergeant, whilst Ratcliffe was an ex-parliamentary soldier. Both had been injured at the battle of Torrington; both had ended up in the same large room being nursed back to health. Surprisingly, the two had formed a close friendship and had left together – Brown to go back to his birth village, Ratcliffe to accompany him part of the way as he intended to go back to Hampshire. Neither saw any future in staying soldiers.

Brown had arrived back in Trusham in the early months of 1646, only to find his parents deceased and his brother gone, heaven alone knew where. Ratcliffe had stayed on for a few days – and that had stretched into a full-time commitment when they had started up the hurdle business. Hurdles, made from mainly hazel, were in constant demand throughout the countryside. Brown had taken over the old cottage and the two had slowly but surely made a success of their little business.

"Shall we chance it?" Ratcliffe said, looking through the window once again at the wind-driven snow.

"Aye – tis not that far!" Brown argued. "Parke is a large estate – and has an important lord. It may well bring us more business – and we cannot afford to let down any customer, especially one with Vickery's influence."

"Aye – suppose you be right," Ratcliffe gave a reluctant look at the fire which was filling the room with warmth and cheer. "I'll go and fetch old Gaffer's cart."

Whenever they had a load of hurdles to deliver, they would borrow the horse and cart owned by Old Gaffer – a long-retired shepherd.

They had received a visit from the Parke steward, Luke Barton, three weeks previously. He had heard good reports of the quality of the hurdles and fencing that the two produced. He had inspected a few samples and had placed an order for fifty, six foot by four foot hurdles – and they were due to be delivered that day and the next.

Large though the cart was, it would take two loads to satisfy the order. Ratcliffe donned his heaviest coat, wound a think scarf around his neck and face, and set off to the end of the village. He was back soon afterwards so that he and Brown could start loading twenty-five hurdles. When the last was safely aboard, Brown jumped up on to the driving board and set off.

"We'll change over half-way, Ratty," he shouted down to his mate who was walking alongside the horse. It was far warmer walking than just sitting on the board.

The safest way was to head west for the River Teign and to follow it south along the track to Chudleigh Knighton – then follow the westward track to Bovey Tracey. The whole journey was just under eight miles – three hours at the speed of the old horse.

By the time they went through Chudleigh Knighton, Brown was almost frozen to the seat. He changed places and started off at a trot to get his blood pumping. It took another hour and a half to trudge through Bovey Tracey, down over the river and into the Parke estate gates.

"I wager you two be frozen and hungry," Luke Barton greeted them.

"That, Master Steward, is a wager you would win," Brown grinned.

"Then, drive up to the main house and tell cook I said you were to be fed a warm meal. Then I shall rustle up hands to unload you so that you may be on your way back."

That sounded very welcome – as was the large bowl of beef and vegetables they found waiting for them in the huge kitchen. Thanking the cook, they made their way back outside into the courtyard to find their old horse had been fed and watered. Two men were starting to unload the hurdles. They took one each and stacked them against the wall of a large shed. Then they turned around to come for another pair.

Ratcliffe stopped dead in his tracks. "Bloody Satan's Bollocks!" he gasped. The two looked at him and also stopped.

"Ratty?" Sam Garvey could not believe his eyes.

"Sam – and Haddock?" Ratcliffe pumped hands with his two old comrades. Sam Garvey, Robert Hook and Ratcliffe had been a part of a tracking detail that had followed the royalists under Lord Wentworth all the way back in the January of 1646 from Exeter to Bovey Heath – where the king's men had been taken to bits by an army under Cromwell.

Sam Garvey and Robert Hook (nickname Haddock) stood and gawped at one another. Their old leader, Richard Lovelace, had been promoted to sergeant and had been at both Torrington and Launceston – where the royalist army had been finally and utterly defeated.

"We have kept our old loyalties secret in this part of the country," Haddock muttered.

"Mum's the word," Ratty nodded. He pointed out his mate. "He's called Michael Brown – and he were at Bovey with the king's lot. Makes no difference to us!"

As they unloaded the hurdles, Ratcliffe told how he and Brown had met, and how they had started their business. They made plans to meet half-way at Chudleigh Knighton the coming weekend to have a proper catch-up. As they were about to leave with the empty cart, Brown pointed to a gate that led to a large field.

"Who is that?" he asked.

"Oh, him – that's Bray Cooper, the shepherd. Doesn't often come that near to the house," Garvey replied.

"Funny – I seem to recognise him from somewhere," Brown muttered. "No doubt it'll come to me. It were nothing good, though – I'm certain of that!"

* * *

The snow started again in earnest two days later. By the Saturday, it was inches thick. Up on the moor it was about the same thickness, but the wind had blown it into massive drifts, especially against the many granite outcrops. All work ceased up there – not that there was much tin mining any longer. That

activity had been mainly displaced by the quarrying of granite –
and that had come to a stop with the weather.

In Trusham, Ratcliffe was wondering whether it would be
feasible to meet with his old mates the next day. He talked it over
with Brown, who said that a true soldier would never be put off
by some snow! In Parke, Garvey and Hook were having the same
conversation. In both places, they determined that they would
keep to the arrangement – unless there was a really significant
fall of snow before the Sunday meeting.

In Bovey, Gil and Ella simply piled the snow up over the
crops that were above ground – in the fond hope that this would
somehow keep them safe and a bit warmer. Nell spent much of
her mornings in the chicken coop. She talked to each of the
broody hens in turn, convinced that her chatter kept them
interested and informed! Rosie spent nearly all of her time in the
cottage, being looked after by a diligent Maud. Neither really
liked the confinement, Rosie giving vent to her displeasure by
stamping up and down the stairs and shouting.

The only really happy people were Abel and Simon Smith.
They worked on happily, the forge almost sweltering hot with
the furnace going full blast. Most other businesses and shops
simply got on with their lives – bitterly cold when they arose,
slightly warmer as they broke their fasts with fires lit.

In Brimley, things were kept going by an indomitable Lady
Violette. Not for her any shirking and huddling around fires! She
went from room to room, ordering cleaning and dusting. In a pair
of huge old boots, clad in layers of clothing, she went from
outhouse to shed to barn – making sure everyone was busy doing
what she had ordered – and to the standard she demanded.

"Bloody hell!" muttered old Rob Garside, the head gardener.
"Prune back all the shrubs! I know tis the right time of year to do
it, but we've got to shake all the snow off first or we cannot see
where to cut! That is going to make us very cold and very wet!"

Garside, a tiny fellow in his fifties, was known as Goliath. He
was also a very knowledgeable gardener – but one who liked his
creature comforts. His workforce consisted of Kit Warden and
Nick Andrews – both ex-soldiers who had been with the king's
forces until the final defeats in the West Country. The other ex-
soldier who had arrived at Brimley with them – Luke Farmer,

was a sort of assistant to Thomas Carpenter, Lady Violette's steward.

Meg, Luke's red-headed wife, was crooning to little Hal. The baby was lying on a rug by the fire in the main hall of the manor house, kicking his legs and making bubbling noises. Meg, apart from looking after her son, was busy cleaning and polishing the brass fitments around the fire. Every now and again, Luke peeped in as he passed. He was busy replenishing candles throughout the house – in holders and lanterns – plus scraping old wax off the holders.

"Again – no church service on the morrow," he mentioned as he passed through the hall before the noon dinner hour.

"We must do what we always do now," Meg answered. "Lady Violette will hold a prayer meeting this afternoon. Tis not as if we are not even allowed to say our prayers!"

"And then we wrap up very warm and take Hal for a walk through the snow. I shall carry him before me, slung nice and warm in a blanket."

The three set off from the manor house on their walk after dinner. They took the usual path that led towards Bovey Tracey. Little Hal peered out from his cocoon of blankets and made chuckling noises every time a snowflake landed on his head – for it had started falling again, but only a very light dusting.

Neither Meg nor Luke saw the figure again lurking on the northern side of the path – a figure well hidden from view behind a stand of bushes. The figure looked and licked his lips at the sight of the red-headed young woman. He was turning over in his mind how he would engineer a meeting with both this one and the other flame-headed girl from the tavern. He waited in the cold for them to pass again on their return journey – then crept back to his tumbledown hut near his flock of sheep.

* * *

A meeting of a very different kind was taking place that late afternoon in the large parlour behind the smithy. Abel, Faith and Simon stood by the door and greeted their guests as they arrived. First were John, Evelyn and Mary from the bakery next door; then came James, Avril and Nell from the apothecary's; Gil came with Ella and Rosie. Finally, came Josiah Grubb, the shoemaker, with his wife Alice and daughter Imelda.

There was a roaring fire in the large grate, over which was warming a big iron pot filled with ale. On the table were small pies and sweetmeats. Abel and Faith made sure everyone had a mug of ale and then asked for quiet, and for Josiah Grubb to join him.

"Friends – these may be unhappy times. Our king is to stand trial against all reason and proper law. But here, in this house today, we have something to celebrate – and nothing parliament may do will stop us! Let us now hear from Josiah."

Standing beside the massive blacksmith, Josiah Grubb looked like a dwarf – although he was well over five feet tall!

"Two months past, Simon came to our house and asked that he may be permitted to pay court to our Imelda. Alice and I, knowing Simon all of his life, knowing Abel and Faith. Knowing them all to be the very finest and honest of folk, readily gave that permission – but first asked Imelda whether she welcomed the advance. It will come as no surprise to one and all that Imelda readily accepted the advance. And now, Simon is to speak for himself."

Simon had been dreading and relishing this moment. Although now nearing his seventeenth birthday and almost as big as his massive father, Simon was normally shy and withdrawing. Therefore, he had dreaded being the cynosure of all eyes – but desperately wanted to do this for his deep love of Imelda. Like Simon's sister Ella had known Gil all her life, he similarly had known Imelda all of hers – and had, for at least the last three years, never wavered in his intention to marry the fair-haired Imelda. So, taking a very deep breath, he walked over to the girl, took her hands in his and made his well-prepared speech.

"Imelda – will thou marry me? Will thou take me as your betrothed? I swear I shall be honest and true to you, never give you cause to regret this day!"

Imelda, almost as shy as Simon, looked him in the eye and gave a smile.

"Aye, Simon. I will marry thee. I accept thee as my betrothed with all my heart!"

"Then let us all toast the pair – and give them all our blessing," Abel declared.

Abel, Josiah, Faith and Alice gathered together after the toast had been drunk, and the cheers had died away.

"We shall have to see Reverend Forbes so that the banns may be read," Josiah said. "That, at least, is still the law. But with the churches supposed to be closed, how may the wedding be performed? This is the first time in the months that the new laws came about that we in Bovey have this problem. There have been no funerals or baptisms, and no weddings either. How may it all be properly celebrated?"

"The problem will come about sooner than this wedding!" Faith stated. "Old Polly Grimes is not likely to last more than a few more days. This cold weather has proved the last straw."

"Then we must all call on Reverend to see how things may be arranged," Abel grunted. "Our daughter Ella wed in the proper way. I do not like to think that Simon be denied the proper service – nor that Imelda may not have her day as should be!"

The four decided that they would indeed call on James Forbes after work ceased the next day. Josiah Grubb was a master shoemaker. He was correctly a cordwainer as he worked on leather goods other than shoes. However, his main work was making and repairing shoes. Like Abel, his work had earned respect from much further afield than the town – hence his never being out of work. Unlike Abel, he had no son to take as apprentice. He had steadfastly refused to seek one, but now with his daughter leaving the home, he had second thoughts.

The four then joined the throng around Imelda and Simon – the two were standing in the middle, holding hands. Ella looked at her young brother and remembered doing the same with Gil when they had declared their betrothal. She silently took Gil's hand and glanced down at Rosie – who was happily playing with her wooden doll.

"May they be as happy as we are," she murmured into Gil's ear.

"Aye – they will be lucky indeed should they be," he whispered back.

* * *

Later that evening, John and Evelyn sat around their own fire. Mary had stayed next door with her brother Gil and Ella. She never tired of playing with Rosie.

"Well, that's all of the Smith family settled – or nearly so," Evelyn laughed as she poured two small glasses of honey mead.

"Ella has made a wonderful wife for our Gil – and they have been blessed with little Rosie, although I swear that sometimes both Gil and Ella could wish for a more compliant daughter!"

"Rosie is certainly not a child to remain silent in the background," Evelyn nodded. "But tis a good thing – think how well she will cope with a little brother or sister!"

John gave his wife a sideways look.

"And you see signs of that happening?" he asked.

"Maybe I have – then maybe I have not," Evelyn gave him a mischievous grin.

"Wife – you have never lost the skill to madden me sometimes!" John grunted. "Have you or have you not?"

"Aye – or I do believe I have. We must let Ella say first to Gil in her own time – that is if I read the signs correctly."

"Talking of reading signs – I know us men are supposed to be blind as far as they are concerned. But what is afoot with our Mary and young Henry Hoggs? Not so long past, they seemed inseparable!"

"Mary is, as she always is, very close-mouthed where young Henry is concerned. I did venture to ask some days past and received merely a shrug of the shoulders and little else "

"The lad be not playing with her affections?"

"Nay – I do not think tis so. Mary is as happy as normal. She would not be so if anything with Henry were amiss!"

John relapsed into silence, contemplating the patterns made by the flames above the burning logs. His son had made a wonderful marriage. He had no worries there – but daughters were different. They needed care and protection. Perhaps he would have a chat with Hoggs Senior – a quiet and friendly chat. Nothing bad would ever happen to his Mary, of that he was determined.

CHAPTER XV

The vast majority of the population of Bovey Tracey, like the vast majority of the population as a whole, tried to close their eyes and ears to what was happening at the seat of power – parliament. Earlier that year, parliament has declared that 'England be a Commonwealth'. That simple declaration did away with the institution of monarchy and established England as a republic. That notion was completely alien to most of the population; England had been ruled by monarchs of all descriptions ever since the Romans had abandoned the country.

Along with that declaration, had come other edicts – churches were to be strictly controlled, fetes and festivals were forbidden, theatres were as good as outlawed. But – most folks simply had to get on with their lives. Crops had to be grown and harvested; wood had to be felled and chopped to provide heat and cooking; the dead had to be buried and mourned; new lives had to be welcomed and nurtured. Most people had little time to stop and think about the wider issues. Keeping life and limb safe and nourished was paramount.

Early on the Saturday, there came a clattering of hooves down the main street and into Parke estate. They stopped at the first two cottages as one of the two estate ostlers came running out to take charge of the horse. The rider, having dismounted, went straight to the front door of the bailiff's house and rapped on the panel.

The door was opened as usual by a tousle-headed lad.

"Master Bailiff," Hob hollered. "Captain Potter be here!"

Cove hurried out to greet his visitor. Mark Potter had been a captain in the king's forces and had been with Sir John Vickery ever since the final capitulation of the royalists. Potter was twenty-five years old, a soldier of some renown, tall and dark – with the pointed beard of his sovereign.

"May we meet at the main house with Master Steward?" he asked.

"Aye – Hob, go and rouse Master Steward and tell him the Captain needs us at the House."

Hob, even though the steward's cottage was no more than twenty yards away, ran like the wind.

"One of these days, that lad will learn that walking is also an option!" Peter grinned.

Some time later, the steward, Luke Barton, joined the bailiff and Captain Potter in the main hall of the House. A fire was crackling in the large grate, as the three sat in chairs warming their feet and supping spiced ale.

"Well, Cap'n Mark, what news?" Barton enquired. "Not that anyone expects good news!"

"For a start, I suppose I have not been a Captain for some time now," Potter pulled a glum face. "Ever since the Commonwealth was declared, we have no official king – and therefore no official king's army! I am plain Master Potter in the eyes of our parliamentary masters."

"In our eyes, you be still Captain Mark Potter!" Barton grunted.

"I left Exeter very early this morning, wanting to spend as little time on the road as possible. I left Sir John at his old London house at daybreak on Thursday, breaking my journey at Salisbury that night. The further I travelled from London, the more distant all the problems seemed to be. In Salisbury, the tavern was filled with farmers – and they were talking mostly of the weather and how it would affect the ground for early planting – and what it forecast for lambing. Only a few ever spoke of the politics! Last night in Exeter, the politics were hardly mentioned at all. I would expect that, were I to travel on to Bodmin, it would not even register! However, you will be wanting to know how fares Sir John."

"Aye – twas what we thought," Cove nodded. "There is talk hereabouts, but only very rarely. The concerns of daily life take precedence."

"Well, as far as any of us can make out, the trial of the king is set to start in two weeks from today. The case is to be prosecuted by the Solicitor General, a Master John Cook. The Indictment is almost exactly word for word as was published throughout the land. Sir John, for some reason, is keeping a very low profile. One cannot place blame on hum for that as his position is precarious, to say the least. As you all know, Vickery has a foot in both camps – being a king's supporter on the one hand and an advocate for change on the other. Being now a common man, I can come and go almost as I please. As you see, I neither wear nor carry the appurtenances of an army officer. To do so would end my usefulness!"

"What hope may there be for the king? And where be the Prince of Wales and the Duke of York?"

"The general feeling is that our king will refuse to even answer to the charges – he does not recognise the right of anyone – be he parliament or general – to hold him to any sort of account. He is the anointed sovereign king and, as such, is beyond anyone's reach!"

"My knowledge of law is weak, to say the least," Barton acknowledged. "But in a common case, should an indicted prisoner fail to respond, is he not deemed to have pleaded guilty?"

"Aye – that be so. But the king is *not* a common felon. And that is the point that is worrying all of the few supporters. Can parliament hold that he *is* in fact a common person – and thus to be treated as such?"

"Let us assume the worst case and parliament holds that he is such a person. That surely entitles him to representation, does it not?" Cove persisted.

"Again, I have to tell you what is the current feeling. The only way anyone can be allowed to speak in his defence is if the king replies that he is not guilty as charged. A plea of not guilty gives any man charged with an offence the right to speak and be represented. I have to tell you that the king will *not* make any plea whatsoever – he does not recognise the right of any court in the land to try him!"

"But what of his sons – and his wife?"

"Ah! Prince Charlie! His whereabouts are a matter of conjecture. Some say he is still in the Isles of Scilly; others that he is in France; others assure me he is in Scotland. James, likewise, is somewhere in hiding. As for the queen – well she is probably with her family in France."

"And is there no voice in parliament who is prepared to give the king any leeway at all?"

"There is but one small hope. General George Monck is known to be of a more lenient disposition – despite his hammering of the Scots, and especially the Stuarts. He has a loud voice, but may well be drowned out by the others, the more vociferous opponents of the king. Cromwell, Bradshaw, Ireton, Ingoldsby, Irestead, all are strident in their condemnation."

"Then banishment is the likely outcome!" Barton sighed.

"Aye – tis the most likely. That and the tightening of parliament's stranglehold!"

It was a sober and reflective group that broke up that Saturday after eating a silent dinner. Potter said he would stay for two more days, then return to see what else he might glean. Whatever the outcome, he promised to return when he was able.

* * *

Just before the noon dinner hour, there came a sound that had not been heard in Bovey Tracey for many a long day – and a sound that simply froze one small girl in her tracks.

"Pots to mend! Kettles to mend!"

Nell had last heard that cry on the day her father had fallen from the wagon and had died without ever regaining consciousness. It filled her with absolute horror.

She ran out of the chicken coop where she had been tending the hens, just remembered to latch the door, then fled into the warm kitchen, where she collapsed sobbing on the floor.

"Whatever is the matter?" Ella paused from adding a handful of barley to the pot of stew hanging above the kitchen fire. And then she heard the cry from the street and knew exactly what the matter was! Ignoring barley and stew, she went to Nell and gathered her into her arms.

"Hush, Nell – nobody here will let anything bad happen. Just stay silent and the old devil will pass as he did before."

"Why Nell crying?" Rosie came toddling over.

"Tis just something that scared her," Ella replied. "Tis nothing for you to worry about."

Gil, who had also heard the cry from the street, came hurrying into the kitchen from where he had been cutting a few cabbages. He took in the scene at a glance.

"Keep Nell and Rosie within. I shall make sure nobody says aught they should not!"

His uncle and aunt had also heard the cry and were themselves outside their apothecary shop. Gil hurried down to them.

"What shall we do if the old man demands we hand back his granddaughter?" Avril asked, her face creased with worry. James and Avril had quite literally adopted little Nell – and had sought blessing from both Reverend Forbes and the Lord of the Manor.

"Then we must ensure that no one tells of her whereabouts," James grunted. "And that includes those miserable devils in the bookshop. Causing trouble of that sort is meat and drink to them!"

"Should we not go and make that certain sure?" Gil wondered.

"Nay – will only make them more determined to stir the pot!" James shook his head.

The wagon stopped where it always had – about a hundred yards further up the main street where a junction to the left created space for a small marketplace. The three watched as the old travelling tinker dismounted, put wooden chocks under the wheels, then started to set up his 'workshop' – hammers, a small brazier for melting lead, tongs and other impedimenta.

His repeated cries had resulted in a small queue, each holding dented or holed cooking implements for repair. The three walked slowly up to where the old man was hammering out a dent in a large cauldron. As they watched, more people from further up the street came down, either to watch or to use the services. Gil spied a massive figure behind the small crowd and made his way over to his father-in-law.

"Nell?" Abel asked quietly.

"Safe with Ella – and staying well out of sight," Gil whispered back.

"That miserable devil simply abandoned his grandchild with never a thought for none but himself," Abel growled. "What if he now asks after her?"

"Then we must ensure that he is met with shaken heads – we do not know," Gil answered. He was sure that, should Abel take the lead in that denial, most would follow. And then he saw what he had dreaded – Hubert and Mercy Green were walking up the street from their shop. He nudged Abel and nodded with his head.

"Bollocks and damnation!" Abel growled. "I shall go and have words!"

"Should not we wait until such words become necessary?" Gil prompted, thinking James' and Avril's advice was the course to follow.

"Aye – maybe. But if the old bastard asks and they speak up, then we all must deny it. Tis not a sin to lie to protect a little one!"

Three hours later and the crowd had all dispersed - those with things mended and those with simple curiosity. They watched from a distance as the old tinker bit into a cold pie, then loaded his wagon again, removed the chocks, climbed up to the driving seat and moved up the street.

Gil espied young Hob who had just merged from the small grocer's shop clutching a paper twist of comfits. He waved to the lad and walked over to meet him.

"Hob – you see the old tinker up there? We need to see that he leaves the town. Will you follow him unobserved and see where he goes?"

"He's the old fart who abandoned Nell," Hob said. "I shall also be happy to see the back of him. And he shall not see me!"

So saying, Hob darted down between two cottages and disappeared.

Gil walked back down to his own small cottage, to find not only Ella, Nell and Rosie, but James, Avril and Abel as well.

"Hob is dogging the tinker. I do believe we may have seen the last of him for another year."

"Has he really gone?" Nell raised a tearful face.

Avril knelt down by the side of her 'adopted' daughter.

"Aye, my sweet. I do believe he is gone. Let us wait to see what Hob says when he gets back here."

They had not long to wait. Hob arrived at his usual gallop. He burst into the cottage and almost skidded to a halt.

"He be gone – on the road towards Chudleigh Knighton."

"May the heavens be praised!" Avril raised her eyes towards the ceiling. Nobody would have been surprised had she crossed herself in the old way.

"But tis not all," Hob went on. "Those two at the bookshop hailed him as he was just past the church. The old man obviously thought they had more work for him and stopped. I was behind the wall opposite and heard all that was said. Master Green asked the tinker if he wanted to know about his granddaughter's whereabouts. The tinker said that she was still far too young, and he had no use for her. He spat in the road and drove onwards."

"Did he indeed!" Abel growled. "Tis indeed time I had words."

"Hob – you have done a good job. You have our thanks," Avril gave him a big smile.

"You also have earned an apple pie," Ella added, handing one to Hob.

"Wow! Thanks, Mistress! But I would have done so for nothing at all."

Nell, nearly seven years old, went over to Hob, just over twelve years old. She stood on tiptoe and gave him a kiss on the cheek. Hob went bright red and even stopped cramming pie into his mouth.

"You have gained an admirer, Hob," Ella laughed. "But you deserve our thanks for what you have done."

"I give Hob a kiss!" Rosie demanded. She held out her arms so that Ella could lift her up to put a sticky kiss on Hob's other cheek.

"I'm off to pay a call on our booksellers," Abel declared. Gil and his uncle James went with him. They both thought they might have to somehow restrain the massive smith from tearing Hubert's head from his shoulders. To their surprise, Abel did not kick the door in. He opened it quietly and walked inside the shop. James and Gil followed him in, Gil closing the door just as quietly behind them.

Hubert and Mercy both answered the little bell that had tinkled with the opening of the front door. Both looked defiantly at Abel, who stood on the other side of the counter.

"I hear tell that you wanted to inform the tinker where he may find Nell," Abel stated quietly.

"Aye – that we did. He has every right to know and every right to claim her back!" Mercy retorted.

"Little Nell has a home and the love of her adopted family. Tis what every child has a right to. That vicious old man would destroy her in a week – and that I shall never allow!"

"That old man has the right to his granddaughter – and the right to beat her as needed!" Mercy shot back.

"Then tis indeed a blessing that you have none of your own – or we would have to take them from you. Is there nothing in your precious bible that tells you to treat little children with love and kindness?"

"What is contained in our bible is strict instructions to force obedience and godliness!"

"Some many months ago, we had to tell you to leave Nell to the love and care of James and Avril. I shall now tel_ you that again – and for the very last time. Should I hear that you have not, I shall rip your heads off so that the children may play football with them!"

"Then you have already committed a crime, Master Smith. By making such a threat, you give us reason to report it to the bailiff. He will have no option but to report it again to the sheriff – and you will face his court!"

"Threat? What threat? I made no threat! I gave you a solemn promise."

"You did so threaten! And in the presence of witnesses!"

"What witnesses?" James looked astounded. "I heard no cross words nor threat! Did you hear such, Gil?"

"Nay, Uncle James. I heard no threat whatsoever!"

"Pay heed to what I said and that these two gentlemen did not hear. Make one move against our Nell and I shall that ensure your lives become a living hell!"

Abel left as quietly as he had entered. He said not one word more but strode up the street to his smithy. James and Gil went back to the cottage.

"I believe that this time, the message has been heard and noted," James grinned.

"What message?" Gil laughed. "I heard no message!"

Nell was quiet for the rest of that day. When Avril went up to say goodnight, she found Nell on her knees by the window, looking up at her favourite star – the star that shone brightest in the night sky.

"I have just told my dada what happened," she said quietly as she hopped into her bed. She spoke quietly to her long-dead dada every night, whether or not she could see that star.

Avril said nothing, plonked a soft kiss on Nell's blonde curls, and crept quietly downstairs again.

* * *

Hob relayed everything to his master, Bailiff Cove and his wife Laura that evening.

"How can anyone not say that Nell should not be with Avril and James?" Laura Cove declared. "That little child deserves a happy and loving home – and she has that where she is. What sort of life would she have with that despicable old tinker?"

"A very miserable life, I would imagine," Peter Cove grunted in reply. "You did well today, Hob."

"Nell gave me a kiss," Hob admitted with a fierce blush.

"Then twas no more that you deserved!" Laura grinned.

CHAPTER XVI

On the Sunday the weather took a turn for the better. It was considerably warmer, and the sun shone from a pale blue sky. Brown and Ratcliffe set out for Chudleigh Knighton roughly at the same time as Garvey and Hook set out from Parke. Both sets knew that their journeys would take about two hours at a good walking speed.

It was therefore just after ten in the morning when they met at the small tavern in the little village. As taverns and inns were the only places able to offer overnight accommodation to travellers, it was impossible to insist that they remained closed, otherwise all long-distance travel would have become impossible.

Hook, Garvey and Ratcliffe renewed their old friendship, accepting Brown as the fourth member of their circle. Over platters of roast pork and vegetables, plus mugs of warmed ale, they compared notes on their situations.

Brown and Ratty could scarce contain their delight in how their little business was growing and flourishing. Garvey and Haddock gave hilarious accounts of their experiences at Parke. Inevitably, their talk turned eventually to what had been their shared experiences in the not too long-ago battles. Brown gave a hair-raising account of Torrington, where the church had simply exploded as the barrels of gunpowder stored within had ignited from a stray spark. Not only were the church and the immediate buildings utterly destroyed - hundreds of people had lost their lives – including royalist soldiers held prisoner within.

"You made some comment about the shepherd when you were at the estate," Haddock reminded Brown.

"Aye – and I've thought long and hard ever since. You know how it be – something niggles inside your head, and it will not go away. What name did you give him when we were there?"

"Bray Cooper," Garvey replied. "We hardly ever set eyes on him as he's away with his flock most of the time."

"His name be not Bray Cooper! Of that I am certain!" Brown stated, nodding his head. "Back in '45, I were at Exeter – before you hooligans chased us out. Early that year there were what was almost a killing. One of the tavern wenches outside Rougemont was attacked and near strangled. Sheriff and two of his bailiffs arrested one of our soldiers and he was charged with the attack. They held him in the castle dungeon until he was brought to trial. Just as he was being brought into face the judges, he gave his escort the slip and was not seen again. His name was Brooke Carter – and if your Bray Cooper and he are not one and the same, I shall eat my boots! As I said, I have been racking my brains to remember the likeness and it came to me days past like a sudden ray of sunshine."

"One of the young maids in Bovey was attacked not long past," Garvey mused. "Could it be that he's up to his old tricks again?"

"Were she badly hurt?" Brown asked.

"Nay – despite being only eleven or twelve, she managed to bite the bastard before screaming her head off."

"We must get that news to Master bailiff as soon as we return. Tis up to him to investigate. But the girl's father is intent on castrating the bastard."

"Something we would all like to witness, if you ask me," Ratcliffe growled.

* * *

After the Sunday dinner had been eaten and cleared away, Mary put on a thick scarf and warm coat. Tucking her hands into the sleeves of the coat, she set out from the bakery to meet Henry Hoggs down by the mill. As she passed the bookseller's, she noticed that the shop was not only open, but there were customers inside. Obviously, Hubert and Mercy were following the letter of the law and working on a Sunday. Outside, secured to a post, were three saddled mounts; obviously, the customers had come from a fair distance.

Henry, very nearly nineteen years old and a journeyman saddler, was standing at the path that led from the mill down onto the Heath. He was a serious, quiet, and very well-mannered young man. He had known Mary all her life – most folks in the small town knew one another, apart from one or two newcomers.

Mary greeted Henry with a smile and a 'good day'. In times past, it would have been scandalous for them to meet without some sort of chaperone. With some families, it still was. But John and Evelyn knew and trusted Henry – as did Mary.

The two walked down the path by the side of the river until they came upon the large boulders where, over two years previously, Gil had sat with Ella. Henry made sure that a boulder was clean before offering it as a seat for Mary. He sat on another, facing her. They had met by agreement for what they both knew was to be a serious discussion. Neither knew how to start that conversation.

"Tis a lovely day, and the river be flowing very fast," Mary observed, failing to look Henry in the face.

"Aye – tis indeed a lovely day and the river will not flood the Heath, I'm thinking," Henry nodded, looking anywhere but at Mary.

There followed a strained silence, both looking at the trees, the river, anywhere but at one another. Mary knew that one of them *had* to broach the subject.

"Henry – everyone expects us to announce our betrothal – but I'm thinking tis not what either of us wants," she burst out. "I love you as my dearest friend – and that is how I want us to stay – friends but never lovers."

Henry gave a huge sigh. "That is also my dearest wish," he managed at last to get the words out. "We have been friends ever since I saw you playing outside the bakery with that little woollen doll. No matter what everyone expects. I could never in all honesty ask for your hand in marriage. Not that there be anyone else! What you want and what I want are one and the same – to remain lifelong friends."

"Thank the Good Lord above that we have at last come to our senses," Mary laughed. "Like you, I have no one else in mind. But for us to marry would not be right. Shall we now go and tell our families?"

"Aye – and let us end this with a friendly kiss!"

Two much relieved young people went first to the saddler's and then to the bakery. Both sets of parents were somewhat taken aback but accepted the wish of the two with hugs and laughter.

"Tis but what I had thought," Evelyn remarked. "Gil and Ella played together as little ones, as did Mary and Henry. But anyone with half a brain could see that Gil and Ella were a perfect match. These two be what they always were – the best of friends. It is right that they remain so."

By nightfall, the news was all over the town. It reached Parke estate as the stars started to show in the clear sky. It brought joy and hope to another young man. Harry Cove, the bailiff's son, went to bed wondering how he might make his thoughts plain to Mary – who he had loved for years past. Mary, asleep in the bakery, was completely oblivious to the fact that she had aroused such passion in someone else.

* * *

The first thing Garvey and Hook did the next morning was seek out the steward.

"And to what do I owe the pleasure of your attendance?" Luke Barton asked as the two shuffled into his office.

"Master Steward, we have to report what we learned yesterday," Hook set the ball rolling.

Barton just sat there behind his desk waiting for more. So far, he had learned nothing.

"Tis what we learned from a friend of ours when we met at Chudleigh Knighton," Garvey continued.

Barton, being still none the wiser, rolled his eyes upwards and waited.

"This friend was a sergeant in the king's army," Hook stated, as if this explained everything.

"So far, I have learned that you learned something from a friend who served the king as a sergeant. I have learned nothing more than that!"

"Sorry, Master," Garvey stuttered. "This sergeant is one of the two who made the hurdles. He came with them, and we helped to unload them. After the job was completed, this sergeant happened to espy Bray, the shepherd. When we met yesterday, the sergeant said that 'twere not Bray but someone else."

Barton closed his eyes and prayed for patience.

"So, this sergeant says Bray be not Bray – have I got that right?"

"Aye, Master – you have that right. The sergeant remembers the man well from some years back when he was stationed at Rougemont. Seems like a serving maid were attacked and badly injured and Brooke Carter were a soldier and were charged with the crime. But it seems he escaped somehow when he was being brought before the judges. We both thought you should be told."

"Aye, indeed!" Barton grunted. "Your friend alleges that Bray Cooper be in fact this Brooke Carter – and fled from justice after attacking a serving maid."

"Aye, Master. That be it!"

"Then this be a matter for the bailiff. You must come with me and make sure I relate it all to him."

Peter Cove listened carefully as Barton went through the tale.

"This sergeant is living at Trusham, you say?"

"Aye, Master Bailiff – with one of our old soldier mates Ratty – er, that is Ratcliffe."

"They have the hurdle business?"

"They came well recommended," Barton nodded. "Their work was excellent."

"Then I must have that sergeant – Brown, you say his name is – brought here and we shall confront the shepherd – whatever his name may be. Say nothing about this to anyone!"

Garvey and Hook were dismissed to go back to their work. Barton sat down in a chair opposite the bailiff.

"Peter – you do know that, should there be truth in that story, then our shepherd may well be responsible for that attack on young May."

"I know that well, Luke. What do you know of this shepherd?"

"He has been here for about three years. He was originally taken on by the farm manager – you remember that Gavin disappeared after going to help out down at Berry Pomeroy."

"There is one other unfortunate thing must be done," Cove grimaced. "I shall have to tell Sergeant Larkin – he is charged with keeping peace and good order hereabouts."

"If we find the man be responsible for the attack on May Fletcher, who has jurisdiction? You as bailiff under the lord, or Larkin?"

"I'm buggered if I know the answer to that!" Cove growled. "But first things first. We need this Brown here to confront the shepherd. Tis still possible that he has mistaken him for the other man!"

* * *

Sergeant Larkin listened to what the bailiff had to say, without any interruption.

"I suppose that, like me, you have to know who has jurisdiction," he said with a wry smile. "And I also suppose that, like me, you have not the foggiest notion!"

"Aye – we are both swimming in a large pool of ignorance," Cove agreed. "How may we resolve this?"

"Tis no good me asking my Captain – for he will automatically take the authority upon himself – no matter whether that be right or wrong."

"It would be the same with my Lord Sheriff," Cove agreed. "But I'm sure it would be best if the guilt or innocence of this man be determined first."

"With that, I agree. I have the means to get Brown here. I shall send one of my men to summon him here. Is it possible you can get this shepherd to attend?"

"Luke Barton, the steward, is his master. I can get Luke to call him to his office on some pretext or other. And then we can confront him with Brown's testimony."

"Then, let us proceed with that plan – and arrange it for the morrow so that the man has no idea the true purpose of the meeting."

Larkin grabbed Trooper Glass, who was not on patrol. He was instructed to ride early the next day to Trusham with a spare horse – and to bring Brown back with him. Glass was happy with that – it would give him something to do other than monotonously patrolling the little town.

CHAPTER XVII

The weather was holding well – cold and bright. Tuesday morning saw both bailiff and steward again in conversation. Larkin had reported that Glass had departed to bring Brown back immediately after dinner. All that remained was to make sure that the shepherd was in attendance. They shared a laugh, and both shouted, 'Hob!'

Young Hob, sneaking back from the bailiff's kitchen with a purloined small loaf and two rashers of bacon, hurriedly stuffed another mouthful and secreted the remainder under his jerkin. He dashed to answer the summons.

"Hob – do you know where the shepherd might be?" Luke Barton asked.

"Aye, Master. He were in the twenty-acre field yesterday, looking to see which ewes were likely to lamb first."

"Then I have an errand for you. Go and find him and tell him that I want to see him immediately after dinner to discuss his plans for the lambing. Then run back here with his answer."

Hob did his usual stunt of standing on one leg as he silently repeated the message over to himself. Then, with a nod, he was off like a whippet.

"That lad would have been useful at any battlefield," Barton grunted. "I've never seen any messenger go so fast, not even on a horse!"

* * *

Nell arrived at the kitchen door as Ella was preparing a pot of stew for their dinner – it would be left simmering for the whole of the morning.

Filling a small sack with grain, and filling a small pitcher with water, she made her way down through the rows of vegetables, through the gate, and into the hen coop. Her first job every day was to top up both water and grain. She was half-way through this task when she happened to glance at the broody hens. In two places, tiny yellow chicks were sitting with their hens.

Nell's first inclination was to scream with delight – but managed to stifle the impulse. Instead, she carefully finished her tasks and went back to the kitchen.

"Ella – we have two baby chicks!" she said, her face beaming.

"May the heavens be praised," Ella beamed back. "What we must now do is to get those chicks here into the warm. I do believe we must have their mothers with them for a day at least – until we be certain the chicks can peck the grain and sip the water for themselves."

In one corner of the kitchen, a small, triangular space had been set with a wooden board set between the two walls. The space inside was already covered with clean straw. The baby chicks would be kept warm until they were large enough to be returned to the coop.

Ella and Nell had already devised the way they were going to accomplish the task of getting chicks into the kitchen. They both went to the coop and made sure that Trumpet the rooster was already outside, pecking at the grass. Ella took hold of the mother hen to safeguard Nell from her beak. Nell very gently took the fluffy chick in her hands, then walked back to the kitchen and set it down on the straw.

The chick, probably only hours old, sat still and did nothing. Ella came back, her hands empty, having locked the coop behind her.

"The mother is sitting on another egg," she reported. "We shall have to go back for the other chick."

It was not long before the small area held two baby chicks, both just sitting apart from one another. Rosie, by that time, had joined them and was sitting just outside the wooden board, staring at the chicks.

"They be very tiny!" she observed.

Nell filled a small bowl with water and placed it on one corner of the triangle, then another with small grains. She dipped a finger in the water and held it at the beak of the first chick. Nothing happened, so she wet her finger again and pressed it into the bowl of grain, a few bits adhering to the moisture. This time, the chick got the hang of it and pecked a grain into her beak.

"That can be your job, Rosie," Nell told the little girl. Ella nodded – it would involve her daughter in the whole business – and would keep her out of her usual mischief.

By the noonday dinner time, Rosie was feeding three new chicks. Gil arrived back from his usual hoeing and digging and praised both girls for a job very well done. Ella had left them to it and had delivered cabbages, onions and leeks to some of their customers. It then remained to be seen what they had got – male or female chicks. They really needed hens to quickly swell numbers. But another rooster would be a distinct advantage. They could exchange it for another from a different flock so as to mix the blood strain. It would also give Trumpet something to think about!

*   *   *

Glass returned with Brown just before dinner – and Brown had to be hidden away out of sight. Larkin and Cove briefed him on what they proposed to do, having first listened to what Brown had claimed about the shepherd. Peter Cove took both Larkin and Brown to his cottage to have a meal.

Bray Cooper arrived just as dinner had finished. He knocked at the steward's door and was taken into the office and given a seat.

"You wanted to speak to me about the lambing, Master Steward," he seemed completely relaxed. After all, the steward had every right to poke and pry into every aspect of the estate.

"Aye – how many ewes are in lamb?"

"Close on one hundred and ten," Bray answered. "I reckon 'twill take more than a fortnight to see them all lambed."

"And where is the best field this year?"

"The long, fifty-five-acre will be best. Tis ready to be cropped and has good shelter along the hedgerow."

Hob, who was behind the shepherd, peering in at the window, saw the steward scratch his head. He shot off around the corner and gave the nod to the bailiff. Cove, Larkin and Brown made their quiet way to the steward's office door and knocked.

"Come in," Barton called.

The door opened and in came the bailiff, Larkin hard on his heels. Barton took up a stand beside the seated steward, whilst Larkin stood with his back to the closed door. A very confused shepherd sat in his chair and wriggled.

"Someone else wants to have a word," Barton explained as Larkin stood aside and admitted Brown. Larkin immediately stood again with his back to the door.

For a few moments, nothing registered at all on the shepherd's face. And then sudden realisation dawned as he recognised the newcomer.

"You are not Bray Cooper!" Brown stated. "You be Brooke Carter – wanted for assault in Exeter. I remember you well escaping trial."

"Nay – you have it wrong," the shepherd faltered. "I am who I say I am. I have never been to Exeter in my entire life!"

"You were a member of a troop under Sergeant Clarke."

"Nay – I have never worn any uniform – not the king's nor parliament's!"

In his agitation, the shepherd lurched to his feet – a huge mistake as it turned out.

"Face about!" Brown roared.

Without a second's hesitation, the shepherd made to swivel on his right heel and left toe.

"Never worn a uniform my arse!" Brown almost laughed.

Cooper – or Carter – drew out a long knife and turned to face the room.

Larkin drew his sword. "Really?" he asked.

Finding one sergeant with a sword facing him, a bailiff with a club on his left and an irate steward with another long knife on his right, the shepherd let his own knife fall to the ground. Brown swung a large fist and sent him sprawling.

"Hob!" yelled the bailiff.

"Aye, Master?" one tousled head poked around the door.

"Fetch young May Fletcher – and her father."

Scampering footsteps could be heard disappearing at Hob's usual frantic speed.

"We shall face you with your latest victim – see what she has to say!" Cove said to the recumbent shepherd.

"Then she will lie!" came the muttered reply from the floor. "You cannot trust a word that falls from the lips of a young whore!"

Barton, who was not only steward bur also May's godfather, aimed a kick at his head – and connected with a hand raised in defence. The room stayed silent and motionless for quite some time until Hob knocked at the door and ushered Wilf and his daughter into the now crowded room.

"May," Barton spoke quietly. "Could this be the man who assaulted you?"

May peered down at the shepherd and frowned.

"I cannot say with him lying there," she replied. "May he be brought to his feet?"

Brown and Larkin heaved the man to his feet, standing one on either side and holding an arm each. May walked purposefully forward and stopped inches from him.

"He wears the same sort of coat – and he has the very same smell. I shall never forget that smell!"

"May I have the use of your Hob?" Larkin asked. Receiving assent, he asked Hob to go and get two of his soldiers – and to bring rope. Once again, the room listened to Hob tearing off on his errand.

"Then we shall have to call you Carter from now onwards," Barton almost spat at his employee.

"May I ask who knocked the bastard over?" Wilf Fletcher enquired.

"Oh – that were me," Brown admitted. "He is also wanted for assault back in Exeter."

"Then, whoever you may be, I owe you a tankard, or five, of the finest ale!" Wilf extended a calloused hand to Brown.

Tamplin and Young arrived soon after, with Hob inserting himself into a corner – a very interested spectator.

"Secure this bugger and take him to the cottage – and lock him securely in the cellar," Larkin instructed.

"Aye, sergeant," Young grabbed the arms and drew them behind the back of the now trembling shepherd. He was marched out.

"This room be far too small for what we must now discuss," Barton stated. "The hall at the House is better suited."

Barton, Cove, Larkin, Brown, Wilf and May sat around the large table with mugs of ale and a selection of small cakes that had been sent up from the kitchen. Somehow or other, Hob had managed to creep into the big hall and squatted out of sight behind a large bench. There was no way he was going to miss any of what followed.

"And now, we must decide where this man be taken – and who has the authority to take control," Cove started the ball rolling.

"The original crime were committed at Exeter – under the command of the king's officers. But they be no longer the ruling force," Brown stated. "Therefore, surely he is to be tried by the Sheriff."

"I am not so sure about that," Bailiff Cove rubbed his chin. "The first assault resulted in real, physical injury, whereas the assault on May resulted in nothing but fright."

"He laid hands on my little girl!" Wilf shouted. "Why cannot you try him right here as Bailiff?"

"Nobody knows for certain where authority lies," Cove answered. "Sergeant Larkin does not know and I'm sure I do not!"

"Aye – that's a fact!" Larkin nodded. "But – two crimes have been committed and he has to pay for one – or both!"

"Why do we not keep him here in confinement and consult the Sheriff – without saying we have a man for trial? Just that we need advice *should* the need arise." Luke Barton suggested.

Larkin and Cove looked at one another, then nodded.

"That seems a good suggestion," Cove gave a sigh of relief. "As bailiff, it has to be my task to go and enquire. I shall set off in the morning and hope to be back with advice by late afternoon. And, in the meantime, I shall send to the tavern so that that wretched man may be fed."

"Then all is settled but for one very crucial matter," Barton grimaced. "I have over one hundred pregnant ewes and no shepherd!"

"Old George were shepherd some years ago," Wilf remarked.

"Aye – that he were," Barton nodded. "That were at least fifteen years past – and tis likely to be a cold task for such an old man!"

"But he may know of someone," Wilf persisted. "I can call at his cottage and ask."

"That would be helpful," Barton nodded.

"Before you and May leave," the bailiff interrupted, "May – how do you feel now that the man is apprehended? Do you now feel safe again?"

May looked at her father, then faced the bailiff.

"Aye, I feel safe. I shall feel safer when he is gone from here. Who did he hurt before? Was she badly injured?"

Brown was the one who could answer that. "She were a serving girl at one of the taverns just outside Rougemont Castle. And aye, she were badly hurt – raped, cut, bruised, and bones broken."

"Then he must stand trial for that crime as 'twas far worse than he did to me. Will he hang for it?"

"He will for sure!"

"Good!"

Everyone was startled at the amount of venom she put into that comment – all except Wilf.

"I shall try to witness it and know my little girl be properly avenged," he snarled.

Wilf and May made their farewells and went home via the cottage of Old George. He said that he knew of many shepherds and would make a list for the steward.

It took but an hour for the whole town to know that the Parke shepherd had been held for the assault. Quite naturally, some said they had wondered about the fellow long before. Others, being more honest, said that they were very surprised.

Many called at the Fletcher's cottage, where Patience received sympathy on behalf of her daughter. Maud, acting as a very junior nursemaid to Rosie, flew home to give her big sister a hug.

* * *

Harry Cove was two months short of his nineteenth birthday. He had 'walked out' with several of the local girls over the previous few years – but he had always hankered after Mary Ramsey. Not only was she a pretty girl, she had intelligence, wit,

121

and was kindness itself. He had heard that the supposed liaison between Mary and Henry Hoggs had ended – and that it had ended very amicably. That evening, he sought out his mother and father.

"Er – ah – there be something I need to seek your advice," he stammered.

Peter and Laura Cove were sitting either side of the fire, sipping glasses of wine. Laura looked at her son and gave him a big grin.

"And would this advice concern a certain Mary Ramsey?" she asked.

"Well, er, um, ah, aye, it would," he admitted.

"And why the shyness and hesitation?" his father enquired. "Mary Ramsey is a lovely young lass. And now that Henry Hoggs is no longer a contender for her hand, why should not the bailiff's son believe he has a chance?"

"Why not, indeed," Laura nodded. "Are you seeking our blessing – or are you asking how you may approach the task?"

"Well, both, actually!"

"Then, the very first thing you must do is to speak directly to Mary. Tell her gently of your feelings and that you wish to approach her parents for their permission to play court to their daughter. Mary is a truthful lass, and she will tell you whether or not she would welcome such an approach."

Harry looked at his mother, then at his father.

"Um," he said. "Put all my eggs into the one basket! Tis a mortal big risk!"

"Aye – that it is. But there is really no other way."

Harry went to his own bedroom, sat on his bed and started to compose mentally what he might say.

CHAPTER XVIII

Matthew Kent pushed his empty platter away from him, then drank the final dregs of his ale. Then he sat back feeling, if not exactly replete, moderately satisfied with life in general. He beckoned the tavern keeper and dropped coins into the open hand.

"One more thing – which road would you recommend I take; the one that leads to Salisbury, or the one that leads to Bristol?"

The tavern keeper, a rotund and morose individual, stroked his short beard.

"You said last evening when you arrived that your destination be Exeter. May I enquire why you have already taken a northern route? After all, Newbury is hardly on a direct route between London and Exeter!"

"That, my friend, is easily answered. I have never in my life travelled south or south-west before. My home and my work have always been in London, Westminster, Essex or further north. Therefore, I am not at all familiar with these roads."

In fact. Kent was a native of Norfolk. He had been born in Wroxham, had studied at Cambridge, and had worked as a senior clerk on the estate belonging to Cromwell – before being recruited into the government's service.

"Then, master, I recommend that you head south on the road to Salisbury. Then proceed west through Yeovil and Honiton. There be excellent taverns where you may stay to rest. To go west to Bristol would mean you then have to go south – and that is a longer route with fewer acceptable taverns on the way."

"Then I am indebted to you for the advice. I bid thee a good day."

Kent stood up – a youngish man of middling height – arranged sword and pistol more comfortably and picked up his valise. He exited through the kitchen, dropping a coin on a worktable and taking a bunch of carrots – all with a friendly wink at the scullery maid who was weeping as she chopped a massive pile of onions.

He then went to collect Murphy from the stables. Murphy was an eight-year-old Irish horse that Kent had owned since a foal. Murphy was superb at long-distance travel, having stamina rather than great speed. Murphy snickered as Kent took him out to be kitted and saddled by the ostler. He greedily accepted a large carrot and nudged Kent for his nose to be stroked.

Leaving the stable yard, Kent allowed Murphy to walk sedately through the little town and took the recommended south road towards Salisbury. Once out of the town environs, Murphy elected to trot. Kent sat quietly and let him get on with it as he in turn let his mind wander.

He had been summoned two days previously to an office that was deep within the Palace of Westminster. He had been there many times before and knew how to thread his way through the labyrinth of passages. He had been admitted to the inner sanctum by a sour faced clerk.

"You sent for me, Master Secretary?" he had given a short bow to the figure seated behind a large desk that was covered in a small mountain of paper.

"Yes – mission!" had come the terse reply. "Proceed to Exeter. Settle yourself there and find out what is going on!"

"Aye, Master Secretary. But may I enquire why Exeter?"

"Suspiciously quiet!"

And that had been it. Kent had left the office, almost none the wiser. All he had was an instruction and his seal of authority – a large seal which he kept in an equally large inside pocket.

He decided on leaving Newbury that, as he was in a part of England never before visited, he would take his time and enjoy the journey. Thus it was that he arrived in Exeter just before nightfall on Saturday the thirteenth of January. What he had observed of the country he had liked immensely – no precipitous hills. Those hills he had encountered were either gentle slopes or short climbs. He was also fortunate that the January weather, whilst cold, had been clear and bright.

He entered Exeter from the east and immediately was confronted by the remains of Rougemont Castle – where a large company of parliamentary soldiers were garrisoned. He let

Murphy walk sedately past and stopped at the first tavern he came across.

He had carried out similar missions before – fact-finding and reporting back – but always in the Midlands or the North. This was all new to him. As was the brand of English he encountered.

"Be ye seeking a room, master?" he was asked by a strikingly ugly man who was draped in a spotless, white apron. It was the pristine state of that apron that convinced Kent that this was probably a clean and well-ordered establishment.

"Aye – a room to myself. I have as yet no notion for how long."

"Ye be not from these parts, I'm guessing," the tavernkeeper grinned, exposing huge gaps where teeth had either fallen out or had been pulled.

"I am from Norfolk originally. It will take me some time I fear to make myself readily understood hereabouts!"

"Aye, master. That it will!"

The room at the end of a corridor on the top floor was quiet, spotlessly clean, and had bed, chest, pegs, a small table, chair, and washbowl. The supper, served in the taproom, was similarly of good quality. Kent went to bed that night and slept through until woken by the noises from the street outside.

He had first to make himself known to the local army commander, and then the county sheriff. He made sure that Murphy was happily stabled, fed him some more carrots, then set off on foot for the Castle.

* * *

Old George himself turned up at the steward's office that morning. It had taken him thirty minutes to walk the half-mile from his cottage. With two ancient hips and one gammy leg, it was as much as he ever walked in any one day.

"Heard you be looking for a shepherd in a bit of a hurry," he said in his old, crusty voice. "Last one be in custody."

"Aye – you heard right, George. I need one very quickly as you may imagine."

"Lambs about to drop any day?"

"Over one hundred of them."

"Young Bernie Wheatcroft over by Lustleigh be a likely lad. He's been with his da learning ropes. Could be ready to do it on his own."

"That's a good thought," Luke Barton nodded. "I'll send Hob over with a message. Meanwhile, you get down to the kitchen and get some ale and a pie. I've a cart going up past your cottage in a while – give you a lift back."

The shepherd over at Lustleigh was not any part of the steward's area, but he knew exactly who to see. It could indeed be the answer he was looking for – and without too much delay. In the meantime, he would have to go and see the ewes for himself – just in case.

Later that afternoon, having seen for himself that the ewes were content -- not a one lying down and looking likely to lamb that day – he arranged to have the loan of the young Wheatcroft lad for the next month. That, with any luck, would see the lambing done for the year.

* * *

By the time light was fading, Harry had at long last managed to accomplish two things. He had finalised his little speech to Mary, and he had summoned the courage to go and knock at the bakery door.

Evelyn came to answer the knock – and gave Harry a big welcoming smile as he stood there fidgeting.

"Er – good evening, Mistress Ramsey. Would it be possible to have a quick word with Mary – if that would be convenient?"

"I imagine it would be convenient," Evelyn managed to keep a straight face. "Mary – Harry Cove would like a quick word," she called over her shoulder.

Mary came to the door and gave Harry a questioning look. Evelyn gave her daughter a big grin and left them to it.

"Hello, Harry. You wanted a word?" Mary said in all innocence.

Harry managed to stop his feet from shuffling and his hands from twitching.

"Er, Mary," he swallowed and started again, seeing Mary's puzzled expression.

"Mary – I would like nothing more than to pay court to you. But first, I need to ask if that would be pleasing to you. If you say no, I will fully understand and will never pester you again. If, as I hope, you say yes, then I must ask to speak to your father and ask his permission."

There, he said to himself – I've managed it.

Mary was, to say the least, amazed that Harry wanted to pay court to her, was also rather excited at the prospect. She paused for a moment to compose herself and her reply.

"Harry – I'm very flattered that you are interested in me. It never occurred to me that you would want to! I'm also very happy for you to pay court as you suggest. And now, perhaps you should speak to my father."

Mary gave him a big smile, touched his arm and went in to call John Ramsey. As John was a few minutes coming to the door, Harry assumed that Mary had told him what was being requested.

"Harry – I understand you have a question for me," he said, trying to look stern and parental.

"Indeed, Master Ramsey. I would ask for your permission and blessing that I may pay court to your daughter Mary. I have known her since she was born and have admired her character, her grace and kindness. I give you my solemn word that I shall respect her in every way."

"Hm! Then, it would seem churlish for me to refuse, would it not? Take care of our Mary – she is very special."

"Indeed, she be, sir. I shall take every care of her."

John offered his hand and Harry went home a very happy young man.

"Well, Mary," John said. "Yet a second young fellow after your hand. And the bailiff's son! You know your mother and I wish you well – and I have granted permission – and a blessing!"

"Thank you, papa," Mary also went to bed that night a very happy person.

* * *

Kent had spent a day touring the sights of Exeter. The cathedral was obviously his first to go and see. Not only did it have the longest unbroken nave in the country, the west front was adorned by so many statues that he stopped counting.

He walked down the hill to the small dockside. Most sea traffic ended their journey further downstream at Topsham, but some still proceeded further up to Exeter itself. The small city was still partially walled. Further upstream from the quay was the bridge that spanned the Exe. Half-way across was the small Exe Island, home of the tanneries and their noxious fumes and smells.

All in all, Kent decided that Exeter was a rather fine little city. He made a note of the position of the Guildhall – one never knew when the local knowledge contained within those walls would come in useful.

Then, on the Monday, he made his way to the castle to make himself known to whoever was in charge. He doubted whether there was still a resident constable, and he was right – there was not. Instead, having got past a rather belligerent sentry, he was directed to a small room where the local commander was supposed to be. Instead, he was confronted by a young and very smart Captain.

"Lionel Brook," this man said, rising from the desk and extending a hand.

"Matthew Kent." Matthew shook the hand, took out his seal for inspection, then took a chair opposite the captain.

"I have been expecting you," Brook admitted. "A fast messenger came two days past with a message for you from Master Secretary." He handed Kent a sealed letter.

"Begging your pardon, I had best read this first," Kent slit under the seal and read the terse message.

"Hm! Seems there is suspicion of insurrection hereabouts. I have to look closely at Totnes and Brixham."

"I sincerely doubt you will find much in either town," Brook shook his head. "I have small forces in both, and neither has sent any report that would give credence to such rumours."

"I am grateful, but I have my orders. So, apart from these two towns, are there any places I should make enquiries?"

"And there is the problem," Brook pulled a long face. "Devon is a large county – large in area but not in population. My force is small but is supposed to be reinforced soon. From Plymouth in the south-west to Tiverton in the north-west, from the Cornwall border of Bude in the north-west to Axmouth in the south-east – you see my problem. And that is not to mention Dartmoor – and only the Good God knows what goes on up there! There is little or no civilian power down here. Thomas Reynel was High Sheriff and is also a Justice. But he was appointed by Charles Stuart – and nobody yet knows what authority the man still holds."

"Then where may I usefully start my quest?"

"Certainly not here in Exeter – the place is still reeling from its defeat a few years back. Anger may well be seething in Torrington, but my force visits only rarely. Bovey Tracey is a very small town, but the same may be felt there. And speaking of that town, I have a report that they hold a rapist – one whose greatest crime was committed here at Rougemont before the city fell."

"That is a problem!" Kent nodded. "Who has jurisdiction?"

"I have ordered that the man be brought here and imprisoned whilst evidence is gathered. Then he will have to wait for the next assize. If what is reported be true, he will hang for sure."

"Aye – and so he should! Rape is a despicable crime!"

"I am sorely tempted to brief my soldiers to let him engineer an escape on the journey here – and then they can dispatch him. That would be a neat answer!"

"Would it help if I made my first journey to this town? I might be able to kill two birds with the one stone – pursue my enquiries and come back with the fellow."

"That would be of great help – and I thank you. Bovey Tracey is – or was – almost entirely for the old king, like the greater part of Devon. You may have to probe deep and with some cunning."

"Aye – cunning! I am supposed to be quite good at that!" Kent grinned.

"The journey will take you no more than three hours."

"Then I shall depart immediately after dinner. I should then arrive before dark."

Kent again shook hands with Brooke and went back to his tavern for an early dinner. Packing his valise, he set off with Murphy at just after one o'clock that afternoon.

* * *

That evening saw the arrival of Matthew Kent at the Bovey Tracey tavern – where he took a room and some supper. He purposely arrived wearing neither sword nor pistol so as not to draw unnecessary attention to himself. He sat quietly at supper in the taproom listening to the somewhat subdued chatter. It concerned lambing, early crop sowing, chickens, and general farming gossip. No once did he overhear anything in the slightest bit political. He went to bed realising that these folks concentrated on their own lives, families and livelihoods. They seemed to have little time for anything else.

That evening also witnessed a meeting at Reverend Forbes' house – with Churchwarden, Sexton and Verger in attendance. It was a sober meeting, one filled with almost dread and foreboding.

"I am far too well known to put in any sort of appearance," Forbes admitted. "There will be members there who will recognise me from my days with the prince."

Ralph Goodes the verger and Sam Fewings were also ruled out as neither was an accomplished rider.

"That leaves me," Will Garlick grunted. "I'm nowhere as young as I used to be, but I'm more than used to riding long distances. So, I shall go."

"With the trial due to start this coming Saturday, you had better be on your way tomorrow morning," Forbes cautioned. "That will mean you arriving late on Thursday. I just hope you will find accommodation as many people will want to be there."

"That be the very least of my problems," Garlick laughed. "My sister and her husband live not a twenty minute walk from Westminster. I can always beg a bed there. My problem will be accessing information as the trial progresses. I fear it may drag on for many days. But you may rest assured I shall return here as soon as maybe."

"May the Good Lord keep you safe. We will get no news by any other source!" Forbes was almost tempted to bestow a blessing - but held back just in time.

CHAPTER XIX

The cold and dry weather broke that night. By the morning, the temperature had risen a few degrees, but steady rain looked set in for a few days at least. Will Garlick set off immediately after breakfast, the old campaigner huddled inside his waterproof cape, a large hat on his bald head. He hoped to make it as far as the Wiltshire border that day.

Matthew Kent surveyed a soggy Bovey Tracey from the window that looked out from the taproom onto the street. He looked a bit downcast.

Dick Allen looked across at him from the doorway into the kitchen.

"Tis common down here, Master Kent," he said with a grin. "Devon be a very wet county. We have the greenest grass and the best milk as a consequence."

Kent looked back and gave a grunt. "You certainly have very good cheese. That slice you gave me with my breakfast was as fine as I have ever tasted."

"Will the weather hamper your business?" Dick asked, hoping for some indication why this well-dressed man was in their small town.

Kent sidestepped that as neatly as a fencing master.

"You may have guessed from my speech that I am not from the West Country. My normal place is London and the country north and east of there. But one part of your county fascinates me. Is Dartmoor as large and scary as everyone tells?"

"Aye – Dartmoor be both very large and very scary. If you take the west road from the crossroads down at the bottom of the town, you will start to climb up and up and up until you see the first of the granite tors. That one be Hay Tor. Up there, and for many a mile you will find granite quarries, some tin mining, and very dangerous areas. Bogs, pixie holes, a mist that can send you around in circles, driving rain, and all the terrors of the earth."

"Pray – what are these pixie holes? They sound like things from a child's story."

"Aye – they do at that! But they really exist. They are deep holes, some only a couple of feet wide, some many yards wide. Nobody knows why they are there, nor what caused them. Sheep regularly fall into them – as do people who disregard warning not to travel in poor weather. They are very easily missed. Legend has it that the moor is inhabited by tiny folk called pixies – and that they live deep down inside the holes. Tis nonsense, of course. But very strange happenings go on up there."

"Is the ground very wet and treacherous?"

"Aye – it is criss-crossed by many rivers and hundreds of small streams. In good weather, it is easily crossed. But in bad weather – such as today – it can be very treacherous."

"Well – enough of this gloomy talk," Kent laughed. "Where may I find the local manor?"

"Ah – that will be Parke Estate. Sir John Vickery is nearly always up in London, but his steward and bailiff will be there. Go down to that crossroads and straight across – as if you were going onto the moor. Parke gates be a few yards further on your right."

"Then I thank you for that. I shall stay here in the warm and go there after dinner. Maybe this rain will stop by then."

Dick Allen gave him a pitying look.

"Rain be set for many days yet. You must be prepared to get wet here in Devon!"

Kent looked glum as he went back to his room. He slumped on his bed and made a few notes on what he had learned. Then he took out a book and read until it was time for dinner.

* * *

Lady Violette had made up her mind that that was the day she would visit Parke – and nothing Thomas Carpenter, her ancient steward could say about the rain, would deter her. He gave in with a shrug and made sure that the Lady's maid had waterproof outer clothing ready for her mistress. He also donned his own waxed hat and cape before calling for their mounts.

By ten o'clock that morning, the two were seated before a roaring fire in the great hall of Parke House. Their outer garments, like those of the others seated with them, were throwing off clouds of steam as they dripped before another fire in the kitchen.

"And to what do we owe the pleasure of your company, My Lady?" Luke Barton asked, having ensured that mulled wine was on the way.

"The days when my company would be deemed a pleasure are well behind me!" the Lady responded. "Nowadays, it is merely tolerated. The reason is that I seek information and advice."

"Then, anything we may do to be of assistance will be *our* pleasure," Barton replied in similar, stilted manner.

"Fowls!" Lady Violette stated. Barton and Cove exchanged startled looks.

"Fowls?" Luke Barton queried.

"Fowls – chickens and eggs to be precise! I require a good flock and a goodly supply of eggs."

"Then we must get Gil and Ella Ramsey to call on you, My Lady. They have just done what it is you seek to do. With the help of young Nell, they have started raising a flock from the beginning – and they are thriving."

"That young Nell – I have heard of her. Is she not the poor mite who was left abandoned?"

"Aye, she was. She was taken in and given a loving home by the apothecary and his wife."

"And I have also heard of them. Is the wife not Avril Ramsey? I hear that she is the one to call upon for sickness and injury."

Peter Cove, who knew the Ramsey family very well, answered that that was indeed the case.

"Hm! A woman who, a hundred or more years ago, would have been burned as a witch!" Lady Violette noted.

"Then may the heavens be praised that we no longer condemn knowledge of the natural world as a crime against God!"

"Amen to that" she grunted. "So, I have a possible answer to one of my problems. The next one concerns gates and other metal fittings. I understand that you also have an excellent blacksmith."

"Aye. Abel Smith and his son are praised far and wide for their work. Shall I ask them also to call on you?"

"If you please. And now my third and final problem. Poachers!"

"What precisely has been poached?" Cove asked, fearing what he might be told.

"A few rabbits and one of my new kittens."

Peter Cove hid his thoughts well. He would have to have a very serious talk with young Hob!

"Then let me assure you My Lady, that I will personally put a stop to that right away!" he looked as serious as he could manage.

"And now, My Lady, may we offer you dinner before you contemplate a very wet return to Brimley?" Barton enquired.

That offer was immediately accepted, and the steward hurried off to the kitchen.

"Cook – what may we offer for dinner to our guests?"

Cook, swathed from neck to toe in sparkling white, pondered, her many chins quivering.

"I can manage capons in almond sauce, those new potatoes from Ella, plus her cabbage, and parsnips in honey. I can also provide an apple tart with cream. Will that suffice?"

"It will do excellently. Thank you." Barton returned with the news, liking the menu very much.

* * *

Mary, not wishing to have her brother left out of the loop, called late that afternoon at the cottage. Rosie, now very full of her own importance, rushed to answer the knock. She could just about reach the latch by standing on tiptoe.

"Mama," she yelled. "Aunty Mary here!"

Gil and Ella had just about finished for the day and were both in the kitchen watching Nell feed the small flock of baby chicks. Mary picked up Rosie for a hug and went into the crowded room.

Ella looked at her and noticed something slightly different about her sister-in-law.

"Hello, big brother, hello sister-in-law, hello Nell, and hello Rosie. I've got some news," Mary announced. That got everyone's attention.

"Harry Cove has asked papa for permission to pay court to me," she added.

"And that is welcome to you?" Gil asked, giving his sister a bear hug.

"Aye – I really like Harry and I do believe we could make as big a success as you and Ella have."

"Then we are all very happy for you, are we not, Ella?"

"Aye – indeed we are. So – when may you bring him with you to supper?"

"May that be this coming Saturday?"

"It definitely may! I shall cook something special."

"This evening, Harry is taking me to meet his parents. Seems silly really – Master and Mistress Cove have known me all my life!"

"Ah – but these things have a certain formality to be gone through.!" Gil responded. "I well remember trembling at the thought of doing just that with Ella's papa."

After a few more hugs and kisses, Mary skipped off home to await Harry calling to collect her. Nell, who had said nothing, then spoke for the first time.

"Will some young man ask to court me when I'm older?" she wondered.

"James and Avril will have to beat them off with sticks!" Ella gave her a grin. "The young men will be falling over themselves to beg for your hand!"

"No, they will not!" Nell laughed. "Perhaps, one or two, if I'm lucky!"

* * *

Later that evening, with Nell back with Avril and Rosie tucked into her bed with her doll, Ella sat down on the settle and patted the seat beside her, summoning Gil to sit beside her.

"Well, wife?" Gil grinned. "What have you broken? Or what have you done that needs me sit beside you?"

"Believe me, husband – I have broken nothing. Also, I have done nothing. It is what *we* have done that needs your attention."

"The chicks?"

"No."

"The vegetables?"

"No, again!"

"The roof needs repairing?"

"No – the roof does not need repairing!"

"Then, in the name of all that is holy, what is it that I must know?"

"Just look at me and tell me what is different."

Gil inspected her from head to toe. "I see nothing other than the lovely lass I married. No new dress or shoes."

"Oh, for the love of God! How many people do you see sat beside you?"

Gil's face went blank, then slowly cleared as realisation dawned.

"Truly?" he gasped.

"Aye – truly!"

"Then for the third time in my life, I am truly blessed. When will this wonder emerge into the world?"

"By the end of September, or the start of October."

"And how may Rosie deal with such competition?"

"Rosie will revel in being the big sister – of that, I am sure."

It was some time before the two of them made their way to bed. Gil, already treating Ella as if she were made of the finest porcelain, gently smothered his young wife with hugs and kisses. He was a very happy young man.

CHAPTER XX

Matthew Kent knew that he had to make a start by visiting the local parliamentary force. Accordingly, he set out the next morning well wrapped up against the chill wind. All he had to do was to wait until he espied one of the soldiers and ask for directions to the local sergeant in charge. The first person he saw was Wilf Fletcher, shovel over one shoulder, on his way to dig out yet another ditch that had become clogged with the normal winter's detritus.

"Never ending job," Kent observed as Wilf stumped past him.

"Aye – I'm responsible for near five miles of the buggers!" Wilf grunted.

The next he encountered was the morning patrol – Young and Glass. He had to make it look just like a casual conversation, or people would immediately twig that he was there in some official capacity – and he did not want that known yet!

Accordingly, he stopped some few feet from the two soldiers and made it look as if he was just casually greeting them.

"Good morning – where may I find your sergeant?" he said with a smile.

"Er – three doors down on the right – the large cottage. Can we be of assistance?"

"No, I thank you. I just need a quick word with him. Would one of you be so kind as to ask him to meet me down at the crossroads at eleven of the clock?"

"And who may we say you be?"

"Just say a Matthew Kent would be grateful for a quick word."

Without even waiting for an answer, he gave a cheerful wave and went on down the street. He had already noted a bakery, a smithy, a butcher, and a shoemaker. As he continued his slow walk, he passed a grocer, a small tinsmith's shop, a little draper's shop-cum-haberdashery, then a long gap before he came across a bookshop. The last shop he encountered was the apothecary. In between all of these were cottages and, in one very large gap, the entrance to a smallholding where he could see rows of beds for vegetables.

A young girl was walking up the slight incline and was just about to enter the side of the vegetable patch when she became aware of a stranger – and a rather well dressed stranger.

"Hello," she said. "Are you looking for someone?"

"No – I'm just out for a morning stroll," he gave her a friendly grin. "Are you with the family that owns the vegetable patch?"

"No – I live at the apothecary, but I come here every morning to tend to the chickens and the new chicks."

"That's a very responsible job for such a young maid!"

"I'm not all that young!" Nell objected. "Gil and Ella trust me to look after them!"

"Then I'm sure you do a splendid job. You seem very responsible to me."

Just then, the door to the small cottage opened and an even younger little girl scampered out.

"Nell – you've got two more chicks!" she announced in a loud and excited voice.

The door to the bookshop opened and an irate face peered out. Mercy Green gave the two little girls a furious look.

"Cease this shouting!" she ordered. "Have you no manners at all?" She went back inside and closed her door.

"Take no heed of her, Rosie," Nell took the little one's hand. "Your dada says she is a miserable old trout!"

"Miserable old trout," Rosie repeated. "Miserable old trout!" she shouted and burst into giggles.

"Then your dada is a very perceptive man," Kent joined in the laughter. "She is exactly as he said!" He raised his hand and bade the two girls a good day.

"Good day to you, young ladies," he raised his hat and walked on.

"The gentleman called us young ladies," he heard Rosie say.

"Aye – he did. And that's what we be!" he heard Nell reply.

Kent went as far as the crossroads, far too early to meet the sergeant. So, he walked on, passed the gates into Parke and continued gently uphill. Had he gone another few miles he would have passed Ullacombe and then climbed up as far as Hay Tor.

However, he turned around after a mile or so and went back to the appointed rendezvous. He thought back to the little girls and found himself quite liking this small town.

* * *

By noon that day, it seemed that the whole town knew of Ella's pregnancy. Somehow or other, people found some excuse to call by and to offer their congratulations – to such an extent that Ella found it necessary to walk quietly up to the smithy where she took refuge with her mother.

Gil, not too pleased to have been left in the lurch, managed to paste on a smile as neighbour after neighbour called out to him as he worked on the long bed he was preparing for the next sowing of beans.

Maud, having tucked Rosie in for her afternoon nap, came down to where Nell was tending the new chicks. Gil, his work hoeing completed, also joined them.

"Is Rosie excited that she will soon have a little brother or sister?" Maud asked.

"Excited?" Gil thought a moment. "Nay – not exactly. She has demanded a sister and will not even contemplate a brother!"

"What will she do if it turns out to be a brother?"

"I dare not think! It will be as if the heavens have opened, and the world has come to its end!"

Nell, as she sometimes did, had fallen quiet.

"Have you noticed that the town has so many young girls and very few young boys?" she ruminated.

"Aye – now you come to mention it, that is so!" Gil answered.

"My mama says that us girls will have to go far afield to find husbands," Maud stated. "I do not think I want to go far afield – where *is* far afield?"

"I believe she is thinking only of Newton Abbot or Chudleigh – not *that* far away!"

"But I've never been to Chudleigh – although I have been to Newton Abbot. It was very noisy!"

"I should not worry, Maud. By the time you have grown up, other people will come to live here – and they might well have suitable young men."

139

"Then I hope so," Maud replied. "I do not like noisy people!"

* * *

William Garlick gazed out of the front window of his sister's house. Not far away was Kings Walk – that led straight to the Palace of Westminster. He was slowly getting used to the crowds, the noise and bustle of the place. The previous evening, he had stumbled upon a huge piece of luck. He, his sister and her husband, had been on a late stroll and had come across two very earnest young men standing on a street corner and arguing. One had said that the previous king, James I, was the son of Lord Darnley, whilst the other had maintained it was the Earl of Bothwell.

"Pardon me interrupting," Garlick had broken into the conversation. "I served King Jamie for many years, and I can assure you that he was the son of Mary and Lord Darnley."

"See!" the taller one poked his shorter colleague in the ribs. "May I ask sir, in what capacity you served the late king?"

"I was a captain of horse. At one time I commanded his official escort."

"Then it is an honour to meet you, sir. I attend parliament as an usher."

It was as if an angel from heaven had arrived with great tidings. Garlick cleared his throat.

"Then I may assume that your remuneration be not that large, despite the onus placed upon you. May I suggest a way in which that remuneration may be enlarged – and by all legal means?"

"Indeed, you may, sir – as long as the manner of its earning is wholly legitimate."

"On that, I give you my solemn word. All I would ask is that you meet me every evening and relate to me what transpires at the trial – which starts on the morrow."

"Can you not wait until the official report be published?" the young man asked.

"The official report will contain precisely what the writer wishes to convey. What I need is for a verbatim account of what *actually* happens and is said. I take it you understand the huge variation that may occur between the two?"

140

"Aye – I understand that right enough!" the young man grinned. "So, where may I deliver my report?"

Garlick gave his sister's address and said that a sum of ten crowns would be waiting for him every evening for the duration of the trial. Garlick was not a rich man, but neither was he a poor man. The young usher, eyes wide at the sum, agreed readily. Garlick retired that night in a much more contented frame of mind.

* * *

Sergeant Larkin duly arrived at eleven that morning to meet the mysterious Matthew Kent. Needless to say, he did not recognise the well-dressed man who was waiting for him at the crossroads. Kent looked around him and saw that it was hardly the most inconspicuous place for a meeting.

"May we walk somewhere a little less obvious?" he said.

"Ah! Like that, is it?" Larkin smiled. "Then, let us take the lane north and talk as we walk. For starters, I know your name. Mine is Larkin. But I do not know your business."

By the time they were around a corner of the lane, Kent was happy to reply.

"I have been sent here by Master Secretary. No – that is not entirely true. I was sent to Exeter in the first place, then was directed here to Bovey Tracey."

"Then your purpose must be to observe and report," Larkin nodded. "I wondered when we might receive such a visit."

"Why? Have you reason to believe such a mission be necessary?"

"Nay – entirely the opposite," Larkin gave a chuckle. "This little town, with two or three exceptions, is exactly what it appears to be – a quiet, lawful, and mostly happy place. Solidly for Charles Stuart – but I assume you know that already. But far too occupied with the day-to-day business of living to do much else than talk now and again – and speculate, of course."

"These few exceptions – would they be towards Rome by any chance?"

"Exactly the opposite – puritan to the greatest degree!"

"I do not suppose they reside in the bookshop?"

"Aye – two of them do. Hubert and Mercy Green. How did you arrive at that knowledge?"

"The woman – Mercy, you called her. Singularly ill-named, if you ask me. She railed at two little girls who were laughing and playing in the street. One of them said the woman was a miserable old trout!"

"Would one of them be young Nell? She has been adopted as a sort of town mascot – a lovely child who was abandoned here by her grandfather – her mother having died at the birth and her father having died here some two or three years past."

"So, apart from a few of the ultra-puritan persuasion, you have found no unrest?"

"None whatsoever. That is strange in itself. First, there was the humiliating rout of the royalists down on the Heath. The rector here was chaplain to young Charles Stuart – styled the Prince of Wales - before that individual fled to God alone knows where. Sir John Vickery is a strange case – taking his place at Westminster whilst showing sympathy for the older Charles Stuart. No problem at all with the Member of Parliament though! Sir John Northcote is solidly behind parliament."

"Then how about the surrounding villages?"

"Ah! Just a few miles west is Brimley – and that's more a hamlet than a village. There, you will find Lady Violette Charlton. She apparently is some distant relation to the Courtenay family. She is also quite ancient. But do not let her age fool you – she is formidable. To the north is Lustleigh – and that is as peaceful a place as you could wish for. To the north-east is Trusham – and that is very similar to Lustleigh; a village bent on maintaining its own peaceful way of life. There are larger places hereabouts – Chudleigh, Chudleigh Knighton, Moretonhampstead, Chagford, Widecombe - to name but some. There are many much smaller places, but I have heard no reports of activity in any of them."

"What of the local authority?"

"The bailiff is as sound and as capable as one would wish for. Peter Cove is undoubtably a royalist through and through – but he stands for no breaking of the peace. Sir John's steward is Luke Barton – and he is similar in all respects to the bailiff."

"How about observance of the new parliamentary laws?"

Larkin gave a shrug and a laugh. "As I think you would expect! Work ceases on a Sunday – with one or two exceptions. That is not in accordance with the laws! As for the tavern, it simply cannot close. Like all taverns throughout the country, should they close, all travel and trade would grind to a halt. But then we come to the church. That opens on a Sunday. It opens just the once. Most of the town attend the service. They arrive quiet and peaceful and leave again in the same condition. I hear of no seditious sermons, nor of rousing speeches. To my mind, the town is quiet and peaceful. Were I to enforce the letter of all the laws, I would have a resentful and potentially rebellious town on my hands. As it is, I prefer a peaceful and quiet town. In such a place, any potential trouble would stand out like a sore thumb – and thus far more able to be controlled."

"That, sergeant, is what one might term a pragmatic view. It is one I would call eminently sensible. However, if word reaches Westminster, you might find yourself in deep water!"

"I'm prepared to wager that most sergeants and junior officers throughout the countryside are of my view – keep the peace and keep both eyes open!"

By the time they had reached a set of stepping-stones that crossed a small stream, both decided to retrace their steps. They had been walking up a gentle slope for most of the way. Both decided they were hungry and thirsty. By one o'clock, they arrived at the tavern and were pleased to note that some of the stew from dinner was still available. Dick Allen and some of the regulars noted that the sergeant was in the company of the newcomer – and that did not fail to register. Rumours about this gentleman were rife well before supper!

* * *

Peter Cove had not managed to see the Sheriff – Sir Thomas Reynell was not at the castle or anywhere else that he could think of. Instead, he had consulted one of the law clerks. This individual was a bespectacled man in a long gown of black, a permanent sneer on his long, thin face.

"And what brings a bailiff from a small town here?" he asked, deigning to put down his pen and giving the bailiff a look of disdain.

"Simply a matter of law," Cove replied, determined not to rise to the bait.

"And what possible matter of law could interest you?"

Unbidden, Cove sat himself down on a chair and waited until he had the clerk's attention.

"Simply this matter of law," he started. "It is possible that I might have to apprehend a person from the town on a charge of rape. If that were to happen, then to whom do I deliver my prisoner? To the Sheriff or to the Parliamentary representative?"

"And what gives you to suppose that such a situation may arise?"

"It is, as I said, possible!"

"Then who was the subject of the attack? A member of the civilian population, a member of the outlawed aristocracy, a supporter or a member of the parliamentary party? Who?"

"As far as can be ascertained, it was a member of the civilian population – here in Exeter."

"Then why are not we dealing with it?"

"The person accused might be residing in Bovey Tracey."

"Then, who is investigating? And why have I only just been appraised of the matter?"

"Simply because the matter has only recently come to light – and that the person *might* be residing in my bailiwick. Sergeant Larkin, who commands the local force, is also involved."

"As he most assuredly should be!"

"So, I can only repeat my question. To whom do I render my prisoner, assuming I am able to apprehend him?"

That, as Cove was able to see very plainly, put the man right on the spot. He either had to make a decision or refer it to someone else for a determination – and that would put him in an inferior light!

The clerk steepled his fingers and went into what was known as a brown study.

"If and when you are able to apprehend the man, he should be brought here for imprisonment awaiting trial by the next assize."

"Then I thank you," Cove said and made a hasty retreat. He had what he had come for and knew the clerk's name should any further complication arise. He had sought advice and had the name of the person who had delivered that advice. He rode back to Bovey Tracey whistling happily.

CHAPTER XXI

The Saturday started off fine and dry. That made Nell very happy as she was sitting on a small stool outside Gil's and Ella's cottage. In front of her was a large box that had a notice on top. 'Eggs for sale'.

It had been decided that, as they now had over a dozen chicks being kept in the warm, it was time to start selling the surplus eggs. Gil, Ella, Rosie and Nell had eaten an egg for their breakfasts. Ella cooked them on a flat griddle with a pat of butter. Nell said hers was delicious – although the others said they tasted just as good as any they had tasted before.

By eleven o'clock that morning, she had sold every one of the eggs. She didn't realise – and nobody told her – that the reason they sold so quickly was because she – Nell – was selling them. That little girl was a very firm favourite with everyone in the village, with the exception of the Greens!

Of the dozen chicks, eight were hens – and they would be kept to mature and start producing eggs of their own. The four male chicks would be allowed to mature, but only one would be kept as a rooster. The other three would be sold to the butcher to prepare as capons.

It had been Nell's idea to keep an account of the costs and income from the flock. She found paper and, every time they purchased seed, she entered this as a cost. At last, she was able to enter the income from the sales she had just made.

"We're still not making a profit!" she moaned. "Our costs are more than the money I got this morning."

"And we will not make a profit for some time to come," Gil told her. "Go and ask James and Avril and they will tell you that every business takes some while to yield results. Do not worry – it will yield a profit, but not yet."

Out in the vegetable area, Gil relayed this to Ella.

"The one thing she has yet to realise is that she is doing all this at the age of seven years! Would you have been able to keep an account when you were seven? I know I could not!"

"Aye – she is an absolute treasure. Just imagine her life had that despicable old man claimed her!"

Gil found a pair of thin boards and gave them to Nell so that she could keep her account sheets between them. Needless to say, James and Avril were not the slightest bit surprised – they knew what a bright child they had!

* * *

Matthew Kent was well aware that, far away at Westminster, the trial of Charles I was scheduled to start that very morning. Despite that, he decided to take Murphy for a day's outing. His first port of call was the nearest – the Brimley estate.

Clattering into the yard, he was accosted first by the steward, Thomas Carpenter. On the way, Kent had decided to come clean at every place he visited – just to test the initial reactions. At his first port of call, he was pre-empted.

"I see by your sword and pistol that you are on official business," Carpenter observed as Kent dismounted. Luke Farmer who had been hovering about, took Murphy to the stables and tethered him in a stall with a bag of oats to munch.

"Aye – I am on official business," Kent acknowledged. "Would it be possible for me to have a word with Lady Violette?"

"To do that, young man, I shall require proof of your authority!" came a stern voice from the back door.

Kent turned and doffed his hat politely.

"Lady Violette? My name is Matthew Kent, and this is my proof of authority," he displayed his seal.

"Hm! From those wretched men in parliament!" she snorted. "Well, Master Kent, what are you prying into?"

"Simply observing, Lady Violette. Simply observing."

"Well – you have observed one old lady, one equally old steward, one very old house, and a small body of servants. What else have you the need to observe?"

He was about to reply when a small figure burst out of the door pursued by a striking red-headed girl.

"Hal – get you back here this instant," the girl made a grab at the fleeing infant.

"Hal! Heed your mother!" came the voice of the lady of the house.

Little Hal knew that was a voice to be obeyed instantly. So, he skidded to a halt and returned to his mother.

"I'm sorry, My Lady. I just cannot get him to obey me these days," Meg apologised with a small bob of her head.

"Hal – come to me and open your mouth!" Lady Violette bent down and peered into the little mouth.

"Cutting a tooth!" she snorted. "Now you hearken to me, young Hal. When your mother or father call you, you obey. Do you understand?"

Little Hal gazed up at the old face. "Yes, ma'am," he muttered, then sidled over to Meg and tried to hide behind her skirts. Lady Violette tried hard not to laugh aloud, but instead spoke to Meg.

"Get to the apothecary and ask for a tincture of cloves. His gum is sore where the new tooth is trying to burst through. It will taste foul, but tell Hal that, should he complain, I shall have further words!"

Meg looked suitably chastened. "Aye, my lady, and thank you." She hurried indoors taking Hal with her. Luke Farmer, who had witnessed all that, hurried after his wife and son. Kent, who had stood by, came forward again.

"I doubt that I need to observe more, Lady Violette," he said quietly.

"You may not, but I most certainly do. Come within and tell me what is happening – I am starved for news in this far-flung outpost!"

Seated before a crackling fire and supplied with a glass of Rhenish wine, Kent knew instinctively that prevarication would not pass unnoticed by this sharp-witted lady. And so, he gave her a precis of what he believed to be the current situation.

"I am commissioned by Master Secretary to visit Exeter – and other places as I find the need. The obvious reason is to see whether rebellion or insurrection is being plotted and, if so, by whom, and at what level. I have to tell you that, so far, I have found none!"

"And I sincerely doubt that you will," the Lady grunted. "Life is hard for the people of the land. Winter places huge demands on their provisions and fortitude. It is hard enough for any small community to survive until Spring. These people down here will, as they are prudent, hard-working, and have a care for one another. That all leaves little time for plotting and planning."

"I have also noted that the laws pertaining to churches are paid scant attention."

"And what would you have expected? Suddenly, at the whim of this Rump Parliament, the habits of centuries are cast aside. Do they seriously expect people to cease their observances at the drop of a hat?"

"To be frank, Lady Violette, no I do not. I take the view of your local sergeant Larkin. As long as the peace is kept, it matters little how that be achieved. To use a mailed fist would only breed deep resentment – and that alone would likely foment what it is we are trying to maintain – peace!"

"A very sensible and pragmatic attitude! Now – what news have you of our king?"

"All I know for certain is that the trial is due to commence today – and that charges will be laid much in accordance with the notice that was issued some time past."

"And now, speak openly and freely. You are recently come from Westminster. What do you *believe* will be the course of events?"

"Honestly, I have no notion whatsoever. I am far removed down the ladder of influence or knowledge. What I *believe* is that Charles Stuart will maintain that he has no charge to face, that he is – in his eyes – above the laws that appertain to common folk. How his accusers will deal thereafter is way beyond my imagining!"

"And, from your admittedly scant knowledge, who are these main accusers?"

"Oh – Masters Ireton, Ingoldsby, Cromwell, and Bradshaw. Where Generals Fairfax and Monck stand in this order, I have no notion."

Lady Violette took a while digesting this minor litany.

"Let us assume that, somehow or other, parliament gets its way, and the king is put aside – this ludicrous republic or commonwealth continues. Who, in your admittedly scant knowledge, will be the major beneficiary?"

The put Kent very firmly on the spot. He in his turn, thought long and hard how to frame his reply.

"There will be no place for his son – the one who was styled Prince of Wales. I shall deny ever having said this aloud, but I think that General Cromwell shall rise head and shoulders above the rest."

"And why would you think that?"

"Madam – who was it who raised and trained the New Model Army? Who was it who then led them to the crushing defeats visited upon the royalist forces? Who is it who is known to be the staunchest supporter of the notion of commonwealth?"

"And where pray, does that leave the likes of Fairfax and Monck?"

"Again, my denial is implicit – as faithful, of silent, servants of the new regime."

"Well, Master Kent. I thank you for your candour. I shall not attribute any of the foregoing to your lips. And now, I owe you a dinner!"

Leaving Brimley well into the afternoon, Kent rode slowly back to Bovey Tracey with that almost surreal visit wandering about in his brain. He would travel further afield the next day.

* * *

William Garlick was on tenterhooks throughout the whole of that day. Would his informant come as arranged? Would he be willing to recount the day's happenings? Would his recounting be even truthful?

Having hardly touched an early supper with his sister and brother-in-law, he sat and worried until he heard a faint knock at the front door. His sister's servant entered the large parlour.

"Excuse me Master, a gentleman named Arthur Walker is seeking audience."

"Then, show the gentleman in,"

Garlick breathed a hearty sigh of relief as the tall usher was shown in, was offered a glass of wine and a seat by the fire.

"I have come to render what service I may," he said, looking directly at William.

"And have you a report ready at hand?"

"I would not have dared write openly. I cast it all to memory and wrote privately when we adjourned for dinner and afternoon break. I have only just completed my writing – which will be indecipherable to anyone but me. I use my own abbreviations throughout for speed."

He produced a bundle of paper and smoothed it out. He cleared his throat and began.

"It took place in Westminster Hall. One end for the court and the other for the public – that section barred and guarded by armed sentries. The Sergeant at Arms first entered bearing the mace, which he set before the court. Charles Stuart was brought in and was sat facing the court members. I have to tell you that the court was established by parliament as The High Court of Justice. Standing by the side of Charles Stuart was Solicitor General John Cook. He read out the charges in the form that is already well known. Charles Stuart tried to intervene many times, but Master Cook took no notice. And then the accused was given leave to speak and to enter his plea. He refused to do so, saying that no court had jurisdiction over an anointed king. He claimed his divine right to govern given to him by God. He asked by what *lawful* authority he was called to this court. The upshot of all this was that he refused to plead."

Walker paused to take breath and to take another sip of wine. His audience of three sat in silence, waiting for what came next.

"John Bradshaw had been elected as chairman of the Commission. He sat with two other main judges – and I counted about 150 other commissioners. It was then declared that, as no plea had been entered by the accused, that it would be assumed that a plea of guilty had been entered. The hearing continued into the late afternoon."

He again stopped for further refreshment. Still, the others remained silent.

"It was then argued that the state of kingship was an office, and not a person – and that the person occupying that office was just as liable to be held to account as any other member of the population. That, as you may imagine, sparked off the liveliest debate amongst the commissioners – and that lasted until the court rose."

Garlick was the first to speak following a prolonged silence.

"That is a most scurrilous suggestion – the idea that a king is a mere office holder. It is also an extremely clever ploy, and one that may well take firm root. It places whoever holds the supposed 'office' in the position of a servant to that office, and hence liable to be called to account for contraventions to the laws that pertain to the office. Oh, diabolically clever!"

His sister Margaret was never one to sit for long without making some comment.

"If that were to be adopted, it would mean that a king would become no more than an elected office holder. To whom would he be answerable – to parliament, to this new High Court, to the enfranchised members of the population?"

"It falls very neatly into the idea of a republic – which this Rump declared England to be," Garlick growled into his beard. "What would they then call him? An elected king? A president? What he could not be is an anointed monarch. And then where would be the Church of England without an anointed Defender of the Faith?"

"The whole thing is a morass," Margaret stated. "It is an ill-thought, ill-intended, morass!"

There seemed to be no answer to that. Young Arthur Walker accepted the purse handed to him by Garlick, thanked his hosts for their hospitality, and promised to return when he had anything more of substance to report. He left behind him a very troubled house.

CHAPTER XXII

On the Tuesday morning, Nell arrived at the kitchen door with a small basket containing six more eggs. It had started to snow very gently during the night, but there was only a light dusting down in the valley. Everyone knew that, up on the moor, it would be considerably more than that.

She put the basket by the front door so that people coming to buy vegetables would see them and hopefully buy them. Having gone back to the kitchen, she looked carefully at the mass of little chicks that were contained in the 'safe' corner.

"Ella," she called out. "I do believe three of them are now big enough to go back out into the coop. What do you think?"

Ella bustled down the stairs from where she had been tidying the two small bedrooms. Gil was, as usual, out in the garden tending the beds.

"I had a word with Aunt Avril, and she said we needed a sort of 'next step' place for the chicks who are well grown. Gil is going to make yet another small area in the kitchen where the larger ones can be put – before they go outside."

"Oh – then I should not put them out in the coop?"

"Nay, not yet."

Having made sure that the chicks had enough seed and water, she went back out to the coop, tidied things up, then went past the cottage to walk back down to James' and Avril's house. She had herbs to grind up. Someone was bending down at the basket of eggs on the step and putting them into a deep pocket. Waiting to see if coins were left in the basket, she was alarmed to see the figure straighten up, look around, and then start to walk off.

Without thinking, she went after the squat figure and called out, "You forgot to pay for those eggs."

The figure turned and gave her a glare.

"Go away, little girl!" he snarled quietly, then turned and walked on.

"GIL!" Nell shouted as loud as she could. "This man has stolen the eggs!"

Instead of returning to silence the girl, the man broke into a run and fled up the street. Nell, again without a moment's thought, set off in pursuit.

"Stop! Thief!" she shouted, then repeated it every five paces. Curious faces peered out of doorways and saw one squat man in a long coat running up the street pursued by a little girl shouting her head off. By the time the man had passed the butcher's shop, Nell was very happy to see the large figure of Simon standing outside the smithy.

"Simon, stop him. He's stolen our eggs!" she yelled.

Hawkes, for indeed it was he, looked up and saw a massive young man standing squarely in his path. He veered down the side of the smithy, knowing that there was a path across the top of the heath and back into the woods. Simon, who had lived there all his life, was equally aware of that path and where it led. He galloped after the fleeing figure, paused to pick up a small rock and hurled it. It hit Hawkes between the shoulder blades, causing him to pause and look behind him. He should not have paused.

Simon launched himself and brought his quarry crashing down. He struggled, only to find the massive young man sitting on him.

"Nell – call my father, will you," he shouted.

"Get off or I'll stick you," Hawkes panted, scrabbling for his knife. Simon seized the wrist and squeezed. Hawkes screamed in pain and went limp.

Nell arrived with Abel Smith and a large crowd, all eager to see what the fuss was all about. Abel grinned at his son.

"Nicely done," he chuckled. "Let's see what we have here."

He grabbed a handful of the long coat and hauled Hawkes upright, Simon still holding the wrist in a vicelike grip.

"Nell," Abel looked down at the little girl. "You say this thing stole eggs from Ella's place?"

"Aye, Master Smith. I saw him put them in his pocket and ran away when I shouted that he had not paid."

"Well – we cannot have thieves in the town, can we." He looked at the small crowd and picked on one of them. "Henry –

be a good lad and fetch that sergeant here, will you?" He returned his attention to the man now sagging in his grasp.

"Simon, I'll hold this object. Let's see if he has eggs, shall we?"

By the time Simon had found four whole eggs and two broken ones, Gil ran up from leaving his vegetable patch. Nell took the four undamaged eggs and put them carefully into the pocket in her apron.

"Those eggs belong to my wife!" Gil said quietly, bunching a fist.

"They also belong to my daughter, and to Simon's sister," Abel added. "So, which of us takes preference?"

Gil was the first to act. He planted a hefty punch into Hawkes' midriff that caused the man to double up. Simon, not to be outdone, closed a fist the size of a club hammer and landed a solid punch into the lowered face. Blood spurted from a badly broken nose. Abel, displaying unusual restraint, simply cuffed him around the head. Hawkes collapsed in a heap.

"I hear we have a thief in our midst," came a voice from the mouth of the alley. Sergeant Larkin pushed his way through, followed by Glass and Bell.

"Aye, indeed we do," Abel answered. He bent down and grabbed another handful of the long coat. Picked up the limp man and threw him at Larkin' feet. "Stole eggs from young Nell. But she pursued him, and we caught him. He's all yours!"

Larkin motioned to his two soldiers. Hawkes was grabbed and taken away to join the shepherd in the cellar.

Nell was just happy that she had managed to salvage four of the eggs.

*　*　*

Troopers Glass and Bell got the job of escorting the shepherd, Brooke Carter, to Exeter. Larkin penned a letter to the Sheriff, knowing that it would be opened, read, and acted upon by that fussy clerk. The letter explained in detail the charge made by May Fletcher, and the accusation made by Michael Brown of Trusham.

He had no doubt that he and Brown would be summoned to Exeter to 'put the meat on the bones' - but was happy to get one of his prisoners out of his cellar. In the meantime, he had a moaning Hawkes to contend with.

"Do you admit stealing from young Nell?" Larkin asked.

"Yes," mumbled Hawkes, wondering if he could ask for a physician to set his nose.

"Then you deserve all you got. Think yourself lucky I don't add to your woes."

"That lout broke my nose!" Hawkes returned with a bloody grimace.

"Good! Had he not done so, I would have obliged. Now – shut up and wait until I've seen the bailiff. He will have jurisdiction – I think!"

Slamming and locking the cellar door, he went in search of Peter Cove. Peter scratched his head and thought.

"Theft usually goes to the Sheriff – or gets dealt with by Sir John Vickery. But – we have no Sheriff to speak of, and Sir John is otherwise engaged. So, I suppose it is down to me. Has the bugger admitted the offence?"

"Aye – and was caught red-handed by young Nell, apprehended by Simon and Abel Smith."

"Then I'm surprised he is still breathing!" Peter Cove laughed. "I need to think about this – and what I may do. Are you able to keep him for a while – I'll make sure his food and ale are provided?"

"That I can do," Larkin nodded. "I'm actually wondering if that even falls under my remit. I am here to maintain the law – and theft is definitely contrary to the old and the new laws. I need to think also. May we compare thoughts on the morrow?"

And so, Hawkes was doomed to spend the night locked in a dark cellar with only a hunk of bread, a piece of cheese, and a jug of ale for company.

* * *

Matthew Kent had spent the previous day enjoying a leisurely ride up to the small village of Lustleigh. Amongst those he spoke to were the local reeve and the woodcutter, Laxton Groves. This latter was a mine of information. Groves lived a very solitary life, spending days in the woods coppicing and felling. His daughter, the flame-headed Meg, had left to marry Luke Farmer and the pair lived at Brimley with their little son Hal. Once a fortnight, Groves would walk to Brimley to see them. He spoke at length to Kent about all he saw and heard, never realising that he was talking to an agent of parliament. He was a naturally talkative man and was a keen observer.

Having left Lustleigh, Kent had decided to go on further north to Moretonhampstead – where he found a thriving little town, utterly at peace with itself. However, there was not an eloquent Laxton Groves at the tavern – so he found out little else than what his eyes could tell him.

As Hawkes was being bundled into a cellar in Bovey Tracey, Kent was riding into Trusham. There, he had better luck. He espied two men cutting and bending hazel into hurdles. He dismounted and watched, fascinated at the speed and precision.

"May we help you?" Brown asked, having been aware of the stranger ever since he had appeared along the track.

"Aye, mayhap you can," Kent replied, allowing Murphy to wander a few paces to nibble the snowy grass. "Is there a reeve hereabouts?"

"Nay – place be too small for that!" Brown grunted as he split another hazel stem for twisting around the uprights.

"This seems like a peaceful village," Kent probed. "No trouble hereabouts?"

"Why? Be you of a mind to settle here?" Ratcliffe glanced up from his work. "Or are you just nosy?"

Kent decided to play it safe. "I'm just a very nosy man, as you so rightly observe," he laughed. A thought occurred to him. "Would you be the two who supplied hurdles to Parke? The steward there spoke very highly of you, if so."

"Aye – and we're doing the same for that old lady over at Brimley. She is quite a character!"

"Aye, she is that!" Kent grinned, then could have bitten his tongue off.

"So, Master Nosy – you've been to Brimley, been to Parke, and you come from the direction of Bovey. You are not just nosy

– you be on a mission!" Brown accused. "Snooping for parliament, are you?"

"Would it concern you overmuch if I were?" Kent asked, eyeing two men armed with billhooks.

"Nay – tis no business of ours who you snoop for!" Brown grunted, splitting another length. "We both were at Torrington and we want no more of all that nonsense!"

"Ah! The place where there was a huge explosion," Kent replied, nodding. "Little wonder you want no more of it. Royalists?"

"Aye – I were, but Ratty here were one of your lot. We decided long past that neither wanted any more fighting. We teamed up and have made a success of what we do."

"I served General Cromwell," Ratcliffe admitted. "I were part of a small group of trackers. Got blown up with Michael here. Makes you think differently, does that!"

"I can readily understand that it would. So, here you both are in a peaceful little village and nothing to disturb that peace?"

"Nay – nothing ever happens here. Oh – I lie! Old Martha had her roof collapse some weeks past with the snow. The rest of us put it back to rights."

"Then I shall leave you to your peaceful lives. I have a thirst that needs slaking."

Kent gathered Murphy's reins and walked him to the local tavern where he enjoyed a jug of ale and a meat pie. Much more of this, he thought to himself, and I might just as well go back to Exeter. Nothing to see or hear – just people trying to get on with their lives.

* * *

William Garlick was getting anxious. He had received notes on the Sunday and the Monday evenings saying that his informant had nothing to report. Had the young man got cold feet, he wondered? Had he been discovered?

It afforded him massive relief when his brother-in-law's servant ushered the young man into the large parlour on the Tuesday evening.

"My apologies – I really *did* have nothing to report," he started as he was handed a glass of wine and offered a chair.

157

"Was that because the trial has been suspended?" Garlick asked, more in hope than expectation.

"Unfortunately for you, sir – no it has not. What has happened is that witnesses are being interrogated, but not in the main Hall. They are being seen in the Painted Chamber – and in private. Neither the accused nor anyone apart from the witness and the panel are permitted entry. As yet, there is no report of what has been said or witnessed. We are going to have to wait until the panel resumes its place in the Hall before we are made privy to what was witnessed."

"You are saying that the king is not permitted to see and hear what is being said against him?"

"Precisely that, sir. You are doubtless aware that, where an accused is deemed to have pleaded guilty, he may not be privy to the evidence offered against him!"

"Aye – I am aware of that. But – this is the king we are speaking of, not some ordinary miscreant!"

"I would beg your pardon for being blunt," the young man said. "But here we come to the whole crux of the matter. The High Court of Justice maintains that the accused *is* an ordinary miscreant. They are holding him accused as being an offending holder of office."

"Then, they mean to continue with this ridiculous argument that an anointed monarch is no more than a jack-in-office?"

"Yes, sir, they do. I can only report faithfully to you what you asked me to do. Whether or not I hold one view or another is beside the point!"

"Yes, young man – we all fully understand that. We would have nothing from you but a faithful recounting."

"Then I have to report that the notion of an anointed king is a holder of office is one that is very widely held by the nearly all of the commission."

"It serves their purpose very well!" Garlick grunted. "Have you any notion when the hearing will recommence in public?"

"From what I can gather, sir, it will be tomorrow. I shall report what happens."

He left behind him a very gloomy parlour. What, they wondered, had been said in the Painted Chamber?

CHAPTER XXIII

By nine o'clock on the Thursday morning, Avril knew that she was going to be a busy woman. But that was nothing new. Bovey Tracey was not anywhere large enough to support its own physician – the nearest one being in Newton Abbot, and he was as often drunk as not!

The first call for her services came via Hob. He had been taking a message for the bailiff when he had been hailed by the verger, Ralph Goodes. Hob arrived at his usual gallop and pushed open the door of the apothecary. Not even remotely out of breath, he said that 'Master Verger wants Mistress Ramsey urgently as Mistress Goode and young Paul have the winter fever'.

James looked up from his work, crushing seeds in the pestle and mortar.

"We've been wondering when it might strike," he said to Avril. "Tis late this year!"

Avril immediately took a small valise and started to put various jars into it. "I shall report what I find," she said, putting a peck on her husband's cheek. Throwing her warmest cloak about her shoulders, she took the valise and hurried out of the shop, turned up the street towards the larger than usual cottage where the verger lived with his wife and young son.

Anne Goodes was twenty-six and her son Paul a mere six. Ralph ushered Avril up the stairs to the larger bedroom where mother and little son huddled together in the large bed. Both were flushed of face and shivering – that strange combination of symptoms where the body burned and shivered at the same time.

Avril stopped at the doorway and immediately wound a length of linen about her nose and mouth. Then, approaching the bed, she laid her hand on Anne's forehead – it was *very* hot, Paul's hot but not as fierce. This was quite definitely the winter fever, Avril knew instantly. She also knew that there was no immediate cure for it, only the relief of the symptoms. Whether or not they survived was in the hands of God. However, she did have the means to alleviate the suffering. She took out two small pots from her valise. She turned to a hovering and anxious verger.

"This one contains crushed willow bark," she said, handing the pot to Ralph. "It will help with the headache. It may also reduce the fever a little. The other one contains poppy juice. One drop in a large spoon of weak ale. Four times a day. That will help sleep – and sleep is probably the best medicine of all. Keep them covered and warm – do *not* open windows to cool them down. The extreme cold will do much harm! Call for me again if there is need."

"Aye – winter fever is amongst us again," she reported to James when she arrived back. "I have the nastiest suspicion I shall be out and about many times in the days to come. Are you able to hold the fort here – I shall need Mary with me as she needs to see and learn. She will be able to tend the sick herself when I have shown her what to look for and what to do."

"Aye – I shall make sure I make plenty of the necessary. Luckily, we have a goodly supply ready to hand."

Mary arrived soon after, having completed her work at the bakery. She listened carefully to Avril, then packed her own small valise with little pots and stated that she was ready to act as nurse to Avril's physician. She also knew that she would be at increased risk herself – and dismissed the thought.

Nell had meanwhile gone to the hen coop to do her morning chores. She cleaned out, replenished seed and water, collected eggs, and went into the kitchen to find both Gil and Ella sitting with Rosie, eating a late breakfast.

"Avril and Mary be off tending to winter fever," she announced.

The previous winter had been exceptionally mild and benign; but the one before that had seen a spate of the fever that had carried off three people in the town.

Nell put the eggs for sale outside the front door, then came and joined in what was her second breakfast – before seeing to the mass of chicks. The second space was now occupied by five larger chicks, whilst the first contained nearly twenty little ones. Rosie was slowly learning how to keep the small seeds topped up, and to replenish the water in the bowls. She did these jobs whilst singing to the chicks – a little song she had made up.

Gil had given up fussing over his wife – Ella had loved him for his care but had railed when he had demanded that she take three rests a day on the bed. 'I am not ill – I am pregnant. I will know when I should take rest. Let me be master of my own condition, or I shall be driven mad!"

Gil, to his great credit, had surrendered with good grace and a kiss for his wife. Rosie asked every day when she would have her little sister and seemed greatly put out when told – repeatedly – that it would be many months yet. She still utterly refused to countenance the possibility of a brother!

The second call came just after dinner. Simon Dingle, the town's butcher was sick, along with his daughter Felicity who was just four years old. Avril and Mary hurried to the butcher's shop and a harried Stella Dingle ushered them through into the back parlour. Simon was sitting and shivering in a chair by the fire, whilst little Felicity lay on cushions by his feet.

Faces wrapped in linen, Avril and Mary went first to the butcher, leaving Stella to kneel and comfort her little girl. Mary watched carefully as Avril did her checks, asking if the headache was bad. Simon merely nodded and started coughing. Then she watched as Mary did the same checks on Felicity. The little girl was burning up and shivering like an aspen leaf.

"Does you head hurt?" Mary asked – she received a nod. Avril then said that the two should immediately get into bed and keep covered up and warm – it was no use trying to lower the fever by sitting in the snow! She again left pots of bark and poppy with the usual instructions. Then, making sure both she and Mary had thoroughly washed their hands, the two went back home.

"Why do we wash our hands so carefully?" Mary asked.

"I am not entirely sure," Avril replied. "But we have laid hands upon sick patients, and I believe that we may spread contagion if we do not. In any case, it is no hardship and might indeed be a wise precaution."

By evening, the two had visited ten more cottages. One was occupied by an old widow. Avril, after the next two visits after the Dingles, sent Mary on her own as she could not deal with them all herself. The two went to bed that night utterly exhausted

– knowing full well that the exhaustion could render them susceptible to catching the disease. Some called it 'winter fever'; others called it 'the shivering sickness'; yet others called it 'shaking fever'. All knew it could be deadly.

* * *

Matthew Kent was completely oblivious to what had been happening in the town. He had left early on his way back to Exeter, where he arrived in time for an early dinner at his chosen tavern. Soon, he would have to demand more payment for his services, his original purse being somewhat depleted. His first port of call after his dinner was to the Sheriff's clerk.

That morose individual listened to what Kent reported – precisely nothing untoward! He said that he required a written record – which Kent promised to deliver the next day. It seemed that the clerk was a firm believer in the maxim that, if it were not written down, it had never happened!

When Kent raised the subject of money, he was met with a sharp intake of breath and a frown of anguish.

"I have not the authority to disburse monies," he said, mournfully.

"I have not the means to carry out more work unless I am paid!" Kent replied. "It would sit ill with Master Secretary should I be disabled from carrying out my mission."

"I shall have to seek authorisation," countered the clerk.

"From whom? The Sheriff is not here!"

"I shall have to seek out the Deputy Sheriff – and he is a hard man to locate."

"I have just enough to see me back to Westminster. Shall I report that I have been thwarted from doing his bidding by a lack of funds?"

The clerk blanched at the thought. "Pray return here in one hour and I shall seek to obtain the funds for you."

"That, master clerk, is very gracious!"

Kent chuckled as he strolled the snowy streets around the ruined castle. How many times in the service of the state had he encountered people like the clerk, he wondered? Puffed up with their own importance, but singularly unable to make a decision, or to accept any responsibility that might rebound upon them. Pitiful little men, he laughed aloud, startling a group of passing apprentices.

That evening, with a new purse of coins, he ate supper in the tavern and decided that he would choose his own course of investigation. He would stay for a while in Exeter, garnering what information he might from the small docks, the local traders, but mostly from idle chatter in the multitude of taverns.

* * *

Lady Violette Charlton was in something of a quandary. Her knowledge of physick was virtually non-existent. She was one of those old ladies who had steadfastly refused to acknowledge sickness – and had consequently led a charmed and sickness-free life. She regarded sickness in others as something they should either ignore or suffer in stoical silence.

Consequently, when her own steward, Thomas Carpenter reported that he was indeed suffering the winter fever, as was the cook, and two of the gardeners, she was somewhat at a loss how to deal with things. She took one look at the faltering steps of her steward, his flushed face and ague-like shivering, she realised that this was not something she could blithely pass off with a mere shrug. She had witnessed the winter fever many times but had never once suffered from it. She sent Carpenter, cook and gardeners to bed. And then sat before a log fire and wondered whether she should summon help from elsewhere. In the absence of her trusted steward, she sent for his helper, Luke Farmer.

Luke immediately feared for his wife Meg and little son Hal. He was sent on an urgent mission to seek the apothecary in Bovey Tracey. But first, he scampered upstairs and told Meg to stay in their attic room and not come in contact with anyone. Then, in warmest clothes, he saddled a horse and set off for Bovey Tracey.

He knocked loudly at the door and was relieved when a light showed through the window. James opened the door and ushered a very cold Luke into the shop. Luke told of his mission and was relieved when he was told that either Avril or Mary would go to

163

Brimley at first light. He rode back and reported to a sleepy Lady Violette.

"I shall rely on you to maintain the house until Thomas be recovered," he was told.

All very well, thought Luke as he went back to wife and son. My first duty is to my own family – not to this household. But when he had told Meg, she contradicted him.

"Luke – you and I need our positions here – and we were very lucky to get them. So, do as you are bid. I shall certainly carry on working at my tasks. If necessary, we shall tend to the sick and make ourselves indispensable."

* * *

Given the emergency, John excused Mary from any work at the bakery next morning. He made hasty enquiries and found that Old Gaffer would willingly release his horse and cart for Mary to use. It was some time since Mary had driven a cart, but she knew the way, could have walked there in her sleep. Also, the old horse was as docile as anyone could wish. So, with valise packed with pots, she set off for Brimley, arriving there one hour after a watery sun had made an appearance. The light falls of snow had ceased, so there was not that to contend with.

She handed the cart over to young Andrews who shot out of the large shed as she drew into the courtyard, then hastened into the house to find Meg tending the kitchen.

"Mistress be up the stairs tending to master steward," she was told.

Having never been inside Brimley house before, Mary went up the stairs, then stood on the long landing and called out.

"Lady Violette – I'm come to tend the sick."

The old lady, in full dress and starched apron, called out in reply.

"Find the last door on your left. You are most welcome."

Mary did as bid and found a fairly large bedroom with curtains closed and an old man lying in a bed, covered with blankets. She immediately put her linen scarf around her nose and mouth, set down her valise and went to feel the old man's

164

forehead, then the side of his neck. He was burning up, breathing with difficulty, and shivering as if to shake himself into pieces.

"This is bad, I take it?" Lady Violette said quietly.

"Aye, my lady – tis bad. He is hotter than any I have yet felt. But he must not be exposed to the cold. I shall be back with some medicines for him when I have mixed them properly."

She took her valise and went quickly down to the kitchen where she took two glasses, mixed powder and water in one, then poppy juice in another, topped with weak ale. These she took back upstairs.

"Tell me how to mix those and what to do with them," she was ordered. "Then I will be able to take that job from your shoulders whilst you tend to the others."

Mary was shocked. "Which others?" she asked. "I was only aware of one."

"My cook, my personal maid, plus one young servant boy – so far!"

Mary told the old lady what were the contents of the two pots, how to mix them, and how they should be administered.

"And the same shall be given to all of them?"

"Aye, my lady – at least, I think so. I will know more when I have seen them all. They must all be kept in bed, warm, and encouraged to drink regularly. Avril says that, should they not drink, they will literally dry out – and their skin will feel like parchment. Very weak ale is best."

It was well past eleven o'clock when Mary at last returned to Bovey Tracey. She found Avril sitting wearily in the parlour, eating a bowl of porridge. Mary, equally wearily, helped herself to a bowl and sat.

"Four at Brimley," she reported. "The old steward is very bad."

"Old Flora passed away during the early morning," Avril told her. "I wonder how many we will lose this time?"

"I really fear for the steward," Mary gulped. "I must go back this afternoon."

"You and I, Mary, cannot cope with all this unaided. There will be many more before this bout leaves the town. I have been wondering who else we may recruit to help us."

"My mother, for one," Mary said immediately. "Then there is Imelda Grubb and Glory from the tavern. They be very sensible and will not panic."

"What we need is Hob! There be no faster messenger on this earth!"

By late afternoon, Avril had mustered her team. Mary would tend to both Brimley and Parke whilst Avril supervised the town. Faith, Imelda and Glory, well instructed, would see all new cases, referring serious ones to Avril. Dick Allen and Sal from the tavern would supply food and drink, delivered to the apothecary shop.

Mary arrived back from Brimley well after nightfall with the news that she doubted the old steward would see the night out. His breathing was, as she described it, gasping and rattling. Lady Violette was a tower of strength, ordering her staff like any good general. Luckily, Parke had only one case – a young stable lad – and he was strong and not too bad.

Hob proved to be just about the busiest of them all – running hither and yon with messages, instructions, reports of new cases. He, with Imelda and Glory, offered to see the night out whilst Avril and Mary got some sleep. These two huddled into their beds wondering what the morrow would bring.

* * *

William Garlick had received no updates from his young informant until that evening. When the usher had delivered his latest news and had departed once again, Garlick sat in silence, trying to digest what he had just been told.

In two more days, the young man had reported, the special High Court of Justice would pronounce its verdict. By Saturday evening, he would know whether or not his king would be declared guilty or not guilty.

The charge was quite specific. The very first phrase – guilty of treason – gave no room for manoeuvre. Any person found guilty of treason would find his or her next appointment was with the executioner. But – would they find him guilty – and therefore paste themselves into that particular corner? His sister, a long-time student of law and language, summed it all up.

166

"William – do not pin your hopes to any false presumptions. Remember the course of events. First of all, parliament has decreed – not merely stated, but decreed – that England is a Republic, or a Commonwealth. A republic has no king! Therefore, before he even came to trial, he was a past holder of an office – and that they have decreed as well. Therefore, the deeds that he stands accused of occurred whilst holding an office which no longer existed. Mark my words – and I utter them in sorrow and anger – they mean to have his head!"

CHAPTER XXIV

When Mary arrived at Brimley the next morning, she was not surprised to find that the old steward, Thomas Carpenter, had not lasted the night. She was surprised however, to find that old stalwart, Lady Violette, sitting by her fire in the main hall, wiping tears from her cheeks.

"I stayed with him all night – as he had stayed with me for more than forty years," she said in a quiet and, for her, very restrained voice. "It was just before dawn that he stopped breathing."

Mary, still only seventeen, had no idea how to respond to that – so she stayed silent. She remembered the time some seven years before when her grandmother had breathed her last. Her own mother had taken many months to recover her spirits.

Lady Violette gave herself a shake – almost as if she had told herself that this would not do.

"The stable lad is as you left him – as strong as an ox, that one. I've left him in the care of my head gardener – the diminutive, little fellow who they all refer to as Goliath. Cook is not at all well. Would you go and see her and perhaps assess her condition. Now, Mary dear. Would you be an angel and do the rounds – see if we have any more cases for you to tend. Oh – and as you pass the kitchen, please ask that flame-headed lass to come and see me."

Mary first went to the old cook's room – up in the attics. One of the very young scullery maids was sitting by her bed and bathing the cook's forehead with a towel dampened in cold water.

Mary looked down at the old woman and noted that her breathing was regular and silent – a very good sign. Feeling her neck, her skin felt no hotter than it had done on the previous visit. Another good sign.

"Are you giving her the two medicines?" she asked the young girl – who couldn't have been more that twelve or thirteen.

"Er, aye, Miss Mary. Exactly as you told us."

"Then you are doing all you can. I think cook is going to recover. But yell for me if there is any change."

The stable lad was sitting up and drinking watered ale. Still hot to the touch, he gave Mary a cheeky grin. No problem there.

As requested, she told Meg that she was wanted, then went on her rounds, relieved to find no more cases for her to tend.

Meg, leaving little Hal in the charge of the other scullery maid, went into the big hall and bobbed a curtsey to her mistress.

"Ah, Meg. As you know, cook is not going to be able to rule the kitchen for some days yet. Are you able to run things until such time as she is better?"

Meg was a bit startled - but rallied immediately.

"Aye. My Lady. I can run a kitchen – as long as plain fare is all that be required."

"Plain fare is exactly what will be needed. Come and see me if there be anything needed that we do not have. Now – another task. Find that tall husband of yours and ask him to come and speak with me."

Luke, who had been tidying up in old Carpenter's room, came down immediately. Lady Violette looked long and hard at him as he stood before her, assessing whether or not she was making a big mistake. Time would tell.

"Luke Farmer. You have been assisting old Thomas for two years or more. How conversant are you with his duties?"

"I have assisted at most of them, My Lady. I think I am conversant with nearly all of them."

"Are you well-lettered?"

"Aye, My Lady. I read and write – and am conversant with figures and the account books."

"Then I wish you to take over the duties as my steward. I will trust you to do things properly. But should you not be certain, come to me immediately. Do not fudge any issue. I would far rather instruct you than repair the damage!"

Luke was astounded and, for a while, could say nothing at all. But realising that continued silence would indicate unworthiness, managed at last to speak.

"I thank you most sincerely, My Lady. I give you my word of honour that I shall try to serve you as faithfully as did Master Carpenter."

"Your wife is at present taking charge of the kitchen. Make a start by producing a list of supplies needed, then muster all the staff here after dinner. I wish to speak to them all."

Luke bowed, then shot off to the kitchen. Meg made a big fuss of him when he told her that he was the new steward. He just hoped fervently that he would be up to the job. Never in his wildest dreams had he ever believed he would rise to such a position.

* * *

Matthew Kent had spent a quiet day on the Friday and, waking up to cold weather on the Saturday, decided that he would wrap up warm and take Murphy for a trot down the Exe river towards the larger docks of Topsham. There would be a far greater mix of nationalities there than at the smaller docks in Exeter itself. Making sure that he looked quite 'ordinary', he set off after a breakfast of porridge and fresh bread.

The short, five-mile journey took just under an hour. He let Murphy stretch his legs for part of the way, the old Irish horse almost turning his head with a polite 'thank-you' for the chance of some real exercise. Arrived at the small town, Kent immediately made for the largest dockside tavern. There were plenty of cogs and sloops moored at the dockside. Some were loading bales of wool; some were unloading crates of heaven alone knew what.

What struck him the most was the air of calm professionalism – the dockers each knew what to do and when to do it. There was no screaming of orders or evidence of mishaps. He went behind the tavern and handed Murphy over to an ostler with instructions to rub down, feed and water. Then, he went into the tavern.

If all was peace and calm on the dockside, the exact opposite reigned supreme in the large taproom. Crews from various ships were shouting across the room at one another, making rude but good-humoured remarks about the others' ships.

However, he heard no foreign tongues at all. It took him some time sitting and supping a jug of ale to distinguish the various English dialects. There were certainly the usual Devon voices, but also he detected many from London and many also from far further north – Norfolk, Yorkshire, and Northumberland. He strained his ears but could detect no Scottish burr – and if there was going to be signs of rebellion, that was the likeliest source.

It was about half an hour before he overheard anything in the slightest controversial. One sailor, further into his cups than his nearest colleagues, suddenly gave loud voice.

"Fookin parliament. Fookin new laws. Fook the lot of 'em!"

"Billy does not like parliament!" one of his neighbours exploded in mirth. "That be right, Billy. You tell 'em!"

Kent immediately placed those accents – Yorkshire, without a shadow of a doubt. He turned slightly away so as not to draw attention to the fact that he wanted to hear more – and buried his nose into his jug of ale.

"My brother – he were at Edgehill. Bastard parliament lot killed for the sake of it – and loved it!" Billy roared. "Now, here we are with these new laws. No fun, no playhouses, no fetes, no fook-all! Where's Prince Charlie? Hull and York can muster thousands. Give us all pikes and follow Charlie to London! Take Cromwell and hang the bastards!"

From the roar of approval that followed, Kent realised that this was certainly a popular view – at least in Topsham docks.

"What say you, friend?" Kent's neighbour on the bench nudged his elbow.

"What say I?" Kent turned to the man - a swarthy sailor with a beard that reached almost to his waist. "I say a big thanks to you sailors. My brother farms sheep and, without you, his business would collapse. I care not a fig who governs. I care for prosperity and jobs for all who want to work!"

As a totally neutral speech, it was a masterpiece – and one that nobody in that tavern could take exception to. He actually did not have a brother and knew little about sheep farming. But he wanted to hear more, and this was the way to incite further comment.

"Hear that, lads?" his neighbour bellowed. "Here be a man who values us of the sea. Here be a man who wants prosperity and work. I say he is right!"

"Aye," Billy roared back. "That be all well and good. But what good be work without any joy at the end of it? This fookin parliament will have us as monks – and that was put a stop to in old Henry's day!"

Kent decided to play a slightly dangerous game.

"These lads in Hull and York. Be they really ready to march south? If so, then I will need to tell my brother to get his fleeces on board as soon as he may!"

"Be they ready, you ask? Aye – they be ready. They just wait for a lead from Charlie!"

Even Kent, with his far greater knowledge of events, had not the faintest idea where the Prince of Wales was at that precise moment. Rumours had it that he was in Ireland, Scotland, France, The Netherlands, Spain, even some said, in Rome.

Kent decided that he had heard enough from these sailors. They were all well on the way to drunken oblivion. But, as he often was reminded, many a truth comes out from the bottom of a tankard. He took his leave and went to another tavern, a much quieter one at the edge of town, where he had dinner.

How much reliance could he place on those drunken boasts? The likelihood was that there were *some* very discontented individuals in both Hull and York. But – enough to start a march south? He mused on the fact that he had heard no such talk in Devon – or in Surrey, Hampshire or Wiltshire on his journey to the South-West.

Before colleting Murphy for the ride back to Exeter, he called in at the Harbour Master's office – where he found a fat and bloated individual sitting behind a desk and smoking a long pipe of tobacco. He had the look of an official who benefited in all possible ways from his access to goods and wines from around the continent.

"The lads in the dockside tavern seem to be all stoked up about a rising in Yorkshire," Kent remarked. "Can there be any truth in that?"

"I neither know nor care a jot!" the man replied, burping immoderately. "Goods come in and goods go out. Will be the same whoever sits in Westminster. Probably a lot of hot air, if you ask me!"

"But should you not report such talk?" Kent probed the man a bit more. "Were it to become widely known, you may well be put to the question as to why you did *not* report it!"

"Like I said – a lot of bluster and cupshot chatter. And who may tell of it? You?"

"No – not me. I'm just interested in proper trade."

"Then, whoever you be, sod off and leave me to my pipe!"

If I had any authority, you would be out of that comfy job tomorrow, Kent grunted to himself as he collected Murphy and started his ride back to Exeter. At least he had something of substance to write in his report.

* * *

Maud came into the kitchen late that afternoon to find both Ella and Gil preparing the supper.

"Rosie is lying on her bed and says that her head hurts – and she feels hot,"

Gil and Ella shared a look – it was what they had feared might happen. The old and the very young were more at risk than anyone else – or so experience had taught everyone in the town. Ella went up and looked at her little daughter.

"Rosie not well," came a croak from the pillow.

Ella confirmed what Maud had told them – Rosie was flushed and quite hot to the touch. Added to which, she was shivering. Ella gathered Rosie up and pulled back the blankets, laid her down again and covered her up.

"What we must do is to keep you tucked up and warm. I'm going to go and fetch Aunt Avril – she will know what to do."

"May Maud stay with me?" came a quiet plea.

"Maud needs to go home. I'll ask dada to come up and tell you a story, shall I?"

"It is the winter fever right enough," she reported to Gil as she returned to the kitchen. Maud went back home to tell her parents. They would now worry if *their* daughter had contracted it from Rosie!

173

James, alone in his shop, said that Avril was with other sick people in the town, but would call in later to see Rosie. Ella asked how many people had gone sick and was horrified when she was told that there were thirty at least.

It was not until well after supper that a very tired Avril called in to see Rosie. She immediately went upstairs and examined the little mite as she was sleeping.

"Hm – hot, but not *very* hot. The little ones always seem to go down very quickly. But they come back up again just as quickly. I'm very reluctant to give her any of the poppy juice – she's far too young. But she can certainly have the willow bark. Put a very small spoonful into a mug of watered ale and heat it up before you give it to her. But do not wake her up specially to administer it. Sleep is by far and away the best medicine. Either Mary or I shall call in again in the morning. Hopefully, she will be no worse. In the meantime, keep her well wrapped up. If she complains, put a cold, damp cloth on her head, but keep the rest of her under the blankets."

"Are not the little ones more at risk?" Gil asked, fearing the answer.

"Aye – they can be. But Rosie is a strong little girl and has strong and fit parents. It's the weak ones who are most at risk – and your Rosie is far from a weak one!"

Many of the younger children in the town and neighbouring villages were far more at risk than Rosie. Many were the children of farm workers, poorly paid and hardly able to feed their families as Gil and Ella could. The children most at risk were those in the large towns and cities – where poverty was rife.

It was still widely believed that diseases that spread rapidly were punishments sent down by God. Avril and James would have none of that nonsense. Why would a caring God visit hardship and illness on those least able to defend themselves?

*　*　*

William Garlick, his sister and brother-in-law, received a final visit on that Saturday evening. It was a very subdued young man who entered and took a seat in the parlour. Arthur Walker was almost trembling – he had no idea what sort of reception his report would receive. It would come as a devastating blow to the three elderly people gathered around the fire.

"Before you commence," Garlick said. "We have been aware of all the shouting that has taken place outside in the street. For the past hour or more, we have deliberately shut our ears to the various things being voiced abroad. We trust that you will give us a proper account."

Walker gulped a bit, then squared his shoulders. These people deserved the unvarnished truth.

"It was just after two of the clock when the panel returned their verdict. I have to tell you that Charles Stuart was declared guilty as charged. As you may appreciate, the chamber erupted in disorder – most were cheering, but a few were solemn-faced. It took a long time for order to be restored."

"Aye – that is the one word we kept hearing. Guilty. Now, young man – was it said clearly which part of the charge he was declared guilty?"

"I'm afraid to tell you that no particular part of the charge was specified. He was declared guilty of the charge *as a whole*."

"Tis like I said," Margaret nodded. "Believe me, I say that with no sense of achievement! The first real word in the charge was 'treason'. But treason against who or what?"

"Can only be treason against the Commonwealth of England," Garlick muttered. "Whether we like it or not, that is the nature of the state in which we now live. What happened after order had been restored – though I fear the answer!"

"As you may imagine, there were demands for the supreme penalty. John Bradshaw, who was declared chairman of the commission, was beleaguered with the demands – not that he seemed reluctant to accede to them."

"They will have the head of an anointed king!" Margaret was close to tears, although she had been the one to forecast that likelihood.

"A warrant of execution – a Death Warrant – was being drawn up. Some members appended their signatures willingly and with much excitement. Others were being persuaded. I saw none refuse outright – but I left before the session was declared closed. As you may imagine, it was turmoil in there."

"Who were the ringleaders clamouring for signatures – although I may hazard a guess?"

"Ireton was quite vociferous. Bradshaw, Cromwell, and some others did so quietly and with some show of dignity. Some were being pushed forward. It was, even to me, an unseemly, even a disgraceful, performance."

"And when do they intend carrying out this act of political murder?"

"It is scheduled to take place next Tuesday, the thirtieth of January."

There was a period of silence in the room as this last piece of information sunk into the minds of the three elderly people.

The young man looked at the three faces, noting that they were near to tears – in fact, William Garlick was in tears. Arthur rose silently and, just as silently, left the room. He had not the heart to ask for his final payment.

Eventually, Garlick wiped his eyes on the back of his hand.

"I must speed back to Bovey," he announced. "I have a duty to relay this information as soon as I may. I shall leave at first light. I am indebted to you both for your hospitality and kindness."

"Did you note that Master Walker left without a word – and without a purse?" Margaret asked.

"Aye – I noticed that. Even out of that accursed parliament there is a small sign of goodness!"

CHAPTER XXV

Rosie had spent the night in her parent's bed, her mother on one side and her father on the other. Neither gave a thought that they might risk contagion. They had all long got used to the clucking that came from downstairs – the chicks were thriving. As the first light crept through the shutters, Ella stirred and immediately turned gently towards Rosie and felt her neck and chest – as she had seen Avril do.

To her, Rosie seemed no hotter than she had done the night before. Ella reached over and poked Gil gently in the shoulder.

"What?" came a sleepy response.

"Feel Rosie and tell me what you think."

Gil put his fingertips to the small neck. "She seems to me to be a mite cooler than before," he whispered.

Ella sighed - content that someone else had confirmed her thoughts. She knew that otherwise she might have been guilty of wishful thinking. Rosie stirred and opened her eyes. As she was facing her mother, she reached out a hand and tucked it around Ella's neck.

"Hungry!" she whispered. "Rosie is hungry, mama "

Avril had hinted that the moment any victim of the winter fever declared hunger, then that person was on the mend – or at the very least, was getting no worse.

"What would Rosie like to eat?" Gil had heard the whisper.

"Grandmama's crusty bread and butter, dada."

"But you must first have another dose of the medicine," Ella insisted. "Aunt Avril said that we must give it to you four times every day for a whole week."

"Tastes nasty! Yuk!"

"But it's making you better, sweetheart. No medicine, no bread and butter!"

Gil gave a sigh, got out of bed and put on warm clothes and left to go all the way up the street to get the bread – which he knew would still probably be in the oven.

By the time he had reached his parent's bakery, the smell of fresh bread nearly drove him wild. Mary was busy in the shop, helping out before starting again on her work visiting the sick in Brimley and Parke. She greeted her brother with a hug.

"Rosie is hungry and wants fresh, crusty bread and butter," he announced.

"That is good news to start the day," Mary smiled. "I shall call in on my way back before dinner."

Gil repeated his news to his mother as Evelyn came out with the first batch of loaves for the delivery cart. Simon had volunteered to help out before laying the fire in the smithy's furnace.

Gil managed to grab two of the new loaves and hurried back home. Rosie was sitting up in bed, still looking flushed, but no longer shivering. She looked very pleased with herself.

"Rosie drunk her medicine!" she announced, making a grab for the small platter of bread that had been buttered for her. Just watching his little daughter demolish that platter made Gil almost fall to his knees to offer a prayer of thanks.

* * *

Mary, still with Old Gaffer's cart, set out from the bakery to make her way to Parke and then to Brimley. She had just passed the butcher's on her left when out of the 'soldiers'' cottage on the right came the tall figure of Sergeant Larkin.

"Excuse me, miss – two of my men are now sick and shivering. Could you look in on them on your way back?"

"Certainly, sergeant. Are they both very hot as well?"

"Aye – that they are. I could almost cook an egg on Young's head!"

"Until I get back, please make sure they are well wrapped up and drink plenty – watered ale, not real ale! Who is the other one?"

"Bell – he's moaning and groaning like an old man!"

"Then Glory at the tavern would make a splendid nurse!"

Larkin was an astute and observant soldier, but that remark had him puzzled.

"And why should that be?"

Mary laughed. "Surely you have noticed that he and Glory have been making eyes at each other ever since you arrived here!"

"No – I had not noticed that," Larkin admitted. "What has her father to say about that as I get the impression that his sympathies lie with your king!"

"Glory is a single-minded young lady," Mary grinned. "If she and Trooper Bell wish to see one another, then she will do just that!"

Mary called in at Parke, tended to the three patients she had there, noted that they were slowly improving, and sighed with relief that no others were yet showing symptoms. She drove onwards to Brimley and called first at the big house, where she was greeted by Luke Farmer, newly appointed steward. Again, slight signs of improvement. Little Hal was coughing, much to Meg's distress. But Mary thought this nothing more than a slight winter ailment as he was cool to the touch and scampering around like a squirrel.

On her way back, a sudden thought occurred to her. She turned into Parke again and went straight to the steward.

"Has anyone thought to check on that young shepherd?" she asked.

Luke Barton stopped, slapped his head and gave a shout.

"Satan's buttocks! I had clean forgotten about that lad. I shall send someone immediately. No! On second thoughts, I shall go myself. Miss Mary – avail yourself of my kitchen and take whatever you need. I shall be back directly!"

Mary needed no second bidding and went straight to the large kitchen where she found a tray of freshly baked pies. Cook picked out an apple and raisin pie for her and mulled a mug of ale. Steward Luke Baton was back very quickly, and from his expression, Mary knew that she had another patient.

"He's lying in the old shelter and looks in a very bad way. I've got one of the home farm workers with him. Luckily, this chap knows a bit about sheep as it's very nearly lambing time."

"Is there a bed for him here?" Mary asked.

"Aye – we can get him up into one of the attic rooms where he will be warm and dry. Are you able to drive your cart up the lane?"

Mary hurriedly finished her ale and pie, then went out to the cart and drove it up the muddy lane, following the steward who led the way on foot. He arrived after about a mile at a gate on the right, opened it and motioned Mary to drive the cart through. Immediately on the left was the tumbledown shack used by the shepherds.

The farm worker came out and lent a hand carrying an almost unconscious young Bernie Wheatcroft. The young shepherd was laid on the cart, ready to be taken back to the big house.

"Are you intending to stay here with the sheep?" Mary asked the man.

"Aye – they need tending as some could drop lambs any day now."

"Then what you must do is to get a rake and pull all that old straw out into the field and set fire to it. Then get a new supply for you to sleep on. Young Bernie has been lying on it and he may have spread contagion."

Back at Parke House, the young shepherd was carried up to an attic room where he was put into a bed and covered in blankets. Mary called for one of the young housemaids.

"Make sure he drinks lots of watered ale. Four times a day, put a large pinch of the ground bark into the ale. Then follow it with a drop of the poppy juice. He is very hot, so use wet cloths on his head to keep him cool."

"Shall I then be his nurse?" the young girl asked. She couldn't have been more than twelve or thirteen.

"Aye – you shall be his nurse. He is shivering violently at present. But, if that stops and he starts to move about restlessly, send for me or Mistress Ramsey immediately."

Back at the apothecary, Mary related her news of the shepherd to James – Avril still being out tending to the sick in the town.

"He sounds dangerously ill to me," James said. "You did all the right things for him. Let us hope you were in time!"

Avril bustled in a few minutes later, bringing with her a farm worker who had cut himself badly with a sickle – cutting back the brambles around a farm gate. The man was bleeding a lot from the deep slash on his upper left arm. Avril fetched a wad of clean linen and, telling the man to sit, asked Mary to press the wad tightly against the cut. Avril fetched a jar of salve and, removing the pad for a moment, smeared some on the open cut.

"See how the blood is flowing slowly and continuously?" she said as she bound the pad tightly.

"Aye – it will stop?"

"It will stop when the blood forms its own crust. Then I shall have to put on more salve and sew the ends of the flesh together. And then I shall cover it and bind it to keep the wound clean."

A while later when the man had walked off home with his arm in a sling, Avril sat Mary down for one of her short, teaching sessions.

"You saw how the blood flowed slowly and continuously? Well, that means that he cut through one of the blood vessels. There are other blood vessels that bleed very differently. They squirt out blood that can be timed exactly to the beating of the heart. I read a paper some time back written by a very learned man. His name is William Harvey and he had discovered that blood courses around the body, propelled by the heart. According to his studies, the heart pumps the blood out through these larger vessels. How the blood is made, he does not say. But – made it must be – as a wound that bleeds copiously drains blood from the body – as we have all seen. But when healed, the body still has again as much blood as before."

"How did he learn all of this?" Mary was fascinated.

"I do believe he did his studies on people injured and killed in battle. I believe he was personal physician to the king."

"But what makes the heart to beat and pump the blood?"

"That I do not know. But some day, we will discover that as well!"

* * *

William Garlick had set out from his sister's home at just after first light. He had been seen on his way with a breakfast that he could hardly eat, and a tearful farewell from his two relatives. The Sunday weather did nothing to improve his mood – a cold drizzle. He was thankful for his old soldier's apparel, a waterproof riding cloak and hat with large brim.

His first task was to cross the river to get on its southern side. He hoped to make it as far as Winchester by nightfall – a big ask as it was just over sixty-five miles of hard riding. Once upon a time he mused, he would have thought nothing of it. But at his age, he knew he was probably overreaching himself by some margin.

As it turned out, he got no further than the small town of Basingstoke. He consoled himself that he had managed over two thirds of his target distance. A large tavern was set on the left side of the road, and he turned into the yard very thankfully. His mount was no less thankful!

Having carried his valise into the tavern and acquired a room for the night, he shed his hat and cloak and sat down in the taproom for a very welcome supper of beef pie and gravy. The tavern was not very full at that early time of the evening, so the landlord came and sat down for a chat.

"Have not seen you here afore, master," he began in friendly tones.

"Nay – I'm from far west of here. I'm returning from London."

He deliberately said London and not Westminster, not knowing how the latter would go down with folks hereabouts.

"Taking the news west?"

"Aye – my little town needs to know what has been happening."

"So, coming from London, you will have better news than we have here. Messengers have been speeding through all day long and never a word of the news they must be carrying!"

"Then you are in the same state as my little town! I must rest up if I am going to get there in another two days."

"And where would your town be, master?"

"Tis called Bovey Tracey – west of Exeter."

"Then you have a powerful ride before you! You say Bovey Tracey? Would there have been a battle there? I seem to recall the name mentioned in the same telling as Torrington!"

"Aye – back in the January of 1646. Parliament routed the royalist cavalry regiments – almost without a fight." Garlick recalled this disaster with some bitterness.

A group of local men came through the door, all calling for ale. The landlord supervised his tapster and the serving wench, then raised his voice.

"Here be a gentleman come from London, travelling west with news for his town. Perhaps he be able to tell us all what be happening!"

Garlick had no option. A hush fell over the large taproom as he cleared his throat.

"Yesterday – Saturday – the Special Commission sitting as the High Court of Justice declared that King Charles be guilty of treason – amongst a whole host of other charges. The Commission then produced the Death Warrant and got many signatures upon it. King Charles is to be executed in two days from now."

That produced a deathly silence as his words sank into the locals' heads.

"And not before time!" one old man growled. "Mayhap now we will get a proper say in how we are governed and taxed."

"Aye," another spoke up. "And an end to popery!"

"One moment," one younger man interjected. "You refer to him as King Charles and not as Charles Stuart. Does that imply you are sympathetic to his cause?"

Garlick had never been one to back away from confrontation.

"Aye – you may assume that young man. Long afore you were born I was fighting alongside his father, King Jamie. Charles is many things – misguided, impatient, inclined to popery maybe. But he has never been guilty of treason."

"But parliament says he is!" the young man bounced back.

Garlick sat back with a sigh. "Let us let our imaginations run wild and dream that we are parliament. All our lives we have hated eating fish. If we pass a law that says that the eating of fish amounts to treason against the state, then treason it is – because we make the laws!"

"He's got you there, Tom!" one old man guffawed. "I bloody hate fish!"

"That, sir, is far too simple," the young man wanted a fierce debate. "Your king declared war on his own people when he started fighting against the representatives we had put in place. That, sir, most certainly *is* treason!"

"Aye," put in another. "He slaughtered may at Edgehill and then declared that he was doing it because he had the divine right so to do!"

"I think you will find that as many royalists died at that Fight as did parliamentarians!" Garlick countered.

"Aye, that be so. But he still made war on his own people!"

"Gentlemen, we are never going to agree. I have no fight with you. I must do as you will no doubt do – relay the news to your families. So, I wish you all a good night and a peaceful sleep. God alone knows, I need it!"

The younger man rose from his bench.

"Were you a younger man, sir, I would call you out," he said forcefully.

"Were I a much younger man, sir – I would respond by smacking your baby arse!"

That drew a hoot of laughter from the room. The young man had the grace to grin at that response – and even wished Garlick a good night.

* * *

It was after supper that evening that Ratcliffe and Andrews tried their luck. They sneaked into the Brimley kitchen and found Luke Farmer sitting alone by the remains of the fire. He had a large ledger open on his knee and was studying a column of figures – trying to make sense of the monthly purchases of vegetables. Loth to call the cook to interpret, he struggled with the figures. Not for the first time he wondered how on earth his predecessor had maintained a grip on the household finances. Old Carpenter's sevens looked like ones; the eights often looked like nines, the strokes being incomplete in places.

"Er – we were wondering whether we might skip off early tomorrow and visit the big tavern at the top of Bovey – the one by the church," Kit Warden ventured.

With a sigh, Luke placed the ledger aside and regarded the pair.

"Why does that need an early finish to your work?" he enquired. "You can walk there in forty-five minutes!"

"Aye, that we can. But we needs be there for the start of the game!" Kit half explained.

"And what game would that be? I have heard of no game!"

"There are three from the town meet there every Monday and play at dice. Unless we be there at the start, they might be unwilling to let others into the game."

"Then let me remind you of two rather important facts. The first is that you owe Her Ladyship a full day's work for a day's pay. The second is that all games of chance are strictly forbidden."

"Dick Allen keeps the game in a back room – no need for that sergeant or his men to know anything about it."

"And what about the duty you owe to Her Ladyship. I hear no mention of that from you!"

"What is one hour more or less? We will make it up the next day. You and I fought side by side. I hoped you might have remembered that!" Warden pouted.

"I shall never forget that as long as I live. But let me remind you that I have been entrusted as Her Ladyship's steward. I have a wife and a child to think of. I shall not put them in jeopardy for you or for anyone else!"

"So, our friendship is for naught?"

"That is a stupid remark. Of course, our friendship is not for naught. But I have been given a position of trust – and that I will not betray!"

Warden and Andrews – the latter having not said one word – left the kitchen and could be heard grumbling as they made their way across the back courtyard. With another sigh, Farmer picked up the ledger again and resumed his scrutiny.

"It seems I chose well," came a voice from behind him.

Luke scrambled to his feet and gave the old lady a bow – not a deep one or the ledger would have fallen to the kitchen flagstones.

"I had no idea you were privy to that, My Lady," he muttered. A thought flashed across his mind. Had the mistress planned a test for him? He dismissed the thought immediately. Subterfuge was beneath Lady Violette. If she had a query, she would ask it in a loud voice.

"No, you were not. So, Master Steward – put that ledger aside for a moment and tell me all about your escapades with those other two. I am fascinated."

She settled herself in a chair opposite Luke and looked expectantly at him.

"I'm sure it will please you, My Lady. Warden and I were members of a four-man squad that was part of the royalist forces. We were aside from the battle here at Bovey – and hence missed the action."

"Oh, tush and piffle! That is now a thing of the past. Parliament has won and that's an end to it! We have to live in the world as it is and make the best of it. So, on with your tale."

Luke started his tale with the two of them, Farmer and Warden, hiding in the woods and observing the royalist forces on The Heath, supposedly under the command of Lord Wentworth."

"Wentworth? I knew him long ago as a very young man. Useless fop!"

It was well past midnight when Luke had ended his tale – with their arrival at Brimley and their good fortune in finding such good billets. Lady Violette yawned.

"That was a very interesting tale. Now – your wife must be wondering what keeps you. Lock up and go to your bed. I say again – I picked very well with you, Master Steward!"

CHAPTER XXVI

Rising just before dawn, William Garlick dressed hurriedly and ate a quick breakfast. By eight o'clock, he was on his way and aiming for Yeovil, some eighty miles distant. He knew that he was unlikely to make it that far, but desperately wanted to get as far as Sherborne. That would just allow him to make it home by the Tuesday night.

With just on eight hours of daylight, he was on target – or so he fondly hoped. As he let his mount alternate between a trot and a canter, he let his mind wander. What, he thought, would be the state of King Charles' mind. Held fast and knowing that at some time the following day, he would be taken out into the public gaze and summarily executed with an axe. Would he be concentrating on his prayers for his future amongst the choirs of angels? Would he be seething with anger at the injustice of it all? More likely, Garlick thought, he would be considering the legacy he left behind him – the fates of this two sons Charles and James and his daughter Mary.

With a start, he became aware of his surroundings – he was riding through a dense wood and was very vulnerable. He clapped his heels into his mount and galloped until again riding through open countryside. Stay awake, you old fool, he chided himself. Have you learned nothing in your sixty and a bit years?

He let his horse walk sedately for a mile or so, then returned to the alternate trot and canter. Hunger and the need to rest, feed and water his horse, forced him to stop at a roadside inn. That lost him nearly one hour of precious daylight. Never had he been so happy to see a large tavern appear on the outskirts of Sherborne. He had made it, and just as the weak winter sun dropped below the western hills – almost directly in line with his route. A long and relaxing supper gave way to a comfortable bed. Falling deeply asleep, he knew that an even longer day awaited him.

Avril and Mary spent the first hour of that day comparing notes. Three of the older residents of Bovey Tracey had died so far. The young Parke shepherd was hanging on. Mary had lost the old Brimley steward and one other.

"I know this is hardly a moment for thanks," Avril commented. "But to have lost only five so far is a miracle indeed."

"How is little Rosie?" Mary asked.

"That little mite seems to have the constitution of an ox! It is another miracle that neither Gil nor Ella have been infected – they have had Rosie sleeping between them every night!"

"How many do you think are ill with the disease?"

"Not all have called upon my help – and I suspect that not all of yours have done so either. But to my certain knowledge, there are still fifty or more in the town."

"I know of seventeen," Mary added. "One of those is an old servant in Parke – and he is approaching seventy years of age. How he has survived is a mystery – but he is up and doing for himself again."

"What is needed is a complete register of all the folk," James butted in. "Who they be, when they were born, what they do, what ailments they suffer. If we had that, we might be in a better position to judge how and why some die, and some do not."

"That would be a huge undertaking," Avril frowned. "But when all is said and done, what is really needed in a physician! Mary and I can do our best with the limited knowledge we have, but we are no substitute for a proper physician."

James gave his wife a sideways look. "And what more could such a person have done for those people suffering the winter ague that you and Mary have not done? Maybe, for such as bones that break and pierce the skin, those suffering a bloody flux, those with internal growths – I will allow that a physician would be of great advantage. But for the winter shivers? You two are more than is needed!"

"Hear that, Mary – we are appreciated!"

* * *

That afternoon, Matthew Kent arrived back in Bovey Tracey, and made straight for Parke and its bailiff. Peter Cove was quite surprised to see him back again as he had believed that Kent's mission – whatever it had been – was over and done with.

"I have need to talk with you and the steward – also, we should ride out together to Lady Violette. The news I have for you all needs to be told once."

Seeing the grim look on Kent's face, Cove called for Luke Barton. The three of them rode out the short distance to Brimley and made their presence known to the new steward. Lady Violette, appraised of her visitors, made immediately for her hall and sat everyone down in a semicircle before the large fire.

"My Lady, gentlemen – I heard the news myself only this morning and I at once came here so that you could hear it from me. I know that my loyalties are far removed from yours, so I beg that you hear me out and refrain from shooting the messenger."

"From your tones and appearance, this bodes ill," Lady Violette stated. "Tell us what you have to impart, and we will listen in silence."

"Then, these are the facts that were relayed to Exeter by the fastest courier. Your king, Charles Stuart, was found guilty of all charges as were set out in the indictment. The verdict was arrived at on Saturday. The gentlemen of the commission then passed the sentence of death and obtained many signatures on the Death Warrant. Tomorrow, Tuesday the thirtieth, the sentence will be carried out. That is the news I bring. I deemed it only right and proper that you heard it as soon as maybe."

None of his audience said anything for a few minutes after he had finished. Looking around, he saw two faces, open-mouthed in almost horror. One – the new steward at Brimley, was actually sniffing back a tear. Only Lady Violette remained calm and poker-faced.

"Inevitable!" she was the first to respond. "The inevitable result of two sets of people too pig-headed to talk - and talk reason. Our king sitting high and mighty on his throne of righteousness; parliament sitting righteous in their House. This was always going to be the inevitable outcome. Had the king won his battles, many parliamentary heads would have rolled. Instead, his own is now forfeit. Stupidity – shameful stupidity!”

“And now, I suppose, we are indeed a republic – or a commonwealth. No monarch to sit on a throne. Instead, a continuance of rule by committee,” Cove was thinking aloud. “But who, amongst all these parliamentarians shall have the final say on laws? Or shall it be a select few?”

“There are rumours aplenty, as you may well imagine. I have heard it said that there shall be a Lord Protector, though who that shall be I have no idea. It is also thought that some may invite the young Charles to sit as a figurehead. But that surely cannot be. I fear that I have no absolute news on that, or any other, score.” Kent sat back and gazed at the ornate ceiling.

“We thank you for the courtesy of your visit,” Lady Violette inclined her head towards Kent. “And I may assure you that we do not shoot messengers, howsoever appalling the news they convey!”

* * *

The news spread like wildfire throughout the small town and, inevitably, to the neighbouring settlements. In Trusham, Ratcliffe and Brown digested the news with their supper.

“Listen to a word of common sense before you gallop off into hiding somewhere,” Brown advised his colleague. “You are known here as a hurdle maker and my partner. I have never given the slightest hint to anyone that we were on opposing sides. As far as I am concerned, that nonsense is a part of the past and has no relevance at all to our lives here.”

“And neither has it relevance to me,” Ratty speared another chunk of pie with his knife. “But there will be fierce resentment hereabouts. If there be any suspicion that I had even the smallest part in parliament’s victory, I could be in some real danger.”

“Then do as I have always suggested. Tell everyone that you care not one whit who sits in power; all you want is for a peaceful life and a prosperous business – and that is something most folks want.”

On the Parke estate, two others were having much the same conversation. Sam Garvey and Robert Hook had also been a part of the parliamentary forces. With Ratty in Trusham, they had been three of the four members of a tracking party that had witnessed the rout of the royalists at Bovey Heath – and who had endeavoured to meet up with their colleagues afterwards.

"Master Steward knows all about our past. He must have told the bailiff as well," Garvey fretted. "Now, with this news, there will be bitterness against all who stood with us. Should we stay and hope for the best – or should we make our escape before there's trouble?"

Haddock – the fish-eyed Hook – regarded his friend with a look of despair.

"For a very sensible man, you talk absolute bollocks at times, Sam!" he replied. "Our course is plain to see for anyone with a grain of meat inside his skull. What we do is to show our sympathy and our solidarity with anyone with eyes to see. We use black cloth to fashion ribbons. We tie these around our arms and parade them as a sign of mourning."

"But Master Steward will know immediately that this be nothing but a ruse!"

"Aye – he will *suspect* that! What we have to do is to show plainly that this gives us no pleasure at all – that we wanted above all else a peaceful settlement – and that devout wish is now an impossibility. That he *will* believe – if we state so firmly and with conviction!"

"Then you be the one to do the talking!" Garvey grunted. "I do not have your way with words – certainly not the words necessary to carry this off."

* * *

Reverend Forbes sought out Sergeant Larkin. He found him walking with a two-man patrol passing the butcher's shop.

"Sergeant – I have to tell you that I am opening the church tomorrow, and that I shall be holding a service of mourning for our king. Sexton Fewings will toll the bell to summon the faithful. There will be no trouble, no uprising of anger. We cannot and will not allow this to pass unacknowledged!"

Larkin stood and thought.

"To stop you doing so would probably arouse more anger than the service you avow will be peaceful. So, I shall stay quiet and do nothing to stop you. But – if I have misread the situation completely and this service leads to trouble, I shall deal with it in the appropriate manner."

And, he thought to himself, I shall be in very deep water for having allowed it in the first place!

Trooper Glass, now fully recovered, gave his sergeant a sideways glance as they walked on with their patrol.

"Was that a wise move, sergeant?" he muttered.

"Probably not," Larkin muttered back. "But I shall be at the side of the church listening through what used to be the leper's squint. The rest of you will be on hand should I have to call on you."

CHAPTER XXVII

News of the service spread just as quickly as had the news from Westminster. By the time the sexton had started to ring the church bell, many feet found their way up the town's main street in answer to the summons. Forbes had deliberately set the time for the service at three in the afternoon- allowing the bulk of work to have been completed by then.

Work at Parke has finished earlier than usual, that at Brimley earlier than that. The church Of Saints Peter, Paul and Thomas was filled to bursting. Lingering at the very back were Garvey and Hook, each with a black armband in evidence.

Forbes entered from the vestry, preceded by young Hob as his attendant. Neither wore anything remotely ecclesiastical. Forbes made his way quietly to the pulpit, mounted the few steps and surveyed a church as full as he had ever remembered.

"Good people, friends and neighbours," he began to a silent congregation. "We are here for one purpose only – to mourn the passing of the life of our King, Charles Stuart. We are here for that purpose and that purpose only. I have no knowledge of the time the deed is to take place – indeed, it may already have taken place. As you all know, I served his son, Prince Charles, as his chaplain. That, more than anything else, makes me profoundly sad that his father should meet his end under such sad circumstances. Somehow, I have to find in within myself to seek forgiveness for those responsible for this act. That I will certainly do, and I ask that you all do the same. What is far harder is for me to find it in *myself* to forgive. Some of you may find that impossible – and that is utterly understandable. But I ask that you try. I have no right to do more than that."

He paused and collected himself for what was to follow. The church was as silent as a grave, waiting to hear what came next.

"I intend to hold no formal service – I would not know which would be appropriate! What I now intend to do is to ask you all to join me in *silent* prayer – prayers of your own devising –

asking the Good Lord to receive and cherish the soul of our departed King. Pray for that, as it is right and seemly. Pray not for revenge, as that is God's own prerogative. Now – let us bow our heads and make our prayers."

He suited action to words, bowed his head, shut his eyes and made his own pleas to his God. Utter silence accompanied this, not even a foot shuffled on the stone floor.

Five long minutes later, he opened his eyes and surveyed the crowd amassed before him. He noted many were silently weeping. He also noted that a few were regarding him with naked anger on their faces.

Standing in the very forefront was Lady Violette Charlton. She returned his look and gave him the tiniest inclination of her head. He was very grateful for that sign of approval.

"And now, my dear friends, let us all turn to one another and offer the sign of peace. If ever there was a time for such, it surely is now. And then, leave here with peace in your hearts. Your lives and mine must go on. Winter still has us in its grip and the winter fever is still with us. Go in peace – and may God bless us all."

Standing outside in the bitter cold, his eye still at the small hole through which in years gone past, lepers were permitted to witness the services, Larkin breathed a sigh of relief. Forbes had been as good as his word; he had used the service to pray for their dead monarch, to seek reconciliation, and to urge peace. He could have asked for nothing more. Whether or not some of the hotheads would hearken to that was yet to be seen.

He stood back and, from behind a gravestone, watched as the large congregation filed out of the west door, nearly all still in silent contemplation. One little girl peeled off from the rest and walked slowly to a small gravestone, knelt at its foot and silently bowed her head, hands clasped together. She remained there for a while, then rose and went after the crowd. Fascinated, he went to read the inscription.

'Here lies Hal Dawkins, Died January 1646. Beloved father of Nell. Sleep in peace, dada'

Larkin knew the story of how young Nell had been abandoned at four years old by an unfeeling grandfather - and had been 'adopted' by James and Avril Ramsey. His admiration for the two rose even further when he brought to mind how stable and

happy Nell was, and how Avril had ministered to the sick people
of the town. All he had to do now was to keep a firm lid on any
bad feelings that arose after the execution of Charles Stuart.

* * *

Josiah and Alice Grubbs were not by any means the only
couple to mull over what had just taken place in the church.
Josiah, the shoemaker, sat before his blazing fire and nursed a
mug of ale. Bustling in the kitchen, as was her wont, Alice came
into the parlour with a platter of gingerbread slices, and her own
mug of ale. They were joined by their daughter Imelda and
Imelda's betrothed, Simon, son of Abel and Faith Smith. As
usual, Simon had difficulty finding a chair that would support his
weight and contain his girth. Simon was built on only slighter
smaller lines than his blacksmith father.

They were joined soon after by their near neighbours, Peter
and Lou Crowley and their son Matt. Peter Crowley was the
town's best carpenter. Matt, a year older than Simon, was just
under half his size.

After some desultory, general chatter, Alice was the first to
mention the subject.

"With our king now dead, does that mean that his son Charles
is now king?"

Peter Crowley, a man given to much thought and little
conversation, was very surprisingly the first to answer

"To all those in England who believe in royalty, yes he is. To
the Scots, he also probably will be. But we now live under a
totally different order of things. Parliament, who now rule the
roost, have declared that there no longer be kings and princes –
so, to all intents and purposes, no he is not."

"But how many in England subscribe to this?" Alice
demanded. "Most of us hereabouts do not. We were for the king
– and still are."

Simon cleared his throat before saying what he had
overheard.

"There is a parliament man at Parke at the moment – I believe
his name is Kent, and you know how Hob likes to run about with
his knowledge? Well, he heard this Kent chap say to the bailiff

195

and the steward that nearly two-thirds of the people are behind parliament. So that makes us a small minority."

"But are those same two-thirds equally happy that parliament has just executed an anointed king?" Josiah wondered. "I can fully believe that they wanted an end to King Charles' rule – his tolerance of Catholics. But are they happy that it ended in his murder? For that's what it was – murder!"

"And his murder should be avenged!" Matt Crowley growled. "Us who supported the king should rise against those who ordered his killing!"

"And how may that be achieved?" Simon asked the hot-headed Matt. "Parliament has a large and very efficient army. They have won almost every battle. To rise up against them would need thousands of men – highly trained and fully armed. Where are they to come from? It's a futile notion!"

"Only those who cower at home would say so!" Matt remarked. Imelda put a restraining hand on Simon's arm as she almost felt his hackles rise.

"Simon is indeed right," Josiah admitted. Alice nodded her agreement, as did Crowley and his wife. "We must simply accept that which we cannot change."

"Never accuse me again of cowering," Simon said very quietly to Matt. "I will fight a battle that has some chance of success. This one would not and would result in many more dead – and to no purpose!"

"If I hear of any group rising against parliament, I shall join it immediately," Matt stated.

"Then you almost certainly will have us mourn the loss of a dear son!" Alice made a grab for Matt's hand. Matt, to his later shame, shrugged off the hand and stalked out.

* * *

James Ramsey was with his brother John in the parlour behind the bakery. Evelyn and Mary were with Avril in the kitchen, preparing a light supper. The conversation earlier had been on the same lines as at the Grubbs house.

"It is almost as if we have no time for the fate of the king," Avril remarked, coming into the parlour with a platter of small apple pies. "Mary and I have our time taken up with seeing to the sick. Anything else seems of little importance."

"That is the same with most folks," John nodded. "Evelyn and I work most of our waking hours baking bread, pies and cakes. James has to spend his day preparing salves and medicines, and seeing to those who come for advice. Abel and Simon next door have hardly a moment to spare from their smithing. It is just as if the rest of the country passes us all by!"

"I rarely see Ella with any time on her hands – nor Gil, come to that," Mary added. "They at least have the help of Nell with the chickens and Maud with young Rosie. But I never see Ella stop, even though she is again pregnant."

James had remained quiet as all this talk went on around him. Everything that had been said was absolutely true – most folks were so busy doing what was necessary to keep body and soul together, they had little time for anything else. Except when, like this time, they had almost been forced to contemplate the wider world.

"England has been ruled by kings – or in a few cases, by queens – for over a thousand years. Ever since the Romans departed, there has been a royal person sitting on a throne. In some cases, there have been three or four! It is going to take a lot of getting used to – having a parliamentary committee being our ruler!"

Mary was learned enough not to let this pass without her input.

"But, Uncle James, many times a king has been put aside or killed so that another may take his place. And this is hardly the first time England has been riven by civil war!"

"No – it certainly is not. But it is the very first time since the Saxons came to rule that a king has been replaced by nobody!"

Evelyn, always immensely proud of her daughter's learning, wanted to know more.

"What of these other civil wars, Mary?"

James gave her a smile and a nod.

"Well – starting with when William came from Normandy. He was succeeded by his son Rufus and then by his second son, the first Henry. When Henry died, there was civil war between his daughter Maud and her cousin Stephen. Later, during the reign of the third Henry, there was civil war between him and the leading barons under Simon de Montfort. Then, the second Edward was put aside in favour of his son, the third Edward. Edward's grandson, the second Richard, was put aside by the fourth Henry. Then, during the long reign of the sixth Henry, there was civil war between him and Edward of York – who became the fourth Edward. His brother, the third Richard, was put aside by the seventh Henry – who began the rule of the Tudors. We all know what followed on from there. Henry the eighth was succeeded by his young son, the sixth Edward, then by his daughters Mary and Elizabeth. During Elizabeth's reign, there were constant fears of civil war – the Scots, the Spanish, the French were always conspiring to end her reign. And then we had a Scot on the throne – James. And now his son has been put aside by parliament."

"So," James almost gave his niece a round of applause. "There has never been a steady succession – an unbroken line of kings and queens. Very like there has never been an unbroken line of succession of popes since Peter. At one time, there were three of them – all at war with one another. What we are now faced with is something this country has not ever seen before – rule by a group instead of rule by a single person."

"We already have the beginnings of a school here," Evelyn said thoughtfully. "Those who want their little children to learn their letters and numbers. If ever that little group manages to expand, Mary should be its teacher. I can think of nobody else more suited to the post." She gave her daughter a pat on her hand. Both John and Evelyn were immensely proud of their young daughter.

"I would second that without a moment's hesitation," James nodded. "It would mean that Avril and I would lose someone we value highly, but the world will not progress without formal learning – and Mary is more suited to lead that endeavour than anyone else in the town!"

Mary by now, was getting red with embarrassment. She had come to believe that her future was to be as the married spouse of the bailiff's son, helping with the health and wellbeing of the town. Perhaps there was now an alternative. Not without young

Harry Cove at her side, but also as the town's schoolteacher. It was a lovely thought.

"But this gets us no further with our discussion about our future as a country," she reminded everyone.

"That, learned niece, is in God's hands. We will have no say in it!" Avril brought the discussion to an end.

* * *

In the dark and cold of the evening, William Garlick at long last reached home. He first saw to the stabling of his horse, then made his weary way to the rectory, where he was welcomed by Reverend Forbes.

Over a glass of mulled wine, he recounted all he knew from his stay in Westminster. Forbes was very loth to tell him that they already knew the details from Kent,

"Do you mean to say that my journey has been in vain," Garlick sighed, wishing for nothing more than his bed.

"No – certainly not. What you have related is of great value in that it confirms what the man Kent told us. He is hardly unbiased – so we needed your confirmation."

CHAPTER XXVIII

Thursday, the first of February, saw a complete change in the weather. Gone were the snow flurries, the biting winds and the early frosts. In had come rain from the far Atlantic, along with a steep rise in temperature. With lambing well under way, the warmer weather was a blessing. The older ewes, wise to all this, huddled against the east side of high hedges and walls. Those who had birthed three lambs had one removed and carefully handed over to those who had birthed only one.

Avril, and Mary once she had been made aware, tried unsuccessfully to find some correlation between a rise in temperature and the fresh outbreak of the winter fever. The two were again having to almost run from cottage to cottage in response to calls for help. Avril really feared a rash of deaths as the new outbreak seemed to cause severe symptoms faster than had the initial outbreak.

Rosie was almost completely over her bout of fever and was running about much as normal. Gil and Ella showed no symptoms – neither did Nell. She went about her tasks with the chicks and hens with no signs of illness. That could not be said for the butcher, the smith, the churchwarden, and the bookseller.

Old William Garlick, probably weakened by his long and bitterly cold ride from Westminster, went downhill fast. Avril saw him in the early morning and by noon dinner time, he was gasping for breath and scorching hot to the touch. By mid-afternoon, he was close to death.

Abel Smith, normally a pillar of strength, lay on his bed beside Faith. Both of them were shivering and very hot. Avril had no real fears for either of them as they were far younger than old William, and strong and fit. Simon toiled alone in the smithy, seemingly immune to the ailments of his parents.

Avril's next call was to the butcher, Simon Dingle and his wife Stella. Both were shivering and hot, but nowhere near as hot and shivery as their little daughter Felicity. Only just four years old, she was mercifully fast asleep, but very hot to the touch. As there was nobody else in the house to minister to them, Avril had to call on their nearest neighbour to keep a watch and to administer the drops of medicine. Avril went on to her next call, fearing for the little girl's life.

Passing the booksellers, she noticed that the shop door was closed and fastened, no lamp lit to illuminate the shelves of books. She knocked at the door and called out, standing back to see if there signs of life anywhere. She was rewarded moments later by a window opening above the shop door.

"The shop is closed as my husband and I are indisposed," came the acid tones of Mercy Green.

"If you have the winter fever, I have medicines that may help," Avril responded.

"We have no need or want for your medicines. The Good Lord God shall answer our prayers and render us well again as and when He sees fit!"

"Are you sure you would not like some assistance?"

"We need nothing from you – or your quackery! Begone and leave us to our prayers!"

"And bugger you, too," Avril muttered under her breath as she went to call at the carpenters.

* * *

Matthew Kent had left early the previous day and was well on his way back to Westminster. He was profoundly grateful that he was travelling eastwards with the rain at his back. His long riding cloak shielded him from the worst of the rain. It also helped by stinging the rump of Murphy, encouraging him to trot faster than normal. Kent was confident that he would reach his destination by nightfall the following day.

* * *

Mary was equally thankful, but for entirely different reasons. The young shepherd was at last showing signs of recovery. However, three more of the staff at Parke, and two more at Brimley, had gone down with the new outbreak. One of those at

Brimley was young Nick Andrews, and he was mumbling incoherently in his fever, wrapped up like a cocoon in bundles of blankets.

"How long has he been like this?" Mary asked Kit Warden.

"Since early this morning. He were fine yesterday!"

Mary managed to use a small spoon to get some of the poppy juice mixture into his mouth, making sure she held his jaw shut until he swallowed automatically.

She went down into the big hall in search of Lady Violette.

"Another?" that old lady asked as Mary came towards her.

"Aye, My Lady, another. Tis young Nick Andrews and he is very unwell."

"And what of the little one?"

"Oh, little Hal is not too bad. He has his mother by his side all the time – and she is very competent with administering the medicines."

"Aye, that Meg is as competent as her husband. Now, young Mary – you look in need of some rest and refreshment. Ring that bell by the fire."

The summons was answered promptly by a serving girl, who bobbed a small curtsey to her mistress.

"Bring some warmed wine and a platter of those gingerbread biscuits," she was told.

Mary gladly sat down in a chair facing the old lady. When the wine and biscuits appeared, she was even more glad for the few minutes of respite.

"Are you not afeared that you may catch this fever?" Lady Violette asked.

"Nay – Aunt Avril and I are spared to do our work. We both believe that the Good Lord is watching over us and keeping us safe."

"And I also hear that you are betrothed to the bailiff's son. Is he not afeared for you?"

"Aye – he is, My Lady. But this is my mission, and I will not shirk it!"

"Then he is indeed a lucky young man – and you may tell him that I said so!"

Mary gave a small giggle of pleased embarrassment, then buried her face in her wine glass. She needed to change the subject.

"Is that right that you have made Meg's husband your steward, My Lady?"

"Aye – I have. And, so far, have not regretted it. How is the rest of the town faring?"

"That I do not know until I get back and speak to my aunt. But I fear that this new outbreak will be more severe than the last. Why this should be so, I have no idea. But one thing is clear already. None who suffered from the earlier fever have contracted it again. Perhaps the Good Lord keeps suffering away from those who have already suffered? Perhaps the first infection makes them safe from the second."

"I also hear that you are highly recommended for the position of schoolteacher. If that be so, then you will certainly have my support – and that of the bailiff and the reverend. I can think of nobody better suited to it!"

Once again, Mary had to resort to hiding behind her large wine glass.

* * *

Avril was walking down through the main street later that afternoon having seen to William Garlick again. The old man was literally gasping for breath and nothing that Avril could do could ease the passage of air into and out of his lungs.

Pressing her ear to his chest, she had been aware of a gurgling noise – almost as if he was breathing through water. She knew just enough about human anatomy to know that there were two lungs and that they should not sound like that. In effect, she knew far more about the human body than anyone else in the small town – and probably as much, if not more than, the physician in Newton Abbot. It was not that long ago that it was considered sacrilegious to probe the mysteries of what was regarded as God's perfect creation!

As she slumped wearily into a chair by her fire, she counted on her fingers the number of patients she had seen in the town that day. She stopped when she reached thirty-five. James, having finished with a customer in the shop, came in with a large mug of warm ale and a hunk of bread and cheese.

"You look just about done in!" he said, sitting by her side and feeding her a slice of cheese.

"Not as done in as old Will Garlick," she replied. "I sincerely doubt he will see the night out."

"Any others that you have grave doubts for?"

"Little Felicity – she's only just four. If she lasts the night, she will probably recover. Still no more word from the Greens. That miserable Mercy told me her husband is ill – but how ill I have no idea. She sent me away saying she had need of nothing but prayer."

"Then she is as stupid as she is miserable. Her God gave us brains to think with and to work out what needs doing. You have the means to ease suffering and she is a fool to ignore that."

"Has there been any word from Mary?"

"Nay – not since she left early this morning. I hope that does not mean that Parke and Brimley are keeping her so long."

Avril had nodded off in her chair for only ten minutes when Mary returned. She also slumped into a chair. James fetched more ale and food.

"Young Nick Andrews at Brimley is very unwell. One old woman who works in the kitchens is also in her bed. And this is what I cannot understand – one young and fit man is very unwell, whilst one old woman with the same fever is a lot less affected. How can this be?"

Avril and James looked at one another and shrugged. They didn't know either.

"The young shepherd at Parke is much restored," Mary went on. "But two of the servants, one in the fields and one in the kitchen, are very bad. These two are what kept me there so long."

"So – how many at the two places are affected?" Avril asked.

"Seventeen," Mary answered.

"Then, with the town, that makes more than fifty. Have we enough poppy and willow to see us through a whole week?" Avril asked.

"I do believe, just about," James answered. "I shall ask Faith to come and help me prepare more batches."

"Then, like Mercy Green, perhaps we should also start praying!" Avril said, just before dropping off to sleep again.

* * *

A watery sun had appeared late in the afternoon. Rain had ceased but had left deep puddles along the lanes and in the fields. Kit Warden had finished his duties and had hurried back to see how Nick Andrews was faring. To his surprise, the young man opened his eyes and peered out from his cocoon of blankets.

"Feeling better?" Kit asked.

Andrews looked at him and shook his head. He just about managed to croak out a 'no', before closing his eyes again. Kit watched as the youngster started shaking almost uncontrollably. Rushing down the flights of stairs, he went in search of his other old mate, Luke Farmer the steward.

"Luke – Nick's in a very bad way – shaking like his bones have all come adrift!"

Farmer followed Kit back up the stairs and saw for himself.

"Kit – run as fast as you may to get that young maid here. She may know what to do. I have not the slightest clue!"

Not even bothering to don a coat or a cloak, Kit tore down the stairs and out into the courtyard. It would take him a half-hour to reach the apothecary in Bovey. Having been a soldier for some years, and a hard worker ever since, Warden was still a very fit man and could easily keep up a pace between a jog and a run for the distance between Brimley and Bovey. Still, he was out of breath when he at last arrived to hammer on the apothecary's door.

Young Nell, finished for the day with the hens and chicks, answered the urgent summons.

"Mary," she called out. "The young man at Brimley is very bad and you are needed."

Mary, who had only just sat down after a sleep to eat some supper, collected her valise. Throwing a cloak around her shoulders, she got Warden to run to the sergeant's cottage to borrow a horse. She used the old horse and cart during the day, but that would be too slow for such an urgent summons.

Avril, woken from a sleep, peered down the stairs and asked Mary if she needed company.

"Nay – I can manage, aunt. That young man I told you about is shaking badly. I need to get a large dose of poppy into him to put him to sleep. Isn't that the right thing to do?"

"That is the *only* thing you may do. Only deep sleep may stop him shaking like that."

Barely twenty minutes later, Mary ran up the stairs to the attic room where she found Luke the steward sitting by Andrews' bed, in which the patient was literally shaking like an aspen branch in a high wind.

Taking out her bottle of poppy juice and a spoon, Mary put three times the normal dose into the glass that was by the bed, then added ale from a jug.

"We have to sit him up, or else the mixture will spill everywhere," Mary said.

Farmer went behind Andrews and easily lifted his shoulders until the young man was sitting almost upright. .

"Please – use one hand to hold him tight like that and the other to keep his head still."

Using one of her own hands, she pinched Andrews' nostrils together so that he was forced to open his mouth to breathe. After he had taken a gulp of air, Mary held the glass to the open mouth, poured in some of the liquid, then released the nostrils. Apparently, this ruse worked as, when the mouth came open again, only a little liquid dribbled out. Mary repeated the procedure another five times until the glass was empty. She sat back on her heels and offered a sigh of relief.

"That seemed to work," she said with a satisfied smile. "You can lay him down again now."

A few minutes later, Warden joined them, gasping for breath as he had run all the way back again. He looked at his friend and noticed immediately that the violent shaking had subsided quite a bit. And then Andrews again opened his eyes.

"Must tell you all about it," he muttered.

"Tell us all about what?" Luke came around to stare at his young friend.

"Must tell you afore it's too late. All about what happened up on the moor."

"But that were three years past! We all know what we did up there! We were trying to make our way across the moor to reach the others."

"But I went with Herrick and Porter – we went off into the mist!"

"Aye – so you did. I remember Sergeant Brown cursing you for leaving when he said we should stay put until the mist lifted."

Andrews' eyes were starting to droop as the poppy juice began its effect. He struggled to open them wide.

"Must tell you!" he repeated. "We wandered off and got lost. That idiot Herrick led us into the mist and got us lost. Porter got so cold he just laid down in a hole and died. Herrick said he was glad as we would not be burdened with him any longer. So, I kicked him in the head and left him. I am sure I killed him. When the mist lifted, I tried to head east to where we had come from. I spent days with some miners before I got down off the moor. I killed that man."

The effort had exhausted him, and he closed his eyes and drifted off into a deep sleep.

"So, that's what happened to those three," Farmer grunted. "I have wondered about that."

"But we never heard him say anything, did we?" Warden pleaded. "He is our friend and he must not be blamed for taking the life of that evil sod!"

"I heard nothing," Farmer nodded.

"And I have just been stricken deaf!" Mary smiled at the two. "This poor fellow must not be burdened with such things. He should sleep now for many hours. I only hope he wakes again!"

"You believe he may not?" Farmer queried.

"He is very ill and weakened by the shaking. It is in God's hands now. I can do no more."

"Shall I watch over him during the night?" Warden asked.

"Nay – he is deep asleep. And you look as if you need that also. All you would watch over is a young man sleeping. If he wakes again, it will not be until way into the morrow."

"Then, thank you for all you have done. May we see you safely home again?"

"Nay – I shall ride back quickly as I need my bed as much as you do. I shall return before dinner. I shall also pray for him."

Kit Warden, asleep in his own bed was not aware of anything during the night, not even when at about four o'clock in the darkness, Nick Andrews took his last shuddering breath.

Mary, also dead to the world, had gone to bed as soon as she reached her home in the bakery. She had returned the horse to the sergeant, who had said that she could use it every day for as long as it was needed. It was much faster than that old cart, he laughed.

One thing she did notice as she was at the soldiers' cottage. Glory, the daughter of Dick and Sal Allen from the tavern, was trying not to be seen. She had been there for an hour or more, nursing Trooper Bell – the young soldier she had taken a real fancy to. Mary gave her a smile and a wink before making her way to her bed, where she collapsed into a deep sleep.

CHAPTER XXIX

Friday carried on much as Thursday had left off – steady rain sweeping down on Bovey Tracey from the moor. It was not too bad if going eastwards – the rain was at one's back. But head anywhere towards the west and the rain was swept into one's face.

Friday, the second of February, was the day that the death toll mounted again. The first indication that things were going badly was when Avril was passing the saddler's shop. Jake Hoggs hailed her as she was about to walk past. Tears were streaming down his face.

"My Eleanor has been taken," he managed to say, before burying his head in his hands.

Avril was shocked. She had visited Eleanor Hoggs only the day before and, whilst hot and shivering, had appeared to be no worse than many of her patients. Eleanor was only thirty-three years old and had married Jake when she was fifteen. Their son Henry was in his late teens and had been apprenticed to his father for years.

Finding her own way to Eleanor's bedside, Avril looked down at the serene and peaceful face of the woman she had known almost since she had been born. Jake stood on the other side of the bed and did his best to compose himself.

"It was early in the morning," he mumbled. "Probably about four o'clock. Eleanor started coughing and writhing about, then seemed to just collapse. She never moved again after that."

* * *

Mary was about to start her day when she received a visitor. Her betrothed, Harry Cove, stood outside the bakery with two horses – one from the soldiers that Mary had used the previous day, and his own from the bailiff's stables.

"I have come to accompany you today," he announced. "The weather is not good, and you should not be alone doing your work with the sick."

Mary called him into the shop and greeted him with a kiss on his cheek.

"Believe me, I am not at all sorry to have your company today. I do not relish having to travel to Brimley day after day on my own."

"I have also brought you a waterproof cloak to go over the one you normally wear in the cold weather."

"Then you are doubly welcome!" Mary grinned at him. "Before we set off, have a small meat pie that has just come from the oven."

John and Evelyn were eating a late breakfast as Mary brought Harry into the parlour, Harry taking large bites from the crusty pie.

"This is the finest pie I have ever tasted," he mumbled between bites. "Although should my mother ever hear of it, I shall deny having uttered the words!"

"It is good that you are to accompany Mary. We have always been nervous with her going about all on her own," Evelyn said.

"I should not have waited this long to see her safe," Harry replied. "I shall take as much care of my future wife as I shall when she is indeed my wife!"

"Then I shall worry no longer! Mary – how long will it take for this sickness to pass?"

"Aunt Avril and I have speculated every day on that very subject and the only conclusion we have reached is that it will cease when it ceases, and not a day before! Uncle James said that, despite all his reading and researching, he can add nothing to that judgement."

"Then it is as some say – it is a visitation by God and only He will know when it may pass!"

"Nay, mother. That is like saying that the rain that ruins crops is God's punishment for our wickedness. We have to read and learn so that we may understand the workings of this world. Tis far too easy for us simply to sit back and put the blame for all our misfortunes on a vengeful God."

"Then you be exactly the right person to teach the children of this town," her father gave his daughter a smile of pride. "Teach them to ask questions – as you have done almost since you drew your first breath!"

"Some say it is the mark of a heretic!" Mary warned. "That everything is happening the way God intends – and that we have no power to alter one single thing! Tis heresy to even pose a question! Look what happened to Signor Galileo. He observed and proved that the earth revolves slowly and moves around the sun, not that the earth is the centre of creation. He was disgraced and said to be a heretic. But he was right. He asked questions and suffered grievously for it!"

"But the Catholics declared him heretic!" Harry pointed out.

"Aye – the horrible Inquisition declared him heretic. But many of our own and Presbyterian faiths also declared that what he said was against scripture." Mary argued.

"And in the meantime, your patients are awaiting their ministering angel!" Evelyn laughed.

Mary and Harry rode side by side down through the town and made first for the further of her two stops – Brimley. Bad news awaited her as soon as she arrived.

"Young Nick Andrews died during the night," Luke Farmer told her as the pair dismounted.

Mary was very sad to hear that news but put it aside immediately. Her efforts were far better spent with keeping those who were still alive in that state for as long as she could. A phrase from the New Testament occurred to her – 'let the dead bury their dead'. It seemed heartless until one thought it through, she mused. The dead were the business of God; the living were in the care of the living. It made complete sense to her.

She visited two of the house servants who were in need of extra willow bark. This had been used for centuries for reducing fever – and nobody ever questioned why this should be. It just did. The same for the juice of the poppy. It promoted deep sleep.

She also made a courtesy visit to Lady Violette. That redoubtable lady was, as usual, ordering things done to her liking.

"Ah – young Mary! Come to check that I'm still breathing? As you see, I am as fit and hale as ever. But I thank you for all your efforts."

"Would that all my patients had Your Ladyship's indomitability!" Mary gave her a grin.

"Ha!" Lady Violette barked a laugh. "Indomitable! I like that. It shall be my epitaph!"

Harry and Mary then rode back to Parke, where more patients needed her ministrations. Unfortunately, the old stable hand had passed during the night. The young lad who had been his helper, was now rushed off his feet trying to cope.

Grace Barton, wife of Luke the steward, was slowly recovering and waved Mary away with a smile.

"Off with you, young miss – I am on the road to health again, thanks to your efforts."

Their last call was to Harry's home – the bailiff's house. No sickness there. Hob was, as usual, off on one of his errands.

"Aha! You bring my future daughter in law to see us!" Peter Cove gave Mary a kiss of welcome. "Harry suggested that he wanted to see you safe and to render whatever help may be needed. Come and sit with us and take dinner."

Laura Cove came in, having supervised the kitchen and the cook. She also gave Mary a kiss of welcome. As they sat down to a bowl of thick vegetable soup, Mary brought the bailiff up to date with the latest state of the illness.

"More deaths? It is inevitable, I suppose," Peter Cove grunted. "There will be more ere this fever passes!"

"Unfortunately, that will certainly be so," Mary nodded. "Aunt Avril and I have had many a long talk about it – trying to fathom why one is taken and one is not. Some young and strong are taken whilst some old and feeble are not. It maddens me that I cannot fathom it!"

"Perhaps they were ordained to die?" Laura wondered.

"Please forgive me when I disagree with that," Mary replied slowly. "There *is* a reason – and it has to do with the person and the state of that person. What that may be, I have no idea. But I will not subscribe to the notion that God is responsible for every ill that befalls us. It is our lack of understanding that is at fault!"

"Bloody Mary would have had you burned at the stake for such utterance!" Peter Cove laughed.

"Aye – she would," Mary agreed. "But she died over ninety years ago. She burned many who did not subscribe to her beliefs! May the Lord be blessed that we are now beyond that!"

"You think so?" Laura said quietly. "In Scotland, we have a Presbyterian regime that would slaughter Catholics if it could! Our own parliament is heading in just as strict a direction!"

"Our own Sir John Vickery is a part of that regime – and he is strictly Presbyterian – although he wanted no part in executing our king – or so it is reported!" Peter reminded everyone. Vickery had been close to parliament for years past.

A rich lamb stew followed the soup, then a cream and raisin tart. Mary felt almost sinful that she was sitting there stuffing herself with rich food when so many were struggling with poverty and illness. And then another thought occurred to her. She and her aunt and uncle were able to help those in need – so it made a sort of sense that the three of them maintained that ability. And then she chided herself for such complacency. She gave herself an internal grin – I am able to rationalise anything if I try hard enough, she chuckled.

* * *

It was just before dinner when a messenger arrived from Exeter. It was not the usual young trooper and this one made the same mistake as his predecessor – he arrived with his horse quivering and sweating. Larkin was furious. Before the unfortunate young man could open his mouth, Larkin was glowering up at him.

"If this be a matter of life and death, I shall forgive you. If it be anything less than that, I shall flay the skin from your back.!"

"Yes, sergeant," the young trooper gasped, looking down into the furious face.

"Yes, sergeant, what? What is the news you bring that requires you to render your horse in such a state?"

"Sorry, sergeant. I have orders from Captain Brookes. You and your troop are to report back to him by this time tomorrow."

"And that news meant that you flogged your horse near to death? Take him immediately to the stables and see that he is properly cared for. Then report back to me."

"But, sergeant, there is more of the message."

Larkin turned to Glass and Tamplin, who were hovering nearby.

"Is this man deaf?" he asked. "Did I or did I not just give him an order?"

"Aye, sergeant, you did," Tamplin grinned.

The young man knew that he was in even deeper water, so wheeled his horse around and walked it sedately to the stables. He was back within ten minutes.

"Right. Now that your poor horse is being tended properly, give me the full message!"

"Captain Brookes' compliments, sergeant. You and your troop are to report back to him by this time tomorrow. You are to bring with you a plan of this town with the names and status of every person residing. That is the whole message."

Larkin blinked in surprise. One of the first things he had done was to draw up a plan of the town and who lived where. It was simply common sense for him to have done so. But it was information that *he* had needed if he was to control effectively. He had no idea why anyone else would ever need it. But he knew it needed to be brought up to date.

"Now – having delivered a message that could have waited a full hour so that your horse would not have had to be flogged half to death, it is now your job to spend the rest of this day cleaning out the stables. You will ride back with us on the morrow!"

"But, sergeant, I have had no dinner!"

"Again, you appear to have lost your hearing. Must I again repeat myself?"

"Er, no, sergeant," the young man trudged back up the street to the stables to begin his chore.

"Tamplin – get the news to the whole troop. I expect them ready to leave after breakfast. This large cottage will be cleaned and left as we found it!"

* * *

Reverend Forbes sent messages to a few of the most senior of the members of his congregation. What he had to tell them was going to come as a very rude shock.

John and Evelyn, with Abel and Faith, were the first to arrive at Forbes' house. They were closely followed by Adam and Olivia Gates from the mill, then by Simon and Stella Dingle from the butchers.

"This will come as great a shock to you all as did the death of Will Garlick," Forbes began. "I have been removed from my living as your vicar – by order of the powers that now be in Westminster. I can only assume that it is my past association with the Prince of Wales that has caused my fall from grace."

Abel Smith, by one year the oldest of the congregation present, was the first to respond.

"They mean us to be bereft of all associated with our church," he rumbled. "First of all, we lose our churchwarden – may God rest him. And now we lose our vicar as well. That leaves this town without any spiritual leadership whatsoever!"

"Within the week, I am to report to some committee or other," Forbes explained further. "What more they can do to me, I know not. I would guess that they will need to examine me to see what I know or recall from my association with the prince. That is very easily answered – I have not the slightest clue what was, is or may be, in the prince's mind. I was merely his chaplain, never his confidante!"

"Are we to have a replacement?" Abel asked.

"I have as much idea as any of the sheep grazing hereabouts."

"But what is to happen to the church?" Simon Dingle queried. "We are left with a sexton and a verger only."

"I intend to ask Ralph Goodes to keep the church in good order. He has been verger here for a long time. He will have to act as temporary churchwarden until the matter is settled."

"Then why is he not here with us?" Faith asked the obvious question.

"Again, simple to answer. He is ill with the fever – but I am assured that he is well on the road to recovery."

By mid-afternoon, the news was all over the town – as was the news that the soldiers were being recalled to Exeter.

* * *

Mary and her parents were again entertaining Harry Cove to supper that evening, the news having reached them that Mary's horse, on loan from the soldiers, would no longer be available to her.

"That is no problem," Harry was keen to tell them. "I shall either beg a horse from my father, or Mary can ride with me. As I said, I shall be with her every day until her ministrations be no longer needed."

"And how do you fancy riding with Harry?" Evelyn faced her daughter with a broad grin.

"I think that I would be able to survive such an ordeal," Mary replied, with as broad a grin.

CHAPTER XXX

It was early on the Saturday morning that Larkin made the final call before he led his troop back to Exeter. He rode briefly down to Parke and knocked at the bailiff's door. As usual, a tousle-headed lad answered.

"Master Bailiff – Sergeant Larkin be here!" Hob yelled over his shoulder. He scampered back to the kitchen where he was in the process of begging an extra bowl of porridge.

"That's two things he just may grow out of," Peter Cove laughed. "Running everywhere and shouting his head off. Good morrow, sergeant. What may I do for you?"

"Just a courtesy visit," Larkin replied, drawing a paper from his pocket. "As you know, we are recalled to Exeter. The messenger who brought us the tidings yesterday also brought a paper with him – a paper which he completely forgot to hand to me until late last night. You will remember that shepherd that was escorted to Rougemont, to be charged with murder? Well, the stupid oaf again tried what he apparently did two or more years past – he endeavoured to escape again. This time, he was not so lucky. Somehow, he had armed himself with a blade, but was shot down before he reached the gate. So – he will be facing the final judgement rather than that of our circuit judges."

"Well, I am not that sorry to hear this news," Peter Cove replied. "What he did to terrorise young May was unforgiveable – perhaps not worthy of a hanging, but certainly a very severe flogging and imprisonment. I will make sure it is known – especially by that fellow over in Trusham – the one who identified him as a murderer."

"Then I will bid you goodbye. It has been one of my more pleasurable postings – this is a fair town, and its people are, on the whole, good people."

Larkin gave a sort of salute, mounted his horse and rode back to pick up his troop, plus messenger - and Hawkes to be delivered to face trial for theft. Many people saw the troop riding out, armed and with all their panniers and baggage. They were soon informed that the town was again free of soldiers.

Cove penned a letter to Michael Brown and sent Hob on his pony to Trusham. He then called on the Fletchers. When he had them all together, he gave them the news about the shepherd.

"So, the bastard is dead!" Wilf grunted.

"Good!" May almost jumped up and down with glee. "Then he cannot do to others what he tried to do to me!"

Maud, her younger sister, heard the news in silence, then bade her parents and sister goodbye, and went down to look after little Rosie.

What she found was a house in a slightly worried state. Nell, her chores with the hens and chicks done, was sitting by the fire looking worried. Gil was pacing up and down, pausing every now and again to put his arms around Ella. Ella was sitting on a chair with a bowl on her knees – every so often, retching into it and looking wan. Rosie was sat at her mother's feet and looking very scared.

"Have you caught the sickness?" Maud asked, hovering by the door.

"That we do not yet know," Gil answered. "We have sent for Aunt Avril to come and see to her."

Ella looked up with a sigh. "For the hundredth time, will you not listen! I am sick because I am pregnant! Do you not remember how it was with Rosie?"

"But twas not this severe!" Gil argued.

"And who is to say that it will be the same every time? Rosie lay quietly inside me until the seventh month. This one is starting to move much earlier and it is upsetting everything else. I am *not* sick!"

Then, to defy her words, she retched again into the bowl.

"I should have said that I am not *ill*. I am obviously sick, but it is normal, and I do not need Aunt Avril or the Archangel Gabriel to confirm it!"

Avril arrived a few moments later, looked into the bowl and gave Ella a big grin.

"Mainly bile," she announced. "Early movement?"

Ella nodded and gave her husband a look that said, 'I told you so!'

"Take a drink of milk – it will help to restore the balance. There's nothing at all for you to worry about!" This last aimed at her nephew.

"Sorry, Aunt Avril," a chastened Gil muttered. "But with all this fever about, I could not help but worry."

"Men!" Avril snorted, making Ella laugh and nod. Nell joined in the laughter as she dreaded sickness of any kind. Maud grabbed Rosie and took her outside to play with some of the older chicks who were big enough to weather the winter.

Avril picked up her bag and made for the door.

"Right – on with my rounds. Now that the soldiers are gone, I will have to find other volunteers to help if things get worse. Oh – have either of you seen Hubert or Mercy? I was told by Mercy that Hubert was ill but have heard nothing since. I shall call again. Maybe she will let me into the house this time!"

"We have seen and heard nothing, have we, Ella?"

"Nay – Nell – have you?"

"I have not seen them for two or more days – and I am not sorry for that! She calls me horrid names!"

"She calls almost everyone horrid names," Avril laughed. "It is in her nature. Mercy by name and unmerciful by nature!"

*　*　*

True to her word, Avril knocked at the bookseller's door – which was locked, with a sign 'closed' in the window. Getting no response, she knocked louder and called out.

Hearing a window open above her head, she stepped back to see Mercy Green looking down at her. Avril was shocked at the appearance. No longer the prim and proper countenance topped off by a pristine white wimple. A haggard face and hair in a mess.

"I shall be down to admit you," came a cracked voice. "Hubert is indeed very sick, and my prayers are not being answered."

At long last, admitted to see her patient, Avril was shocked by what she found. Days of fever had resulted in bedclothes drenched in sweat – and smelling to high heaven. Hubert was lying there and breathing with great difficulty, still shaking and muttering in what looked like delirium.

Avril choked back the words that immediately occurred to her – to call Mercy all shades of an idiot not to let her administer medicines that *might* have reduced the fever much earlier. Instead, she placed the back of her hand at Hubert's neck – it was extremely hot.

"Have you tried to get liquid into him?" she asked.

"I have been on my knees beseeching the Almighty to make him better."

"You would have done much better to have forced weak ale down his throat – or cold water, if you prefer. He urgently needs to have that fever reduced – he is raging hot! First of all, fetch me a mug of water and a spoon."

When the mug of water arrived, Avril spooned some of the willow concoction into it and stirred it, then started feeding small spoonsful into Hubert's mouth, making sure most of it was swallowed.

"What is that stuff?" Mercy asked, peering suspiciously into the open jar.

"That is willow bark – crushed and infused in boiling water. It has been used for centuries to relive pain and fever. It is *not* a creation of the devil! Your God and mine gave us these things growing naturally for us to discover and use."

"And will it make him recover?"

"It might have done, had you allowed me to administer to him when he was first sick. We can only hope it is not too late! I see no point in giving him poppy juice as he is already deeply asleep most of the time."

"Then I shall continue to beg the Almighty to let him be better."

"As well as praying, make sure you spoon a good quantity into him every two or three hours. One dose will not be sufficient – it may take days yet. I shall leave you a small quantity in your kitchen and shall drop more into you this evening."

As Avril packed her bag and went down the stairs to let herself out, Mercy was already on her knees – eyes tightly shut, hands clasped in prayer.

"And not the slightest word of thanks," Avril muttered as she went to her next call.

Matthew Kent answered a summons that was delivered to him at his lodgings near Westminster. He was surprised to find that there were many in the room, all seated around a very large table.

At its head sat the forbidding figure of John Bradshaw, who was rumoured to be elected soon to the post of Lord President of the Council of State. With his black clothes and the white rabat at his throat, he looked as sternly puritan as anyone could imagine. At forty-seven years of age, he wielded considerable power.

At Bradshaw's right sat another stern figure, Colonel Sir Richard Ingoldsby. He had been one of the judges at the trial of Charles Stuart – and one of the signatories on the death warrant. A disciple of Cromwell, he had fought superbly in the New Model Army.

On Bradshaw's left, sat another that Kent recognised – the fanatical Henry Ireton, another of Cromwell's military commanders, and Cromwell's son-in-law.

The other five places around the table were taken up by 'agents' similar in rank to Kent himself.

Bradshaw opened proceedings by going around the table, addressing each of the 'agents' in turn. When it came to Kent's turn, Bradshaw spoke of the information Kent had managed to glean concerning possible uprisings in York and Hull.

"Nowhere near as serious as we first imagined," Bradshaw said in his dry voice. "There were altogether less than two hundred prepared to instigate trouble – and it was very quickly dealt with. Nevertheless, it was well worth your visit."

Kent breathed a small sigh of relief.

"As far as the part of the country you visited – Devon in particular, there seems little or no interest in rebellion of any kind."

"Which I find strange," Ireton interposed. "Devon and the rest of the West Country were a source of rabid royalism. Are we absolutely sure that they are pacified to the extent that you seem to propound?"

"No evidence has been found that contradicts this assumption," Bradshaw stated – and looked at Ingoldsby.

"I would agree – strange as it may seem," Ingolsdby nodded. "However, I would propose that, of all the areas of the country, the South-West deserves ongoing vigilance."

"Then, Master Kent, back you shall go. This time, I suggest that you centre yourself further west. Tavistock, or even as far as Bodmin."

It was after a late dinner that the meeting reconvened. Bradshaw had satisfied his hunger and thirst with bread, cheese and water.

"And now we must turn our attention to the remnants of the Stuarts," he frowned at the mere mention of the name. "First, Henrietta Maria. She is seemingly back where she belongs – France. And long may she remain there amongst her religious cronies. Then there are Charles and James. From all I can gather, the damned Scots have declared Charles to be their new king – as Charles the second."

"And how may he reconcile that with the Scottish Covenanters?" Ireton gave a bark of laughter. "They were fast enough to hand his wretched father back to us!"

"Realistically, what other option does he have?" Bradshaw wondered. "There is no place for him in England. France will soon tire of his pleadings. Scotland is his only option – as far as I can see it."

"Agreed," Ingoldsby nodded. "Scotland *is* his only option – unless he simply renounces all claims and settles for a life of debauchery – which, from what we know of him, might suit him admirably!"

"That may be so," Ireton said. "But I cannot see his younger brother James settling for that! He is by a long chalk the most able militarily, despite his youth."

"The Presbyterian Covenant – with Lord Warriston as its most voluble mouthpiece – will exact promises that Charles will be hard pressed to agree. He will be forced to add his imprimatur to their covenant – and that means his support for the Presbyterian cause, both in Scotland and in England. Without that promise, he is sunk," Ingoldsby noted.

"Perhaps we should widen the scope of our agents' investigations," Bradshaw took pen to paper. "Not only should they be searching for royalist support, but also support for Covenanters."

"But, sir, the two are surely miles apart," Kent could not stop himself from speaking, as he thought that such a double mission very tricky. "The Scots have done away with the idea of an episcopalian church – no bishops or archbishops above their presbyters. That is in direct conflict with the role of the remaining Stuarts, who adhere strictly to the Anglican regime that holds both of those ranks. I have not heard of any such rivalry anywhere!"

"He makes a valid point," Ireton grunted.

"He also has pointed out a conflict between the two that, should it arise, will reduce our detractors to fighting one another!" Ingoldsby guffawed.

Bradshaw frowned at such levity but conceded that it was – possibly – a consummation devoutly to be wished!

By early evening, the meeting broke up, with the agents going off to make whatever arrangements they deemed necessary. Kent was faced with a long ride back, past his old area around Exeter, and to the west of Dartmoor. He was not in the least enamoured with the idea – as were his colleagues, one of whom was faced with a journey to the wilds of Cumberland and Northumberland – with the Pennines in between. Winter made this a horrible outlook.

* * *

Hubert Green worsened by nightfall. Avril answered a frantic summons from his wife and arrived to find the man in dire straits. He was still extremely hot to the touch, his breath rattling and as shallow as Avril had ever experienced.

"Have you been making him drink?" Avril asked Mercy, who was almost prostrate on the floor.

"The dose you gave him did no good, so I saw no reason to continue with it!" she answered, looking up at Avril with a malevolent glare.

"No – as I told you, it needed to be repeated constantly to have any effect. I fear it is now past the point of remedy."

"You shall be held accountable for his death," Mercy wailed. "Your potions are nothing more than a sham!"

Avril refrained from answering that charge – as she was charitably inclined to suppose it was grief talking.

"I shall have you charged as a charlatan and a witch!" Mercy screamed.

Avril left quietly and went home to tell James what had occurred.

"Nobody in this town will hear a word against you," James put his arm around his wife. "It is surely grief – and perhaps her own sense of guilt. Had she asked, nay begged, for your help days ago, this might well not have happened."

Hubert Green died in the early hours of the Sunday morning – having been given nothing since Avril had tended to him earlier on the Saturday.

CHAPTER XXXI

James, Avril and Nell were woken just after daybreak by a furious hammering on their front door.

"Dear Lord above," Avril groaned. "Not another one in dire straits!"

James quickly donned breeches and shirt, then hurried down to the shop. There, her face ravaged with both tears and anger, stood Mercy Green, almost speechless with rage.

"Hubert has passed to the Lord – and it is all the fault of that wicked wife of yours," she spat out the words.

"Avril has told me the story, so before you go too far with your accusations, let me remind you of the laws against slander and false witness."

He held up his hand to stem what promised to be another burst of invective.

"Calm yourself, or I shall have to turn you out of here!" he warned.

Mercy turned on her heel and marched out of the shop, walked purposefully up the street and stopped at the small square. There she stopped and started shouting at the top of her voice.

"My Hubert has been taken from me! That witch with her potions killed him as surely as if she had taken a knife to his throat!"

She continued in that vein, drawing a small crowd. Most of them had been affected by the illness in one way or another, either by contracting it themselves or by a relative being stricken. In a pause between mouthfuls of hate, Lou Crowley walked up to Mercy and faced her.

"My Peter was similarly taken by this foul disease," she shouted over Mercy's voice. "Mistress Ramsey, in all the time he was sick, treated him with the utmost care. That she was unsuccessful is no fault of hers. I shall be eternally grateful that

Peter had someone like her to tend to his last days. You, uttering these foul remarks, should be ashamed of yourself!"

"Aye – ashamed!" came a chorus from behind Lou. "Mistress Ramsey has been the cause of many a cure – as has that young Mary. We should all be thanking God for them, not shouting foul abuse!" That came from Alice Grubbs, whose husband had recently recovered from the illness.

"That was well spoken indeed," Wilf Fletcher added his voice. "Mistress Green – instead of mouthing foul words about the supposed failings of others, why do you not meet up with those similarly bereaved. There you will find solace, friendship, and true Christian charity. You are in sore need of all of those."

"And what solace shall I find amongst worshippers of Satan?" Mercy shouted back. "Hubert and I were the only ones in this accursed town to worship the Lord in the proper manner! The rest of ye are doomed for the pit of hell itself!"

"I cannot remember the last time I worshipped Satan," came a voice from the back of the crowd – it caused some laughter. "Mistress Green – we are all sorry that you have lost your husband. But to cast about for someone to blame is fruitless. Look no further that yourself. From what I hear, you failed for days to call for help – help that would have been readily and selflessly given. And do not blame your God, either. Maybe Hubert would have died anyway – but you never afforded him the chance for life. Look no further than your mirror!"

Mercy could just about make out through her tears the massive figure of Abel Smith at the back of the crowd. She gave a piteous wail and ran back to her shop and locked the door behind her.

"Someone – and I suppose it is I who shall be responsible – will have to arrange a proper burial for Hubert Green," Ralph Goodes, the verger – and now temporary churchwarden – shrugged. "Although, how I may do it is a puzzle."

* * *

After dinner, Mary and Avril again took stock of the situation. James, guarding the shop, left the door to the parlour open so that he could participate.

"I have had no new cases for two days now," Avril started the ball rolling.

"And I have had none for the past three," Mary added. "May we even dare hope that it is passing away from us at last?"

"Beware complacency," James called out.

"Aye – that could be a big mistake," Avril agreed. "However – we are but simple humans, and hope is sometimes all that we have!"

"In Parke and Brimley, there have been a total of nine deaths. But on the brighter side, there have been twenty-three who have recovered," Mary stated.

"And in the town itself, I have recorded nineteen dead and well over forty on the road to full recovery," Avril made a note of the figures. At some time, she would pass these statistics and the names to the bailiff.

"Have we any idea of the situation in the furthermost villages?" James asked.

"Nay – that we have not, and it is about time we found out," Avril admitted. "We have been so occupied with those nearest to us that we have not had the time."

"I can undertake that task," Mary offered. "Harry will readily accompany me to the other villages."

"Riding with him or alongside him?" James laughed.

"Oh – with him seems so much more appealing!" Mary grinned.

* * *

Harry Cove brought Mary back to Parke with him that evening. As usual, being the perfect gentleman, he dismounted and lifted Mary down gently. Mary gave him a slightly puzzled look.

"Why are we here and not at my home?" she asked.

"Aha! Your curiosity shall be satisfied in but a moment," he laughed, taking her hand and leading her into the large cottage where, along with the bailiff and his wife, she was surprised to see her parents being entertained with mead and cakes.

"Oh – so this is to be a conference, is it?" Mary exclaimed.

"Indeed so," Harry grinned. "We have all been making enquiries as to the timing and location of our wedding."

"Given that Reverend Green has been deprived of his post, we have made sure that we can get the services of another vicar to conduct the ceremony," Bailiff Cove explained. "The vicar up at Chagford is more than willing to come to our church and officiate – making it all properly legal and binding."

Mary was both happy and a bit puzzled that things had been organised without her knowing. Harry obviously had been privy to the arrangements. He was immediately aware that his betrothed was concerned.

"We all thought that it would come as a lovely surprise to you," he explained.

"It is a lovely surprise," Mary nodded – then added, "And when is this all planned to take place, or is this something else to which I am to be kept in the dark?"

Everyone was then made aware that Mary was both happy that it was all going ahead but displeased to have been kept out of the planning. Harry took her hand in his.

"Believe me, that is the last time I ever keep anything from you," he promised.

"Then may I suggest that we plan for the wedding to take place on the first Saturday after the May celebrations. I should not want to overshadow that – it's far too important to the town," she offered.

"That is a very good suggestion," Laura Cove gave her a warm smile. "And now some other news that we have not been able to announce until today. We have only just received approval for the wedding feast to take place here at Parke – in the big hall. There will be a very large crowd for the occasion – so the Hall is most suitable to accommodate everyone."

"Oh – that's wonderful," Mary gasped. "We were expecting that we would celebrate in the tavern – it's the usual venue for weddings."

"Our daughter is still unaware of the esteem she is held in by everyone!" Evelyn laughed. "Mary – what you and Avril have achieved in recent weeks has ensured that you are the toast of Bovey Tracey."

"There is one other small item that we have to impart," Peter Cove announced.

Even Harry and Mary's parents were not aware that there was more to be learned.

"It has been long mooted that the town needs a formal school for the children – so that as many as possible may learn to read and write, to do their sums, and learn something of the history of our country. I have obtained permission for that large cottage that the soldiers have just vacated to be set up as a school – with desks, pens, paper, ink, and all the other things necessary. Not only that, Laura and I canvassed views from the more senior members of the town. There was only ever one name that was put forward – yours, Mary. When all is prepared, you shall become the schoolmistress – if that is what you desire."

Mary had heard something of the kind being mentioned before but had never thought anything would come of it. She was almost rendered speechless. Harry again took her hand.

"Just think how proud I shall be knowing that my wife is the most learned person in the town."

"Mary – you *must* agree to do this. There is no one more suited or deserving," her father prodded.

Mary found her voice at last.

"How could I refuse," she replied with a smile as wide as a crescent moon. "I have to admit that some such has been mooted in the past, but I never dared think aught would come of it. I shall be happy indeed to accept the position and will do my utmost to prove worthy."

"Excellent – then all is settled. One more small thing – the ground floor of the cottage is big enough to accommodate the school – and the upper floor more than large enough for your and Harry's home."

"And you shall be the one to plan it all," Laura added. "It will be your school and also your home. It needs to be done as you would wish."

"But how will Uncle James and Aunt Avril react when they learn that I am not to be their pupil apothecary?"

"Believe me, they will be as happy as we all are," Mary's mother retorted. "Who do you think started the rumour of just such a possibility?"

"And anyway, they have little Nell to teach. She will soon be eight years old and is as bright as a button – and has already been helping out and learning," her father added.

"And do not think that Gil's chickens will feel the loss – Maud Fletcher will be only too happy to take on the task. She already acts as nursemaid to Rosie. I'm sure she will be delighted to take over the chickens."

Mary sat down on a vacant chair.

"This really has been a strange evening," she observed.

* * *

A totally different meeting took place the following evening at the smithy. Imelda stood beside Simon, whilst Abel, Faith, Josiah Grubb and Alice Grubb stood in a group facing the young couple.

Abel was the first to give voice.

"Were you not able to keep it inside your breeches until you were wed?" he growled.

"But we are to be wed soon," Simon countered. "The child will be loved as much whether it be conceived before or after the ceremony!"

Faith gave her massive husband a sideways look to remind him that *he* had not kept it inside his breeches. The fact that she had attended her own wedding ceremony without a child growing inside her had been a matter more of luck than judgement. Abel gave another grunt – seemingly acknowledging her unspoken reminder.

"This wedding needs to happen very soon," Alice Grubb insisted. "Imelda tells me that she is not yet far gone, so it all may appear as normal if we put it about that the child has emerged early."

"I should by rights take a horsewhip to you," Josiah had the grace to say this with a deprecating laugh. The idea of the diminutive shoemaker taking a horsewhip to the massive Simon certainly lightened the mood.

"However," he went on. "Imelda has made her feelings well known to us. She loves Simon and wishes nothing more than to bear their child. But as Alice rightly says, we must hurry this wedding. I have already made enquiries of the vicar in Newton Abbot. He is willing to conduct the ceremony this coming weekend."

"But what about the legal requirement of the banns?" Faith queried.

"Ralph Goodes, our own temporary churchwarden, can be prevailed upon to fudge that issue," Abel grinned. "He owes me more than one favour. All he has to do is to write them and post them on the church door – suitably smudged and dated back."

"But that will mean a quiet ceremony. Are Simon and Imelda happy to forego the usual large celebration?"

"Yes!" came from the two young people.

"Then both of our chicks will have flown the nest," Faith sighed.

"Are you out of your wits?" Abel laughed. "Where else will they live but here with us – until they are able to get a cottage of their own? Simon will one day become the smith – and I cannot imagine anyone else I would rather have as a daughter-in-law living here with us!"

"We both thought you would be angry with us," Imelda said quietly.

"And why should we be angry?" Abel responded. "You are soon to present us with another grandchild. Rosie was the first and Ella's next will be the second. Yours shall be the third. The more the merrier!"

"Expect me to fight you for cuddles!" Faith gave Imelda a hug.

Left to their own devices, Simon put his arm around Imelda.

"That could have been a whole lot worse!" he grinned.

Back in their own cottage, Josiah and Alice faced one another with a secret grin.

"Tis just as well that nobody ever suspected that Imelda was created in similar circumstances," He laughed.

"Aye – and just as loved despite that!" Alice grinned back.

CHAPTER XXXII

Matt Crowley was not a happy young man. His father had died from the vicious fever that had taken many of the population; his mother Lou, was becoming more and more adamant that she and others of a like mind, would take sail from Plymouth to join the burgeoning colony across the Atlantic. Matt himself burned with indignation at what had befallen the king.

What Lou had feared was about to come to pass – the fact that she would soon be all alone, with the very distinct possibility that her son would join up with similar hotheads and come to the inevitable end.

Matt had at one time been hopeful that something would happen between him and Mary Ramsey – and that had fizzled out. Mary was now firmly and happily betrothed to the son of the bailiff. He had intimated to his parents some time past that he was intent on joining *any* group that was opposed to parliament – and the more bloodthirsty that opposition the better.

In his spare time, he had visited various towns and villages that were not too far from Bovey Tracey. In these taverns, he had simply eavesdropped on any conversation that he could – hoping to discover those of a like mind to his. He had been to Hennock, Newton Abbot, Ashburton, Trusham, and Moretonhampstead – and had drawn a blank in all of them. Ranging further afield, he had at last struck lucky in a tavern by the small docks in Totnes. There, one weekend, he had overheard what any parliamentarian would have classed immediately as inflammatory remarks bordering on possible insurrection. He was elated and made up his mind to endeavour to insert himself into that group.

Consequently, he set out very early on the following Saturday morning to walk the seventeen miles, hoping to cadge a lift from any carter going his way. Walking the entire distance would have taken him a minimum of six hours, so he was extremely fortunate to get two lifts that deposited him at the bridge spanning the River Dart just after one o'clock that afternoon. He made his way down the side of the bridge and entered the tavern where he celebrated with a large mug of ale and a fresh mutton pie.

By three in the afternoon, he was outside the tavern, sitting at the edge of the small dock and watching as two little boats were rowed up, moored safely and the men inside unloading their catch of fish. None of the men resembled in any way the men he had seen and heard before. He gave a shrug and determined to sit and wait until – if – any of the men appeared. On the point of giving up as the sun disappeared to the west, his patience was at long last rewarded. Two young men ambled onto the dock area from the roadway – and he recognised them immediately. The two went into the tavern and, after a few moments, Matt followed them.

The two were sitting together in a dark corner of the taproom, each with a mug of ale. Matt took a deep breath and went to sit on a stool opposite them. Two faces looked up and stared at him.

"Do we know you?" one of them asked.

"Nay – you do not know me – nor do I know you," Matt replied quietly. "The last time I was here I heard you speaking softly amongst yourselves – and there were five of you. What I overheard filled me with hope that I might join up with you, for what you were saying matched exactly what I wished to hear."

"And what did you wish to hear?"

Matt dropped his voice a further notch.

"That the death of the king needs to be avenged; that there needs to be an uprising of revolt against parliament."

"And why would you wish to have heard such?"

"It matches precisely what is in my heart!"

"Then, if you speak truly, we would indeed welcome you into our group. But you will understand that we shall have to first make sure of your commitment. For all we know, you could well be a parliamentary informer!"

"Aye – that is sensible. I should have expected nothing less. How may I convince you that I am in true earnest?"

"You must first meet us all and be prepared to answer as many questions as we may put to you."

"That I will readily agree. How may this happen?"

"On the morrow – Sunday – you must travel to Dartington. Tis a small village not two miles from here on the road towards

Rattery and South Brent. When you arrive at the crossroads in Dartington, take the left track and walk up the hill until you see on your right a stand of ash trees. Enter the stand and there you will find us. Be there by twelve of the clock.”

“I shall be there,” Matt promised. He left the two and went in search of somewhere he could pass the night. He turned to the left as he reached the road and walked through the small row of cottages that lined it on both sides. They soon petered out, the main town being up the hill on his left. He walked onwards past meadows until he reckoned he had travelled the two miles, and came to the crossroads that he had been told.

“Now – where to pass a cold night?” he wondered.

* * *

Bailiff Peter Cove sat nursing a mug of warm milk. Sooner or later, he mused, he was going to have to bend his mind to a small problem that his wife Laura had raised the previous evening. Not to be put off, Laura, sitting opposite him at the large fireplace, reiterated it again – just in case it might have slipped his memory.

“If Mary is to run this new school – and is to live above it as you outlined – where does that leave our Harry once the two of them are wed? Harry needs be here, learning to take over as Bailiff once you have retired from the post.”

Cove looked over at his wife and gave a small shrug.

“Harry knows probably more about the business of Bailiff than I do, even after my years in the job. He is more literate than I am – and certainly more numerate!”

“Peter – as usual, you avoid the issue!” Laura gave him her smile that meant, ‘you know full well what I meant’.

“Aye – I do,” he returned the smile. “Being Bailiff is far more than writing and numbering. It is about knowing the estate, the town, its surrounds, the people within it, the way they work, who does what and with whom, who is plotting what – and why. Our Harry is luckier than I was when I took over. I came here with you from elsewhere and had to learn all this slowly. Harry has been here all his life and knows everyone. And where did you get the notion that his elevation to Bailiff is a done deal?”

"The whole town already thinks of him as successor to the post. He is highly regarded and, with Mary at his side, will be even more highly regarded. That lass is a gem!"

"Aye, she is that!" Cove grinned. "But I sometimes wonder what ideas she will instil into the heads of the children. Certainly, she will teach them reading, writing, and numbers. But some of her other thoughts are – shall we say – a trifle radical!"

"Such as the notion that a king is not to be regarded as God's right hand?" Laura grinned.

"That and others," her husband acknowledged.

The two in question made an appearance before any further 'outlandish' thoughts could be voiced. Harry gave his mother a kiss, then poured Mary a small mug of the warmed milk. The two sat side by side on the settle.

"Were we the subject of your thoughts?" Mary enquired.

"Definitely a witch!" Peter Cove regarded his future daughter-in-law with a fond smile. "Defines our innermost thoughts!"

"Disregard that," Harry's mother laughed. "We were indeed wondering how the two would manage to combine your various roles once you are wed."

"Where we will live, you mean?" Harry went straight to the point. "That has been our own topic this morning. Mary and I have been to see the large cottage and have reached a decision. Despite the cottage being large – both on the ground and upper floors – we have decided that, with your approval, we will live here in this large house. Mary will run the school and I will be on hand to help with the job of Bailiff."

"I would have thought that you would want a home of your own – to run as you would wish," Laura looked directly at Mary.

"I shall have more than enough on my hands with the school – at least during the first year," Mary replied.

"Certainly, you will," Cove nodded. "Even more so when your first child arrives upon the scene!"

It said much for Mary's world-wisdom that she didn't even blush at the mention of a child.

"How much better for me and the child to be in a house of love and care – and a wise mother-in-law to ease the burden!" she replied.

"But back to the here and now," Peter Cove put on a serious face. "We come to the business of how the school may be financed. There will be considerable cost in setting it up – then in the day-to-day running. Are the children's parents to be asked for a subscription? What of those too poor to pay? Are those children to be denied an education? I have decided that a serious conference is needed – where all interested parties have a chance to offer opinions. Make no mistake, the whole town is very keen for there to be a school – but monetary considerations cannot be ignored!"

"To that end, I have already drawn up my plans – both practical and financial," Mary stated. "What is needed to start with and how much cost is involved; what monies will be needed to run the school for ten, twenty and thirty pupils."

"And can you present that to the meeting?"

"Aye, it is all prepared."

"Then I shall call such a meeting without delay – and invite any who wish to contribute in any way whatsoever – wherever they may live."

"And when you have done that, Mary – perhaps you would do the same for parliament – they are in sore need of a cool and logical brain!" Laura laughed.

* * *

James Ramsey was attending to a customer who had somehow or other managed to wrench his ankle. Inside the apothecary shop there was a small counter, behind which were rows and rows of bottles and jars full of ointments, pills, and potions, prepared at a side table where there were scales, pestle and mortar, spoons, empty jars and a whole host of other small things. To the side of that was a small cubicle that was screened off so as to afford some measure of privacy.

"Bloody Jericho!" yelled the man as James' fingers probed the large swelling surrounding the offending ankle. "I came here in search of a cure, not to be put to torture!"

James, kneeling on the floor, looked up at his seated patient.

"How did you manage to do this?" he asked.

"Chasing a bloody fox away from my lambs. Turned my foot over as I stepped into a coney's hole."

"There is a steady pulse at your foot – so no damage to the blood vessels. I can find no broken bone – so you have just wrenched the muscles, and that will account for the swelling. This will take a considerable time to heal itself."

"And in the meantime, who is to look after my flock? I have one son and he's about as much use as a donkey with three legs!"

"That, I have no answer for," James grunted. "What you must do is to keep your weight off it for as much as possible – fashion a crutch and remain sitting or lying as much as you can. When lying, keep that foot elevated on a pillow."

"And still no answer about my flock!" the man growled. Without anyone to tend them, the man faced a very uncertain future.

"Nell," James called.

Nell, wearing a spotless white apron, peered around the curtain.

"What would you prescribe for a badly swollen ankle?" James asked.

Nell puckered her brow and went through a list of possibilities in her mind.

"Willow bark to ease the pain. Keep it tightly bandaged for support. Try to keep the weight off it," she answered.

"Excellent," James gave her a broad smile. Not yet eight and already filled with common sense and knowledge, he thought.

"Why not poppy juice?" he asked.

"Twill only make him sleep – and he does not look in need of that. He has sheep and lambs to tend – somehow or other!"

"See?" James grinned up at his patient. "My prognosis confirmed!"

"Luckily, I have two dogs to help me. They are well trained and can move the sheep as I command. What I do if a ewe is distant and needs my help with lambing – well, that remains to be seen. How much do I owe you for your time?"

"Nothing at all," James gave him a broad grin. "Oh – two pennies for the willow bark. Nell will tell you how to mix it."

The man hobbled out, using a holly stick that needed to be replaced with a properly fashioned crutch. Everyone hereabouts will know how to make one of those, James mused. The benefit of living in the countryside. He left Nell minding the shop and went back into the parlour where Avril was taking a nap.

"Just heard that," she said. "Our Nell is going to be a boon and a blessing."

"She was from the moment we took her into our family," James nodded.

* * *

Matt Crowley was cold and hungry. He had passed the night sheltering inside the stand of ash trees until being woken just before dawn by a fit of shivering. His first thought was that he had contracted the dreaded disease. But, having observed Avril's actions, found that he was not running a fever. Far from it – he was simply frozen. Being young and normally a very healthy chap, he did the sensible thing and jogged all the way back to the crossroads and went in search of a tavern or a cookshop. He eventually found a small bakery a mile further on towards the small village of Rattery – and they were not yet open. The smell of baking bread had him dancing in frustration.

Another consideration was money. He had some, but not much – and it had to last him until he found shelter and companionship with like-minded people. But he was starving hungry! He made up his mind that he would buy one loaf when the bakery opened and, until that happened, he would have to walk or jog to keep warm.

Despite his firm intentions, Matt gave in at ten o'clock – the nearby church clock had seemed to him to have gone into slow speed! He went back to the bakery and bought the cheapest pie he could find – a vegetable one. Being much warmer, he started walking to pass the time until he judged he had enough left to get to the rendezvous at twelve.

Approaching the stand of ash trees, he was surprised to see that it was silent and seemingly empty – until he walked through the first of the trees. A small figure suddenly appeared from behind a stunted bush.

"Give us the password!" the little lad demanded in a hoarse whisper.

"What password?" Matt grunted. "They said nothing about passwords!"

"Right," the little chap nodded. "What's yer name?"

"Matt Crowley."

"Aye – that's right as well."

"I bloody well know it is!" Matt was getting a trifle peeved with all this.

"Foller me!"

The small figure led the way through to the back of the stand of ash trees, then steeply uphill following a barely discernible track. That led to a small granite outcrop. The lad weaved his way through to the centre of the large boulders until Matt found himself facing three seated figures. Two he immediately recognised as his contacts from the tavern. The third was older and far better dressed.

"Thanks Gubby," said the one to whom Matt had been speaking in the tavern. He passed a coin into a grubby hand – a small hand that closed around the coin. The lad gave a sort of bow to the older man, then scampered off.

"So – you are in earnest!" the elder man remarked. "Sit down and tell me all about yourself."

Matt sat down on the nearest boulder and gave him a precise account of name, address, history and political leanings.

"What do you see the best outcome to be, now that our king is no more?" he was asked.

"The immediate restoration of the Prince of Wales to the throne as Charles the Second; the execution of all who sat in judgement; the scrapping of this Commonwealth nonsense."

"And how would this all be brought about – in your estimation?"

"By banding together all who think as we do, forming them into a formidable army to march on Westminster and London, clearing all opposition as we encounter it."

"Would that it were that simple," the man gave a laugh. "Tis indeed something to be devoutly wished, but it will take manpower, persuasion, and a fortune in coin to bring it about. Manpower *is* probably available – but over a long period of time. Persuasion? Well, that also takes time and men of power and standing to utter it. The fortune – well, that will have to come from many sources. Scotland is possible, but that will certainly mean acknowledgement of their Covenant- and even then, Scotland cannot be relied upon for more than a fraction of what would be needed. France? France is heading downhill at a fast rate. No – the money will have to come from within England itself, unless the Netherlands can be turned into an ally. What you propose is an ideal. It is one we all share. But we also acknowledge that we have to plan for a very long-term strategy."

"But I thirst for action!" Matt growled.

"Yes – I can see that you do – in your youthful exuberance. But have you the patience to wait until the time be right? That is what I must know! Small bands doing mischief will not serve! First, they will be annihilated swiftly. Second, they may well alienate the very people we need to bring about to our view – the ordinary working English."

"Then I will have to wait until we are strong enough – although it will eat like a canker in the meantime!"

"That is what I wanted to hear. So, Matt Crowley, are you willing to make your way to Bristol where you would join a group that is slowly getting bigger and better trained – and in secret?"

"Aye – I am willing. It's what I most want!"

"Excellent. Then join with these two and three others of their band and make your way quietly and slowly to Bristol, beyond that along the river to Avonmouth. You will be met there and conducted to a secret place well away from all seagoing and road traffic. When we reach fifty in number, I plan to move you all even further north. Now – you must travel openly and peacefully, not attracting any notice from parliamentary officers. To do that, will require money. Your leader has the necessary coin so that you may reach there lawfully."

The man stood up and prepared to leave but added what seemed to be a sort of prophetic statement.

"The other alternative is that the people of England will themselves tire of all these new laws and Puritan strictures – and the Commonwealth dream will fade quietly into history. I shall meet you all again in some weeks from now."

Half an hour later, Matt and his new colleagues set out on their very long journey, wondering what they would find when they eventually arrived at the empty land around Avonmouth.

* * *

It said much for the standing and reputation of James Forbes that he was able to pull strings – even though he was unable to conduct services himself, he had managed to obtain the services of the vicar from Chagford to come down to Bovey Tracey to conduct the marriage service for Simon and Imelda.

That it was a matter of some urgency was made perfectly plain to him by both Abel and Faith. He had turned a blind eye to the spuriously dated banns that the acting churchwarden had produced. After all, he reasoned, I am not the vicar – so it'ss really neither my fault nor my business!

So, on a blustery Saturday afternoon, Simon and Imelda proceeded to the church where they were duly joined in matrimony. Avril had been told of the slight predicament. She had readily undertaken that she would attend Imelda in approximately seven and a half months, to make it known that the baby was coming very early. Not that some folk would be taken in by that – but they were certainly the ones who could be relied upon to express believable surprise at the news!

The wedding feast held in the tavern afterwards was one that would remain in memories for some time afterwards. Throughout the afternoon and evening, nearly every member of the population came to drink the health of the couple – some even managed to snaffle some of the food that was left over. There were two notable absences. Mercy Green was inconsolable in the bookshop dwelling. It was rumoured that she had already received several lucrative offers for the cottage and the business. Lou Carpenter, now the widow of Peter, and mother of the disappeared Matt, also stayed away. Everyone knew that she was also selling up prior to a move back to her birthplace in Teignmouth.

Dick and Sal Allen were rushed off their feet. Glory, then nineteen, and Zachary at seventeen did what they could to help their parents run the feast in the tavern. It was noted that Glory was not her usual self. The flame-headed beauty was herself saddened and almost inconsolable by the absence of trooper Bell – who had gone back to Exeter with his squad. Everyone knew that it would take her little time to recover completely – especially as Henry Hogg, son of Jake Hogg the shoemaker was 'available' and showing great interest. Despite the loss of their mother, Henry and his sister Primrose had rallied around their father Jake and were slowly pulling him back to something like his former ebullient self.

It took the combined efforts of four stalwarts to carry an almost comatose Abel Smith back to the smithy. Simon, fully aware of his new responsibilities, remained relatively sober as he and his new bride were walked ceremoniously back to the smithy for their bridal night. Faith, well used to Abel's periodic drinking bouts, merely shrugged her shoulders and stayed at the tavern to help the clearing up process.

Gil carried Rosie back to bed on his shoulders, one hand clasped by Ella. They tagged along at the back of the convoy that was accompanying the newlyweds to their lodgings.

"Why Imelda going in there?" Rosie demanded. "Imelda lives with her mama and dada!"

"But Imelda has just married Simon – and that is where they are going to live," Ella explained as those nearest to them burst into giggles.

"Oh!" came from Rosie. "So, Imelda lives at the smithy now?"

"Yes, sweetheart -Imelda and Simon both live there now."

"Will Imelda help with the big fire and the hammers? I want to have a big fire like that – and lots of big hammers!"

"You, my little cherub, are going to learn all about chickens and baby chicks. You will not need a very big fire, and certainly not big hammers!"

"Big hammers are more fun than little chicks!"

And so it went on until Rosie was tucked in for the night. Ella and Gil sat down on the settle before going up to their own bed.

"Let us hope that number two is just a bit more cooperative than Rosie. She is just the most perfect little mite – but she is hard going!"

"Aye – perfect, but hard going describes her perfectly," Gil sighed.

CHAPTER XXXIII

It was on Wednesday of the following week that Avril and Mary finally were able to leave their valises of medicines in the shop. There had not been a new case for three days – not in Bovey Tracey, Parke, or Brimley. Both had made a point of visiting as many homes as they could to make assurance double sure. They sat around the parlour fire behind the apothecary shop and shared a glass of mead in silent celebration. It was only then that they realised what it had taken out of them.

"No more rude awakening in the night," Mary sighed in relief. "I swear that I will sleep with one ear poised for the knock!"

"We seem to have come through it though," Avril commented. "So many gone from us – and we still have not the remotest idea why some were taken, and others were not."

"I wonder if we will ever be wise to that," Mary said, almost to herself. "Still and all, I can now start planning the school properly – with my whole mind on the subject."

"And not a portion of that mind on your wedding?" Avril gave her a smile.

"Well, of course – but I must get the school ready first so that I can concentrate properly on my marriage to Harry."

"And - please pardon my asking - are you still as happy with *that* prospect as you were?"

"Aye – I am more than happy with the prospect. Why? Have I given you cause to think otherwise?"

"You are a very different person to me – that is all. You concentrate single-mindedly on one thing at a time, whereas I flit from one thing to another."

"I have a very concise timetable in my mind. First, I have to get the large cottage properly fitted out as a classroom. Second, I have to prepare the lessons for the first term. Third, I have to enrol the children and wonder where the money is to come from to support all that activity. I have set four weeks for completion of all that. And then I shall devote all my thinking to the wedding.”

“You have the most orderly mind I have ever encountered,” Avril laughed. “I, like a lot of folk, envy you that!”

Mary looked at her with a frown.

“It is hardly a blessing,” she replied. “The thing that is in my mind at any one time assumes an importance that is sometimes not merited. The thing I find hardest of all is to categorise the tasks ahead in order of real importance. I need to school myself to do just that, or I stand a real risk of putting off the one thing until it appears in my list – and it turns out to be worthy of immediate attention!”

“I caught the gist of that,” James said, coming through from the shop. “I found myself falling into that trap when I first started out as an apothecary. So, I schooled myself to spend a little time each day listing all the things that I needed to do. Having done that, I attached to each a mark out of ten, ten being vital and one being the least important.”

“And now you know where your orderly mind comes from,” Avril gave her husband a broad grin. “You inherited it from your uncle!”

* * *

Hob was off on one of his irregular forays into the countryside north of the Parke Estate. Irregular, because he was never sure when he would have the free time to indulge himself. He had taken to heart the bailiff’s stern warning to cease prowling the Brimley Estate – and to refrain from trapping coneys. Not that he had admitted to having ever done so!

He had searched his mind to find an alternative – and had come up one day with the idea of collecting birds’ eggs. They fascinated him – the difference in colour, size, and markings. The countryside around literally teemed with birds of all shapes and sizes – from diminutive wrens to much larger buzzards.

His recent forays had concentrated on discovering the location of nests. And now that it was getting towards early spring, he planned to take just one egg from a clutch, mark its location on a rough map he had drawn, and make a note of the species of bird that had laid it. It was a far cry from his usual pranks. Perhaps he was growing up!

He left the bailiff's house and struck out north for less than a half mile until he reached the River Bovey. Turning left, he followed its curves upstream for about a mile until he was near the top end of Blackamoor Copse. Pulling out his drawing from his pocket, he found the first marked nest – he had seen a pair of blackbirds building it deep within a clump of blackthorn. Both birds were away from the nest, so he very carefully parted some of the thin stems until he was able to peer into the cup – no eggs yet. Just as carefully, he withdrew the stick and wandered to the edge of the trees to locate the next nest – high up in the fork of a tree – buzzards. He stood there for some time trying to work out how he would be able to climb up it at some time in the future. And then he became aware of a wailing noise.

Being only a few yards from the river – which was running fast over rocks – he listened again until the same noise alerted him – it sounded very like the anguished cry of a very small child. And then he became aware of something he had never noticed before. About a hundred yards across clear ground stood a small shack right by the riverbank. He ran across to the shack, the wailing growing louder as he got nearer.

Stopping just short of the shack, he looked to his left where, about another quarter mile distant, stood the tiny hamlet of Pullabrook – where he could discern absolutely no movement whatsoever. That in itself was very strange. And then he went inside the open door of the shack.

As his eyes became accustomed to the gloom, he was able to make out that the shack was almost completely empty – except for a pile of old straw at the back wall, in front on which was a small wicker basket. It was from within that basket that the wailing was emanating. Hob went over and peered into the long basket to see a little face screwed up and crying for all it was worth. Being familiar with lots of little children, he guessed that this infant was not quite a newborn but nowhere near as old as Rosie.

Looking around, he could see no sign of anything else in the shack – no evidence that anyone else had been there. Obviously, someone else *had* been there or the infant would not have been there either. On closer examination, Hob could see that the infant was swaddled tightly inside a cocoon of cloths. He bent down and lifted the small bundle and pressed it to his chest, making soothing noises that had no discernible effect whatsoever.

"Cannot leave you here, can we?" he muttered. "Let's get you back home and see if we can find you some proper comfort."

Screwing up his face at the smell coming from the bundle, he left the basket where it was and started walking as fast as he could back to his home with the bailiff's family. On the way, he kept up a meaningless chatter, holding the child close and tight, hoping to pass on a physical message of 'you are safe with me'.

By the time he dashed into the house, the child had gone quiet – it had dropped off into an exhausted sleep. He called out as he arrived at the parlour, only to find Laura Cove already there mending yet another rent in a pair of Hob's breeches.

"What on earth have you found now?" she said, dropping breeches, needle and thread into her work basket.

"I was up near Pullabrook looking for nests when I heard a child wailing fit to rouse all the angels," he started to explain. "There is a shack up by the river and inside, I found this poor little soul in a wicker basket. There was nobody around and no sign that anyone else had been there – so I brought it home. Couldn't leave it there, could I?"

"Nay, you most certainly could not," Laura agreed. "Not a living soul around apart from the babe, you say?"

"Not a sign of anyone," Hob replied.

Laura called for her husband and repeated the story, at the same time taking the child from Hob and slowly peeling off the layers of swaddling until a naked little boy child lay on the pile of cloths on the floor.

"I would guess about three or four months," she said. "Well nourished and clean – apart from the mess down below – and that is easily dealt with. Hob – go and find Harry and ask him to come here. I shall tend the child whilst you go with Master Cove and show him where this all happened."

Hob shot off on his errand, whilst Peter Cove watched as Laura fetched a bowl of water, clean cloths, and cleaned up the infant. Wrapping him up again in fresh swaddling, she hugged him to her.

"See – all that is needed is attention, loving kindness, and a tight hug!" she grinned up at her husband. The baby looked around, feeling obviously safe, nodded off again. "Have you heard of anyone losing a child?" she asked.

"Nay – and this one is a real puzzle," Cove scratched his head. "I'll take Hob and a few of the hands so that we may start a proper search. It may be that the mother is ill and has simply wandered off to get help. It may be that the father did the same. Who knows!"

"When he wakes again, I shall feed him warm milk, then give him a bath. I shall also find that old crib that Harry vacated all those years past."

Harry bustled in and was told the story.

"Fetch Mary here when you have told her what has happened," his mother instructed him. "She will know what to bring so that she may check the babe over."

"And now, young Hob," said Bailiff Cove, "fetch my horse and that pony you ride. Then rouse Garvey and Hook from whatever they be doing. We shall all ride out and start a proper search".

* * *

It was some two hours later that the four gave up their search. Nobody had found any trace of a mother or father to the child – or anyone else come to that - within a quarter of a mile radius of the shack.

Peter Cove was at somewhat of a loss as to what to do next. It was no earthly use widening the search with only the four of them – he would need many more to cover the woods, river banks, and open fields. That was a job for the next day as soon as it was light. He would muster as many as he could that evening and tell them to make their way to the shack as soon as it was light enough to carry out a detailed search. In the meantime, he sent Hob, Sam Garvey and The Haddock back to the estate.

He rode slowly over to the buildings that comprised the tiny hamlet of Pullabrook – the farmhouse and three cottages that housed the workers. It formed no part of the manor for which he was bailiff, so he had no right to demand – he could only ask.

Not for the first time, he regretted not having Larkin and his soldiers, they would have been of great help. And then he

247

remembered that both Garvey and Hook had been expert trackers. He would put them in charge of small groups and make use of their expertise.

There was no response to his knock at the farmhouse, nor at the first of the two run-down cottages. But at the third, a young face peered around the door in answer to his knock and call.

"Mama and dada are working in the fields," he was informed by a young girl of about seven. She had on a grubby pinafore over an equally grubby dress, her hair not having been visited by a comb in many days. Cove bent down to get level with the freckled face.

"Where may I find the farmer and his workers?" he asked.

"Hoeing the badger field," he was told.

"And where may I find this badger field?"

"Down yonder lane and on the left."

Thanking her for the information, Cove remounted his horse and trotted down the lane until an opening on the left gave on to a large field that was in strips, young sprouting plants just showing above the mounded strips. Leaving his horse to explore the overgrown verges, he walked over to the nearest strip where he found seven adults and three older children busy hoeing weeds between the sprouting crops. One man, seemingly in his forties, looked up and leaned on his hoe.

"You be bailiff of Parke Manor. You have no jurisdiction here!" he growled.

"You be right on the first part – I am indeed bailiff of Parke Manor. And you be right on the second part as well – I have no jurisdiction here. But I do have need of your help."

"We have no time to offer help – we have to get this weeding completed. Get on with it and stop your ear-wagging." This last towards the workers behind him.

Peter Cove realised that he was in for an uphill struggle with this man.

"That shack above Pullabrook – the one at the river's bank. We have discovered a babe there – abandoned, as far as we can tell. I was just about to ask if you or anyone here had seen or heard of a man or woman – perhaps both – there this morning. The babe would not have been there all night."

"Nay – we have not!" The man bent to his task again. "You have your answer, now let us alone to our work."

Cove glanced along the line of workers. Only one woman was young enough to be the possible mother – and she was probably the mother of the freckled girl in the cottage. That did not discount any of the others – the mother could well be the daughter of any of the others. However, he decided that enough was enough and went back to ride back to the last cottage.

"Did you find them?" freckles asked when he had knocked again.

"Aye – I did – and exactly where you said they would be. Tell me – has there been a little babe hereabouts recently?"

"Nay – why?"

"My lad found one in that shack up by the river. He looks to be about three or four months old."

"That old shack be empty for ages – nobody uses it now."

Cove again thanked her and rode slowly back home. He had no doubts at all that the little girl had spoken the truth. So – where could that babe have come from?

He found Mary with his wife, Harry being an interested spectator. Mary had the babe cradled in one arm and was holding a very thick piece of straw in the other as the little mite sucked on one end.

"Until we can find a wet nurse, this is the best I can come up with," Mary explained. She gently drew the straw out of the pursed mouth, dipped it into a jug of warmed milk and then put her thumb over the end, trapping the milk within the straw. Back it went into the mouth for the babe to suck on as she eased her thumb off the end to coincide with the sucking motion.

"That is as clever a trick as I have ever seen!" Laura grinned at him. "We are soon to have a genius in the family!"

"I think he is satisfied for now," Mary said as the sucking slowly petered out. She threw the used straw on the fire as she knew that the next feed would be better with a new, clean straw. She handed the babe to Laura who put it over her shoulder and was rewarded by a little burp.

Seeing that he was at best a trifle surplus to requirements, Cove found Hob and told him to go around as many houses as he could to get people to volunteer for the search when it was light enough on the next day. And then, still puzzling over the problem, he went in search of supper.

CHAPTER XXXIV

"Well – that took me back a few years," Laura Cove remarked over a late breakfast the next day. "It is many years since I was awoken during the night to feed Harry. This little one, whoever he may be, is certainly a very amenable child – not one grumble so far. Takes the milk and allows me to attend to his other needs. It is almost as if he is very well used to a variety of people attending to him."

"Harry will be joining me and Hob this morning," Peter Cove wiped the remains of egg from his short beard. "I wonder how many will turn out to help in the search. Are you content to stay as foster mother until later today?"

Laura, the little babe nestled quietly against her shoulder, simply gave a happy grin by way of reply.

* * *

Mary had collected the key to the large cottage the previous day. She unlocked the front door and stood in the main room surveying what was going to be her domain. Facing her was a very large room – she had borrowed a measuring string from Simon; he and his father used it to plan large metal structures that they had to forge – such as gates. The string had knots at every foot and half-foot.

Having measured the rectangular room, she sat down with paper and charcoal stick to make a quick sketch. Twenty-two feet by fifteen feet and six inches. That made just over three hundred and forty square feet. Assuming that only two thirds could be realistically used for seated pupils, and allowing twelve square feet for each child, that gave her space for eighteen or nineteen. She sat back and thought that there was no way on this earth that she would get that many even in the first whole year. Plan for a dozen, she told herself.

She would need four long benches or stools, and a desk for herself. Shelving for books, tablets, quill pens and inks Also, she would need small but long tables for the pupils to write upon. That brought her up very short – Peter Crowley, the long-time town carpenter, had perished with the winter fever. His usual helper, young Matt, had disappeared completely, leaving poor Lou all alone. How could she get the basic furniture made? Come to that, who was going to pay for it all?

She urgently needed advice from the most senior member of the town – her future father-in-law. But Peter Cove was out searching for the babe's parents. Who else?

And then another thought occurred to her – what to do with the upstairs rooms. There were three of them – large enough to accommodate a small family. Should she suggest that these be rented out? The stairs arose from the back downstairs room. So, the school would not be interrupted by their coming and going. Yes – that might bring in some needed income. Again – advice needed. She did what she usually did and, having locked the cottage, went down to the apothecary to consult Uncle James and Aunt Avril.

* * *

Peter Cove, Harry and Hob had arrived at the hut to find that not only Garvey and Hook were there but also another fifteen people from the town – all eager to help search for the babe's parents.

"First of all," Cove started off by addressing his 'posse'. "Does anyone here know this area well?"

"Aye, bailiff, I do," came a gruff voice from the crowd. "My mother still lives up by Lustleigh and I oft times walk there this way."

Cove recognised a quiet young man who worked as a stockman for one of the farmers to the south of Bovey Tracey – indeed, at the south end of Bovey Heath.

"It's Ned Appleyard, isn't it?"

"Aye, bailiff."

"So, Ned – I would want you to lead one group northwards towards Lustleigh. You know what you are looking for. Sam

Garvey and young Haddock here are, as you all well know, professional trackers. Sam – take one group back along the river towards Parke and Bovey; Hook – you lead another group towards Pullabrook over yonder. Go as far as you think it worthwhile. The remainder will come with me back south. We will all meet here again this afternoon – unless one of you makes a discovery, when we all need to be called.”

“What happens, Master Bailiff, if we get challenged as being on another’s land?”

“Good point. Tell anyone you encounter why you are there and what you are seeking. Ask everyone if they have any knowledge of the babe and his family.”

The four groups set off on their various ways. Young Ned Appleyard was feeling quite important as he led his group of four up the track in the direction of Lustleigh. Without even being told, the other three spread out to cover not only the track but the grass and woods to either side.

Sam Garvey felt very much at home as he led his small group along the river back towards the town. “Look for anything discarded, anything that shouldn’t be there, anything at all really,” he instructed.

Haddock led his group first past the cottages that made up the hamlet of Pullabrook – not bothering to stop or question anyone as he knew that had already been done. He and his men received strange looks from the inhabitants as they trudged through and onto the lane beyond.

“Looking for signs of the babe and his family,” Haddock called out as they passed. He received a few nods and took it that this signalled tacit approval. He started off on the track in the same manner as Sam had.

Peter Cove led his group south. He had only Harry, Hob and one chap from the dairy – and they all knew one another very well. He had no real hopes of discovering much in the direction he was going, leaving the more probable routes to his two experts and the man who knew the route to Lustleigh.

It was over an hour later when one of Ned Appleyard’s group called out that he had discovered something. Ned and the others clustered around as the man held aloft a small sack. It was closed at its neck with a cord that also formed a loop so that it could be slung over a shoulder. The man pulled open the neck of the sack and fished about inside it. He pulled out a bundle of cloths.

"They be all about the right size for swaddling a babe," he said. "Our two were in like cloths when they were very small. Sack were by the side of that bush there."

"Let us all mark this place carefully," Ned noted. "Now – did whoever leave it here do so before or after leaving the babe?"

"Bloody ground be as dry as dust," the man grunted. "No marks or tracks anywhere hereabouts!"

"We need one of they trackers!" another growled. That found instant agreement with the whole group. Not one of them had the expertise to read the signs. Ned felt he needed to make a decision. He had been thinking furiously ever since the discovery had been made.

"I believe we should take the sack with us, mark this place very carefully, then carry on to see what else this track may yield. Seems obvious that they came this way – but in which direction?"

"Aye – makes sense," the finder agreed. He shouldered the small sack as Ned led the way further up the track. It was another of the small group that made the next discovery – and it was one that stopped him yelling in horror. By the right side of the track, partially concealed by a mound of stones, was the body of a young woman, fully clothed and very dead. The others clustered around and gazed down at the sight.

Around the head was a large, red and congealing puddle. Ned, feeling he had to take the lead, knelt down at her side and looked at the head.

"Skull be caved in," he announced. "Now, we really do need Bailiff and trackers!"

He dispatched one of the men back to the hut and onwards to the town where the Bailiff had been heading. He would know the best way to get the trackers to where they were needed.

"Until Bailiff gets here, we must guard the body and the scene," he ordered.

* * *

Mary had joined James and Avril at their shop. When she outlined her problem, both uncle and aunt decided that Mary should stay for an early dinner, leaving a willing Nell to man the shop.

"Have you started to make an account?" James asked as they started on a stew and new bread.

"Aye, uncle. It is frightening. The easiest and cheapest way would be to have three or four long writing tables with stools for the children. I can make do with two shelves only to start with. But who is to make them, now that Peter and Matt Crowley are no longer with us?"

"And where is the money to come from for the work and materials?" James added.

"Stools be no problem at all," Avril remarked. "Surely that bodger down by the woods can be relied on to make them!"

"Aye – he can at that," James nodded. "How many did you want to start with?"

"I'm being hopeful – twelve," Mary replied.

"Still does not answer the problem of the long writing tables. But what about the paper, pens and ink – to say nothing of books for reading," Avril cautioned.

"I shall swallow my pride and go to see Mercy Green," Mary gave a grimace. "She is selling the bookshop business now that Hubert has passed. Surely, she has some she could supply!"

"Aye – and they will all be the bible!" James laughed. "I do believe that all the others are far too advanced reading for little children."

Mary had been thinking at the 'school' cottage and with her uncle and aunt.

"One person of note was very keen about starting a school," she muttered, more to herself that to anyone else. "Lady Violette – I wonder if she can be asked to make a donation?"

"It will do no harm to ask," Avril nodded.

They were about to finish their dinner and provide Nell with hers when Hob burst in.

"Mistress Avril – Bailiff wants you urgent like. They've found a young woman – dead and likely murdered. They've also found more swaddling for the babe."

"Dear God in heaven – where?"

"Tis up the Lustleigh track. I've got my pony and another from the stables for you. Bailiff says tis urgent!"

It was a while later when Avril knelt by the side of the dead girl. She slowly stood up and gave her verdict to the Bailiff.

"Stiffness is already almost worn off – so she has lain here for two or more days. Blood is nearly all dry and hard – that also agrees with the timing."

"Still does not answer one important question," Cove announced. "Was she killed after leaving the babe – and on her way to Lustleigh – or before the babe was left? And that would mean that whoever killed her then dumped the babe in the hut. And *that* suggests that she was on her way *from* Lustleigh."

"Then if that be the case," Harry observed, "he is long gone and could be anywhere between Ashburton, Torquay or Brixham – or anywhere else, come to that!"

"What we must do is to take this poor girl for a proper burial," Cove announced. He cast his eyes over his assembled searchers. "Many of you must know how to fashion a hurdle. Let us make one and lift her on it and get her to the church. Also, we must carefully mark both places."

"Done that already, Master Bailiff," Ned spoke up. "Trees about both places be blazed."

It was a very subdued procession that slowly made its way back through Bovey Tracey to deposit the body at the church.

Reverend Forbes gazed down at the shattered skull.

"No matter what decrees are made about my position, that poor girl gets a proper service and a decent burial. I shall hold the service immediately – unless any more can be determined from the body."

"I have determined all that I can," Avril asserted. "She was killed where we found her – no blood traces anywhere else. She was killed two or more days ago – by having her skull caved in. The edges of the wound suggest the weapon was wooden – a stout cudgel or a length of branch."

"Then I shall proceed within the hour. Perhaps all here would form the funeral procession?"

As it turned out, the attendance was far greater than that. Half of the town turned up as the young girl was given the last rites and lowered into her grave. It occurred to Cove on his way home that nobody had even suggested that the girl had been anything else than the mother of the babe

* * *

Mary again called in before going home. She found Laura Cove still acting *in loco parentis* to the little one – and seemingly enjoying that role.

"He feeds very well and seems content," she reported to her husband, her son, Mary and Hob. "He brings up his wind faithfully and makes happy gurgling noises. But he is now without a mother or a father. What will we do with him?"

"Surely someone in the town will want to take him – after all, look how Nell has been absorbed into the place," Cove mused.

"We have no name for the wee mite," Laura observed. "What may he be called?"

Hob had been peering at the child and was rewarded with a broad smile.

"He looks like a contented cat!" he laughed.

"Then he must be called Felix!" Mary announced.

"Why?" Hob demanded.

"Felix – Latin for cat!" Mary grinned at him.

* * *

Matt Crowley and his new colleagues managed to get all the way to Bristol without encountering any problems. They had achieved this by the very simple ruse of travelling in pairs a mile or so apart. Each one had no visible weapon and was therefore seen as no threat to anyone.

However, north of the city, they joined together and slowly made their way to what they hoped would be a final destination – the open countryside around the mouth of the River Avon. Following directions, they arrived late one afternoon at a large wood between the small harbour at Avonmouth and east of the hamlet of Chittening. Matt did a count of the young men that gathered in a clearing and came up with twenty-six in total.

The leader, or the person who seemed to have elected himself as leader, was a man barely into his twenties by the name of

Rufus Riley. He was of medium height and looked as strong as an ox. Naturally, because of his name, he was red in complexion and was topped with a thatch of red hair. He wore a baldric from which hung a broadsword. In the belt was tucked a wicked looking throwing axe and two daggers. Had he but known it, he was the spitting image of a Norse invader from centuries past.

Riley had been almost the first to arrive at this meeting place and was consequently the one with the latest news. He summoned all the others just before night fell and, standing on a fallen tree trunk, addressed them all.

"Friends and fellow royalists," he started. Matt was immediately struck by the accent which he thought came from nearer London. He had got used to hearing the soldiers of Larkin's squad – and they were nearly all Londoners. "This is but the first stop on our long way to join many others of our persuasion. I have been told that we are to remain here until summoned further north. To do that, we will cross the river to Chepstow and then make our way north, staying on the Welsh side of the border. Where our real destination will be has not been made known to me yet. I will make a guess at Chester. The further north we travel the more like-minded folks we will encounter. York and Northumberland are still strongly for the crown."

"All well and good," one voice was raised. "That's hundreds of miles – and mouths to feed along the way. How may we, a small band, manage that without attracting the attention of parliamentary forces?"

"Aye – we would be slaughtered by the smallest parliamentary patrol or garrison!" claimed another.

"Our commander has promised to be with us in a few days from now," Rufus tried to settle matters. "These problems, and other matters, will be explained to us when he gets here. Believe me, this is no isolated force; it is one of very many throughout the country who will rally to our new King Charles when the time is right. Where that shall be, I have as yet no idea. But I am assured it is all well thought out."

"Heard that load of bollocks before," one near neighbour of Matt remarked quietly. "Have faith; it is all planned; nothing can go wrong; load of crap! It will be like any other of its kind. It will all happen by chance. We will either succeed or die. Prince Rupert said he had a plan – and look how that ended up!"

"Then why are you here?" Matt asked, equally quietly.

"Because I have no other option. I have no work and I hate parliament!"

"As for food," Rufus was continuing his address. "We have an abundance of coneys hereabouts. There are fish in the rivers. We have already obtained sacks of flour with which to make bread. We can easily survive here for weeks if necessary."

"But no ale!" came another voice.

"Then we will have to survive on water!" came the response – and that was met with a concerted groan.

* * *

It was later that day that Avril had an idea, but first of all, she tried it out on James to see what he thought of it.

"The little one – Felix as Mary has christened him. It seems obvious that the poor girl we found was indeed his mother. It also seems likely that the father is missing – perhaps even the killer of his wife, and the one who abandoned the babe."

James gave her a knowing look.

"You have had an idea, haven't you?" he grinned.

"Aye, I have. Lou Crowley is all alone now that Peter is dead, and her son Matt has disappeared. How do you think she would take to the idea of taking on little Felix?"

James thought for a moment.

"It would either be dismissed out of hand or grasped with both hands. To be honest, I have no idea which it would be."

"I agree. She is not the sort of woman to do anything half-heartedly. T'will be one or the other for sure. I shall go and ask her now."

Donning a cloak, Avril walked up the street and knocked at the Crowley's front door. It was opened after a few minutes by Faith Smith.

"Lou is in the parlour," Faith ushered Avril into the back room. Lou was sitting before the fire winding wool into a ball. She raised a tired face to Avril.

"Faith has been sitting with me for the evening. All I do is wonder where Matt may be – what sort of company he has fallen into," she said.

"Indeed, that must be a worry," Avril agreed. "I understand he is hellbent on joining others of a like mind – to raise enough manpower to bring back Prince Charles to claim his throne."

"Aye – he was ever full of the idea. I believe it is foolhardy and doomed to failure – we have all witnessed the power of Cromwell and that army of his!"

"I am here on a mission of a different kind," Avril decided to take the bull by the horns. "Would you be willing to take on that babe that was found?"

It was as if she had thrown a rope to a drowning woman. Lou's face lightened immediately.

"Not only willing, but eager," she almost smiled. "It will be just what I need to fill the gaps left in my life. But what will I live on? Peter is gone and no money will come in from his carpentry. Matt is not here to bring in any money either. How will I live? I have just enough to last me for a month or two, and that is not counting the extra I will need for the babe."

"You weave very good woollen cloth," Faith interrupted. "Cannot this support you?"

"It well might, but not with this large house to maintain!"

"Then I have another idea," Avril laughed as it suddenly popped into her mind. "Mary is opening the school as you know. There are two rooms above that you could rent. Surely your work would support that!"

"Aye, it well could," Lou was getting quite excited at the idea. "But are we not getting ahead of ourselves? How is the school to be funded? I understand that the matter is yet to be decided."

"Oh, you know Mary. She will obtain the funds, never fear."

"Then by all means bring this little mite to me and I shall raise it as best I may."

CHAPTER XXXV

For many years England had 'welcomed' Protestant adherents from mainland Europe. The predominant among these were the Huguenots from France. Ever since these religious 'rebels' had been targeted in the previous century by the Catholics of France – and in many cases, slaughtered – they had sought refuge anywhere they might. Other religious 'rebels', such as the Cathars and the Albergensians, had no such luck!

Mercy Green had travelled alone to Newton Abbot, there to advertise her bookshop for sale. Without Hubert, she had no heart left for that enterprise. It had taken but a week before she was visited by a tall and swarthy man who introduced himself as Henri Bessant. He had been renting a small shop in Newton Abbot for the previous five years where he managed to eke out a living by buying and selling books and tracts. He, his wife Eloise and son Gaston, were ready and eager to make a new start. To purchase Mercy's shop would involve securing a substantial loan. But after spending an hour with Mercy, examining books and accounts, was convinced that this was indeed too good an opportunity to miss.

Mercy for her part had put aside her misgivings and her normal sour expression as the delightfully accented English had slowly won her over. They ended the meeting after two hours with an agreement on price and timing – Mercy would have to vacate the premises by the first of the following month. She already knew exactly what she was going to do – make her way to Plymouth and join the very next available ship that offered passage to the Americas – where many of her religious persuasion had already gone.

Henri rode back to Newton Abbot well pleased with his agreement. Now all he had to do was to raise the loan – and for that he had to turn to a fellow Huguenot who had already been very successful with his own business – importing and selling wines from the Italian States, from Spain, from anywhere that produced wines of high quality. This worthy individual had known Henri for years, had indeed been a fellow escapee from France. He readily agreed the loan – to be repaid over three years and at zero interest. Henri and his family looked forward to a more secure future.

*　*　*

Lady Violette Charlton was feeling at a loose end. During the previous two years she had very successfully 'resurrected' the large house in Brimley. Despite losing her confidante of many years – Thomas Carpenter – she was quietly happy with the way things had developed. The house ran smoothly; the grounds were well kept; produce from the fields were sufficient for their needs. Not that this satisfaction was ever expressed to the staff – they needed to be made constantly aware that standards were to be maintained at all times and at all costs. Still and all, she was at a loose end.

One morning, having finished her correspondence, she happened to glance up to see below her in the courtyard the welcome figure of Mary Ramsey – obviously come to see that her erstwhile 'patients' were recuperating properly. Her hand hovered towards the small bell on her desk. At its tinkling sound, her new (and very satisfactory) steward knocked and entered.

"You rang, my lady?"

"Yes, I rang. I see that young Miss Mary is visiting. Be so good as to ask her to come and see me when her business is done."

"Certainly, my lady." Luke Farmer went down the broad staircase and out into the courtyard where he delivered the message.

Before Mary put in an appearance, Violette sat and wondered about her new and to her, very impulsive, idea. Was it foolish? Was it even practical? She made up her mind to see the first part through and to discover where, is anywhere, it led.

"Mary – come in, my dear and sit yourself down," she said as Mary entered and made a small bob of greeting. "Now – tell me all about the wellbeing of my staff."

"Wellbeing indeed, Lady Violette," Mary grinned. "All seem to be well on the road to complete recovery."

"That is good to hear. Now – how are the wedding plans going?"

"To be honest, I have had little time to dwell on them. The end of this illness, thanks be to God, has taken much of my time – as had the planning of the school."

"And it is the school that I wish to discuss with you. I understand that you have found the premises and have planned what is needed. Indeed, all that is now missing is the wherewithal to bring those plans to fruition. Would that be a fair summary?"

Mary's heart beat a little faster; was it possible that this conversation was leading in a certain direction, she wondered?

"That, my lady, is a succinct summary."

The old lady's face split into a wide smile.

"So, I am now both indomitable and succinct! What woman could ask for more? But to come to the point of my enquiry. Would you be willing to share with me the details of your financial needs? Which children are likely to enrol? Are their families able to pay? And if so, how much? What is needed for the school to even open its doors?"

Mary, now almost convinced that the conversation was heading the way she hoped, was only too willing to discuss even the most minute detail. The figures were imprinted on her brain. Lady Violette dipped pen into ink and made notes as the details emerged. As she at last finished, Violette sat back and went silent as she drummed elegant and beringed fingers upon the desk.

"I have a proposal that you might like to consider," she eventually spoke. "As you must realise, I have no close family of my own. I also have considerable funds that are sitting doing little but earn paltry interest. So, let us take things one at a time. First, I understand that the Parke steward and the bailiff have received Sir John's approval that the cottage be made available for the school, rent free. Is that correct?"

"Aye, my lady. That is the case, and very welcome the news was."

"Good. Second – I see that there are no alterations needed to make the cottage suitable for classroom and kitchen. There is also a substantial privy. So, no funds needed there. Now we come to the furniture required. That consists of long, low tables for writing, stools for the pupils, a desk and stool for you, plus various shelves. Is that all that is needed?"

"To begin with, I can manage very nicely with just those. But there is the problem of who is able to make them. The village carpenter, Peter Crowley, died of the illness; his son has simply vanished."

"I have to confess that all carpentry I had completed here was accomplished by a very good and reliable man from Ashburton. He would do a splendid job. I shall despatch my steward tomorrow and ask the man to come here to see you and to get your specific requirements. And now we come to the most delicate matter – that of your stipend and that of the running costs. This is assuming that *some* of the pupils will be paid for by their families."

"Actually, my lady, I was not seeking any stipend at all. I shall soon be married to Harry and we will live at Parke with his parents in their large cottage. Harry already earns a stipend as he is learning the job of bailiff. All that would be needed is the initial cost of paper, inks, pens, books and a few other things."

"Piffle and nonsense!" snorted Lady Violette. "What you will bring to this town is worth more than a polite 'thank-you'. Of course, you must have a stipend. So, here is what I propose. I shall defray all the costs of the carpenter and his materials. I shall also happily pay for the initial stock you require. Furthermore, I shall contribute a monthly amount to the running costs. Now – please do not tell me that this is unacceptable!"

"Believe me, my lady, nothing could be further from my mind. It is the most generous offer and is accepted with gratitude. Now, if I may presume to make a counter proposal, may I propose that you become the patron of the school to whom I shall render a monthly accounting?"

Violette's old face transformed into a broad smile. "That is also accepted – and with eager anticipation."

Later that day, Mary related all of this to her betrothed, his family and her own family. Needless to say, the news was received with real pleasure.

* * *

It was exactly three weeks later that Bovey Tracey saw the back of Mercy Green and the arrival of the Huguenot family. There were many people in England at that time who made up their minds to start new life in the North American colonies. Nearly all of them went for religious reasons, and Mercy was no exception. Despite the Puritan nature of parliament, England was still a very 'Anglican' country – churches abounded as they had always done. Mercy had managed to join company with two other families who were on the same mission. One was from Newton Abbot and another from Teignmouth. With the money from the sale of the shop (and its stock), she was able to purchase a small cart and a pony to haul it. With her scant belongings loaded, she bade a silent farewell to Bovey Tracey and drove off to meet up with the others at Newton Abbot – there to journey together to Plymouth and obtain passage across the Atlantic. Very few inhabitants witnessed this departure.

Henri, Eloise and Gaston Bessant arrived the same afternoon. They were greeted by a small welcoming committee – all eager to meet this family who they fondly hoped would be a distinct improvement on the previous occupants of the bookshop. Many hands volunteered to help with unloading the two large wagons that contained furniture, cooking impedimenta, and many closed chests. Before long, the new family were comfortably settled into their new home. They walked up to the tavern to make themselves known – Eloise having no appetite for cooking supper after their strenuous day. It also took very little time for Glory to make the acquaintance of the twenty-three-year-old Gaston. With his dark hair, broad shoulders and enticing French accent, Glory had dreams of a very pleasant future.

* * *

The following day saw the arrival of Matthew Kent. He had, following the dictates of his parliamentary superiors, stationed himself in two places – Launceston and Tavistock. From these two places he was able to monitor what was going on in both east Cornwall and in west Devon. However, his curiosity got the better of him and he had determined to ride to Bovey Tracey to renew old acquaintances.

His first call was to Parke where he knew he would receive a polite welcome. He was not to be disappointed in this assumption as he was greeted with smiles by both Peter Cove and Luke Barton. The three of them repaired to the tavern for dinner in a quiet corner.

Dick and Sal Allen both were curious about the purpose of this small gathering and told their son Zachary to loiter now and again to see what he could glean.

"And what brings you back to this small town?" Peter Cove asked as platters of beef and vegetables were deposited on their table.

"Curiosity, I suppose," Kent answered with a grin. "I am now a way to the west of you but could not help thinking about this place. Any more trouble with shepherds?"

"Absolutely not," Luke Barton replied. "The young lad – Wheatcroft – is proving to be very able and trustworthy. I shall offer him a permanent position soon."

"And what news from the far-off Westminster? Or are you not able to disclose such information?" Cove prodded.

"Oh, there is no secret about one matter," Kent replied, "For years now, Ireland has been in turmoil. The Catholics have been causing murder and mayhem for years – massacring Protestant settlers and seizing lands. It seems they are banding together more and more under Ormonde. In the very near future – or so I am informed – General Cromwell is to go there himself to settle matters. Knowing the general, his methods will be as effective as they will be brutal. His son-in-law, Ireton, is reportedly going with him."

"Then may the Lord have mercy on the Irish," muttered Barton.

"Apart from that, matters are proceeding much as expected. John Bradshaw is about to be named President of the Council of State."

"Any news as to the whereabouts of Prince Charles – or as we should call him, King Charles II of Scotland?"

"I would not wish to be quoted on this, but my parliamentary masters seem to have dismissed him from their minds – as being of no importance. Scotland is quiet, believe it or not. And if it ever becomes not so, it will be dealt with."

Kent then changed the subject, enquiring into the wellbeing of other previous acquaintances. Cove and Barton, sensing that there was little point in probing further, sat back and enjoyed a pleasant afternoon.

* * *

Matthew Kent sat on the bed in his rented room in Tavistock. He had chosen, against better advice, to traverse the moor instead of going the easier (and longer) way all along the southern edge and then turning northwards. He was not sorry that he had done so.

"One of these days, I shall learn all about that moor," he made himself a promise. It had fascinated him – its ruined stone huts from perhaps two thousand years previously; its standing stones; its bogs and hollows, crags and tors. It was a place of mystery, and it drew him like some sort of magnet.

"But in the meantime," he muttered aloud to himself, "not a whisper of insurrection anywhere – at least, not that I can find. This part of England fascinates me, and I shall spin out my so-called investigation for as long as I can."

And with that comforting thought, he drained the last of his mug of ale, rolled into bed and slept peacefully.

* * *

Just before evening, Nell visited her father's grave – a small mound in a corner of the church cemetery where a small, lettered headstone had been placed to identify that young man. Nell made a point of visiting it every week to put a small flower against the gravestone.

"Hello, dada," she said, kneeling on the grass. "I've been learning all about different plants that help with headaches and stomach ailments. James and Avril have said that I am coming along very nicely. I hope so, as I want to learn. Mary is going to open the school soon and is going to marry Harry Cove. Simon and Imelda are married and already are going to have a baby. Isn't that wonderful? Never worry about me, dada – I am happy and very well. I love you, dada."

AUTHOR'S NOTE

This, like its predecessor *A Shameful War*, is a work of fiction. The doings of parliament, and the trial and execution of Charles I, certainly happened – and much in the manner I have narrated. However, down in Devon, nearly all characters in the book are from my imagination. There never was any dignitary in Bovey Tracey called Sir John Vickery. The only person in the small town of Bovey Tracey, or in any surrounding area, who really *did* exist is the Reverend James Forbes – and his name will be found prominently displayed in the church of Saints Peter, Paul, and Thomas - and a knight by the name of de Tracey certainly existed and was reputedly one of the gang that murdered Becket in Canterbury – December 1170.

What was the 'right' side in the conflict? That of a 'divinely appointed' king, or that of a parliament supposedly representing 'the people'? Parliament was far more popular than many would have us believe. To choose a side after three hundred and seventy years is utterly pointless. Whoever held the reins of power made the laws and, if you broke them, you became a lawbreaker – whether or not you believed that law to be lawful. The law was what the person (or persons) in power said it was. Some cynics would say that not a lot has changed!

What is important is the way in which the ordinary folk simply had to get on with life – whether it was producing food or making things. Not to do so resulted in poverty. I have tried to concentrate mainly on the lives of the 'ordinary' folk – and how their day-to-day existence was their main concern. Other matters waited until there was either the time or the inclination.

If you would like to find out how these folk carried on through the early Commonwealth, then Book 3 – *A Time Of Acceptance* – is to follow soon.

Thank you for your patience and perseverance.

Jim Marshall
Devon
Autumn 2023

www.ingramcontent.com/pod-product-compliance
Lightning Source LLC
Chambersburg PA
CBHW070606170726
48291CB00003B/727